THE MYTH MAN

THE
MYTH
MAN

ELIZABETH SWADOS

VIKING

VIKING
Published by the Penguin Group
Penguin Books USA Inc., 375 Hudson Street,
New York, New York 10014, U.S.A.
Penguin Books Ltd, 27 Wrights Lane,
London W8 5TZ, England
Penguin Books Australia Ltd, Ringwood,
Victoria, Australia
Penguin Books Canada Ltd, 10 Alcorn Avenue,
Toronto, Ontario, Canada M4V 3B2
Penguin Books (N.Z.) Ltd, 182–190 Wairau Road,
Auckland 10, New Zealand

Penguin Books Ltd, Registered Offices:
Harmondsworth, Middlesex, England

First published in 1994 by Viking Penguin,
a division of Penguin Books USA Inc.

1 3 5 7 9 10 8 6 4 2

PUBLISHER'S NOTE
This is a work of fiction. Names, characters, places, and incidents
either are the product of the author's imagination or are used fictitiously,
and any resemblance to actual persons, living or dead, events, or locales is entirely coincidental.

LIBRARY OF CONGRESS CATALOGING IN PUBLICATION DATA
Swados, Elizabeth.
The myth man / Elizabeth Swados.
p.   cm.
ISBN 0-670-84202-8
1. Theatrical producers and directors—New York (N.Y.)—Fiction.
2. Americans—Travel—South America—Fiction.   3. Girls—New York
(N.Y.)—Fiction.   I. Title.
PS3569.W17M98   1994
813'.54—dc20   94–7873

Printed in the United States of America
Set in Minion
Designed by James Sinclair

In memory of Robbie Anton
A genuine magician, my soulmate, and creator of
my first New York romance
I will never forget his genius or his laughter.

ACKNOWLEDGMENTS

To David Stanford, my editor, for his guidance, his sketches when words wouldn't do, and his unique understanding of what would help the manuscript become a book. To Charlotte Sheedy and Jim Silberman, who saw me through the first drafts in 1982 and had the courage to tell me to wait and the graciousness to let me move on. Many of their notes helped the book evolve ten years later. To the many readers and advisers who provided encouragement. To Cindy for her patience. And Laura for her industriousness. To Daniel Neiden for spelling tutorials. And to Roz Lichter for helping secure the right home for the book and for me.

The Myth Man

conceived and directed by Sasha Volotny

with

Juno Blackbeak Crayton, Christoph Alan Denoir, Reeva Jahkhar, Tashi Kun Kataro, Bruce Levin, Mustafa Muhammad, Robin O'Rourke, Charles Solomon, Rikki Nelson, Sasha Volotny

Chorus: Sheetan El Bahar, John Braken, Carolyn Colliner, Ben Hardallah, Rocko Metroni, Sheila Nathanson, Carl Patterson, Jonas Stern, Tatsara, Barnett Samuel Valcome, Annie Weber, Zebra

Sets Designed by	Costumes & Makeup by	Puppets, Wigs & Masks by
Sasha Volotny	Charles Solomon	Koshero Texicali

Music by	Choreography by	Texts Adapted by
Robin O'Rourke	Reeva Jahkhar	Bruce Levin
Tika		
Obana Kunshay		

Dramaturgy by

Randy Paul

Note from the Director:

All heroes and villains are descendants of the gods portrayed in the ancient mythologies of the world. If we study these stories we will see that no matter how much human beings may have advanced technologically, we are still ruled by the same forces which tormented our primitive ancestors. It is humbling to realize that despite discoveries in science and medicine we are more helpless and terrified before the darkness of death than ever, as a child who wails when the night surrounds him. And the broken-hearted lover believes no one has ever felt the scourge of betrayal but him. He is the first. He is the only. And despite all the grief and destruction left behind by war, human beings remain ambitious, stubborn, fanatical in their pursuit of power. They have always wanted to be gods.

These aspects of human nature are pitiful, perhaps, but our common weaknesses are also cause for rejoicing. We are, after all, one being.

Neither race, nor religion, nor climate, nor language can erase the universality of our mythic unconscious. We may claim individual territories, styles, and inventions, but all boundaries crumble when we manage to touch one resonant, universal sound or image.

This little vaudeville, or revue, attempts to present just a few of the deities who are the basis for our fear, our strength, our lust, and our struggle for revelation and redemption. They march through our psyches as if in a parade. Some create the catastrophic disasters which render human beings helpless. But there are also those gods who manifest enough wit and compassion to provide the inspiration which sets our imaginations on fire and incites us to act as the kind of heroes who reach out and create miracles. Welcome to Travels with the Myth Man.

Sasha Volotny

THE THEATER OF THE
MIRACULOUS
AND THE MUNDANE

CHAPTER 1

A thin strip of carpet was laid out across the middle of the plywood floor. It was mustard color and stained with gray spots. Otherwise, the old loft was empty. I stood at one end of the rug and a Japanese man waited for me at the other. He was short, square, and dark. His silver hair nearly covered his eyes. He wore a white kimono. His calves and forearms were smooth and stiff as clay. His feet were bare. He was so muscular he seemed carved, like a puppet. He gestured to me with his hand. His fingers were like claws. All the wrinkles and lines on his dark face looked at me. He had too many eyes. He jumped up and down impatiently.

"Sta-n-nd up st-laight," he ordered. His voice came fast in a thick angry accent.

"Now waaark."

I stepped onto the carpet as if I were balancing on a beam.

"Stop, stop, stop!" the Japanese man yelled. I leaped off the carpet. He let out a high-pitched giggle. I didn't dare to smile.

"You—puppet—no?" he said. "You—have—stling—attach to

3

head—it hold it up! You have stling attach here"—he pointed to his pelvis—"all movement she start from here—legs—they forrow behind, no? Alms they are roose. Whooo . . . whooo."

I practiced being a puppet at the edge of the filthy carpet in the dingy loft with the Japanese man barking "Yes, yes, yes" or "No, no, no."

When he decided I was ready to cross the carpet, he said, "Now I tell you most important thing. When you closs this lug—I want you think onry this: I step on calpet, I boln. I get to other side, croser I get to death. End of calpet, end of my rife. After I step off calpet—whooo! whooo! mystely!" He giggled again.

I was nine years old. (But it's not like I'm remembering. I'm doing it again. Full-out costumes and sets in my mind. According to them, memories were useless. Nostalgia was called sentimental and indulgent. You had to use the past for research, and use memories to make masks, gestures, and attitudes. Even at twenty I'm not rid of their opinions yet. Their voices drown out my own. I never know when I wake up whether I'll be nine, twelve, or fourteen years old. I'm still waiting to add up to one age—to have some quiet for a change.) I may have been nine but I knew this was a weird audition. I found comfort knowing my father was downstairs waiting in his cab. This audition was nothing like the one where the lady in a big sweater and thick glasses with a stopwatch told me to make faces as if I were laughing with joy when I played with Mattel's "Bozo the Balloon." Performing for the Japanese man was even more terrifying than when I had to "cuddle up" to five or six different cake-faced men with bright yellow-toothed smiles. They were supposed to serve me a new, hot, gooey breakfast cereal and then give me a puppy. At least I wasn't being dressed up in a rainbow T-shirt and being shouted at to "bake your damn brownies" in a Barbie Easy-Oven. But this audition was odd, because I had no idea what it was for.

I stepped up to the carpet and tried to keep the little Japanese man out of my sight. Jonah (my father) always said that it was crucial to show these casting people what a sweet girl I was and how much I sincerely cared about their product. So I chanted a tune to myself as I walked like a puppet across the grimy mustard carpet. I always made songs up in my head. If anyone heard them, I'd probably end up in the Florida Children's Home—which was exactly why Jonah had stolen me. He said the kids were chained to cement posts and were forced to eat iguanas. I remember that day I was singing to myself.

> *This is the beginning of the beginning of the beginning.*
> *This is the middle of the beginning of the beginning.*
> *This is the end of the beginning of the beginning.*
> *This is the beginning of the middle of the beginning.*
> *This is the middle of the middle of the beginning.*
> *This is the end of the middle of the beginning.*
> *This is the beginning of the end of the beginning.*
> *This is the middle of the end of the beginning.*
> *This is the end of the end of the beginning.*

I reached:

> *This is the beginning of the middle of the end.*
> *This is the middle of the middle of the end.*
> *This is the end of the middle of the end.*

And I crashed directly into the Japanese man. His body was hard as a rock. He smelled of sweat and menthol. He caught me easily, as if I'd flown off a trapeze into his arms. He giggled. I lost my balance in his grip. My muscles shook as if I'd been walking for several miles across sand.

I noticed that the Japanese man was no longer alone. Another man stood a few feet behind him. He stepped from the shadows into the light. He wore a royal-blue kimono with clean white Japanese letters. His arms were folded. I thought of a great heron when I saw him. He was so tall. His hair was straight blond, thick, and fell to his shoulders and was streaked with white. His nose was like the beak of a hawk. His eyes were large, almond-shaped, and very light gray. His blond eyelashes were long and completely straight. He had the lips of a woman, thin, but the lower lip pouted. He was skinny, but, like a giant heron, he unfolded himself into a creature of great strength and vibrance. He stepped toward me. The Oriental man, who'd had so much power, became like a servant in his presence. The new man was only in his late twenties, but he behaved like a prince or some kind of wise man born to power. He had a stillness and grace which made the Oriental man seem clumsy and obedient. He raised his thin blond eyebrows at the Oriental man. The Oriental man laughed and pointed to me with a stubby finger.

"No con-cent-tla-tshun," he reported. "She think she think she think, but she not *do* . . . do not *do* . . ." Then the Japanese man squeezed my arm. "You wolk hald. You good gill."

"So what do you think?" the blond-haired man said. He spoke pleasantly and lightly, as if nothing that had happened mattered very much. He had a slight accent. I didn't know accents, but it sounded like a combination of British and French to me.

"No concentlatshun," the Oriental man repeated. "Tink too much. She's too old. But velly pletty, velly smaht." He bowed. He abruptly left the room. The blond-haired man squatted down on his haunches. He pulled his kimono around him and grinned. He shook his head, laughed, and nodded toward the door. His huge almond eyes watered as if with dew. "That's Kosher," he informed me. "A great master. He escaped a strict noble family in Japan to join my troupe. Generations of dead and living masters went into crisis. They sent obese mindless sharks to kill him. Hit men. He's changed his whole identity. My silly brother, Charles, gave him the name Ko-shera Texicali." The man smiled at me. His teeth were even and white and shiny. I shrugged. I couldn't tell if his story was true or not. I tried not to appear too interested.

"Poor Kosher," the man said. "He can't figure you out. They start them at age three in the Bunraku and he can't understand why American children are so spoiled. In fact, he thinks that most Western people are brats." The man's accent came and went as he talked. Sometimes he sounded like the Russian pilot on *Star Trek*, then he'd grin and remind me of a Florida surfer. The blond bird man looked directly at me. His eyes were curious and very kind, but he was examining me—as if looking for something cracked or soiled. I was supposed to know how important this moment was for me.

"What do you think?" he asked.

I shrugged again and looked at my feet.

"You're very beautiful," the bird man said. His accent returned full force. His voice was high and light. It sang. "It's like someone cut you out of the wrapping for a Swiss chocolate bar. Wholesome. Blond-haired, blue-eyed. And yet—a little sultry, no? Maybe you know a thing or two."

I lifted my head. I wasn't about to smile.

"I'm Sasha" the bird man said. He extended his hand. His fingers were much longer and thinner than I'd seen on any man. It was as if they grew from his wrists like plants. His skin was white and pale and smooth. The veins showed through. "Tell me your name."

I pointed to my throat and my mouth and I shook my head.

"You don't want to?" Sasha asked. "Or you're mute?"

I lowered my eyes. I was embarrassed and confused.

"Is it illness? Were you born this way?" Sasha leaned toward me and touched my throat with one thin finger. He blinked fast. He was thinking hard. I didn't know what was so interesting.

"Where are your parents?" Sasha asked. I gestured toward the street, where Jonah was probably snoring in the cab. By now he'd have drunk a six-pack and combed through *Variety* and *Backstage*.

"Well, let's go. Let's go," Sasha said. He raced in front of me down the steep metal stairs to the street. He paused just before he opened the door: "You could be perfect for us," he said. I followed his speed, afraid I'd catch my foot and crash headfirst onto the cement landing. I had no idea what the job was or why I might be perfect for it.

CHAPTER 2

A couple of years later the *East Village Other* did a cover story on Sasha. The writer said that Sasha "took an autistic mute under his wing and cured her." In the same year a long profile appeared in *The New Yorker* and it quoted someone as saying that Sasha and I had "a unique camaraderie." He seemed to be able to penetrate my severe dyslexia or autism and "transform it into a unique poetic language." A photographer from the *Village Voice* took pictures of us performing a reading of my words. In the picture I'm crossing a long, dark proscenium to where Sasha stands in the light. We both look like patients in a Victorian sanitorium. Sasha told me that lots of doctors, social workers, teachers, theater directors, composers, painters, and writers wanted me to read my sound poems, exhibit my paintings, and lead sound and movement exercises for their classes. He would not let them exploit me. When I first started speaking again, I chanted a song about money, Mallomars, Mustang convertibles, Magic Markers, millionaires, and mother. Sasha laughed in his high easy manner, placed his lips on my forehead, and called me his "capitalist canary."

In the late summer of 1971, Jonah had sped me away from Florida in a beat-up Dodge he'd rented or borrowed at the last minute. It was a fast escape. Jonah was an expert at running. The truth was—and Jonah always told me the truth—that he'd spent a good many years as an actor in New York before I was born. He'd been part of an ensemble that performed scenes from all the great American plays. However, the "studio" was poor and Jonah developed a serious alcoholic problem and couldn't remember his lines. He was broke too. He bounced from city to city until he ended up in Sarasota, Florida. He managed to get a job conducting theater games and film instruction in several retirement community recreation centers. He met my mother in Sarasota. She was waitressing at one of the seafood restaurants on the harbor. Jonah said he knew Florence was a prostitute, but the job was a "means" to her and she was open and practical about it. She painted landscapes in watercolor and designed comical erotic postcards and greeting cards with India ink pens. She was waiting to get into art school or to start selling her work at boutiques and galleries. Like Jonah, she was a heavy drinker and that slowed down her progress. But Jonah believed she had a real artist's persona. She was nearly six feet tall with long, dirty-blond hair and odd gray eyes set wide apart. Jonah said she was already thirty when he met her, but she looked like one of those Italian porno stars—all bosom and hips. She liked to make all kinds of men pose naked for her landscapes. The retirees thought she was exotic and I guess standing wrinkled and naked in front of a picture window was a happy memory to take to their graves. Jonah was the opposite of my mother. He was plain, paunchy, and bald, with watery blue eyes. He looked like an Irish cop on TV. It wasn't his looks that won my mother's heart. He had a kindness—a softness. He said he sacrificed himself to her until she wanted to hurt him. He explained that he gave her so much money, admiration, and protection without question or complaint that Florence was driven to destroy his dignity and mock their relationship. Jonah said it was a peculiar fitting of parts. But it was an engine that kept them going for a while. He said it was as old as the Bible and he didn't want me to live out the same kind of story.

Jonah told me, in all honesty, that he couldn't guarantee he was my blood father. It didn't matter. He'd been around since I was born. It was my mother who named me Rikki Nelson, after the rock-and-roll singer from the happy postcard family. She liked the way his upper lip sneered when she saw him on TV. Jonah insisted on the spelling R-i-k-k-i to give me a little class. He lived in vacated rooms in the retirement condos and Flo kept her three-room apartment in a stucco project overlooking a canal. Jonah insisted I live with her. I got to see motorboats and pelicans and herons, but when I was old enough to swim, I swam in a pool filled with old men and ladies with sagging skin and bloated bellies. Flo said she'd rather die than look like that, but I loved the floaters and swimmers. They were like inflatable animals and I longed to crawl on them and row from one end of the pool to the other. Jonah or my mother lay on a deck chair pretending to watch me, but both of them were so drunk, they usually passed out with their heads back and mouths open exactly like many of the elderly sunbathers who lay half naked and snoring around the pool. I talked quite a bit in those days and I liked to ask the lifeguard, who was young and bored, to drop me off the diving board so I could pretend I was an astronaut circling in space as I practiced my cannonball.

When I was a baby, Jonah was the one who fed me, diapered me, and watched me take my first steps. Flo liked to show me off at the seafood restaurant to the waitresses and customers. She dressed me in pink frilly petticoats. But unless she called on me, it was better if I kept my distance. She closed me in my room while she "painted." I liked hearing her sing Beatles songs to the men who were her models.

My mother invited many men to the apartment to pose for her paintings. The paintings were distorted, childlike depictions of palm trees, canals, the bay, and houses. I didn't know what she needed the men for, since they never showed up in the paintings. But they stood there for hours while she painted and I stayed in my room teaching myself history, ballet, mathematics, which was all phony and had nothing to do with the real subjects. I just pretended I knew what I was talking about. Flo didn't like the fact that Jonah called me "precocious" or that I drew and sang and danced at an early age. "She's a kid. What's so special about her?" I heard her tell Jonah. "Annoying, greedy, and determined to suck the life outa me. She's affecting my damn looks too." I never wanted to hurt her. She was my mother and I liked her long hair and her smooth neck. I wanted to crawl up on her lap and put my head on her breast. She painted, went out on her job, and stayed away as much as she could. Sometimes she brought me paper umbrellas with Japanese phrases hidden in the top (you had to tear the little sticks apart), but Jonah took care of me. I don't know why I didn't move in with him.

My mother had this one "guest" named Walter. He was an older man with stringy brown hair over a shiny bald head and glasses that slipped down to his nose. He was a tall, clumsy guy who talked loud and liked to hear my mother sing. Long after she'd be snoring noisily in the next room, Walter would come into my bed. He moved like Frankenstein. He asked me if I liked to play peek-a-boo and hide and seek. I found him stupid and annoying, but there was something scary about his yellow smile and the odor of his sweat. It was like burned almonds and turpentine. There was a tease and a threat to his whisper as if he knew things about my life, although I was only seven at the time. When he put his mouth on mine, we touched teeth (I thought of the marimba player at my mother's restaurant). He didn't really kiss me. He'd just mumble some little nursery rhyme about "Mr. Snail, Mr. Snail, has a tail, has a tail." He'd repeat it until he jumped and soaked the bed. Then he'd cry. He left quickly. It gave me time to change my pajamas and wipe the sheets. Walter always told me he'd kill my mother if I told anyone about his visits. He swore he'd suffocate her in her sleep or stab her. I didn't believe him. He was an underfed animal, mangy and terrified. I wouldn't have told anyone, anyway. There wasn't much to say.

And it wasn't like Walter was the only one of my mother's friends who played night games with me. He's the easiest to remember. The others are thick, sickening, and cloudy like cigar smoke.

One night my mother stumbled past the room when Walter was swimming on top of me. (He flopped like a whale.) My mother shrieked from the bottom of her throat, grabbed him by the skin over his spine, and pulled him off. His glasses crunched on the floor. Barefoot, shirtless, and blind, he ran from the house. My mother sat on the edge of my bed and wept and wept. Her performance was so convincing, I almost believed she hadn't known about Walter all along. Or her other friends. I thought she'd recommended me the way I'd seen her offer the Two-For-One Early Bird Special at the Sarasota Diner. She seemed to want old people to have a good time.

"Look, it's like this," she sobbed. "I don't work for myself—but when I tell you the truth you gotta keep it to yourself. Otherwise I'm really finished. I mean he'll kill me.

"Look, here's the thing—Jonah sets up those dates for me. He works with this enormous drug ring off the coast that includes Cuban crooks, Mafia, and the CIA—Jonah says I got to entertain them and then he uses my profits to pay our expenses—you see? I'm a prisoner. The one thing he says, the one *rule*—no—*law* is you're not to get involved in any of this. If he finds out—he won't just have me murdered—I'll probably get sold first, get my tongue cut out and my private parts mutilated. I'll be sold into slavery."

I couldn't believe Jonah would hurt anyone. He said he wanted to direct long plays by a man named Eugene O'Neill. Jonah spent most of his time sitting in a chaise, bleary eyed, smiling to himself, and sipping on a clear drink with a lime in it.

"Jonah?" I asked.

"Look, babe, it's the gentle ones who are the real freaks," my mother said. "You don't have to worry about the bastards who yell and break bottles over your head. It's the 'good men.' The ones who wait for you, forgive you, take care of you. They're the ones with the cuffs and branding irons."

Despite my faith in Jonah, my mother was my goddess. I gave in to her deal and became her partner. Up until then I talked fine. But speech had begun to wear on me. Too many grown-ups growled and moaned on top of me, warning me to keep my mouth shut, not to tell my mother, my teacher, or my friends. Conversations with Jonah became filled with stretches of silence and meaningless smiles. My mother always let me know that Jonah could, with one phone call, have her abducted and tatooed all over her body with an Arab's saber.

I didn't make a decision. Eventually my voice decided for me. Talking was treacherous. I chose silence. Like nuns or monks. If words didn't slip out accidentally, I might be able to keep my mother in one piece and I would be her cherished heroine. I withdrew from little-girl activities and stayed in my room drawing owls. I liked to draw their ears and disconnected eyes. I stopped raising my hand in first grade, and I didn't answer when called on.

Jonah took me to throat doctors in Sarasota. They sent us to specialists in Miami. Dr. Greenblatt in Miami told Jonah that due to the amount of alcohol and drugs my mother had consumed during her pregnancy, I probably suffered from brain damage. I'd simply stopped developing. He recommended a special school or a state hospital. Meanwhile, Dr. Zenoff in Miami tested my motor functions and neurological reactions. He sent us to a special psychiatrist, an old doctor with elephant skin named Dr. Zotoff. He asked me to undress and showed Jonah the sores on my rectum and vagina and the black and blue marks on my thighs. Dr. Zotoff worked for the Florida Youth Council and angrily told Jonah he was going to call the police and Social Services Department. While he was on the phone, Jonah grabbed me, wrapped me in my clothes, and we rushed toward the old Dodge he'd borrowed or rented for the day. Then he drove us to New York.

Jonah swore he'd drink nothing but wine and beer. I didn't know why it mattered. He decided to work toward opening an acting studio in the style of Lee Strasberg. He'd teach young actors sense memory and scene analysis. He thought he could supplement the studio by coaching. He said coaches helped actors on their Broadway plays or movie sets if they were having trouble with character. Jonah got a job driving a cab and I sat with him all day long. We bought

Backstage, Casting News, Billboard, and *Variety* and during traffic jams and red lights he circled commercial auditions for little children who wouldn't have to talk or sing. Jonah made enough money to get us a cheap suite at the Hotel Earle. It was a four-story residence hotel on Waverly Place in the Village. The halls stank of urine and there were drunks and junkies screaming at each other saying they would "kill you motherfucker," but it was across the street from a restaurant called the Coach House. I loved staring out my window at the Coach House. It was a small brick building with white shutters. There was one black lantern lit with real fire like an old-fashioned street lamp. Limousines drove up to the heavy antique wooden door. I never saw anybody famous get out, but I didn't know that many famous faces. Washington Square Park was down the block. On Sundays Jonah took me to watch the guys on unicycles and the folksingers and poets. I preferred to watch the old men playing chess. They moved through the hours like the intense and silly grouper fish in the Sarasota Bay. I also was entranced by the pigeons. I wanted to feed them bread crumbs. But Jonah said if one bit me I might contract tuberculosis or a septic infection of my blood.

I didn't go to school. Jonah wanted to teach me at home. He was afraid of drawing attention to our "predicament." I learned how to add, subtract, divide, and multiply. I learned how to read and draw a map of the United States. After a few months Jonah called my mother and afterward he asked me if I really wanted to know what she said. I missed her. I wanted to hear her, even if only through Jonah's voice. He was bleary and sad. He took me on his lap and told me that Flo was relieved I was gone. She didn't want a daughter who was retarded or a man who was a wimp and a parasite. Jonah was much more hurt than I was. I was used to Flo's sharp tongue when she drank. Her barbs made me laugh. Her mind was quick and mean on booze. When she was sober she was either sparkly and flirtatious or she whined and lied.

Jonah leaned his head against mine and sang a verse of "Together" from Gypsy. He said he was glad we had each other. He pinched my cheek too hard and I got mad. I gave him an elbow in

14

the gut. He turned red and started chasing me. I ran around our tiny room as if there were somewhere to go. Jonah's face was shiny and wet. He swung his loose arms at me. "Why didn't you do that to the other guys?" He yelled at me. "Why didn't you fight them?" He seemed more jealous than indignant. I just stared at him and he backed down. "I'm very sorry," he said quietly. "I know Flo made you think you had no choice." He went out, leaving me alone in the Hotel Earle. The sounds outside the door were mysterious and varied. I heard fragments of mumbles, moans, laughs, screams, running, falling, and very slow, quiet steps. I began to write stories out of everything I heard in the hallways and in my head. The scrawling, primitive letters exploded with sound. I didn't show my work to Jonah when he returned. He was much too drunk. He tousled my hair and lurched toward his room. "You're an innocent, babe. Don't you forget that. There's no crime in being innocent and young."

We traveled around New York for a year in his cab. I went to TV and print auditions for Baby Breck Shampoo, Barbie, Maxwell House Coffee, Ajax, print ad auditions for Macy's, F.A.O. Schwarz, Angelico Photographers, Sealtest, and a bunch of other sweet, peaceful, happy, family-oriented products. I got enough jobs to buy new clothes and toys. Jonah decided to become my "manager." We had head shots taken with my hair up, down, curled, in pigtails, and with a bow. He coached me on smiling, pouting, and flirting with the camera. He taught me to eat cereal "expressively." He showed me how to "romp" in new overalls and how to love a stiff little teddy bear. He was an awful teacher. I was tall and thin and pale and he insisted I imitate Shirley Temple. When I went to an audition, I did exactly what the casting director ordered me to do. I got a national commercial for Blue Cross/Blue Shield by lying down on a gurney with an IV attached to my arm. I didn't even have to raise my head. Jonah took us to Peter Luger's to celebrate and we ate T-bone steaks, French fries, and onion rings paid for out of my advance. Jonah drank eight beers and a shot of bourbon with each one. He had a bottle of wine with dinner. On the way home he rear-ended another cab and got into a fistfight with the Arab driver. At the Hotel Earle, he asked me to put a cold compress on his sore jaw. He kissed my hand and wrist and pulled me onto his lap. "You're my best pal," he sighed. "But I'm a miserable father and I need an 'out clause.' I pray to God for a rich, gentle, childless couple every night." Then he started to cry. "Forgive me," he said. "Maybe it's time for a foster home for both of us." But we went on with the coaching and the cab and the circling of ads until Jonah found one particular call for an "extremely special child" wanted by a theater troupe in lower Manhattan.

Sasha Volotny's famous experimental shows aren't difficult to understand ten years later. He's featured in almost every book written about the theater of the seventies. He incorporated the dark imagery of Eastern European directors, the stark stylized movement of the Orient, and the sounds of third world music. He made paintings and ritual. He designed huge collage canvases as backdrops and hired untrained people whom he drilled in his own athletic physical style. They often wore masks or elaborate makeup and operated towering puppets. He wanted his people to be forces of nature, not modern human characters, and they acted out his stories and dreams. The moving creatures were orchestrated into his still landscapes. It's been said that professional actors would never endure his demands or relinquish their egos to his philosophies. He subjected his recruits to arduous schedules and rules. They sat for hours to learn the value of stillness. They worked on the gestures of one hand for days at a time. Some days they were allowed to only whisper. Others to scream. Biographers point out that Sasha wasn't a hypocritical demagogue. He worked more hours than anyone. His commitment to theater was his life. He believed the stage was holy and anyone who agreed to perform upon it had to give up the distractions of the outside world. The audience watching Sasha's theater was supposed to be awakened, cleansed, and changed. He talked about the risk every performer took when he or she became "possessed" by the madness of performance.

When I auditioned for him, he was already quite famous. His ensemble lived and rehearsed in a converted warehouse on New York's Lower West Side. His new show was already booked for a full tour through Europe. His first fall show, the one that made him famous, had been a cruel and bloody adaptation of Artaud's *Fall of the Aztec Empire.* Sasha had won many prizes and grants. He was considered a great young genius and his "images" provoked ecstatic journalistic comment from everyone, from writers like Susan Sontag to Richard Rauschenberg and Ionesco. Sasha's brother, Charles, once told me that the best way to destroy an artist's work is to co-opt it. He said if you put an artist in jail or censor him, you make him sharper and stronger. But if you want to weaken his impact, lithograph his paintings onto a coffee mug or write his character into a sitcom. Charles said the American public is very hard to shock and that their attention span was changing from full meals to bites. You have to keep inventing new catastrophes, new diseases, new duets between death-row cellmates, new wars, new assassinations, but neither pity nor love lasts beyond a few months. Perhaps that's why Sasha suffered so intensely each time he had to invent a new project. Charles once said that Sasha wanted so badly to be original that he went nuts when he realized there was no such thing. "Sasha didn't invent masks or puppets, you know—or huge canvases or slow motion or African drums. He stole from Robert Wilson, Peter Schuman, Peter Brook, Andrei Serban, Joseph Chaiken, Fred Astaire, Shari Lewis, and Wilson Pickett, to name a few. He didn't invent shadows or fire. He didn't discover sand or backlight. It's too late in history to do anything new. He's a copycat. But an inspired copycat. A copycat with a beat that Dick Clark can dance to."

I can feel what it was like—racing behind Sasha as he leaped down three steps at a time toward the front door of his warehouse. He was so anxious to meet Jonah that he raced the last few yards from the door to the cab with his hand already extended. His smooth, shiny skin was covered with red blotches and his wide smile was boyish and shy. Jonah struggled through his haze to greet Sasha. He tried to get out of the cab, but Sasha was blocking the door. Sasha realized what he was doing and let out an enormous guffaw.

He covered his mouth with his long fingers and took a step back. Jonah managed to get out of the cab. He yawned a little and leaned back. His eyes were watery and his face was bloated. His clothes were wrinkled and unwashed.

"Whatdya think of my girl there?" Jonah asked. Sasha nodded his head up and down and placed both of his hands under his head as if cupped in prayer. I stayed behind him and watched Jonah.

"Extraordinary," Sasha said. "Something fresh. Very bright. A truly original heart."

I watched Jonah carefully. He tried to appear aloof, but he wasn't doing a good job of faking.

"Your ad in *Backstage* said the commitment's for at least a *year?*" Jonah asked. Sasha's face transformed into a thoughtful expression. He looked as if he were trying to translate his thoughts from a foreign language into English. His accent became very thick.

"Oh, it must be," he said. "That's the only way to create a theatrical experience that has real depth and commitment. Do we want to imitate life or create life?"

Jonah's eyes clouded. "I'm a coach myself, you know. I've given her a lotta tips."

Sasha smiled, but his eyes remained wide and serious. "Yes," he said quietly. "That's very evident. She already has a kind of reverence for craft that has clearly been passed down to her in an almost tribal fashion. That's why she's so unusual for her age."

I backed farther away from the two of them and leaned in the corner by the door. I suddenly realized I had to go to the bathroom.

"I'd need to talk about money—school—" Jonah began.

"Yes!" Sasha interrupted. "But really, must we do that here? Please come to my office and share some Stoli!"

Jonah grinned.

"I'm most interested," Sasha went on, "to discuss her . . . silence."

Sasha opened the front door and I jumped to get out of the way. Jonah took quick little steps to keep up with him. I followed. I started to look down the long anonymous hallways at the painted doors. I needed to find a bathroom. I wasn't that interested in their conversation. I knew Jonah had been looking to sell me for a long time and now he'd finally found himself a buyer. Jonah and Sasha stayed behind a closed door for a long time. I could hear laughter and mumbling. Finally I walked as far as I dared and found a cold cement corner. I squatted, took down my tights and underpants, and peed on the floor.

An hour later Jonah patted me good-bye on the top of my head and then let his hand flop on my shoulder.

"This is a good break—kiddo," he said. "There's a nice steady salary, travel . . . you'll get to see some places and these are educated people. Me, I'm gonna head over to Jersey. They've got a hell of a state-run arts program there."

I didn't look at him.

He gave me a short, gruff hug and was gone. He hadn't told me when I'd see him again, and I didn't want to make a big deal out of it. If I pushed or acted clingy he'd never come back.

Sasha gently led me to a wooden cell. "This is where my new beautiful girl will sleep. But she will not sleep much!" He kissed me on the cheek and dashed off. I dropped to the bare mattress on the floor and stared for a moment at the mattress opposite mine. It was covered with exotic Indian and Persian fabric and the sunlight from the window glittered off the tiny mirrors and beads of glass attached to the colorful throw pillows. The wood wall beside the bed was painted in a complicated mural which featured Bugs Bunny, Minnie Mouse, Porky Pig, Janis Joplin, Malcolm X, and Judy Garland. A desk next to the mattress was piled high with dresses—I noticed a tutu, a red sequined evening gown, a sailor dress, a nurse's uniform, and a flowered house robe. A handmade bookshelf held books with titles like the *Kabala, The I Ching, The Teachings of Lao Tse, Zen, Haiku, The Book of the Dead,* and books of myths from the Greeks to Romans to Eskimos. There was a whole assortment of children's books like *Winnie the Pooh, The Brothers Grimm, Alice in Wonderland, The Complete Fairy Tales of Hans Christian Andersen,* and several thick books with titles like *Porno Movies From the 30's Until Now, Pornography and the Orient,* and *Classic Pornographic Sketches from Around the World.* There was also a clay pot with fat, thin, short, and long wooden flutes sticking out like flowers. The floor was lined with small drums that looked as if they'd been carved by hand. There was also a tiny dressing table attached to a wall of mirrors. I saw more mascara, blush, eye shadow, false eyelashes, lipsticks, base, and liner than I'd ever encountered on secret raids of my mother's bathroom.

I turned away from the busy world of my unknown roommate and closed my eyes. I dropped off wondering how I'd find sheets and a toothbrush and how I'd pay for clean underpants.

I woke to hear a shout.

"No you may not 'just take a look.' She's a little girl and this is not a *zoo.* If you are so profoundly curious about children, find yourself a man with a good pedigree, make him lasagna, and then rent several thousand of his sperm!"

I awoke to see a character weighted down with shopping bags. He was trying to maneuver the door while holding a huge ring of keys in his mouth. I jumped up to help him and was shocked by his appearance. He was absolutely identical to Sasha except his hair was wildly curly and he had a wispy mustache. The tall, thin, blond-haired man dropped all the bags at once, not caring where they fell, and collapsed onto his mattress.

"That's your linen, flannel granny gown, toothpaste, toothbrush, and magnum," he said. "I've been appointed your official nanny. I'm Sasha's older brother. By three years and two months and a day. My name is Charles, but you can call me nothing since you don't speak."

I stared at him. He grinned and stretched in an overdramatic imitation of a cat.

"It's disconcerting how much we look alike, I know. Except I'm much, much, much more beautiful. Don't you think? My nose is more delicate. My hair is bushy and has angelic twists and curls. My eyes are hazy gray and have a slightly feminine, Oriental slant. I'm taller and thinner and more exotic and I steal the attention of elderly women wherever I eat lunch."

Charles sat up.

"Of course, Sasha is smarter. But I'm nicer. He's deeper. I'm hilarious. He's heartbreaking, silent, and mysterious. I talk too much. Hungry?"

I nodded yes. Charles jumped up and raised his fist in victory.

"Good. I brought you a lunch which, I hope, will be nutritionally correct, environmentally sound, and fun for all. Since I've never been nine, I can't imagine what the people of your culture eat. How's tuna fish, chips, a Coke, and a Ring-Ding?"

I showed my appreciation by grabbing the brown paper bag he held out in front of him.

"Bwana," Charles yelled. "The creature has communicated. Bring the electrodes! Bring the Polaroid! Call the anthropologists!

"Don't worry," Charles said. "I'll calm down once I get used to being a nanny. It's worse than a first date. But then how would you know? I mean, what if you choke on your sandwich? What if you choke on your sandwich and vault out the window? You're not killed, but you somersault through the open car window of a fabulously handsome, talented, and rich real estate broker who loves you, wants to marry you, but isn't Jewish? What do I do then?"

Charles disappeared under his pillows and began shaking with terror. I didn't laugh. Charles peeked out from under his pillows.

"Just don't spit the sandwich out," he warned me, "or blow the Coke out your nose. It doesn't go with the sad Victorian image my brother so adores. I can tell, Miss Prim and Proper, you are going to be a very dull roommate."

I threw what was left of my sandwich at him and blew soda out the striped plastic straw at his head. Charles's face was covered with tuna fish and Coca-Cola. He could've been one of the Three Stooges. He put on delicate horn-rimmed reading glasses as if that would make it better. He gave me a thumbs-up sign and licked his blond mustache.

"Thank God you don't talk," he said to me happily. "You'd probably be a bitch." I pulled away as Charles approached my bed. He gently cleared away the garbage. He managed to gather the wax paper and plastic cups and brown bag without touching me. He left as quickly as he came, saying "good night Chet, good night David" and before long I fell back to sleep.

I woke to the sound of a low echo resonating through the narrow hallway. The sound was metallic and circular. It repeated, got louder outside our door, and then disappeared. It sounded like a dinner gong.

"Wake up, little one," Charles whispered. "Watch me." It was dark, but the streetlights reflected dully through the blinds. Charles was a black shadow against an orange hue. He held out a piece of cloth. I grabbed it and he pulled me up from my mattress.

"Do this," he whispered. And he dropped to the floor. I started to laugh.

"Shh," he said. "It's a Tibetan prostration. We do it every morning before dawn. It's like brushing your karma instead of your teeth."

I fell to the floor next to him. He hummed through his nose. I tried to follow. We rose and collapsed several times. My elbows became sore. I had a splinter in my left palm. The long flannel nightgown Charles bought from Macy's tore at the hem. The eerie metallic noise vibrated through the door again and I covered my ears.

"Not to worry," Charles whispered. "That's a gong. Very Eastern. Very chic. It's a school bell for the enlightened."

Many footsteps drummed lightly in the hallway. They were soft but rushed.

"Let's go," Charles said. He pushed me out the door and began running. His back was straight and his knees lifted high as he pranced. We jogged quickly down the pitch-black hallways and up cement stairs, around blind corners, and down more stairs. We joined a crowd of silent shadows. There seemed to be about twenty of us. The group ran up a last steep, narrow flight of stairs and, one by one, climbed an iron ladder. My feet were cold and I slipped on the ladder, but someone caught me and I was lifted through a trapdoor onto a rooftop. The city sky surrounded us—black and gray, spotted with lights. The faces of the actors were hidden by shadows.

In the predawn hour I saw water towers and smoke, skyscrapers and fading stars. Someone played a deep pulse on a drum. One by one, the group began to spin, each in his or her own style. I spread out my arms and joined the spinning. Dark buildings and blinking lights whizzed past. Bodies and faces I didn't recognize rotated around me like the inside of a clock. The spinning got faster and faster. My feet couldn't keep my weight moving in even steps. My throat felt thick. The inside of my head began to rock. My body lurched. I was sick to my stomach. Someone grabbed me by the shoulders.

"Look at my eyes," a voice said. "My eyes."

It was Sasha.

A siren moaned in the distance. The drums pounded, unrelenting. The spinners tipped their heads back as if drinking rain. Sasha touched a spot behind each of my ears with one of his thumbs. His eyes were gray, light, and calm.

"There is a place—here." He touched the bottom of my spine. "Fire, ice, and rock. It is very old. You are attached to the earth like the root of a tree. This spot gives you great power. Turn your eyes inward and concentrate on that place when you move. The outside pictures should not disturb you. Nothing. Only this place—the spine—here—fire, ice, rock—the root of the tree."

Sasha began to spin. He was a heron. The sky was turning red. It blazed behind his circles. I followed him. I tried to look inward, but I was too fascinated by the light emanating from his long arms and long golden hair. When he sped up, I followed. I was chasing the sun. After a while I didn't hear the drum anymore. Sasha had taken off. I was behind him. He was circling Manhattan higher and higher. I was on his wing. We were going to burn up and God was waiting in the flames.

I found myself standing still in my flannel nightgown soaked with sweat. An ugly yellow stain spread out where I'd urinated. A dreary yellow sun beat down on the tarmac floor. Sasha's actors lounged silently. They stretched their limbs and rubbed each other's backs. Some of them stared at me and others purposely looked away. I tried to cover the stain. Sasha had disappeared. Charles loped forward, held out a can of Coca-Cola. I grabbed it and drank with thirst. He signaled with his eyes and took me in a corner, where he removed my nightgown. He gave me his soft, long Indian shirt. "Next time, we make a pee stop before journeying toward God," he said, and grinned.

"This is Rikki Nelson," Charles announced to the group. "She's our Kalabash virgin. Sasha's going to throw her down a volcano the next time we need a grant from the National Endowment." I could see faces sculpted in diverse shapes and tinted in an array of colors. The people here were no different from the tourists in south Florida. My mother once wrote out a list of body types and smells.

Asian—Small and hairless. Soy sauce and English Leather. Precise ice.

Muslim—Prickly hair on soft skin. Bread and stale sweat. Zing kings.

African—Hard muscles. Hot peppers and listerine. Nothing with the lips, only the hips.

Danish—Downy, grainy, thick powdered sugar, and dirty underwear. Slaps with clap.

Greek—Small rolls of fat, poodle hair, salad dressing, and incense. In and out. Scared the Virgin Mary will find out.

Jews—Hair all over. Bones protrude. Leather, Old Spice, onions. Rude. Brains in pain.

Italians—Bushy, ruddy, acne, sweaty palms, wet lips. Roses, tomatoes, garlic, Armani. Romantic fakers, oversure. Insist you eat their pasta. Like it fasta.

Irish—Smooth, soggy, greasy hair. Ale, vinegar, and mint. Their aim's a shame. Too drunk to dunk.

When my mother showed Jonah her "guide to lovers of the world," he said she was being simplistic and making rascist stereotypes.

"You don't know shit," my mother said to him. "*I'm* the U.N. *I'm* UNICEF. *I'm* the fucking Red Cross."

At breakfast I met Reeva, an actress born in Nigeria, and Juno, a storyteller from northern Canada. Charles told me that the women rotated staffing the kitchen and were expected to sew the men's clothes, serve their meals, and tuck them in at night. Reeva and Juno scowled at Charles.

"You're corrupting this one," Reeva said. She had a lilt in her voice that wasn't quite an accent.

"You're the slave around here, Charles," Juno said in a low, heavy voice. "You're the seamstress, accountant, and shrink."

Charles bowed and left me with the women. Reeva was very muscular and wrapped in bright, embroidered clothes. Juno was short and pudgy, with dark bangs. She wore an old serape. They spoke very little to me and called me "daughter." I fetched spices ground on wooden boards which Reeva poured into steaming pots of rice. Juno steamed hunks of onions, carrots, zucchini, and tomatoes in a deep, sizzling wok and dumped them in the mix. They pried open the wide, greasy oven and pulled out crisp pita bread on fat wooden spatulas. They chopped away at blocks of feta cheese with carving knives. And then they removed pitchers of iced tea and fruit juice from the 1950s refrigerator.

I had no appetite. I served. Sasha sat at a small wooden card table in a corner. An extremely tall gray-and-black-haired woman sat with him. She was covered in necklaces and bracelets with exotic symbols and stones. She was wrapped in a cape of black burlap. She looked to be over six feet and had as many muscles as a man, but her expression was soft, nervous and womanly. Her eyes were lined with black kohl and her long, thick, frizzy hair was interwoven with feathers which she pulled at delicately with her thick fingers. Sasha beamed at me, delighted to see me in action. The woman was in the middle of an urgent monologue.

Sasha interrupted her. "Robin—say hello to Rikki Nelson."

The woman looked up. Her green eyes flicked nervously. She

showed a row of perfect teeth. "Yeah, Rikki," she said in a man's raspy voice. "Charles told me." She took my hand in hers. Every one of her fingers had a different ring. Her hands were large, flat, and cold like the belly of a fish. She had tatoos between each thumb and forefinger. I could smell the wine in her sweat and I recoiled.

"Children know," Sasha said.

Robin bowed her head and picked at a hangnail on her thumb. I turned my back with a heavy serving tray on my shoulder and tried not to stumble as I moved from table to table.

Sasha said I was to begin sessions with the Japanese man named Kosher. He was the "master carpenter" and puppeteer. He also taught exercises that Sasha said were essential to his style of work. He directed me down a dimly lit flight of stairs.

Kosher's studio occupied the whole basement with worktables, handmade saws, fabrics, paints, and the skeletons of his artwork. The dark basement reeked of glue and the master seemed to work by large black candles and torches. Dressed in a filthy gray kimono, Kosher made me bow to him. He never smiled, but gave me a quick, indifferent physical exam. He measured me and tested my muscles and flexibility. He said "Tsk tsk—oh—chi," as if he were annoyed with the inferior body of a little American girl. The shadows of bamboo poles and the plaster of paris gods and goddesses wavered in the firelight. I could see the outlines of snake, spider, and crab puppets. Masks with gray skin and red slits for eyes were lined up against the walls. They leered at me; their blue, orange, and green lips half smiled.

"Rittle mosquito," Kosher snapped. He tapped me on the shoulder. "You concentlate on me—hele." He pointed to a place in the middle of his forehead. Once again he ordered me to walk a straight line toward him. He sent me back and I walked again. I had to balance an imaginary egg on my head. I was pulled by an invisible string. He told me to keep my feet close to the ground. I walked miles for him. Sometimes the cement felt like sand dunes. Sometimes it became hills of slippery rocks, sometimes I was slogging my way through mud; sometimes the floor became vertical. My legs shook, my feet became numb. I gulped and my lungs burned. Kosher kept sending me back and I would inch forward again toward his crouched little body. "Sasha wants this." Kosher sighed. "It is lidiculous in short time rike this . . . five yeals of work in one month." Kosher grinned. "We both die young, eh?"

He led me through a slow-motion series of poses. I held the "earth as a beach barr." I was a "rion with craws." I fished in a "liver with my teeth." I turned on an axis and "prucked the moon flom the sky." I "pranted a low of seeds." I "attacked the emney with a swold." I didn't know what I was doing or why, so I relaxed into a game of Simon Says. Kosher swatted me across the back of my head. "Don't you imitate me, razy gill," he said with disgust. "You find movement in you."

I wasn't allowed to rest. Every hour or so he rationed out a few sips of a bitter tea. I hated his silver hair and grinning eyes. I missed Jonah's lessons. I wanted to munch on Kix, lift my eyebrows, widen my eyes, rub my tummy. It made more sense to hug a fat Mattel Baby Doll than "plance on the blanch rike a cat." Tears blurred the candles and painted faces in Kosher's stuffy prison. "You cly!" Kosher yelled. "You spoiled! In Japan we start at thlee. They take us flom our homes!"

He rapped my bottom with a long bamboo pole. Red silk cloth was tied to its end. Then he handed the pole to me.

"Make fry," he commanded. "Make frying bird." The muscles in my arms shook. I didn't have the strength to hold the pole upright. The silk hung limp.

"Swing. Swing. Swing," he shouted. No matter how hard I tried, I couldn't bring the piece of red silk to life. I smashed the bamboo pole on the ground and it splintered.

"Punish you," Kosher said softly. I winced and took a step backward, but he didn't hit me. He sat me at one of his long worktables and had me paste sequins—one at a time—onto the crown of a puppet. She had huge crossed eyes painted on a bumpy papier-mâché face. Her nose was like a banana. Her teeth were uneven tiles. She had a stupid, arrogant expression. Her long red hair was woven with rubber fish and real shells. She was some kind of sea goddess and no friend of human girls. I despised putting sequins on her crown more than all of Kosher's games. The glue fuzzed up my vision, slowed my breathing, and burned my fingers and chin. "Punish you." Kosher sneered. "Lespect for the object much more impoltant than rove of self. Object has many rives. Knows many things. Been many praces. Bloken stick is bloken ancestol." I went on pasting sequin after sequin. I never seemed to make progress. My nose and eyes ran. My ears rang. I was wheezing. I lost track of time. Kosher's voice startled me.

"Time for you to go to music crass," Kosher said cheerfully. He led me out of his basement, but didn't tell me where to go. I could hear him laughing and talking to himself in Japanese as I surveyed a stairway down the dark hall, looking for wherever I was supposed to be going. Finally I heard music from behind a door directly up the stairs. I found the source of the sound. The door was open.

Robin, tall and powerful, draped in capes and jewelry, sat cross-legged in a tiny cell. Sunlight streamed through the bars on her windows. Bottles of wine lined the windowsill. Posters of Janis Joplin, the Jefferson Airplane, Jimi Hendrix, Virginia Woolf, and Emily Dickinson covered her walls. Guitar, banjo, and mandolin cases lay open on the Persian rug. Wood and steel drums lined the walls. Robin's cell had bookshelves overstuffed with paperbacks and old hardcovers. She burned incense. She grinned a quick loving smile at me and motioned like an octopus with long slow arms that I sit near her. She would've been a stunning woman if it weren't for a sadness that pulled her whole face down, but her round eyes and gray-streaked hair made her earthy, motherly, and exotic. I wanted to crawl onto her lap.

"Rikki, Rikki, Rikki," she sang. "Rikki Raccoon checked into his room, only to find Gideon's Bible. Rockin' Robin, Rockin' Robin." Her voice started in her belly and flowed through her throat. I'd never heard anyone up close with such a gravelly, vibrating, chilling voice. She sounded like one of those blues or rock-and-roll stars I'd heard on the radio. She reached into a deerskin pouch that lay next to her and pulled out a slim Sherman's cigar. She lit it with a candle, took a deep drag, and offered it to me. I shook my head.

"These things are great for Tibetan singin'," she said drunkenly. "You mess yourself up enough, you can get two or three pitches at the same time just like the monks. Some people study for fifteen years to achieve what a pack of Shermans and a bottle of Chablis a day can do in a year. I ask myself what God wants. But God's in anything that works. I found my calling in a coffeehouse in Brentwood, California. I was waitressing there and singing on talent nights. Sasha and Charles used to hang there after rehearsals at USC. I think they were doing some kind of gymnastic Kabuki-style Chekhov—*Three Sisters,* maybe? The three of us fell in love. With Sasha it was intense and physical. With Charles it was like . . . mirrored souls. The three of us went to Japan—Charles and Sasha found Kosher. He'd been kicked outa the Bunraku scene for doin' late-night Kabuki cabarets with outrageous humor. I studied koto and sang with a blind shaman. Then we came back to San Francisco and did street theater, story theater, revamps of Shakespeare and the Greeks. The Shah's wife gave us money to do weird improvs on ruins all over the world. I loved the Greek island of Hydra. I sure as hell met ancient voices there."

Robin let out some harsh guttural syllables. She was an avenging angel and I jumped because I could almost feel her consonants sting me. She laughed and coughed.

"I tell you all this," she said in between coughs, "because there aren't any accidents. There's a reason you came to us right now. Sasha says to wait and the reason will reveal itself in its own place and time. I'm a more aggressive seeker. Tomato, tomahto. Both are valid." Robin leaned back.

I noticed she was very interested in the sound of her own gravelly voice, her pauses, louds and softs. She leaned forward and stroked my cheek with her big hand. Her eyes were all pupils. Her skin was flushed.

"I swallow the rainbow," she sang. "The rainbow, the rainbow. Sasha and I've decided to get married after *The Myth Man,* the new show. It's a perfect time astrologically except that Sasha treats women like shit. Me, worst of all. But I tell myself that's just part of the journey I'm on. Charles says I may as well wear a black veil that just shows one eye. It could've been Charles. It could've been. If, if, if . . . You haven't collected enough 'what ifs' to know what I'm saying, but I look at you and I know you know what I mean."

I didn't.

Robin looked at the cheap Mickey Mouse watch covered by leather bracelets and beads hanging from her thick waist.

"Shit, shit, shit," she growled. "I'm supposed to teach you chanting. Except you don't talk. How bizarre. Sasha says to see every obstacle as a step toward making our work deeper. Very Catholic. Did you know I almost became a nun? I entered a convent and the whole bit. I was heavily into masses and subservience, marrying Jesus, signing up with the Lord. . . ."

Robin breathed in hard and her eyes darted around her cell. She heaved her large frame to a standing position and grabbed a small drum. She placed it in front of me and tapped her flat, dirty foot on the Persian rug. She was so tall, it strained my neck to look up at her.

"Well, folks, we can't chant today," she said, "so we'll just learn another voice."

She stepped over me and squatted close to my back. She smelled of wine and musk oil.

"I'm going to drum on your head and you repeat the beats. I'm not just drummin'. I'm talkin' to ya, Rikki Rickoon. So listen with all of you, all of you, why not take all of you?"

Her fingers tapped clean beats on my skull. I hit the drum in response. The pressure of her fingertips sent bell-like sounds into my ears and down my nose. My hands wanted to sing. The rhythms became more complex. Their melody was soothing and fun. I answered as best I could. Robin never stopped to correct me. I had the feeling she'd forgotten I was there.

Robin kept pounding on my scalp and my head started to hurt. The sounds of her pounding got faster and faster. I couldn't keep up. Finally I stopped drumming and, for the second time that day,

I sobbed. Robin threw her long, muscled octopus arms around me and rocked our bodies from side to side.

"I'm a flake, but I'm a healer and I'm psychic and I'm ancient," she said calmly. "You have a lot of poison inside, little one. When we know each other better, I'll throw the *I Ching* for you so we can have some timeless assistance in our diagnosis. But remember, you're not here by accident. This is the beginning of the unknown. It's always scary." When I'd recovered, Robin wiped my eyes, stood me up, and told me to meet Mustafa in the theater. Once again I plodded in the darkened hallway feeling like I was playing a live game of Clue, but since I didn't know the crimes, I couldn't begin to figure out the identity of the killer.

"Praise Allah—they take a little girl and treat her like a woman. This is God's wish? No. God wants you with your mother." I was standing in the darkened theater. A couple of glaring light bulbs lit the empty stage. Mustafa, the carpenter, was carrying planks of wood and depositing them in piles according to their length.

"I am going to teach you to build a stage?" he said despairingly to the empty space. "No, first I will teach you to get me tea."

Mustafa had brown, kinky hair and sad, slitted eyes. His nose was pointed and his lips were thick and small like a bad drawing of a woman. He looked like a clown without makeup. He moved his burly frame with an arrogant, stiff stride. His belly hung over his khaki pants and his dirty white undershirt rode up, revealing curly hairs and a thick scar like a red worm. His biceps and forearms bulged with muscle.

"You stare at my skin—you invite Satan," he warned me. "I said go get tea."

I hurried through the wing of the stage and found a hot plate.

I boiled tap water in a cheap aluminum pan and poured it into a glass. There was an unlabeled jar of leaves and herbs. I pinched some into the water. It turned brownish red. The glass was hot. Gingerly, I carried it to Mustafa and handed it to him. I looked away. He said nothing. He sipped at the tea. I could feel him staring at me.

"Now we will hammer a nail into a piece of pine"—he sighed—"and, God willing, the wood will not cry."

Mustafa took a thick piece of wood, a thin little nail, and a heavy hammer. With expert aim and a strong wrist, he drove in the nail with one stroke.

"Arnold Palmer, no?" He grinned.

He handed me the hammer and I could barely lift its head up. I held the nail between my thumb and forefinger and let the hammer drop. I smashed my fingers and the nail went flying.

"Go find," Mustafa ordered.

I got on my hands and knees and searched for the nail. I saw it under a platform. I slid on my stomach in the sawdust and dust balls and retrieved it.

Mustafa thrust the hammer at me.

"Again," he said.

This time I let the hammer fall, but got my fingers out of the way. I dented the wood and embedded the nail sideways into its surface.

Mustafa shook his head. He pointed a crooked callused finger at me. "You hurt the wood, you ruin the nail. It does not go in like a clean kill. If you were a boy, I beat you with my belt, like so."

He lifted his arm and I winced. Mustafa lowered his arm slowly, grinned, and lay ten tiny blocks of wood in front of me. He gave me a small plastic bag full of nails.

"You practice," he said, and strutted toward a black curtain in the back of the house. Then he was gone. I stayed alone in the empty theater aiming the hammer at one nail after another. I never got one in. When I'd used up the nails, I balanced one block of wood on top of another like a house of cards. I scratched the words "I'm sorry" onto the linoleum floor with a bent nail. Then I hid in one of the hundreds of folding chairs used for the audience and waited for my tower to collapse. When Mustafa returned, he looked at the tower and my message.

"Tomorrow," he shouted into the darkness, "you learn cut linoleum, sand wood, and replace floor." Then he rearranged my tower so it stood nearly a foot taller. His sense of gravity and balance amazed me. He had some blocks standing on one corner. "Always remember—you girl," he shouted. "No girl wisecracks in my theater. Go to dance class," he said more quietly. "As is right." He mumbled something in Arabic and disappeared behind a black drop.

Reeva was a petite, impatient woman. They said she came from Nigeria. She swung her head and a waterfall of intricately braided snakes slapped against her smooth black arms. She walked briskly in small steps. Her dance studio was lined with mirrors and she examined herself as she talked. Leather and beaded bracelets wound in layers from her wrists to her elbows. Ten or fifteen amulets and stones hung from her neck. Each ear was pierced many times and her earlobes were ripped by the weight of the ascending circular earrings. Her nose was pierced too. Sometimes she fidgeted with the stone inserted in her nostril.

Reeva didn't speak to me at first. She argued with her drummer, a bald black man with only a few teeth and blue tattoos on his cheeks. Even though he was squatting like a frog, I could tell he was tall and lean. He wore patterned cotton pants that looked like pajamas. His eyes drooped at Reeva. He seemed to be mocking her. The two of them argued for quite a long time while I stood and watched. Finally she grabbed me with her sharp little fingers and indicated I should take my slippers off. Then she stood in the middle of the floor and the drummer began to issue commands from his flat talking drum. Reeva showed me how to swing my hair from one side to another as if there were no bones in my neck. Then she had me separate my rib cage from my waist and rotate my upper body. Then we pulsated our stomachs up and down like a river going over rocks. We swung our hips around and threw back our heads. Our bare toes pounded the floor with our knees crooked, our pelvises extended, and our thighs tensed and spread apart. We rushed across the room in a diagonal with our elbows bent, our hands on our hips like proud birds. The drum demanded we come over and shake our bottoms at it and then we retreated. When we finished dancing, I was elated.

"This is the fertility dance," Reeva said, glaring at the drummer. He was picking what was left of his teeth with a twig. "All girls learn this first. It prepares them—" The drummer laughed and said something in another language. Reeva spat at him. She yelled something back. "It prepares them for the marriage, the birth, the time of becoming woman." Reeva would not look at me. She pushed me to the door.

"Tomorrow you will work harder, I hope." She and the drummer commenced yelling at each other and he blasted noisy rhythms in her direction. I could hear her whole body rustling at him like a string of shells. I had no idea what she was so mad about, or why she hadn't noticed that I'd tried very hard to please her.

CHAPTER 3

I stumbled into the dining room. Like all other spaces in the theater, it was wide and drafty with cement floors and aluminum and
wood walls. I could tell factory workers once ate on the colorless,
long metal tables. The kitchen could be seen through a long window
and the ugly metal trays once used to hold hot food hadn't been
removed. There was enough space for at least two hundred people,
but the dining room was less than a quarter full. I didn't recognize
many faces. Most of the people were dressed in light karate clothes
or beat-up sweat pants. They were in their twenties. One Jewish boy
with curly hair and rimless spectacles introduced himself as Bruce.
He ate his brown rice and vegetables and pored over a book by
someone named Artaud. He repeatedly glanced at his watch. "Nice
spinning," he said to me.

Juno balanced a tray covered with plates, spilling over with food.
She fell into her chair. "I'm Eskimo." She shrugged. "I'm addicted
to my own lard." She began to tell me a story about the coyote who
ate all the fish in the North Pole and when the gods demanded he

throw them up he refused. The mouse found one last fish and attached it to the coyote's tail and then the coyote was forced to eat himself tail first and all the fish were restored to the waters.

"Please," Bruce said. "Please, I'm just a boy from Brooklyn."

"And I'm"—the plump girl grinned—"just a soothsayer from the north. I have told your future. You will marry Reeva, but you will have to take a dance class every time you wish to sleep with her."

Bruce grimaced and lowered his head. "Agony and humiliation," he moaned. "I'm just a poor guy who reads a lot."

An ageless man slid into a chair, making noises like Dracula. He was very handsome, dark with dimples and bright, small eyes. His hair was cut short and uneven with a cowlick. As soon as he'd finished biting Juno's neck, he lapsed into a quiet melancholy. He lit a French cigarette and waved the smoke out of his eyes.

"I left my wife and daughter in Europe," he said to me in a raspy French voice. "You make me think of her."

"Which one?" asked Bruce. "The wife or the daughter?"

The French actor half rose from his chair and raised his fist. He pretended to be insulted, but he liked the joke. He sat down and began to shovel food into his mouth. His eyes became thoughtful.

"I do not understand what we are working on," he said.

"Chew your food, Christoph," Juno said.

A large gong broke through the murmuring in the room and the people immediately stood up, scraped their trays into nearby bins, lay them on a rack, and rushed out swinging doors in four directions. The French actor took just a little longer than everyone else and I could tell that he paused for no other reason than to be noticed. He wanted to be out of place. He acted like a great star who had taken this job for an adventure. He wanted me to know he was a deep thinker, and the one who despised authority. He purposely spent a great deal of time chasing a crumb with his fork.

I backed out the two main doors. Sasha was waiting in the narrow hallway perched on one leg like a flamingo. He wrapped me in an Indian blanket and led me to his room. The wide space was spare and divided by Japanese paper screens and furnished with pillows. A low, empty table, handcrafted from wood and tiles, sat in the middle. A white telephone was plugged into a blank wall and was placed on the otherwise empty floor. A painting of elephant heads attached to naked human bodies hung over his square mattress.

Sasha grinned at me and sat cross-legged on the floor. He indicated that I should follow. He poured clear liquid from a half-empty bottle with foreign lettering.

"Vodka," he said. "You want a little sip?"

The warm drink slid down my throat and then burned my stomach.

"I want you to go to bed early tonight," Sasha said. "So our session will be brief." I noticed that the clock on the table read past midnight.

"Most new members train for several days and nights without rest, but I've never worked with a child, so we must improvise. It's clear you are much older than your age." Sasha reached out and touched my cheek. His fingers were cool and dry. "Those eyes keep much concealed," he whispered, "and still you are such a baby. Do you know when you smile your whole face lights up? You should smile more." He pulled his hand away. "Yes, that's right—smile, little one. We do nothing here but theater and I am no more than a skinny clown who likes to pretend he's king." Sasha rolled a cigarette and leaned forward. He smelled of shampoo and vodka and garlic. He took a swig of vodka, lit the cigarette, and then flipped the glowing butt under his tongue. He exhaled fire. I jumped. He reached into his mouth and took the cigarette by two fingers. He took a drag.

"That was a trick, Rikki Nelson," Sasha said. "It has a perfectly simple scientific explanation. But I am fascinated by the things that have real mystery. Like your eyes. And your silence."

I lowered my gaze.

"You know, I had a terrible childhood, Rikki," Sasha said. "My parents were divorced. Charles lived with our mother, but for some unfortunate reason my father wanted me. He thought I was too weak, so he treated me as if I were in a military academy. I had to stand at attention from the moment I woke until I went to school, from the end of school until bedtime. I had to do my homework standing and eat my meals standing. I had no friends, I wasn't allowed to speak, and the only playtime I was allowed was when my father drilled me in wrestling holds, track, or calisthenics. If I became fatigued or lost patience, if I was caught sneaking a call to Charles or a girl at school, my father dragged me into the bathroom and whipped me with his belt. He had terrible rages. Sometimes he grabbed me by the hair and yanked my head into the toilet bowl. Sometimes he forced me under a freezing-cold shower and, if it was winter, locked me out of the house to fend for myself in the ice and snow. My stepmother had a son who was a year younger than me. He was quite mad. He used to sneak into my room at night and say, 'They love you more than me. Your grades are better than mine. You are taller than me. God has deprived me so that you may have my riches and now you must pay me back.' Then he would bite my arm—because that's what he wanted to do to make things even. Later, when Social Services put me back with my mother, I had to have many, many operations to cover the scars on my arms."

I kept my head down. I didn't know whether to believe Sasha's story or not, but I felt privileged that he was telling it to me.

"I support my father now," Sasha said. "He is very ill and I fly to California to be by his bedside. He is my father and I accept the legacy of his cruelty. The mystery is how I learn to transform the pain of his inexcusable acts into something useful and beautiful. A theater artist is an alchemist of human behavior. We take what is horrible and make it into something deep and beautiful. Sometimes, however, we must take golden moments and change them into something savage."

I was trying hard not to sleep. Trying very hard not to sleep. Sasha got up slowly and in stages, like a giraffe. He stretched his long limbs and breathed one deep satisfied syllable.

"What if none of my story is true?"

I peeked up at him. His eyes were closed and his mouth was set in a pleased, luxurious smile.

"What if I lied to you about my whole childhood?" Sasha asked. "Does it make the story any less interesting?"

I didn't know. I was too tired to care.

Sasha reached down and pulled me to my feet.

"Good storytelling is the ability to live other lives during the moments you tell your story. You can transform into other characters —even creatures. No single life is any more interesting or important than any other. It's how you tell the story of that life. Or you can take bits and pieces of lives and collect them into one grand event. The event becomes your life. Its stories are your stories. Your troubled past no longer exists. You can steal things from stories and keep them for your own. I will teach you great stories and they will replace your haunted past. I will help you remake your life in the way that I've succeeded in changing the story of my own life over and over. None of it matters. Really. It's what we call temporary."

He walked me to his door and stopped in front of it. He held my gaze for such a long time that I began to laugh, then twitch, then I worried I might urinate. Then I got weepy, angry, then my face went numb, and finally he smiled and pulled me into a deep warm embrace. His arms could've wrapped around me twice. "We are very much alike," Sasha said. "You are already my own little girl. I intend to protect and defend you." Then he quickly released me and closed his door. I was too tired to think about Sasha's stories. But I knew his words had to be very important. I felt suddenly exuberant and safe. I raced down the hall and up a flight of stairs. Miraculously, I found my room with no trouble. I was convinced Sasha knew magic.

"Look at that blush!" Charles said. "You must've had a good audience with the Pope." Charles was dressed to go out. He wore a fringed deerskin shirt, embroidered with beads, bells, and tiny seashells, which he'd made himself. His blue jeans were faded and tight. The brown two-toned cowboy boots on his feet had pointy toes and thick high heels. The leather was old and soft. He'd messed up his blond hair so that it was a fluffy mop of waves and curls. A diamond earring glittered from one ear. He stopped in front of our mirror.

"I'm very beautiful," he said to me, "but Sasha says I'm Dorian Gray. If you don't know who Dorian Gray is, I'll write down the name and author. As your nanny I feel obliged to provide you with a reading list and exams at midterm and the end of the year. By the time you're ten you should be reading Harold Robbins in Latin, Greek, and Aramaic. No?"

I sat on my mattress and saw that there was a box of Junior Mints on the pillow.

"All the best hotels supply mints at bedtime," said Charles. I passed out with my head next to the unopened candy. I didn't feel Charles remove my shoes or cover me with the Barbie blanket. Charles told me he'd bought the blanket on Orchard Street. He said Orchard Street was the mecca for bargain-hunting housewives like himself. He told me the blanket appeared to him like a vision of perfection for just $12.99. It was soft white flannel with blue waves painted on it. Barbie was waterskiing. Ken was driving the boat.

When the gong sounded several hours later, Charles's bed was empty, but he'd left me a note.

> Anytime they work you too hard, roll your eyes toward the ceiling, stretch your hands out straight, and fall over backward. They'll think you're having a fit. It's much more exciting than a cold and more up their alley. I bought you some Flintstones vitamins. They're in my bead drawer. You chew them. Please take Fred or Barney or dinosaurs or rockmobile as you wish. Until you reach full enlightenment a little dietary supplement doesn't hurt.
>
> Charles

CHAPTER 4

The company was silently running, but not toward the roof. I felt like I was in a herd of penguins rushing toward the sea. Sasha, in a white kimono and sandals, was in the lead. We jogged into the misty night. Cars breathed gray fumes. Streetlights and signs blinked behind the fog. My joints ached. It was hard to swallow. There was a bleary-eyed drunk shuffling slowly, looking for a stoop or a corner on which to pee. He grinned happily when he saw the herd of sleepy actors emerge from the warehouse.

"Hello, hello, hello," he growled. He let out a wild laugh that echoed in the silence of the deserted neighborhood. There was a dog too. He was medium-sized, part terrier, part shepherd or fox. He was starving. He cowered at the size of our group and froze with fear. We had to run around him.

Sasha led us with a brisk, excited pace. A truck driver honked at us and a couple of streetwalkers on the Henry Hudson Parkway cursed in Spanish. We ended up on a burned-out pier. The river was a few feet below us. The night made it appear black and slick.

Small boats, tied up to other piers, creaked against their ropes. The lights coming from New Jersey were dull and sparse.

"Close your eyes," Sasha commanded. "Stay still and memorize your boundaries by the sounds. Then walk freely—keep your eyes closed."

"We're gonna need tetanus shots if we fall in," Bruce complained.

Sasha ignored him, but I couldn't. I thought I'd fall off the pier and drown in the river. Or I'd catch my foot on a rusty nail and cut open my heel. I was more worried about Sasha's disappointment than my own injury. I squinted, with my back to Sasha, and marveled at the sight of all the adult actors breathing noisily and playing a slow-motion game of blind man's bluff. Twice I caught Sasha, eyes open, leaning up against a pole. His mind was far away. Another time I saw Christoph the French actor trying to grab for Reeva's breasts. Reeva ducked him. She was determined to continue the exercise in a proper way.

As we ran back to the warehouse, Robin charged up to me.

"Charles isn't with you?" She gasped. Her neck and cheeks were bright red. She was wearing a turquoise mumu and leather sandals identical to Sasha's. Her long hair was pinned up in a lopsided bun. She looked like a hostess for a Tahitian-style restaurant in Florida.

"*Damn,*" she hissed. "He and Sasha really ought to meditate together. Their Cain-Abel karma gets out of control. I love them both so much. And they're both incredible geniuses—in totally different ways—it should be a yin-yang thing—a balance thing. Anyway, you shouldn't worry about it. They both love you. And they both love me." She let out a panting, hearty laugh. "I'm having a Bloody Mary for breakfast." She was beginning to trail behind me. "I don't care if I puke in tai chi class."

Charles stood in front of the warehouse with one long leg crossed in front of the other. He smoked a thin Sherman's cigar and seemed very relaxed. As we approached the front door, he gave us all a quick curtsy.

"Finished with the handicapped Olympics for today?" he asked.

Sasha walked right up to Charles and I could see Charles cringe a little.

"Charles," Sasha said quietly. "Do you have to break the concentration?"

Charles flung his arm over his eyes.

"Don't blind me, brother," Charles cried. "There's a reason for my betrayal."

I'd never seen two such beautiful-looking men in my life. In the gray light, they looked like sun gods. Their bodies were identically long and lithe and although Sasha was more controlled and Charles dramatic, they possessed the same graceful gestures and poses.

"It wouldn't hurt you to do the work, Charles," Sasha said calmly. "You won't survive the new show on cheap histrionics."

Meanwhile Sasha signaled to the group that we should keep jogging in place.

"My cheap histrionics haven't hurt your vision or your box office," Charles answered cheerfully.

"See what I mean?" whispered Robin.

Sasha swung his whole body around and glared at Robin.

"It's bad enough that you demean your own life," he said to her, "and trivialize the lives of everyone around you, but you will not corrupt a child."

Robin said nothing. Her neck and face turned scarlet and then sickly white. She kept jogging in place.

Charles winked at Robin.

"You know I believe in your workshop," he said to Sasha. His voice was gentle. "No need for A*i*-da-da."

"*I* never want to quarrel," Sasha said. "We have a huge journey ahead of us and so little time." He lowered his voice and put his hand on Charles's shoulder. "How can I handle it alone?"

Sasha opened the front door and signaled for us to go through. As Robin passed him, he patted her affectionately on the rear. Her smile was immediate and bright. Charles shook his head and then made the devil sign with his finger behind Sasha's head. I pretended not to notice. Sasha grabbed Charles and lifted him in a fireman's carry. Charles pretended to struggle and called out in a distressed diva's voice, "Oh, help me, Rikki Nelson."

"You see how close we are?" Sasha grunted, carrying his brother.

"Tweedledum and Tweedledee." Charles coughed with Sasha's bony shoulder in his stomach.

"Abbott and Costello," Sasha said.

"Leopold and Lo . . ." Charles sang.

They started screaming some kind of scat and broke into "You say toh-mah-toh—I say toh-may-toh." Inside the warehouse lobby, Sasha dropped Charles to the floor. They broke into a wild tap dance as they continued their song. I was surprised to see that their dancing seemed as professional as any variety act I'd watched on TV. Each arm and leg was able to pound a different rhythm. The company gathered around and clapped their hands, keeping time and hooting.

"Did you know we were on *The Ed Sullivan Show* when we were boys?" Charles shouted. Sasha slowed down his dancing to catch his breath, but Charles was just taking off. He squatted into Russian kicks and turns.

"Did you know we were chorus girls on Broadway?" Charles mimicked a grinning, kicking showgirl. Charles began to sing the newsboy's theme from *Gypsy* and tried to grab Sasha. "Extra! Extra! Hey, look at the headlines—incredible news is being made . . . da da da." Sasha didn't move, but smiled at Charles. Soon the smile became frozen on his face as the company whooped and cheered Charles's version of Dainty June, Gypsy Rose Lee, and a dancing cow.

"Enough, Charles," he said. "We've got to work."

"Okay, okay," Charles sang—he did an Al Jolson cakewalk on his knees down a narrow hallway toward one of the rehearsal rooms. The group quickly disappeared. I was left standing in the lobby with Sasha. He straightened his posture. His whole face tensed up. The expression in his eyes became distant. His long, thin hands tightened into rigid claws. He posed there—preoccupied. He pretended not to notice me until several minutes had passed.

"Aren't you supposed to be with Kosher?" he asked softly.

I nodded my head.

He touched my hair softly and gave me a gentle push, but didn't look at me.

"Well, then, hup-hup," he said. "You are not quite an expert yet." His voice had regained its odd accent. Charles called it his "fundraising voice," but I found his uneven sentences and odd vowels very mysterious.

"You must get beyond waiting for the orders," Sasha said. "The hunger to learn must come from within."

I backed up toward the stairs to Kosher's basement studio. I wanted to keep my eyes on the morning light. I was sorry that my glimpse of joy had ended so quickly. Sasha stood alone in the lobby as still as a pillar. I watched his tall, thin body, waiting to find out if I could catch a god making a creation. I expected planets and stars to circle around his head. He shifted his weight from one leg to another and snorted quietly. I realized that he could be sleeping, standing up like a horse. I was mesmerized.

A loud "Tsss" snapped in my ear. I jumped. Kosher, his dark face all lines and leather, took me gently by the collar of my T-shirt and led me down the stairs. "You sneak into the dreams of a man," Kosher whispered, "someday you won't get out." I changed into my gray cotton training outfit, took off my shoes, and bowed for him.

"Okay, again with you." He sighed. "But I don't know why."

During the next eight weeks, my music, dance, and stagecraft classes were cut back and Kosher became my principal teacher. I dreaded him. He led me through an arduous regime of physical exercises. I did squats, kicks, circles with my arms. I learned to balance on my hands and stand on my head. Kosher gave me the long bamboo pole and barked at me while I lunged with it, swung it around my head, and lifted its weight toward the ceiling. He manipulated my spine with his quick, skillful fingers so I'd learn perfect posture. I had to sit on my knees with my legs crossed without curling my back. He led me through the basic moves of tai chi, aikido, and karate. He disappeared for long periods of time, leaving me frozen in a position (sometimes balanced on one leg), and I was not to move a muscle until he returned. He barked at me as I progressed through strange square-shaped Japanese and Indian dance poses imitating pictures of gods and goddesses. I repeated the difficult poses over and over. Often I became sore, sick to my stomach, or weepy. If I limped, Kosher gave me a eucalyptus grease to rub into the correct accupressure points. If I threw up, he gave me a rag to clean the vomit and then taught me how to brew a camomile and mint tea to settle my stomach. He saw illness and pain as proof that I was working my body harder than my mind. Sometimes he'd let out a high-pitched giggle when I'd stumble or collapse. "Body go east—mind go west," he'd say mockingly. He despised crying. He just stood and stared with his black eyes squinting and blinking. "No such thing," he'd say. "No such thing." He'd stomp to his workbench, muttering to himself in Japanese. He wouldn't return until my tears and hiccups had completely subsided, and then kept his distance as if I'd had an infectious disease.

We went directly from exercises to mask work. Kosher carved a small, expressionless face out of wood. I held it on by clamping an inside ridge with my teeth. After an hour my jaw ached but I disappeared behind the neutral wooden face. I learned to express hunger for a bowl of rice, fear of thunder or a beast, wonder at a delicate flower, fatigue from planting, curiosity at a wrapped package, and other reactions and gestures from the details of human life. He insisted that I only use simple angles of my body. I wasn't expressing *my* emotions, he told me. I was to transform into the mask's character. If I did it right, the blank wooden face would come to life. Kosher shoved me in front of a mirror and left me alone with the dead faceless mask. When I couldn't awaken it, I felt mocked and tormented. Now and then if I saw a flicker of expression in the mask I'd get excited, botch my movements, and watch the life fade from the mask. Then I'd beg her to stay with me. But it was Rikki Nelson's arms outstretched toward the mirror. The mask wouldn't accept my pleas. The mask rejected anything but the total sacrifice of my feelings. I had to become empty inside in order for her to come to life.

"That is why actor has thousand hearts," Kosher said. "You give one evely time mask needs it."

One morning Kosher didn't lead me in exercises, meditation, or mask work. He was crouched on his stool painting an exotic bird.

"You rook alound," he said, not glancing at me, "memolize evelything, okay?"

46

I didn't know what Kosher wanted from me. I never did, but following his orders seemed essential to my survival. He and Sasha worked together every night. I was sure Kosher reported on me. If Sasha was displeased, I'd be thrown out. Therefore, I did exactly as I was told. So I examined the room, as Kosher had ordered, memorizing what I could.

Kosher's workshop was like a graveyard for ancient creatures. Half-finished masks with horns and beaks peeked out from behind jeweled muslin capes. Wooden and papier-mâché claws, tails, and hooves lay in broken angles against the brightly painted heads of bulls, lions, and dragons. Headless torsos of sculpted rubber lizards and fish were lined up against cement walls. Swords, bows and arrows, and helmets hung down from the ceiling on nails. The long worktables were laid out with neatly stacked tools. Unfinished lizard claws, human hands, half masks with bulging eyes, odd-colored noses, screaming lips and colored teeth, and long wigs lay between the tools as if someone were preparing for a cannibal feast. There were even some disembodied rubber intestines and imitation human hearts hung on wire above washbasins. They were painted to look like they dripped red blood. These masks, props, and set pieces jumped out at every turn—like the ghouls and skeletons in the haunted house ride at the local amusement arcade back in Sarasota.

After a while I became weary of my tour. I trudged back to where Kosher was intently painting blue feathers on his bird mask. He made me stand silently and wait for him. Then he got up, reached into a drawer, and pulled out a black hood. He put it over my head. He walked soundlessly away from me and I heard him switch off the light. There was no hum from the electricity. My hood was sewn from several layers of black muslin and cotton. The darkness surrounded me like a solid mass.

Suddenly I heard Sasha's voice. "Find me," Sasha said. He could've been right next to me or at the farthest end of the room. He could've been standing on a table or lying on the floor. I'd lost all sense of distance and direction. "Don't hesitate," Sasha ordered. "You must learn to feel my voice." I edged my way along what must've been a worktable. My hands touched the cold metal of tools

47

and the rough surfaces of wood carvings. My feet shuffled unevenly, stopping nervously every three or four steps. I feared I might fall off the edge of the cement floor and plunge down an elevator shaft or a deep crevice. I'd never thought I was afraid of the dark, but under the stifling hood in the silent dark basement, I felt pursued. Any one of Kosher's puppets or masks could come alive. Strangers could step out from the walls, the floor could turn to snakes, predators with spider arms might be curled in corners. Kosher or Sasha might throw me to the floor and bind my hands and feet. I quickened my pace and knocked over a stool. I waited to be struck, but I wasn't. I sidestepped in an empty space and rammed into the corner of a table. My left hip burned. "Concentrate," Sasha said. "Are you trying to feel my vibrations?" I groped along a cement wall and pulled down some kind of netting. I untangled myself. I was breathing hard and fumbling. My hands burned from the rope. "The dark must be your cradle," Sasha said. "She is your mother." His voice sounded muffled and distant, as if I'd been traveling in the wrong direction. I made a sharp turn and cracked my head on a shelf. My forehead throbbed and I felt warm blood trickle into my eyes. My throat tightened and my hands tingled. I lay down on the cold cement so I wouldn't faint.

"That's better," Sasha said. "Stay in that place and feel my vibrations." But I was lying in the pitch-black and I was bleeding and helpless. I lay there expecting the weight of a stranger on my ribs and hips. I felt his breath on my lips. Men were weeping on my chest. They threatened me in whispers. I couldn't see my mother in the doorway. I didn't dare call out to her. The hood was suffocating. I imagined someone stuffing the cloth into my nose and mouth. I was losing consciousness. I heard Sasha's voice.

"Don't give up," he said. "Find me. Find your way out of the dark."

I crawled on my hands and knees. Then I pulled myself up by a worktable. Any object that got in my way I hurled to the floor. It relieved me to slam object after object to the floor. I threw some things into the air. I crawled over a table—I didn't care what I stepped on. I got to the floor again. I crawled a short distance and began to shake violently from head to toe. Then I grabbed Sasha's legs and held on to him.

"Bravo, little girl," Sasha said. He gently removed the hood from my head. I didn't recognize him. I couldn't remember what he looked like and the room was very dark. Kosher snapped on the lights. I bit Sasha hard in the leg. He kicked me lightly and laughed. I let go.

Sasha's blond mane glistened under the light. It was too bright. I had to squint. He put a gentle hand on my shoulder and called over my head to Kosher.

"Did she destroy our show?" he asked pleasantly.

Kosher was picking up various masks and tools from the floor.

"No plobrem," he said, giggling.

Sasha fixed his wide gray eyes directly on mine. I was still squinting from the brightness as well as the blood and sweat that was running through my lashes.

"You found me." Sasha grinned. "Few do. That means we are able to work within a special closeness."

I went deaf. A wall of white light rose in my eyes. I felt very calm and strange. I kicked him hard in the leg and punched him with both fists in his stomach. Then I turned around and, although I was dizzy and breathless, I ran as fast as I could out of the workshop and to my room. As I was making my way through the basement, I heard Sasha and Kosher laughing and talking to each other in rapid Japanese. I decided I would quit before I was fired, but I didn't have an address for Jonah. I lay painfully on my mattress and waited for sleep. The room jerked, lurched, and violently rocked. I felt sick. I told myself I was on a huge white ocean liner strung with Christmas lights. A dance band was playing.

I awoke a short time later. The light in the room was a soft gray and blurry. Someone was patting a cool cloth on my forehead. Each tap brought a soothing and pain, simultaneously.

"You have quite a little lump there, Cassius Clay," Sasha said. I didn't move or smile.

"Of course you are very angry," Sasha said. He washed the scrapes on my arms and legs with a cold, stinging astringent. I was surprised by the ease and gentleness of his nursing. "And you have every right to be. Sometimes I forget you are a child." He stroked my cheek lightly with the tips of his fingers. I could see his face now. His skin was pale, his eyes had a shadow beneath them. He was ashamed. I struggled to sit up. My joints burned. He lifted each arm and leg, rotating it gently, pushing it in and pulling it out, loosening the muscles and freeing the pain.

"We call that exercise a 'trust' exercise," Sasha continued. "The idea is that we know each other so well and we trust each other so much that we can *sense* each other in any situation. If the lights go out; if a crowd rushes the stage; if there is a bad storm or someone is hurt or the set collapses midperformance. We also use the exercise to learn how to feel each other's rhythm and vibrations. That way our work is always a real dance between people who like and need each other and not just an automatic imitation of relationships."

Sasha let me lie still. I felt oddly calm. As if he were talking to me from inside a dream, from several different directions at the same time.

"Do you understand even a little?" he asked sadly. I liked the attention and wanted to drag it out as long as possible, but I was keenly aware that Sasha was urgently busy. I'd be selfish if I demanded too much more time, like Robin. And Charles said Sasha treated neediness with scorn and impatience. Reeva wanted nothing to do with him and therefore he frequently sat in on her classes listening to the drums and songs, watching her dances, saying there was a land in her heart where he wanted us to travel.

"Do you understand?" Sasha asked again. I kept my eyes away from him, but I nodded very clearly yes. If he wanted to get religious about a game of blind man's bluff, that was his business. I remembered the sound of Sasha and Kosher laughing and talking in their fast-clicking Japanese. I was not completely convinced by Sasha's seriousness.

"By the way, Kosher says your progress is nothing short of remarkable," Sasha said.

Now he had my full attention.

"He's never worked with a little girl." Sasha grinned. "They don't do that in his country. He's very ornery and very sexist, but I deeply respect him because he knows more about dance and theater than anyone. He was my teacher. He *hated* working with you at first, but now he would kill for you. . . ." I tried to conceal my pride. Sasha had just taken a huge leap in winning my heart back. I wanted to remain withdrawn and aloof like Reeva, but it was going to be hard work.

"So, are we friends?" He put his hand on my shoulder and stared into my eyes.

My mouth twitched into a smile. I shrugged.

"Good!" Sasha said. "Now I have something I really want you to see."

He lifted me up and carried me from my room. I felt triumphant to see that he was limping where I'd kicked and bit him. He carried me silently through the cement-block hallways to the floor that Mustafa had torn apart and restructured as the small proscenium theater. Now metal and fake velvet chairs had been installed. There were about two hundred of them. There was also another addition—a small balcony with a lighting booth and wrought-iron catwalk. Sasha sat me down in the back row. He tousled my hair and walked away. The stage was empty. It was lit by a single bulb, but many people were milling about and stretching, chanting and practicing moves. Sasha summoned Bruce. Bruce carried an old thick notebook with lots of scribbles on the cover and odd papers that were pasted onto other papers. He wore old, ripped blue jeans, sandals, and an Indian shirt. His rimless glasses slipped down onto his nose. He had a pierced ear. A heavy embroidered shoulder bag hung on him. He looked in my direction and smiled as Sasha spoke rapidly to him. He lumbered toward my row. "Excuse me," he said in a Groucho Marx voice, "is this seat taken?" I rolled my eyes in disdain.

"Yeah," Bruce said. "I don't know why people always feel like they have to make jokes around kids. It's very demeaning." He sat down and crossed his legs over the velvet seat in front of him. He wore sandals. His feet smelled like wet wool. He offered me a Life Saver. I refused. "I live on 'em," he said. "I'm sure their fascist corporate manufacturer includes some kind of chemical in their recipe that causes addiction. And probably the paper wrapper is man-ufactured by the same company that supplies the wrappers for the government's napalm capsules in Vietnam. You work in the the-ater—you compromise."

I yawned. Bruce bit his lip. His feelings were hurt.

"Yeah," he said. "People must talk at you all the time—given you are a child and also can't talk back. We should be more militant about the rights of the handicapped. Do you know what the show is about?" I shook my head. Up until this moment I had given up on the idea that there was a show. "Sasha said you might not. I'm the dramaturge and the stage manager—that means I'm not allowed to act yet. So I keep track of all the character and plot interpretations that everyone, except Sasha, remembers. The name of the show we're taking on tour is *The Myth Man*. You know, like Robert Preston? *The Music Man*? Anyway—our show is a kinda revue. A metaphys-ical follies." I blinked at him. "Ed Sullivan for snobs?" I smiled. He looked relieved. "The way it goes is that there's a small child—guess who?—and the kid won't go to sleep. So her ancient, wise grand-father conjures up some Greek gods to teach her about life, death, and the here, there, and everywhere after. The gods become so real, the grandfather has no power to help the little girl. She must save herself and her grandfather with what she learns on her journey." Bruce slipped a red Life Saver into his mouth. "Don't ask me if the girl ever gets to sleep because I don't know. And I don't know who the gods are because they keep changing. I'm supposed to supply the ancient Latin and Greek text for the scenes, but so far there aren't any scenes. But it's like the last show we did, all those little decisions will be made ten minutes before the first audience walks in." Bruce took out a bag of potato chips from his shoulder bag and opened them with a nervous jerk. Half the chips scattered to the floor. "You didn't see that—okay? Mustafa will execute me." I put my hand on my heart.

Bruce raised his fist into the air. "You rock, you roll," he chanted. The lights onstage began to come up to a bright amber color. Bruce stood hurriedly, squashing the potato chips with his sandals, and glanced nervously toward the lit platform.

"Shit," he said. "I've got to study my Euripides, Aeschylus, Aristophanes, Homer, and Seneca for some Top-Forty lyrics." He half ran toward Sasha and then stood waiting for what seemed like a half hour until Sasha had finished an intense consultation with a mousy-looking girl. She had long brown hair pulled back in a thin uneven braid. Her eyes popped out and she blinked a lot as if she wore contact lenses. Her teeth were large and when she smiled, you could see a lot of her gums. She wore an old shirt with short puffy sleeves and embroidery. Her skirt was black and neither long nor short. It hung a bit below her knees. She held a tape recorder and every time she talked, she pointed the microphone at her mouth. When Sasha talked, she directed it at him. When Sasha talked, her face took on the kind of rapturous pain you see in pictures of Mary in a Catholic church. I didn't like her. I was relieved when she packed up her tape recorder. She walked down the aisle with the posture of a dancer, but her body had no life. She blinked at me and attempted a friendly smirk, but I turned away.

Drums started beating. Strong, relentless low bells chimed in unison. Sasha motioned for me to sit closer. I'd become so accustomed to viewing his world as an outsider I wasn't sure I wanted a closer view. I moved to the third row. Robin was flailing at huge flat red drums and shining gongs. She was hidden behind a wooden frame that looked like a hut made of instruments.

Bruce ducked over to me and leaned down. "Do you know how Zeus gave birth to Athena?" he rasped. I shook my head no. He looked like he was about to tell me, but got distracted and hurried with his clumsy side steps to Sasha.

Mustafa leaped onstage. He wore a black cape and full mask. The nose was painted and the nostrils flared like a bull's. The mouth scowled and the beard and the hairs of the wig stood up from the mask as if caught in a violent wind. The wild mane and beard were knee length, woven in earth colors and smeared with mud. Mustafa stomped furiously as if a large insect clung to his back and he wanted it off. He clenched his fists in agony and shook his upper body. His cape flew open and his body was naked, but painted with mud underneath. His muscles and veins bulged. He let out cries of pain.

He made his skin shiver like a horse. I'd never seen a man move his muscles and skin separately the way Mustafa did.

The drums doubled in speed. The crashing of the gongs became one continuous thunderous wave. A piercing high note sang above the chaos. Suddenly a head peered out from the center of Mustafa's waterfall of hair. It was a small head. It was greasy and brown and covered with blood. A rat could've been wriggling its way out of a pile of garbage. It was disgusting. The creature began to undulate from side to side like a snake, and as it grew larger I realized I was watching Reeva. She was naked, painted with red and covered with grease. As she struggled to release herself from Mustafa's wig, the music changed to steel drums and harps and music of breath and relief.

Reeva's arms and hands became birdlike. She jerked her head from side to side, blinked her eyes, and rotated her rib cage slowly, showing off her dark breasts. She was transforming from a wormy creature into a beautiful girl. She was still attached to Mustafa. She turned and crawled up the front of him, spread her legs over his mask, and hooked her knees over his shoulders. She hung upside down and then sat up and thrust herself forward. Then she placed a foot on his left shoulder, trying to stand. Her balance was off. When she put the other foot on Mustafa's right shoulder, she and Mustafa rocked back and forth unevenly until Mustafa fell flat on his ass and Reeva landed on top of him. The two of them began to shake quietly with laughter. Within moments they were rolling on the floor screaming and whooping. The house lights snapped on. The music stopped.

I could see that Sasha was trying to smile, but his neck and face broke out in splotches of pink and red. He let Mustafa and Reeva carry on for a while before he jumped up on the stage and clapped three times. Kosher appeared from the wings. Mustafa and Reeva stopped laughing. Kosher lovingly checked the mask and wig. Reeva wrapped herself in a terry-cloth bathrobe and wiped the blood off herself with paper towels. Sasha started talking rapidly. I heard bits and pieces. "You don't fall," he said, "unless a part of you wants to or unless you need to sabotage this rehearsal . . . a lack of attention is not only dangerous, it's an indication of an overall cynicism . . . a denial of life . . ."

I heard Mustafa say, "Man, I just lost my *balance*." Mustafa hung his head and Reeva looked away as if she were uninterested.

"Hey," Reeva said to Kosher, "you expect me to hang from his shoulders, then *stand* on his shoulders with all that *grease* on my feet? How am I supposed to get traction?"

"Kosher," Sasha said evenly, "Venus is supposed to come from Zeus's *hair*, not stomach. From hair—top of head. Okay?" Kosher squinted at Mustafa's head and lifted off the mask and wig. Mustafa took a deep breath of relief. Kosher hoisted Reeva to her feet and with two quick lifts managed to balance her on his flat, silver head. Then he helped her jump to the floor. "I fix," he said. And he dragged his tangled mask and wig offstage as if it were a disobedient child. Sasha rubbed his eyes. He seemed tired.

"What's next?" he called to Bruce. Bruce lifted his sloppy notebook close to his eyes.

"Narcissus," he shouted.

"Is Charles ready?" Sasha asked.

"Charles doesn't seem to be here," Bruce said timidly.

Sasha's eyes flashed and then went cold. Bruce anxiously scanned a page of his notebook.

"I mean, we could do Orpheus or—Robin's here—we got Minerva, or we could work Rikki Nelson into the beginning," he suggested.

"No," Sasha said quietly. "When Charles gets here, have him practice his scene without me. In fact, you all can go over whatever pieces you choose without me. I really have to decide whether we should keep this group together." He smiled sadly. "Sometimes things just run their course."

"Sometimes people have off day," Mustafa yelled. "Every mistake not telegram from God to Sasha."

Robin stood up from behind the racks of instruments.

"This work is our life, Sasha."

Sasha looked straight ahead.

"Maybe you believe what you say," he replied. "Maybe the decay in our commitment is so deep, we can't see the rot or make ourselves clean again." After he walked out, the theater sank into a dark silence. I remember feeling fidgety and itchy, the way I did in school when a teacher punished the whole class after only two kids had misbehaved.

After about ten minutes, Charles dashed onstage, loaded down with shopping bags and packages wrapped in brown paper and string. He was out of breath from running. He wrinkled his nose and cupped a hand over his eyes as if looking into the sun.

"How late am I?" he called out.

"About twenty minutes," Bruce answered testily. Charles stamped his foot. "Oh shit, shit, shit, shit, shit," he growled. "Where's Sasha?"

"He left," Robin answered from behind a drum. "I guess we're all sitting here trying to understand how we contributed to this breakdown of the dream. Sasha's not sure he can keep going, Charles."

"Oh, for God's sake," Charles moaned. He dropped his packages and gestured toward the ceiling. Then he stood up straight and clenched his fists.

"Would someone go get my brother," he said through clenched teeth, "and tell him the lines on Orchard Street were impossible? He *knew* I was buying fabric on Orchard Street."

Reeva strutted across the stage and patted Charles's arm.

"He's being a diva," she said. "Let him stew."

Charles shook his head tearfully. "No, you know he has this absolutely obsessive thing about time," Charles said. "He can't help it. He's under a lot of pressure right now." Charles's voice half begged, half ordered a command. "I will get into my costume. And while I am doing that I want someone to go and find my brother. Please? When you get him, remind him that I was on Orchard Street buying fabric for the new costumes and that I have been standing in lines since eight A.M. this morning. Also, tell him that I am very, very sorry. *Make* him come back here. Now, *go*." Bruce took off. I was surprised at Charles's authority. He let out a loud breath, gathered up his bulky packages, and headed for the dressing rooms.

"Hi, Pussycat," he called to me. I waved.

I sat in the tense theater for the next half hour. I was somewhat worried that Sasha wouldn't come back. Mustafa and Reeva were sulking. Kosher was talking quietly to himself in the wings. Robin and her musicians were meditating and chanting. The rest of the company wandered in and out murmuring to each other. I'd been sitting in the darkness watching these little plays for what seemed like hours. I was pretty bored.

Bruce came through the back with quick, heavy strides. "He's here—he's here," Bruce announced.

I turned around and Sasha was standing under the exit sign. Charles walked out onstage. He wore only a kimono. His legs and feet were golden and bare. His eyes were painted like a Japanese woman. His skin was brushed with white powder. "I went to Orchard Street," he said gently. "I had to buy fabric for the costumes. I left at seven o'clock this morning and I thought for sure I could make it. But it must have been a sale or something because everything took forever. I must've gone into twenty stores to find that black silk we talked about. I'm *really* sorry."

Charles seemed to be telling the truth and I was surprised to see that he seemed genuinely concerned about Sasha's mood. Charles talked to his brother like a man coaxing another off a ledge. Sasha padded reluctantly down the aisle at first, stopping and listening. Then he sat himself on the edge of the stage where Charles stood.

"What did you find?" Sasha asked.

Charles turned toward his pile of packages, which lay directly in the wing. He meticulously unwrapped them. He gracefully held out each bolt of colorful fabric, knelt down, and laid it before Sasha like an offering. Sasha and Charles examined the texture and weave of each of Charles's purchases. They shared the pleasure of touching the silks and cottons and argued excitedly over who could wear which colors. Mustafa let out loud coughs and belches from time to time, and Reeva paced in an upstage circle, cursing under her breath. I squirmed and tried to sleep with my chin on my chest. Finally, after every single bolt of material had been examined, Sasha announced that we'd begin with Narcissus. Charles piled his fabrics neatly in a corner and loped off to fix his makeup.

Kosher and Mustafa rolled a beautiful miniature garden onto the stage. In the center of the garden was a real pool filled with water and rimmed with rocks. I think the bottom of the pool was made of mirrors. Sasha checked the garden, nodded, and then he flopped into a seat next to me as Kosher fidgeted with the mechanics of their invention. He kicked out a trapdoor in the stage and rolled the whole garden over it. Sasha put his hand on my knee and patted me distractedly.

"So how do you like our little soap opera?" he whispered. He grinned at me and his gray eyes were full of mischief. He was mocking himself. "A child would find all this ridiculous, no?" he said. His accent was thick and musical. "But we are all children. Otherwise how could we believe so much in a game like this?"

The lights went black. A field of light projected a golden path from one side of the stage to the other. Charles stepped into the light. He was transformed. His body was naked except for a short white silk skirt. The fabric glistened under the light. His curly hair billowed around his head. His painted eyes appeared very youthful and innocent. Yet if he turned his head to the side, he could be a sly girl. His elegant nose and painted flowery lips brought out the sharp angles of his cheekbones and his smooth high forehead. He'd shaved his mustache. His face was without blemish. He was neither man nor woman; he flowed from one to the other. His chest and arms seemed hairless, delicate, and a rosy peach color. He managed to be lean and hard and silky at the same time. He gave off a golden glow and his hands and wrists wove delicate gestures in the light. He was wrapped in bracelets and necklaces of fresh white daisies and babies' breath. He loped through the lighted road like a young boy, but when he paused or made a turn, he became a wild young horse. He went from floating to galloping without any effort at all. Every inch of him was beauty, but he didn't know he was stunning. He leaped and danced innocently, transfixed with the light, the air, and the joy of movement itself.

And there was an oddness to this boy-man. Despite his frolicking, his eyes seemed empty or lost. It was as if his soul had been stolen or blocked by a spell. His face reflected less emotion than a clean white mask, and there was a deeply listless human heart buried inside.

I glanced over at Sasha. He sat rigidly in his seat. His eyes were moist and he was mouthing silent syllables. His hands doubled every movement of Charles's hands. His feet danced in place every time Charles slid forward. When Charles turned to the left or right, Sasha's body shifted a tiny bit in his chair. He was incredibly tense. A thin vein throbbed on his forehead. An odd smile appeared on his lips from time to time and he nodded his head.

Then the story changed. Narcissus discovered the rock garden and sank to his knees in front of the mirrored pool. He glimpsed at his reflection and gasped. When he gasped, Sasha gasped. Charles leaned forward with curiosity and stared into the mirrors. Every time he made the most minuscule of movements, he became more deeply involved with his acquaintance in the pool. With one finger he lovingly sketched the outline of his reflection's golden ringlets, wide eyes, nose and lips, long neck, shoulders and arms. Sasha leaned forward in his seat and subtly duplicated Charles's caresses. Then Narcissus' placid expression seemed to shatter into pieces over the mirrored pool. His features became soft, as if someone had taken off a mask to reveal a human face underneath. He was no less beautiful; in fact, his innocence and anguish seemed to enhance the perfect face. His eyes burned with love. His need for the creature in the pool pulled him toward the water like a magnet. Narcissus was so in love he longed to join with his reflection in the water. He began to do a soft erotic mating dance.

I heard Bruce whisper to someone, "He's the best. The fucking Callas and Nureyev of this group. Everything we could ever know is in his left hand. The rest is totally beyond us. Shit. I'm watching history."

I turned to Sasha and watched him lean farther in his seat. His hands were raised slightly and he was touching invisible water with his fingertips. I began to shiver.

Charles played with his love in the pool a while longer. At one point I remember he took off his skirt and swayed, naked, over the reflection. He ran his fingers over its chest and thighs and ran the tip of his forefinger along his penis. I could feel his need to hold and be held by his lover. I wanted to shout out and warn him that it was just a reflection, but I wasn't sure anymore. I was becoming convinced that there was a real lover in the mirrored pool. Charles remained calm and graceful, but I sensed his frenzy growing. Sasha looked as if he were going to explode from the tension. It came as a relief when Charles finally dove into the mirrored pool. I could hear people sniffing and sobbing quietly in the house. Sasha sank back into the seat. He glanced over at me and gave me an exhausted smile. I looked up on the stage and saw that Charles's feet were sticking straight up out of the trapdoor hidden by the mirrors. He began to do a little puppet show with them. His voice echoed out from the tunnel underneath the stage. "Oh, Kosher," he sang. "I detect a small problem in our measurements. Or maybe my body doesn't bend correctly. Oh, Kosher, darling, I'm stuck."

Mustafa and Kosher ran onstage and gently tried to lift Charles out of the trap door by his feet, but he was at an odd angle and wouldn't budge. They didn't want him cut by the mirrors that surrounded the small hole into which he'd tried to disappear. Kosher started to laugh—an odd, high-pitched trill. Mustafa snorted like a bull. Soon I could hear tight bursts of laughter from all over the theater. Fearfully, I glanced out of the side of my vision at Sasha. He grinned and shook his head.

"Let's take dinner," he announced. "Someone is playing jokes on us today."

As I was leaving the theater, I watched as Kosher hurried offstage to slither into the crawl space. I hoped he knew how to teach Charles to pull himself out. I wondered if they'd have to chop up the floor. The idea intrigued me. I liked the idea of Kosher in trouble. I felt shy when Charles came in to dinner. He had a round pink lump on his forehead and his makeup was smudged. He bent over me, gingerly, as if his back hurt. He kissed me on the top of my head.

"Nanny heard that you trashed Kosher's workroom and neutralized Sasha today. I'm so proud."

The exercise with the black hood might as well have happened weeks in the past. I stared at Charles's forearms and hands. They were cut up and scraped from dragging himself out of the tunnel under the stage. Charles caught me gaping.

"Not to worry," he said. "I just forgot my parachute. You can't dive into the floor without a life jacket. The tide is too unpredictable." Then he sang:

> Roun' roun' git aroun'
> I git aroun'
> Roun' roun' git aroun'
> I git aroun'—ah ah ah ooh

He smiled and nuzzled me while simultaneously stealing the carrot cake off my tray. He reached tenderly into his pocket with his red and swollen fingers, pulled out a Kit Kat, and placed it where the carrot cake had been.

"I'm your nanny," he whispered. "I'm here to see you have a normal childhood."

CHAPTER 5

We never kept track of the days or the weeks or the names of months. We didn't celebrate birthdays or holidays. But I noticed there was a fresh coolness in the air I'd never experienced in Florida. Charles said it was autumn. He sang what he claimed was a French cabaret tune: "I love autumn in the springtime, in the stairways and the hall/ I love autumn all year over; autumn's best when it falls in the fall." Charles told me that autumn in New York was a buffet of sensual pleasures. The light was imported from Jerusalem. The smell of burning leaves from Burgundy. The shadows came from the Painted Desert. He told me about flea markets, outdoor art exhibits, farmer's markets, street fairs, and parades. He wanted to take me to the pier to watch New Jersey turn from an industrial wasteland to a polluted rainbow of rotting leaves.

But I wasn't allowed outside the immediate area of the warehouse. Sasha said I was at a crucial stage of my training and shouldn't be distracted. He told Charles there'd be time for tourist trips, but for now I had to concentrate on my "internal journey." Charles got mad and asked Sasha when he'd decided to become Mother Superior. They bickered over my upbringing like two parents, but Charles was the one to give in. I didn't care that much. I knew they both loved me. And I was often too tired to enjoy the souvenirs Charles brought me—a T-shirt with the Statue of Liberty on it, a ticket stub from a big outdoor concert of the Grateful Dead, a tiny pumpkin with a curved stem, and a green plastic necklace that lit up in the dark.

Meanwhile, my training advanced. I started each morning with Kosher, who not only gave me tai chi, kung fu, and Kabuki steps to enhance my strength and coordination, but insisted I imitate every acrobatic stunt I'd seen the older actors do onstage. I fell and hit my head so many times, I thought I was going blind. Then, as always, at the end of the session I was to stand absolutely still until he released me. Sometimes he got so overwhelmed with his duties he forgot all about me. My muscles would begin to shake with fatigue as I prayed for him to return. When he'd rediscover me, he'd try to cover his surprise: "Oh, you," he'd say, his face crinkled in a half smile. Sometimes he'd rub my shoulders and calves with eucalyptus oil, or if he was in a foul mood, he'd gruffly expel me from the room as if my being here at all was my own fault. Some days he kept me with him for hours. I'd stand in front of the mirror trying on masks for him. "No ego, no ego!" he'd bark. I'd stare into the mirror, trying to make my heart into a piece of wood so the masks would transform into whatever petulant frog or terrified lizard he was creating.

There were mornings when Sasha ran in to examine a mask and he and Kosher would talk hurriedly in Japanese. Kosher often painted a face on a blank mask as I stood obediently holding it in my teeth. Sasha would nod, clap Kosher on the back, and leave without ever saying hello to me. I was invisible. On one rare and special occasion Sasha slid in and watched my whole session, his arms folded, his back soldier straight. After several hours, he smiled, tossed his long straight mane from his eyes, and whispered, "That's not bad." I felt a rush of energy and rediscovered the reason to do whatever Kosher ordered with extra effort and commitment.

63

I dreaded working with Reeva because her moods changed so unpredictably. She could be mischievous and tough, teaching me sexy moves and wisdoms I didn't understand about male musicians and actors. ("Don't trust the ones who smile and show their gold caps.") Or she'd snarl at me and behave as if it were her duty to hate little white girls. On those days, dancing was misery. There were black students who interned with the company, but Reeva wouldn't let them talk to me. If I didn't perform a step correctly, Reeva acted as if I were mocking the culture of her ancestors. ("Those racist pilgrims wouldn't dare shake their butts. It was sacrilegious. They just killed colored and Indians and prayed to phony rascist gods. That's your people, Miss Nelson.") If I couldn't find the beat, she acted as if I were treating her with defiance. ("I'm not your cleaning lady, Blondie.") Some days, she'd discipline me by hitting me with a long switch. She said that's how it was done in Africa. The switch stung the backs of my legs, but didn't do too much damage. She could be sulky and remote and then her tiny strong body would explode into violent outbursts. She was always throwing coffee cups at the drummer. "Black men," she shouted, "are the white man's weapon to destroy black women." But her haughtiness and fury were balanced by a broad, toothy smile that softened all her features and brought mischief into her eyes. And, on many days, she dashed forward and hugged me for no reason, spreading kisses over my face. When she danced, she'd smile right at me, as if her whole body was telling me stories. Her moods shifted so quickly, I was always careful to not make a move or expression that might set her off. Reeva's mercurial nature seemed to attract men. Bruce and Mustafa were both in love with her. She made fun of them and flirted with them. But she didn't want them, she told me. One was a large clown, the other a white devil.

She was completely devoted to Sasha in her own remote, then noisy, withheld, then violent way. The rumor was that he'd seen her onstage in a Baptist church somewhere along the Georgia countryside. Reeva's foster father, a mad fundamentalist preacher, locked her in a chicken coop in between services. Sasha rescued her and sent her to Nigeria to study. It was a rumor, but I believed it.

64

Reeva behaved the best around Robin. Although tall, big-boned, and muscular, Robin could dance with extraordinary grace and power. She drummed as well as any man and respected African music deeply. Robin said that both she and Reeva were "earth mothers." She gave Reeva amulets and long earrings. Robin's years as a backup singer to several Motown groups gave her a genuine ease with the sways and dips of black dancing, but she didn't imitate Reeva or her friends. And she sang the blues and African chants with a wild but sweet rasp. She agreed wholeheartedly with Reeva's diatribes against white people and apologized many times to Reeva on behalf of her entire people. Reeva and Robin recognized each other as "sister sorceresses." They vowed to be nurturing and wise, but lethal if crossed.

The few sessions I had with Robin were full of mischief and games. She drummed on my head. She taught me about overtones by encouraging me to run full speed into a huge gong. She painted numbers on my fingertips so I could remember single chords on her oud or Kora and made up tap steps for complicated rhythms. She gave me a huge flat tray of Magic Markers, and then she sang her blistering, mysterious scat and I got to draw what I heard. I wasn't very musical, but Robin never berated me. She'd stare at me for a long time (all of them, except Charles, had a tendency to stare) and then she'd take my hands. "Every session opens something up. We don't know why. We don't know where. We are dealing with the layers of bad musical habits and media saturation." Then she'd wrap me in her large, strong arms and rock me. She'd laugh as she did so, as if she knew some secret truth about me. She usually smelled of peppermint and wine. "We are so blessed," she'd say with a sigh. "So fucking blessed."

The only problem with Robin was, despite her physical displays of affection and positive words, she wasn't very warm. She acted exactly like a warm person—belly laughs, embraces, loud expressions of emotion—but she was distantly, quietly angry. The focus of her attention was Sasha. She was a kind of wife to him, but he rarely softened toward her. He mocked her or flared up at her whenever she tried to express an opinion. His tight, hostile comments about her work would've driven a less devoted woman from his life. But Robin rushed to Sasha when he called her, and spent her free time doing his laundry, cooking for him, addressing his letters, and taking care of his personal business. She read books on mysticism and the occult, threw tarot cards and the coins of the *I Ching,* to "be near him" psychically. Sometimes she gave up, listened to Janis Joplin, and drank. She told me that she and Charles were brother and sister, cosmic twins, beyond friends, and deeper than lovers. Robin had a special connection to everyone she met. It was important that she give love and solace and that everyone love her, but she seemed to live a solitary life.

I spent several hours each day helping Mustafa paint his set pieces. He rarely talked to me. He was always hauling, lifting, sewing, hammering, and sanding. Pools of his sweat spotted the stage floor. Charles said Mustafa worked for God. Mustafa said he worked for Sasha because he was his boss and paid him a weekly salary. Day after day he built set pieces that Sasha would have him destroy. Mustafa constructed huts at Sasha's bidding and then he'd silently rip them to pieces when Sasha pretended to be shocked that he'd ever asked for such "Disney set pieces." Mustafa instructed me to hammer beams into walls, then he would pull them apart when Sasha decided on cloth drops. We laid down wood floors that Sasha told us to pull up when he claimed he'd always wanted linoleum. Through it all Mustafa was wide-eyed and obedient toward Sasha.

I thought maybe he was a little stupid or slow, but one time we spent a whole week building a miniature Shinto temple. When Kosher and Sasha came in and told Mustafa they wouldn't be needing it, Mustafa went after Sasha with a hammer. Kosher stood in front of me, protecting me. But he was laughing under his breath. Mustafa chased Sasha all over the theater until Sasha stopped in his tracks, faced Mustafa, and breathlessly said, "Go on, kill me."

Mustafa, who could never touch his boss, hit himself in the head with the hammer. "There," he said, blood trickling between his eyes. "I show you what you do to a man. Make crazy. Make a nothing. Rob of manliness."

Sasha was stunned. Mustafa strutted past him toward the door of the theater. He only began to weave from the blow to his head when he thought he was out of sight. He was gone for over a week, but later I saw him in an isolated corner of the warehouse with Reeva. The top of his head was shaved and bandaged. One eye was slightly black. Reeva was leaning forward and Mustafa's eyes were lowered to her cleavage. Her strong hands held a bottle of ouzo and they were both quietly drunk.

I snuck up close and heard her say, "Sometimes we do things that seem useless, but where else can we go? Two niggers with accents. It's a paycheck, am I right? The man's sincere, am I right? Mustafa, you're a fugitive. The shah or sheikh or whatever would kill you good. You were driving a cab, mister. You picked up Sasha one day and now you're safe, you've got a passport . . . hey . . ."

Soon Robin, wearing a low-cut kimono, joined the two of them. She put her arm around Mustafa and said, "It can be hard. I know. It can be shit."

I watched Mustafa as he shrugged his big bear shoulders and blinked his bleary, clownish eyes. He scratched his curls and stared at Robin and Reeva, who stared back at him, and over him at each other. Both women crooked their heads to the side—just an inch —and Mustafa lunged, grabbed the two of them around their waists, and pulled them up, and they all went staggering off to his room. I wondered if war would break out with Sasha, but later I saw Kosher, Sasha, and Mustafa slapping each other's backs. Mustafa didn't even seem to care that Robin went right back to Sasha, and Reeva called him an Arab fascist when he winked at her.

CHAPTER 6

The opening of the show was soon, though no specific date had been mentioned. Sasha said it was an American sickness to corrupt ourselves with result-oriented thinking. I was passed back and forth from teacher to teacher all day long, depending on who'd been liberated from the marathon rehearsals. Kosher measured and fitted me for masks. Charles held fabrics up against my body. At night I sat in the audience watching characters that scared and mystified me. Bruce did his best to explain Hippolytus, Minerva, Prometheus, and the others, but he was always rushing and scribbling in his books. Just when I'd begin to understand the action onstage, Sasha would stop it and jump ahead to the end or start again at the beginning. I didn't know where I fit in because Sasha never found time to go over my part. My initial excitement began to be clouded by fatigue. My joints ached. My throat was raw and the little dresses and tights Charles bought for me were always damp with sweat. I found it hard to concentrate. My teachers berated me for low energy and lack of commitment. Even Robin shook me gently by my shoulders and warned me that this was no time to hide inside my head. I held back my coughs and sneezes. I didn't want to be returned to Florida like damaged goods.

I wasn't surprised when I was called to Sasha's room. He greeted me silently with a severe and drawn face. He barely let me inside the room. I stood shaking and sweating with my back against the door. I could barely swallow and my chest was playing chords when I breathed.

"Everyone is working very hard with you," Sasha said. "We have adopted you as our little girl."

I didn't look at him. My eyes felt as if they were covered over with film. Like a dead fish's eyes.

"You know that in a chain, if there is one weak link, the chain breaks. It's a trite idea, but true."

My nose was starting to run. I didn't know whether to wipe it on my sleeve or leave it.

"Now is the time when everyone has to sacrifice the most. Western children aren't used to the concept of sacrifice, but you, of all children, should understand by now what it means to be attentive, hardworking, and generous."

I glanced up and nodded at him. My nose was running over my mouth, my eyes were tearing. My head was pounding with pain.

"I'm aware you have a cold," he said impatiently, "but you're young and strong and you have to summon the spirit inside you to work through the sickness."

Something was happening in my stomach. It started as a sensation of tightness and became a flood of burning in my chest and throat. I couldn't control it. My ears began to ring. My feet started to grow cold and the coldness was spreading.

"I say all this with love and concern," Sasha said. "It's clear to everyone that you're withdrawing. You're careless and distracted. This is not the time. It's *never* the time. Our work here is more ambitious than TV commercials or children's summer camp theater—otherwise why would I push you? We're trying to find answers for our lives. No one is too young to begin that quest. You should be giving the most now—not the least. Do you understand, Rikki Nelson?"

He stepped toward me as if to examine my brain. To see if I'd taken in the message he'd given me. I tried to appear humble, but suddenly my head exploded. I vomited at his feet and couldn't stop throwing up. My neck and head felt hot and a white light washed over me. I felt myself collapsing and reached out, but there was nothing to hold on to. Sasha was gone.

I still couldn't get my eyes to open. I didn't know if they were swollen or taped shut. Or maybe the lids were just too heavy. I woke up before anyone realized. I discovered facts in fragments. Puzzle parts of the outside world floated pleasantly in my dreams, but no one was making me stick them together. The doctor had cold hands, but he said my lungs were clearing. Certain nurses entered so quietly that I didn't hear them until their breath was on me and they pricked my arm or rolled me over. There was one who sucked on breath mints. There was another who smelled of broccoli. One nurse had a dress that swished and I dreaded the sound because she was prissy and didn't approve of me. She made tsks and said things like "Really, now" and scrubbed me roughly. Whenever she removed the bedpan she let out sounds as if something inappropriate had escaped from my bladder and bowels. There was a young doctor who listened to my heart and called me "Peanut." I decided to marry him.

Sasha was there day and night. He read to me from Hans Christian Andersen, The Brothers Grimm, and Native American myths and legends. His voice was a drone and I don't think he finished one complete story, never picked up where he'd left off, but I knew he was always there. I could hear him talking to the doctors or whispering to Kosher, Reeva, or Mustafa. They all came by. I wanted to greet them, but it was impossible to wake up. Charles only visited once. He leaned over me and I could smell the sweetness of his herbal shampoo. His bracelets jingled like bells in my ear. I could feel his tears on my cheeks. He and Sasha exchanged hushed but furious words. Charles told Sasha that this should be proof that Sasha had totally lost his mind. Sasha whispered that the doctors

70

said I'd been malnourished and anemic for years. Charles said that Sasha had driven me over the edge—that he was driving everyone over the edge. Sasha told Charles that this was no time for his divisive, jealous behavior. Charles stomped on the floor and said children need sleep and playtime and unconditional love. Sasha slowly and quietly replied that if Charles ever took the time to *really* be a part of the group, he'd see that the work was full of playtime and a deep love and that this wasn't some cheap Broadway play, but a family. What about the sleep? Charles asked. He said he'd begged Sasha to give me naps and days off. You're right about the sleep, Sasha said with a sigh. We'd all been too preoccupied and hadn't paid proper attention. For that he'd never forgive himself. Charles started to scream. You're impossible. You're a lunatic and you're impossible! I heard nurses shuffling toward the door and several voices scolded Charles. I heard his sandals flip-flop out the door. Sasha sat heavily into his corner chair and began to sob. One of the nurses tried to comfort him and assure him that the doctors were certain I'd be quite well, but Sasha didn't stop crying. He seemed to be listening to the sounds of his own sobs. I missed Charles. He was a master of stupid games and he made me the best presents. I began to remember that right at the beginning when I was first getting sick he noticed immediately that I was down and would keep me in our room until Sasha came to get us. We hid under the bed and threw spitballs, but after a while Sasha's silence made the game boring and we were forced to come out and go to work. A few days later Charles sewed me a set of flannel pajamas with slippers attached and a flap over my bottom that buttoned. He'd embroidered Archie and Veronica on the flap. He installed a humidifier in the room which helped me breathe when I leaned over it, but since I worked such long hours, I didn't spend any time in my pajamas or by the steam.

My room at St. Vincent's Hospital was yellowish white. There was a carved Jesus Christ hung by the light switch. He was wooden, unhappy, and he hung on his cross. I found the little statue very intriguing. It reminded me of the Nativity scenes I'd seen in a shopping mall in Sarasota at Christmas. They were roped off so I never got to touch any of the kings or sheep. There was another Jesus above the chair where Sasha sat. This Jesus was painted in the same style as the landscapes, oceans, and ugly ships in the lobby of the Hotel Earle. I wondered if Jesus had actually posed for the portrait. He looked three quarters toward the front and his eyes had a faraway expression. A bluish glow emanated from his nose and forehead. If he were an actor onstage, Sasha would say that he didn't have to do all that holy stuff with his eyes and mouth. A real holy man has an open, normal expression and his intensity comes from within.

When Sasha saw that my eyes were open he didn't jump up, but remained slumped in his chair, cowering, as if afraid of me. He was pale and sweaty and the circles under his huge gray eyes were dark half-moons. His long, lean body appeared crumpled in the chair and he could barely lift his hand. He smiled weakly at me. His eyes were pools of grief. He was better at being sick than I was.

"There you are," he whispered. "My goodness—I thought I had a Rip Van Winkle on my hands."

I turned my eyes from him and discovered that there were several tubes attached to my arm and one running into my nose. I worried about my appearance. I wished Charles would fix my hair and paint the tubes in Day-Glo colors.

"They're feeding you extra glucose, vitamins, and antibiotics," Sasha explained. "It seems you don't like our cooking."

He looked so sad and afraid that I felt an urgent need to reassure him. I wanted to smile, but for some reason, I thought my teeth had turned brown.

Sasha stood up slowly. He walked like an old man with his shoulders stooped and his legs bent slightly at the knees. He kept his hands in his pockets as if he didn't dare touch me.

"I've been praying for you," Sasha said, "praying and praying. And I don't even pray."

I nodded my head to thank him. Tubes swayed back and forth. He grimaced. It was a self-mocking smile.

"Well—so—how do you feel?"

I realized suddenly that I felt nothing. I wasn't numb; I was just distant from pain or discomfort. Floating. I blinked and smiled. Sasha grimaced again.

"I know you feel like you have to be courageous with me. It isn't necessary."

Sasha placed his hand tentatively on my head. Then he carefully placed himself down at the end of the bed. I felt his weight shift my body's angle. I seemed to be acutely aware of details which meant nothing.

"May I sit near you?" Sasha asked. He was already in place on the bed. He folded his hands on his lap and stared down at them. There was a long silence while he bit his lower lip. I experienced impatience for the first time. I wanted to float. He was forcing me to think. Finally he looked up.

"Look," he said, "I've lectured you far too much and what you need now is peace. Your parents didn't feed you well and you came to us weakened and predisposed to serious illness. The doctor said so." He examined my face for a reaction.

"Still, that's no excuse." He chuckled, then became sad and sighed. "Look—my little Rikki Nelson prodigy—I was mean that night—only because—I thought—well—it could heal you. I've traveled all over the world—to many, many lands—many cultures. I shall tell you about them all someday—for research for our plays and to gather our actors. I have seen many rituals with children— many . . . *painful, terrifying* journeys into adulthood, and the chiefs, the shamans—they never *ever* let the children give up—because— you see, it causes great shame—*unspeakable* shame to the families and initiates—"

He stopped for a moment and squinted his eyes, looking far off out the window in back of me. Had I given up? Was I supposed to feel ashamed?

"But if they make it through the ceremonies—I mean, if they endure the weeks and months of abuse and terror—the quality of self-knowing—the inner strength—well—is incredible and it stays and protects them—absolutely guides them and helps them with every obstacle they will meet in their adult years."

Sasha smirked. He pulled his long fingers through his hair. "So, I am a great chief, but a lousy daddy—right?"

I felt very tired. All I wanted was to drift from the throbbing white walls into the soft gray of sleep.

"To expect these things of the Western personality is not just naive—it's almost criminal," Sasha said. He smiled broadly now. His eyes looked clearer. "But I will always expect great things of you." I began to doze, but my body tensed. Was I being less than great if I fell asleep in the middle of our talk?

I felt Sasha lean over and kiss me. "This little initiate shall have all the naps and vitamins she needs." He kissed me again and pulled the covers to my chin. In a way I thought I was off the hook, but I was left with a vague, sour impression that he was mocking me, and discarding me into the garbage of Western civilization.

When my strength began to return, the tubes were removed. I became conscious of the soreness in my nose, throat, and arms left by the invasive procedures. I resented being carried by the nurses to the bathroom. Whether the nurses were cheerful and accommodating or gruff, I cringed when they commented on how light I was, how my bones stuck out, and I grew increasingly upset as they stood over me waiting for me to go, checking my urine or stool when I was done. The doctors were no better. They came in packs and poked me and listened to my chest and heart and congratulated me on my progress. I couldn't recognize the one I'd vowed to marry. The doctors and nurses were white puppets, with flesh-colored heads. For some reason my mood was very bleak and I didn't make any effort to make friends.

Different members of the company showed up each day. Mustafa carved me a wooden dog. Reeva brought me a piece of colorful cloth and wrapped my hair. Robin presented me with a fancy diary made from rice paper and soft red leather. Bruce pulled a plastic matzoh ball from his pocket and wound it with an aluminum key and we watched it waddle across the floor. Sasha was too busy to visit. He'd lost many days of rehearsal sitting by my bedside, but he sent scribbled love notes each day, which said he was waiting for me to return. Strangely enough, I even got a letter from Jonah—it was one of those ugly get well cards with a thickly photographed flower on the front and a sentimental poem inside. I guess Sasha had called him. Jonah said he was living in New Jersey (he didn't say where). He'd married a wonderful woman named Francine and, although he was still coaching and teaching and acting, he had decided to become a therapist. I think Robin read me the letter. I don't remember exactly. But I know my mind kept drifting and I had very little interest in what Jonah wrote. Despite all the good wishes and high spirits of the actors, my mood remained restless and cranky. I tried not to let it show. Outside the atmosphere of the warehouse, the actors struck me as very kind, caring people. The theater just poisoned them in the same way it had infected me.

St. Vincent's Hospital was a Catholic hospital. Besides the portraits of Jesus and Mary everywhere, I often saw many variations of nuns. There were nun nurses in uniform with weird caps like frozen birds. There were nuns in gentle gray habits with soft fabric and knee-length skirts. There were gliding nuns in fierce black habits that covered their feet, and collars that practically speared their chins. One day as I was sulking over a meal (they insisted I eat something every three hours), my attention was caught by a flash of white out by the elevator. I wasn't the only one to be struck by this vision. I noticed that the nurses and attendants stopped their busy routines. Patients on gurneys tried to sit up. An absolutely beautiful nun had just stepped off the elevator. She was dressed in a pure white habit with a long train behind it as if it were a wedding gown. This nun glowed in her starched whiteness. She was whiter than the walls of the hospital. Her oversized gold crosses and medals bounced off her unusually large bosom. She walked modestly, but with a slight shift in her hips. She had an odd body for a nun and managed to display not just her bosom but her huge, round bottom. When she lifted her layers of skirts to avoid the wheels of the gurneys and food carts, she revealed long, thin, muscular legs. I was shocked to see that the nun was sliding along on three-and-a-half-inch spike, pointed-toed, white-sequined high heels. Her hair was tucked into her habit, but the face, from a distance, looked like a movie star's. I noticed that her fingernails were as long as Barbra Streisand's and were polished in a glistening pearl which sparkled like her shoes.

My heart sped up as the sister in white approached my door. She stepped inside, gave me a dazzling smile and batted her eyes, waved to the small crowd that had gathered and shut the door. Then the sister put her palms together and she lowered her head as if to pray.

> *Here's the church and here's the steeple,*
> *the church is a drag and it persecutes people.*

Not only was I mystified by what she had said, but I was confused by her voice. The nun seemed to be Julie Andrews. How did Julie Andrews know about me? The nun began to sway and then suddenly broke into a whole dance routine—a waltz. She sang from *The Sound of Music:*

> *Raindrops on roses and whiskers on kittens,*
> *New vinyl miniskirt, very tight fittin'*
> *Hell's Angel sailors with tattoos and rings,*
> *These are a few of my favorite things.*

Halfway through the song I realized that I knew the mysterious Julie Andrews nun. I turned my head and forced myself not to laugh. She broke her song off after a verse, pulled off her hood, and shook out a tangle of curly blond hair.

"I don't blame you for being furious," Charles said in his normal voice. He still had on false eyelashes and makeup. He was a very beautiful woman.

Without knowing why, I started sniffing. He took my tray off my bed and plopped down in front of me. I began sobbing and he put his arms around me.

"I know I left you to deal with this all alone, but at least I knew you'd be well cared for. I mean, Dylan Thomas died here and a really great playwright named Joe Cino—when he cut his balls off

—he died here and a great lesbian journalist named Jill Johnston had her psychotic break here—it's a very reputable hospital."

I was crying so hard that my tears caused his makeup to drip a trail of blue, brown, black, and pink down the front of his habit.

"I won't leave you like that again, I promise. I absolutely promise," Charles soothed. "I just couldn't stand Sasha's Ballad of the Harp Weaver routine. Day and night. Day and night after he'd beaten you into this. I couldn't be a part of him making your sickness *his* show. But I didn't mean to hurt you. You and I are a *team*. Nanny and child. Mother and daughter. Roommates. Cross-dressers and midget lesbians. Tag team wrestlers. You name it."

My crying let up, but my breath came in gasps. Charles kept his arms around me and rubbed my back. I began to calm down.

"That's it, Pussycat. We've all been left too many times to see the joke in it. I'm not going to leave you like that again. I mean, the scene with me and Sasha can be awful—but I've got to learn to stick things out—for you and for me. Quitting isn't the answer."

I touched his habit for the first time. He stood up and modeled it for me. He could dip and turn just like a female fashion model.

"You like?" he asked. "I never told you this, but I was a very famous drag queen."

I eyed him with suspicion.

"On my honor, Sicki Rikki Nelson, I *was*. I did a show that ran for almost a year off Broadway. It was called *Medea at the Laundromat*. (I killed my children by putting them in the dryer.) Then I was asked to play Queens from the classics in all the best clubs in New York, Paris, Berlin, Milan. I was the first man to do a drag review of Judy, Barbra, Julie, Carol, Marie Antoinette, Catherine the Great, Gertrude Stein, Golda Meir, Clytemnestra, Ophelia, Nora, and Grace Kelly *on Broadway. Do you dare to touch me?* After that, screenwriters wrote character bits for me in movies. I made a fortune. I actually traveled in a *white Rolls-Royce*. I hired a Hell's Angel as my chauffeur."

I knew Charles well enough to realize with amazement that this story was true. I wondered why he'd given it all up, but he cut off his autobiography with a phony yawn.

He lifted my tray off the floor and lay it over my legs. Then he examined it carefully. "I think I've detected a scam," he said in a low voice. "The hospital feeds you this shit so you'll stay sick and then I have to pay more bills. Let's make a soup out of all of it."

We mixed the soggy, boneless chicken breast and the stiff mashed potatoes into the bowl of greasy chicken broth. We topped it with the runny ice cream and a garnish of undercooked broccoli. Then Charles put his nun hood back on and snuck the tray from the room. In a short while he returned with a McDonald's double cheeseburger, large fries, and a vanilla milk shake. While I ate, he crawled under my bed and lit up a joint. He told me we didn't have to be afraid of being caught because the staff on my floor had decided he'd been sent from the Vatican.

Charles visited me every day after that. The other visitors tapered off. He said Sasha had set a date for the New York performances before we left for Europe. "That means," Charles said, "that he must finish the show. He finds that so damn inconvenient."

CHAPTER 7

I was surprised that Sasha came with Charles to pick me up from St. Vincent's. They'd hired a horse and buggy from Central Park. The air was brisk, and Charles covered me with a scratchy plaid blanket. Charles sat next to me and waved to every shopper, vendor, and drunk on the street. He said he felt like Franklin Delano Roosevelt. Sasha wheedled the reins from the young, pug-nosed driver with the oversized top hat. The horses went at a sluggish clop clop clop and Sasha turned around, his eyes gleaming and his face red from the cold.

"We would get nowhere in Russia," he said. "We would never get out of the first scene of *The Cherry Orchard.*" He and Charles began to sing a medley of tragic Russian songs, but it was hard to know if the words were real Russian or made up. Sasha insisted on going around Washington Square Park exactly seven times and then he insisted on steering our carriage toward La Mama Theater on East Fourth Street so he could show his good friend Ellen Stewart that he was driving. She was a powerful black woman with Gypsy black eyes and a mass of curls on her head. She dressed in rainbow-colored robes from the Mideast and her wrists and ankles jingled and jangled from layers of bracelets. Charles whispered to me that she was a mystic and a psychic and also a producer. I decided to avoid eye contact with her. When she came outside, she stood with her hands on her hips, grinning, and shook her head from side to side.

"Honey," she said to Sasha, "you'll do anything not to finish that play."

In an exaggerated gesture she glanced back and forth between Sasha and Charles several times.

"Are Tweedledum and Tweedledee getting along these days, or are they at each other's throats?"

"What do you mean?" Sasha laughed.

"Never better," Charles said with a vague flourish of a hand. Ellen Stewart lowered her chin onto her chest and gave a long look through her false eyelashes. The three of them broke up. She stepped with great ceremony into the back of the cab and leaned over me. She breathed with sounds like a song and smelled of jasmine oil. She kissed me hard on both my cheeks. "She's beautiful," she said to me. "It's just what Sasha and Charles have been saying. Yes. Yes. Yes." She smiled and nodded for a while. She didn't bat her eyelashes at me—she glued her eyes on mine. I scowled. She smiled broader. "Yes, yes, yes," she repeated. "I do believe this little one's gonna talk soon." Then she leaned into Charles and whispered in his ear, "Thank you, baby," but Charles urgently put a finger to his lips and the Gypsy psychic producer nodded with mock seriousness. I could tell she liked teasing Charles and Sasha and I admired her for it. Sasha helped her down as if she were a countess and we took off toward the West Village and the warehouse. Sasha grew bored and let the boy drive. He sat quietly to the side, his face already clouding over with thoughts about the work. After we'd driven past the traffic of Sixth Avenue and were plodding on smaller streets with town houses and small Italian restaurants, Sasha turned to Charles.

"Thank you for what, Charles?" he asked.

I felt Charles's muscles relax, which was what they did when he got nervous. He yawned. "I sent her some money," he said cautiously. "Her boiler blew up."

Sasha's eyes changed for a moment. They became smoky and sarcastic. I saw it and so did Charles. Then they cleared.

"Oh," Sasha said.

He took both my hands. "My theater is a family. You'll never be alone. There's always someone who'll know you because you knew me or Charles. And someday there'll be people who know me and Charles because we knew you."

"Praise Jesus," Charles agreed. He jabbed his elbow into me under the blanket.

We rode along and I could see the gray water beyond the blue and black storage buildings and the iron-colored auto parts store. There was a flat barge being hauled on the river by a cranberry tug. The seagulls swooped over the barge with great interest. They were so white in the cold sky. The carriage stopped at our warehouse. I was glad to be home. Sasha spun me down to the sidewalk. He moved over to Charles as he paid the driver. "It's not like our heat works perfectly," I heard him say with an edge in his voice.

After my prescribed two weeks of recovery, I was ready to rejoin the rehearsals for a "special demonstration" which is what Sasha insisted we call opening night. I always took a seat close up in front to demonstrate my enthusiasm to be there. I worked very hard to appear attentive and energetic at all times so no one, especially Sasha, would consider me handicapped. I was surprised to see that *The Myth Man* hadn't progressed very far at all while I'd been ill. The first rehearsal I came to, Mustafa and Reeva were onstage working with Kosher on how Athena could pop from Zeus' head. I knew we had only a short time left and yet Kosher worked slowly and meticulously, step by step, over and over.

Sometimes Sasha's directions seemed very odd. One night, he took me into a rehearsal studio with Mustafa. Sasha and I sat on the floor and Mustafa stood. Sasha said to me, "Look at him. Now look at me. Now look at him. Now look at me. Look at both of us. Look at him with one eye. Look at me. Look at him with the other

81

eye. Lift your chin. Put your hand to your mouth. Lower it. Lean toward me. Lean back. Lean toward me. Lean back. Look at him. Lean back. Hand on chin. Lower chin. Raise eyes. Close eyes. Open eyes. Stand."

Then he told me to do all of that again right away and, of course, I couldn't remember it. He was furious. "Either you *want* to be treated like a grown-up or *not*," he spat at me. "Either you take direction or *not*."

"You didn't warn her that she had to *learn* it, Sasha," Mustafa offered. "Show her again—she'll get it."

"*I'm* supposed to memorize *directions?*" Sasha shouted. "That's not *my* job."

He stalked off and told Mustafa and me to rehearse by ourselves if we were so smart. But we had nothing to rehearse. We didn't even know what parts we were playing.

As the date for the "special demonstration" came closer, Sasha's energy changed. When he greeted us in the predawn hours, he was already freshly showered and shaved. He ran with us. He ate twice his normal portion of breakfast, standing up. He rushed from table to table signaling with his eyes that Juno should come talk to him in a corner, or Bruce should write an idea down. He stroked and massaged actors as he conferred with them and drew them out. He laughed loudly during each individual session and told jokes himself. The company didn't seem surprised by Sasha's personality change. No one gossiped behind his back. They accepted his generosity as if he'd never behaved any other way. Charles said they'd learned to live in the present tense the way children do. I was a child, and I seemed to be the only one with a memory. Even Charles didn't offer me his usual commentary. He stayed up all night sewing costumes, and during the day shopped for face paint and eye makeup. During our "family" times we usually ate McDonald's or Kentucky Fried Chicken and danced in front of the mirror to the Rolling Stones or Marvin Gaye. "I wish I was black," Charles said. "Then all my mistakes would be justified." Sometimes he'd read me a sonnet from Shakespeare or an Emily Dickinson poem in his breathy voice. Sometimes we acted out final scenes from tragic operas and died all over each other. The whole energy of the warehouse seemed more open, excited, and playful.

I was now an active part of the show. Juno played Neptune on five-foot stilts with hair and a beard the color of a green sea. Fish, coral, rubber octopus, and grass were woven into her hair. Her mask was green with black, ferocious eyes and a fin for a nose. I was taught to approach her timidly. She became a force of destruction. I watched her transform into a vortex of swirling colors and pounding water. I ran from the attack, and every direction I turned there were more lunges and slaps from the green hair and beard. She buried me under the storm of hair. My heart speeded up, but I was uplifted. I began to like Sasha's theater. You got to live inside a fairy tale.

The dull young woman with the beady eyes and the tape recorder was back and came around several times a day. I learned that her name was Randy Paul and she'd just graduated from Yale Drama School. She was a freelance writer on assignment for the *Village Voice*. I really didn't like her Eastern European peasant garb or the way she blinked each time she asked someone a question. She was mousy and arrogant. She always took Sasha off into dark corners and leaned forward to listen.

"Why isn't she talking to you?" Robin kept taunting Charles. "She can't talk to Sasha and leave you out." Charles didn't react very strongly to Robin's provocations.

"He's my baby brother," Charles would say. "I'm proud of him."

"The *Village Voice* isn't my thing," Charles explained to me. "They don't carry enough comics." I don't think Charles liked Randy Paul any more than I did. The only time he agreed to talk to her, he insisted on doing her hair and makeup. I got to sit in on the interview. Every time she asked Charles a question about his past, the show, or Sasha, he'd put a mirror in front of her and ask her which way she wanted to go with her makeover. I don't think Randy Paul got one straightforward answer from Charles and she ended up with her mousy hair teased up and done in a beehive, black false eyelashes, bright rouge high on her cheeks, and creamy pink lipstick. Charles called it his drag version of Brenda Lee.

CHAPTER 8

Kosher was supposed to play Bacchus. Although he and Sasha had whispered about it at meals, he'd never rehearsed a single element of the role. Sasha declared that Kosher's rehearsal would take place at sunset on the warehouse roof. The entire company lined up like schoolchildren in the downstairs hallway. Even Randy Paul was invited to participate (although Sasha confiscated her tape recorder and notepad). We marched up the stairway. Kosher was perched on the edge of the roof against the darkening sky. He wore a padded flesh-colored costume with a foam and wire penis that jutted out several feet in front of him like a wagging tail. His wild wig went to his feet; it was pitch-black and hung over dried breasts and a flabby stomach. Even so, his mask made him a buoyant, childlike creature. He had pudgy red cheeks and a wide, sloppy smile. Then I realized Kosher wasn't wearing a mask at all. The smooth, fat, greedy expression from his mouth and eyes was real. The fat cheeks and funhouse laugh was his own doing. I examined Kosher's face for plastic or makeup and there was none. I looked into the marble, darting eyes of this character, Bacchus, and Kosher had disappeared.

He gestured with his naked toddler's arm that we should come and join him. A table was spread with bottles of wine, cheese, fruits, and breads. The actors ate and drank as the sun disappeared, and I saw that everyone, including Sasha, was getting quite drunk. (Charles primly sipped from his cup, offered me a taste, and then took it away.) Kosher circled his guests, who sat on the pillows beside his table. He encouraged everyone to gorge themselves and drink. He danced grotesque bumps, grinds, and thrusts. When the meal was completely consumed, Kosher ordered that the table be struck. He pulled back a cloth that revealed an enormous tub of wine. Actors began bathing in the wine, painting streaks on themselves and others, kissing it off each other's lips. I saw Mustafa paint Juno's eyes and suck it off. He lifted her to his shoulders and licked the bottom of her feet. Bizarre couples circled me as if I were on a carousel made of mating animals. Bruce had Randy Paul on the floor and he was spitting wine from his mouth to hers. I turned again and saw Robin join Juno and Mustafa. They were all grabbing each other's hair, shampooing each other with wine, catching it in their mouths as it fell. And then I saw Sasha at the farthest end of the roof. He stood completely still. Reeva was with him. She lifted up her blouse and showed him her breasts. He dipped his pinky finger into his cup and placed a tiny dot on each of her nipples. Then he licked it off very slowly. Kosher's laugh became maniacal.

"Enough of this for you," Charles said. He tapped me on the arm. "What kind of day-care center is this anyway?" He prodded me toward the stairs. I saw several of the actors flinging off their clothes. I hesitated. "It's nothing," Charles said. "It's much more fun to watch mating in the wild. Check out a herd of rhinoceroses next time you're in Kenya. *That's* entertainment."

The next day Kosher, Mustafa, and I were the only ones on time for rehearsal. We practiced the small moments of business that I, as the Traveler, was to experience with Zeus and Bacchus. Neither of them looked or acted any differently around me. They didn't even mention the night before.

The company arrived in the usual twos and threes. No one complained of a hangover. No one smiled lovingly at anyone else. The orgy wasn't mentioned. Even Charles treated me and everyone else as if the night before had not existed. This was a strange group of people. Rehearsal seemed to be starting an hour late. Sasha hadn't arrived, and everyone behaved as if the day were proceeding normally.

Sasha and Robin arrived last. They had an odd way of entering a room together. Sasha rushed ahead as if they'd just been walking side by side, but he didn't want to admit it. Robin held back as if to assist his deception, but did it in such an exaggerated fashion that her actions told everyone that they were a couple.

Sasha appeared to be in a good humor, invigorated and snide. He laughed with the actors, kissed them, and cried "Ah!" when he greeted them as if they hadn't seen each other in a long time. Robin looked heavy, thick, and tranced out. The circles under her eyes were a dark brown. Her chin sagged. Her hands hung at her side like fat loaves of bread. She wore a shapeless purple cotton dress that was stained with greasy spots, and her feet shuffled along in large, flat mariachi sandals. She trod up to the stage, hunching over, using her hands to give her balance. She stood outside the lights, staring distractedly past Sasha as he conducted animated meetings with Kosher, Mustafa, Juno, and Reeva. I could hear his open, good-natured laughter. The noise of his conferences died down and he seemed to notice that Robin was occupying a dark block of territory onstage, picking at her dry lips and folding and unfolding her large hands. Sasha walked up to the edge of the stage and spoke so quietly I had to strain to hear. His tone was mild, but odd. His patience, exaggerated and mean.

"Do you want to get into costume now or do you want to make everyone wait for you? I mean, we could start even later if that's what you want." Robin took in a heavy, pained breath. She tapped her heavy flat sandal three slow times. She didn't lift her eyes.

"Of course I don't want to waste anyone's time, Sasha," she said. "I didn't *know* you wanted me to get into costume."

"Of course you *knew*," Sasha replied. "You knew exactly. You just want to destroy two years of work by staging a sixties protest march."

Most of the actors busied themselves quietly backstage or in the house. Everyone thought Sasha and Robin were fighting over his casting her as Artemis. Artemis was the supreme huntress. She was goddess of all hunters. Robin was a strict vegetarian. Artemis caught fish with her teeth. Robin didn't even eat fish. In the beginning, Robin had resisted, in her cosmic, gentle manner, against playing a cold-blooded animal killer. Sasha had explained to her that Artemis, in ancient times, balanced the elements of the earth and therefore was a savior of animals. Artemis was also the one who knew animals, could speak their language, and was profoundly trusted by every living thing. He created a moment where Robin would teach me some of her bird and mammal songs. Sasha's arguments placated Robin.

But there was another issue—Robin hated her costume. Charles had designed a deerskin tunic with beads and feathers, and intricate sacks woven with colorful symbols. The sacks held arrowheads and knives. Robin didn't want to wear deerskin. She refused to carry arrowheads and knives. But most of all, she felt like a fool in a short tunic. "I look like Robin Hood in drag," she shouted at Charles. Charles offered to throw the costume out, but Robin apologized and settled for having the hem lowered to her knees. Robin was characteristically so untemperamental and passive that Kosher, Mustafa, and even Sasha went out of their way to make Artemis comfortable for her. She was allowed to shoot her bow and arrow at targets that were moving shadows.

Her hunting dances had to be wild and ferocious, and when she burst into tears, Bruce explained to Robin that she was *also* the goddess of midwives and she should think of the fierce struggle from the womb to the world while she danced. Think of the pelvic bone. The vaginal wall. The fight against the prison of the mother's vagina. The set was built without any animal heads, legs, tails, or skins. Instead, Sasha and Mustafa designed cavelike drawings of hunters pursuing their game. These gestures seemed a bit much for the other actors, who were not allowed to so much as utter a complaint about their roles, but Sasha said that Robin was a kind of animal herself and had to be treated with the same wariness, trickery, rewards, and punishments. Each rehearsal he cajoled her, mocked her, and bargained with her. She began to find an uninhibited, fierce song and dance, but claimed her childlessness and vegetarianism were tearing her apart inside. I always loved watching her stomp her bare feet, swing her bushy hair in a circle, and rub her bow against her breasts. She made odd delicious sounds as she slapped the string on the bow as if it were a banjo. She built herself into a frenzy. She stalked the shadows of rabbits, deer, snakes, and lions. (Kosher used Balinese puppets.) Mustafa attacked her. He was dressed in a tiny loincloth from the waist down and a ferocious lion head. She wrestled with him and brought him to the ground. She sat on top of him and rocked herself faster and faster until she stabbed him at the climax. Then she lay on the ground and writhed from side to side until she pulled a bloody dove from between her legs and let it fly.

Robin hated herself after every session working on Artemis. She wanted to work on Hera, the wise-ass wife of Zeus, but Sasha found Artemis more interesting. Eventually she stopped protesting and did her job like a confused but loyal soldier. Perhaps that was why I found her behavior the day after the Bacchus orgy particularly strange. Charles was surprised too. He sat in the empty audience leaning forward with his elbows on the seat in front of him. Once or twice he moved as if to get up and intervene, but stopped himself. Robin had an odd look. Her skin glowed with a sickly hue. She whispered answers in a monotone that made Charles ask Bruce if she was on acid or PCP. When she finally slumped offstage to change into costume, Sasha clapped his hands and the rest of us jumped onstage to practice one of the storytelling choruses. Reeva led us through the smooth African-Indian gestures of the choreography. Her voice was nastier and more impatient than usual and when Sasha interrupted to ask her about a change in sequence, she argued that we'd always done it the way we were doing it. No matter what he said, she just kept repeating, "We've always done it this way. We've always done it this way." Finally he shrugged and backed off, but by then Reeva was shouting about white imperialists and artists who rape and steal from third world cultures. She announced she was quitting and leaped off the stage, ran to the back of the house, and disappeared. The company settled uneasily into scattered chairs in the audience. I moved into the darkness of one of the wings.

"This is getting interesting," Charles mused in his low voice. He lit a Turkish cigarette and hid it under his seat, squatting down now and then to sneak a drag. The audience section began to smell like smoking Rosemary.

Robin appeared in full costume. "The goddess has arrived," Sasha called out. His voice was irritable. "She deigns to let us begin." Kosher lifted me to my customary hiding place—high in a Japanese tree Mustafa had sculpted. I waited for the goddess of the hunters to discover me and teach me some bird calls.

But Robin merely stood there. The musicians began her music. A long call on a conch shell. The hollow clattering of seashells. A low, sustained throb—like frogs or a heart. Wooden titters of crickets. Robin didn't lift her head or open her eyes.

Sasha waited several minutes and then jumped onstage. He leaned over so his face was directly in front of hers.

"Are you all right?" he asked, but his voice had a nasty edge. "I mean, what I need to know right now is if you're all right. I need to know if this is your period, or if you've been frightened by one of your *I Ching* readings, or if you're having a convenient nervous breakdown. I mean, do you want to tell me what you're doing or shall we continue with this egotistical opera all night?"

In one motion, with great grace and speed, Robin reached into her pouch, pulled out Artemis' machete, spun Sasha around into a hammerlock, and placed the machete at his throat. No one screamed. Everyone was too fascinated.

"You wanted a killer," Robin growled between her teeth. "You've got a killer."

Sasha didn't dare challenge her. His cheeks burned and his eyes squinted from the pain of her large arms around his upper body. He seemed slightly terrified, but also intrigued and a little pleased with the adventure.

"Really," he choked scornfully, "this isn't Stanislavsky. We don't bring our tiny personal wounds into the work. Our work is much bigger than petty jealousies or selfish needs."

Robin moved the machete slowly against Sasha's throat. A tiny scratch of blood appeared on his Adam's apple.

"You wanted me to enjoy the blood," Robin chanted in her eerie monotone. "Okay, I'm learning. I will cut you until I hear your breath rushing out of you. Then I'll cut off your goddamn balls, Sasha. They're not the biggest prize I've ever had—but I'll make do."

Charles, for some reason, was searching nervously through his shoulder bag.

Sasha was sweating in Robin's hammerlock. "Listen," he said, annoyed, "enough of this melodrama. If you're going to kill me, go ahead, you silly thing. If you want to know about my feelings, then think about what we've been to each other the last ten years. Don't become a housewife now."

Robin lowered the machete, but held it in front of her so he couldn't get near. "You screwed all of them last night and half the time you can't even stand the thought of screwing me."

Sasha held out his arms to her. He spoke carefully.

"Last night was an . . . exceptional . . . odd . . . exercise. It may not have been entirely successful."

Robin let out a scream. She lifted the machete high above her head. It was hard to tell if she intended to bring it down on Sasha's head or into her own chest. Kosher ran behind her and twisted it out of her arm. He forced her into a kneeling position. Robin began to pound her stomach with her other fist. She moaned. Sasha looked on and his eyes were bright with anguish and fear, but despite his genuine sorrow, he couldn't quite conceal his excitement.

"You're completely mad," he said with admiration.

At last Charles found what he'd been digging for in his bag. It was a bottle of pills. He moved cautiously in front of Sasha and held out a white pill toward Robin. "She's completely stoned," he said.

Bruce brought a glass of water from the wings and Robin stopped pummeling and moaning long enough to let Charles feed her the pill.

"What is that?" Sasha asked suspiciously.

"Thorazine," Charles said. "Anyone who ever lived in San Francisco carries a private supply."

Mustafa and Charles helped Robin up and when they began to lead her out of the theater, Sasha held up his hand. He slid his arms under Robin and, although she weighed at least fifty pounds more than him, lifted her like a baby and carried her out, mumbling quiet phrases to her that no one else could hear.

When they were gone, Charles shouted, "Hey, let's have another feast for Bacchus!"

Kosher picked up Robin's discarded bow and arrow and, giggling in his demented way, began to shoot arrow after arrow over the heads of anyone he could see offstage, onstage, or in the audience. There was a great deal of yelling and everyone hit the floor. Arrows continued to whiz by at ridiculous angles, hitting walls, chairs, lights, and bouncing off again. I felt like I was hiding out watching a battle to the death between two blind idiots.

CHAPTER 9

There'd been so many blow-ups and injuries, I couldn't believe we'd ever have a show. But Charles said that catastrophe was an essential element in any of Sasha's productions. He explained that Sasha believed the success of a work could only be measured by the amount of risk that went into creating it. "It's a mathematical equation, Pussycat. The quotient of success in the performance can be measured by the proportion of catastrophe endured during rehearsal." I often had the feeling that, if the progression of work was going too smoothly, Sasha deliberately created problems. I may have imagined his scheming. His ensemble, collected from all over the world, outcasts and refugees, wounded and opinioned, driven by secretive inner voices, was capable of surprising anyone. Sasha relished the eccentricities in each one of us. Sometimes the show seemed like an excuse for Sasha to watch us try to survive in his world.

However, it is misleading to focus only on those early hints of disaster. There was great uncertainty and ugly behavior, but the simple beauty of my first year remains in my memory even now, even after what eventually happened. My memories are clear pictures. Charles and Sasha dressed in white, spinning in the hours before dawn. Each of them made perfect circles and their hair was a golden flame. And I remember sitting on the rooftop, with candles surrounding us as if we were in an Orthodox church, and Sasha's long legs folded up beneath him and his long hand holding a thick, weatherbeaten book from which he read Greek myths. And he spoke to us the way a father tells bedtime stories. In long, exaggerated tones and sliding pitches in very loud and soft fairy-tale voices. He was almost silly reading to us in that manner, but he cared about the stories of the fickle, awesome, slapstick gods. He was trying to induce us to be as frightened and reverent of the myths as he.

One night he and Charles decided to treat us all by taking over the kitchen. They served up a runny, lumpy version of chili, damp pita bread, and a salad with odd-looking mushrooms and greenish gray anchovies. They insisted on waiting on everyone themselves. No one, not even Robin, could eat their rancid recipe. So we all washed the dishes and then Charles took us to a Russian restaurant in Brooklyn, where we ate blintzes and listened to an amplified balalaika, dumbek, and an out-of-tune basso.

Sometimes I watched Sasha and Kosher practicing tai chi or a Kabuki dance step in his studio. They looked like exotic birds. They were so pure and joyous. I remember Robin, picking on her heavy blues guitar. She hummed in her scratchy voice and rasped out songs that chilled me, made me laugh, and warned me about the joys and wrenching sorrows of love. Once in a while she'd sing a blues song and Reeva would join in with an African chant. I remember one chant Reeva sang. It was a grieving song from Niger for the fisherman out in a storm. Robin's and Reeva's voices sang back and forth, talked back and forth, and you could hear other voices emerging— overtones—but the overtones became distant choruses, like ghosts doing gospel or Motown backup, wailing in harmony.

My best times were with Charles. There are so many details I remember. The tiny games, gestures, talks. My memories of him fill shelves, closets, and whole rooms. He had so many pens, pencils,

Magic Markers, pastels, paintbrushes, charcoals, colored threads, peacock, pigeon, and parrot feathers, patches of silk and cotton, fake flowers, wind-up toys, bells, sequins, fake jewels, zippers, buttons, fetishes, phalluses, stories, songs. He connected the dots in my cartoon books, found all the Ninas in the *Sunday Times,* and sewed bizarre outfits for himself, the company, and all his friends. I remember big black bosoms fashioned out of throw pillows and velvet. When I needed to, I could lay my head there because he was my nanny and I was his "girl child." He called the bosoms my "substitute salvation" and sang "Home, home on the strange" when I lay on them.

Sasha had the eye of a painter and he created a whole country out of each small scene. Africa and Japan. Iceland and the Southwest. The Everglades and Pompeii. He controlled the space, color, and movement down to every last detail, and when you stepped onstage you went traveling. As his pictures became clearer, arguments and attitude turned into excitement. Chaos turned into orderly obedience. Sasha kept everyone electric and dangerous. Sometimes Sasha brought me onstage to watch or participate. Sometimes he signaled that I should stay in my seat. I remembered the original story was supposed to be about a child who refused to go to sleep and therefore her grandfather created myths to get her through a long night. Sometimes I pretended he was making the whole show for me. But I'd never seen the beginning or end and I only understood fragments of what I was supposed to do. I'd never seen this grandfather he spoke of, or the spirit of the grandfather which was to be the magical Myth Man, the Great Storyteller. I didn't know if Kosher had even begun to work on his mask. I wondered if Sasha had changed his mind or forgotten to cast the role. The character never appeared in rehearsals and the only reference to his existence was when Bruce would shout from the house, "And now the Myth Man appears—I guess—does he appear? Do we still have him? Hellooo Sasha? What are we doing at this moment?" But Sasha would remain silent. I remember that no matter how pleasant he was to be around, he remained unpredictable and secretive. He smiled to himself as if he were planning a prank, like the Winnebago Trickster god he loved to talk about when he read us stories. He pressed his lips together, mumbled, and made tiny, quick gestures. If he caught me staring at him, he rolled his eyes as if the whole art of theater were annoying and stupid and he couldn't do a thing about it.

During the frantic, sleepless last week, we were invaded by rich ladies. Since the weather was turning cold, they wore different shades and lengths of fur coats. Their attitude was like grown-up candy stripers or, as Charles said, the ladies who run the telephone campaign for the PBS drive. They set up an office in the lobby and spent a great deal of time on telephones. They printed up programs which the actors weren't allowed to see. Since the ladies looked so much alike, I couldn't count how many there were, but Sasha seemed to be great friends with each one of them. He laughed and kidded whenever he saw them, accepted scarves they brought as presents, and pored over the guest lists, discussing every name in great detail. If Sasha asked one of the ladies for a cup of coffee or tuna sandwich, the chosen one took his request as a kind of honorable recognition. Charles called it "Upper East Side/lockjaw slave labor." But the ladies adored Charles too. He'd stand behind one of them, as she sat in her card-table chair making her calls, and restyle her hair or fix the color of her blush. He always knew where each lady's sweater suit came from—Armani or Christian Dior. If Charles didn't approve of a pair of shoes, several new pairs would be brought in to be modeled the next day. Sometimes they exchanged jewelry—although Charles let it be known he really had no use for diamonds.

Sometimes if I was tagging along, Charles or Sasha might introduce me to one of them, but I was much more boring to them than anyone else in the group. A child's silence wasn't as exotic as Reeva's African haughtiness. A little girl didn't have Kosher's mystery or Mustafa's Mideastern violence. These ladies were in awe of theatrical talent. A little girl didn't have that sexy intensity. Bruce didn't evoke much of a response either. Bruce said that Connecticut ladies believed that Jews were radicals and dirty and probably couldn't keep white costumes clean or speak in whispers. As far as I was concerned, the ladies were a matching set of phony blondes—like those Russian dolls that open up and there's an identical smaller one inside and a smaller one inside that.

Charles said Sasha had a way of jump-starting their pacemakers. He pretended he couldn't remember one name—they all had several. Charles said even their sex lives were hyphenated. Mrs. Lindsey Phillips-Johnston. Mrs. Carter Fremont-Shane. Charles said he was changing his name to Charles Teacup Solomon, but Sasha said they were really very nice to "give up their time" and "work so hard for us." As usual, I had no idea where they came from, where he knew them from, or who'd called them. They were very devoted to planning a reception for a show I'd never seen from beginning to end. They chose a caterer, found a boutique which sold black balloons, and designed gift baskets containing miniature wooden Balinese frogs, a book on mythology by Joseph Campbell, and a stylish T-shirt with TRAVELING WITH THE MYTH MAN printed in characters that resembled ancient Greek. Sasha seemed more relaxed and decisive about the reception than the show itself. He involved himself in every detail, including what size the T-shirts should be. He was secretive about his participation and no doubt made his devoted ladies vow to keep their activities hidden from the actors. They loved being a part of a conspiracy with Sasha.

Only one face remains in my memories of the volunteers. There was a woman named Mrs. Preston DeVane who made me uncomfortable because I thought she was going to die. She was the thinnest volunteer, and she chain-smoked menthol cigarettes. Her shoulders stuck out in bony squares underneath her cable-knit sweater, and her legs were like a doll's. Her frosted hair was always pulled back in a proper flowered headband and her skin was tan and a bit leathery. She must've been in her early sixties, though her tininess made it seem more like she'd just graduated from some Seven Sisters college. I liked her hands because the veins stuck out from her tanned skin and she wore no nail polish. Her wedding ring was thick gold with delicate rubies and diamonds. Unlike the other women, Mrs. Preston DeVane didn't work very hard. Whenever I saw her, she was sitting quietly in a chair staring straight ahead. She didn't want to be there. She didn't want Sasha's charms or Charles's fashion tips. And they respected her. But I often saw ladies assign her jobs as if she were a child. She lifted a telephone slowly. She wrote notes and took long pauses in between scratching out large, overly neat words. She seemed sad. Charles told me that she was the richest of the whole bunch and what I was seeing was a combination of brains, boredom, and cancer. She didn't care about the bustling volunteer force. She seemed ready and willing to disappear.

Kosher often sent me to the storeroom directly next to his work-shop to fetch things, like the special glue he used to mend his masks. It was a large closet with spattered iron worktables and sawdust. Tools were packed neatly in hundreds of wooden boxes. Kosher didn't allow many people in his closet. He hated having the order of tools invaded. In my long apprenticeship with him, I'd earned the honor of memorizing the contents of all of Kosher's drawers, bags, and boxes. I was instructed in the art of cleaning and polishing too. I was his geisha slave.

One night Charles was onstage working on Prometheus when his mask somehow cracked. I knew the glue Kosher needed. It was in the smallest wooden box in a small white china urn with a letter that looked like a hand on it. When I dashed down the hall to fetch the glue, I saw the closet door open. I almost slid right inside when I heard a kind of low, nasal weeping. It was like the squeak of oars working an old rowboat. At first I thought I saw only Mrs. Preston DeVane. Her blue Villager skirt was hiked above her thighs and her pantyhose were rolled down to her ankles. Her matching loafers stayed on except the left one hung halfway off her foot. Her toes pointed down. She appeared to be crashing her thin hips against the iron table. She seemed to be smashing herself in two, trying to wedge the table into her stomach and cut herself. I thought this was an odd way for someone to die, but I was too fascinated to run and get help. Then I saw the long pale hands with the translucent skin. They rested on Mrs. Preston DeVane's behind and pushed her hips forward while holding her in the air. I saw the long legs spread wide open bent at the knees, the white kimono floating like a veil, and I recognized Sasha's naked chest and his peaceful face. He kept very still as Mr. Preston DeVane tried to die all over his body with her lunges and thrusts. Her tan hands held on to Sasha's neck and she creaked and moaned and dug her fingers into his skin with terrible pleasure. I could see he was trying to help her, and I couldn't figure out how to get the glue without drawing attention to myself. I heard someone behind me. Kosher had come to find out where I'd gone. He put his fingers to his lips as if to say "Shh" and his eyes crinkled in the nasty way he had when he both condemned and enjoyed the weaknesses of the Caucasian race. He signaled me to leave with him. Mrs. Preston DeVane was still committing suicide on Sasha's body. She was like a shell of a lady. I knew Sasha would stop her before she broke apart on Kosher's floor. I couldn't remember her face. At the time she didn't have one.

Three days before the "special demonstration" and the night before the dress rehearsal, we still hadn't seen the beginning or end of the show, settled on the order, or run through any section of the show the same way twice. Bruce was close to hysterical. "What about actors' *rights?*" he kept screaming. "What about giving the artists the opportunity to *learn* their roles?" Kosher thought Bruce was very funny and imitated his high-pitched complaints in Japanese. Robin carried her heavy *I Ching* book and coins in her embroidered Pakistani shoulder bag, along with a supply of coins, crystals and an antique Russian pendulum. Every day the group gathered around Sasha with the hope that he'd take them through the complete map in his head, but he always got caught up in some detail or ran one scene over and over. Reeva didn't bother coming to the theater anymore. She told Juno to let her know when the audience was actually in their seats and the house lights were out. Charles paced the aisles counting chairs and touching walls as if he were a fire inspector. "Where am I?" he'd moan. "Is this a *theater?* Am I to *perform* here? Are you sure this isn't just one of those anxiety dreams?" The company gathered on the stage. They were waiting for Sasha. They nervously planned a low-key confrontation. He simply had to let everyone try their scenes. They had to be allowed to experience the flow of one scene into another. Why couldn't the actors know the length of the show or the size of the audience? They didn't intend to threaten Sasha or criticize him, they wanted to express their concerns. They elected Mustafa as their spokesman. I was amazed to see that our huge Arab bear had become a nervous little boy. Sasha entered the theater as happy and relaxed as I'd ever seen him. He took us all in with his pale gray eyes, and he smiled with radiant tenderness. He loved us all so much.

He threw back his wild blond mane and shook with laughter. "I'm really making you all crazy, ain't I?" Mustafa lifted his thick, callused hands. He tried to speak. He was shaking. Kosher found Mustafa's nervousness hilarious. He turned his back and chuckled to himself. Charles disapproved. He angled himself into Kosher's peripheral vision, lowered his eyelids, and pursed his lips. But within seconds he let out a weird, high, sustained cry of laughter and then fell on his back and began kicking his legs. Robin let out a low, vulgar growl and then chortled too loudly for me to believe she really meant it. Gradually, the whole group folded into hysterics as if they'd been brought in, one at a time, by a conductor. Reeva, hearing the noise, tiptoed cautiously down the center aisle, her face lit up with an astonished smile as she viewed the collapsed and shaking bodies of her actors' collective breakdown. I don't remember if I laughed. I doubt it. I always found weakness in adults repulsive.

"You're right," Mustafa said. "We've lost it. We're crazy."

Sasha stood up. "But don't you see?" Sasha almost sang. "This is the state a performer strives for. Abandonment. No premeditation. No intellectual censorship. Stripped of any imitations or ambitions. All that is left is what the muscles, bones, and blood have memorized. The mind gives up and the body must do the thinking."

I watched as the whole company stared at Sasha with rapt attention. Even Kosher sat cross-legged and still with his gray, square head cocked to one side. Charles's head was bent as if there were something fascinating on the floor he had to watch. Robin sat on her knees, her large chest expansive, her bright red lips and face forced into a knowing smile.

Sasha held out his arms. "I'm so proud of you," he said. He

glanced briefly at anyone who'd look back. Reeva quickly lowered her eyes and turned her back. Mustafa gave him a tiny thumbs-up. The feeling in the room had transformed. The actors had been allowed to get a glimpse of something miraculous; and if they could just hold on, there'd be more to come. I couldn't figure out what I'd missed.

Sasha clapped his hands together and broke the spell. "So," he said cheerfully, "everyone has the day off except for Charles, Kosher, the little Pussycat, and me." Robin fell over backward. Mustafa started pounding his head and screaming in Arabic. Reeva once again swished down the center aisle. Charles paced in fast circles around the stage.

"Tomorrow . . ." Sasha shouted. He was smiling at the reactions. "Tomorrow, we will have run-throughs. A run-through every hour if you want. We will be a subway station of run-throughs. I will answer questionnaires. I will pass out *published* versions of our show complete with blocking and musical notation and footnotes. Now go! Go! Go! I have work."

"I don't understand why you're putting in a whole new scene now," said Charles. The four of us—Kosher, Sasha, Charles, and me—were huddled on the barren stage. "No, put it this way," Charles said. "I *do* understand, and that's worse."

"So if you do understand," Sasha said petulantly, "why do we waste time arguing about it?"

"Velly compricated," Kosher said. He stood up and tugged his filthy kimono over his underpants and bare thighs. He squinted at the balcony.

"We have to have a God who takes risks," Sasha explained. "How can the little one be taught anything if she doesn't meet a man who dares to fly toward the sun?"

"He doesn't make it," Charles moaned.

"Really, Charles," Sasha said. "Honestly. It's the fact that he has the vision that counts."

"Are we having a philosophical argument here or are we working on a scene?" Charles asked.

"Both," Sasha said. "It is always both."

"God!" Charles yelled. He was dancing in place now. "Sometimes you are so pretentious, you're like a Swami from Long Island."

"I like that." Sasha smiled.

"I could lig a purrey," Kosher said. "Sun could be above barcony—Icalus go up—he come down again."

"Exactly," said Sasha.

I didn't understand a word of what was going on.

"Maybe you're just fulfilling some frustration about never staging Peter Pan," Charles said, and quietly began singing "I Gotta Crow."

"I go to haldware to get cable," Kosher said.

"You better put on some pants first," Charles told him. Kosher grinned.

Now it was the three of us.

"So okay," Charles said. "You're gonna put these wings on me and you want them made out of wire and wax and silk? And I'm going to dance—a dance I'm supposed to choreograph while I'm making the wings. Then I look up into the balcony and I see the sun—what's the sun going to be?"

"Don't worry about the sun," Sasha said. "We'll make a ring of torches or something."

"Or something," Charles repeated. "Okay, I look up in the balcony and I see this sun and I step onto this pulley which will slowly take me over the heads of the whole audience."

"Exactly," said Sasha.

"Then I reach the sun and I start crying out in dyslexic Dante to let everyone know I'm burning. I fall to earth with the help—we hope—of the pulley and dive into a huge pile of sand—where's the sand coming from?"

"It will be there," Sasha said. "I ordered it."

"How does it get onstage?" Charles asked.

"Charles, stop being do damn neurotic—*I'll* make sure it gets onstage," Sasha snapped. He winked at me.

"Anyway, I'll construct the wings so only the outer edges can ignite," Charles said.

"That's beautiful," Sasha agreed.

"And am I to do this in the dress rehearsal without any practice?" Charles asked.

"Icarus only got to do it once," Sasha said.

I cherished seeing Sasha and Charles enjoy each other. I felt as if I were a part of their family—an adopted but privileged pet.

"Little one," Sasha said, "Charles and I need to work on some boring details now. You can go."

I knew this was an order, and Charles looked as surprised as I was.

I stayed outside the door and eavesdropped.

"So," I heard Sasha say. "What do you think?"

"Of what?" Charles asked. "Icarus? How can I tell?"

"No, the whole thing. The endeavor. The process. The work."

"Sasha," Charles exclaimed, "why are you asking me this?"

"Well, we are at a sort of crossroads here, and I was trying to get a summary of your reactions."

"Each day has been each day," Charles said. "Some days lovely. Some days horrendous. There's no 'summary.'"

"So has it been worth it?" Sasha asked.

"Are you asking me as an actor, your brother, your benefactor, the *New York Times* second-string critic—what?"

"No jokes, Charles," Sasha said.

"If you weren't nervous," Charles said, "you'd never be asking me this."

Sasha's tone took on an edge of sarcasm. "I realize, of course, that this is not like a Broadway show or an international cabaret act—" he said.

"Sasha, please don't start," Charles pleaded.

"I'm not 'starting.' I ask you a straightforward question; and, as usual, you play the hippie with me and refuse to answer. Perhaps it is your feminine side that chooses to stay coy."

There was silence.

"All right," Charles said evenly. "You want to know what I think.

I think a lot of things, but I dread this. When you feel better, you won't care what I think."

"You don't have to be simple," Sasha said anxiously. "Say it all."

"As far as the artistic part goes: The conception. The realization. The visual effects. The sounds. I think it is brilliant. I believe you are a genius. You stun me, okay?"

"That's it?" Sasha said. "I am your superstar?"

"Not exactly," Charles replied. "You know very well that you manipulate the actors like some fascist evangelist. You exploit them and overwork them and have no concern whatever for their feelings. You can be an arrogant monster who abuses the women as if they're whores. Your inability to organize their time or a logical progression in the work causes extreme mental stress and ill health. Whenever you are confronted with their discomfort or anger, you retreat to some spiritual high holy ground and behave as if it's their fault. Your moments of genuine guilt and remorse are too quickly contradicted by actions that are humiliating and abusive to the very people whom you've soothed with remarkable gentleness. I don't think you have to behave this way to get the results you get. I think your work would be transcendent even if you were humane."

For a long time I heard no sound from inside the theater. I could picture Charles staring at his feet and Sasha focusing on a far-off point.

"Well, clearly you are jealous," Sasha finally said. His voice was odd—almost cheerful.

"You see?" Charles moaned.

"What do I see?" Sasha snapped. "You're afraid I'm going to become more famous than you."

"I'm not famous," Charles said wearily. "I was a diva for about three years along twenty blocks of the Lower East Side."

"What you can't seem to grasp," Sasha said coldly, "and of course I can understand this, given how you choose to live, is that psychological weakness has no place in real ritual. It is not about the comforts or discomforts of the petty, conscious mind. It's about developing the psyche and the spiritual faculties to the point where they are ready to transcend daily life and soar into universal ex-

103

pression. A few stubbed toes or hurt feelings are nothing in comparison with the enormity of the search for godliness onstage."

"Sasha, you're a boy from California!" Charles yelled. "Just like me. You used to surf and read Ken Kesey and Alan Watts. You staged a leftist version of *The Boy Friend*, and I played all the parts. You can't be taking yourself so seriously. You can't believe there's only one answer and that only you hold the key."

"I don't hold any key," Sasha replied. "I am searching for it. And let's not talk about betrayal—let's not talk about betrayal and abandonment." Sasha's voice had taken on a plaintive quality. "I mean, I don't think we want to have a contest about who has shocked the other more. Do we?"

Charles sighed. His voice was barely audible. "I guess not."

Sasha was practically crying.

"I keep no secrets from you. You know exactly where I stand. I am clumsy and cruel, but my desire is out there for everyone to see. What about you, Charles; are you nearly so honest? Mr. Gentleness. Mr. Mystery. Mr. Humor. Who knows what you really feel or how you spend your time half the time? You have no commitment to me. You have no real commitment to anything."

"I can't believe we're getting into this," Charles yelled. "*You* asked me what I thought of your work. I answered. Now we've managed to end up condemning my moral character."

"Look," Sasha said calmly. "When the performance is over this week, why don't you take a leave of absence from the group? Skip the tour. I'll hire someone to do your part."

"This is a *dance*," Charles screamed hoarsely. "We step back and forth, back and forth, but we don't go anywhere."

"I want you to leave my work for a while," Sasha said gently. "Things just ain't working out as we'd hoped."

"Fine, fine," Charles mumbled. He sounded tearful. I could hear him walking quickly toward the door. I took refuge in a dark corner by some cement steps.

Charles slammed out the door. His jaw was set in a tight, angry line. His hands shook. His eyes were teary behind his glasses.

"Oh, stop hiding," he snapped at me. "You think I'd let you miss an opportunity like this? I want you to write it all down. All of it. Make a movie, but *don't* hire a famous director. He'll spoil it with crowd scenes and Vaseline on the lens. Make a fucking fortune, little one, and then move to Spain. Buy a villa and marry an elderly prince. Visit Princess Grace and tell her I sent you to gather some tips on posture and wardrobe."

The last day before the "special presentation," we only had time for one dress rehearsal. The actors had been waiting around all day when at eight P.M. Sasha finally announced in his thickest, most hesitant accent, "At ten P.M. you get your rehearsal. Then we can talk all night." By then no one believed him. All day he'd been working with Kosher on the pulley for Icarus. The actors, like wind-up toys, practiced their individual scenes in the wings furious that Sasha paid no attention to them. Charles hid behind a table in the costume shop laboring over his wings. Despite his argument with Sasha, he cut and sewed his creations with great enjoyment. I exercised halfheartedly, to warm up, keeping my eye on Charles as much as I could. When he worked with his hands, he became tender and withdrawn. He actually listened to the silk, and he knew the line of a seam so well that the needle led his fingers. As he invented his costume design, he closed his eyes and gently played the outline of his body with his fingertips. Then his hands fanned out, and he flapped his arms. I think all his work was inspired by colors. Charles experienced emotions and characters as colors. I wasn't allowed to stand at the table and "gape." These were the only moments he wanted to be left alone. He told me he believed the muses which helped him sew and staple and paint were lovers and they were possessive and jealous. Charles never lectured about things the way Sasha did, but he believed that the clothes a person wore, in any situation, were like a mirror to the soul. Costumes were just as responsible for shaping characters as anything else. That's why half the company consulted him on their wardrobe and that's why he either sewed my clothes or shopped for them himself. And he laid out an outfit for me every night. Watching Charles sew was like watching a magican practice coin and card tricks with fingers that moved as fast as insect wings. I hid out of the way and took in every gesture I could.

As he sewed his wings, Charles began to sing a calypso song.

> Icarus wings be made of wax—   cha cha cha cha
> cha cha cha cha
> He fly toward the sun but could not fly back—
> cha cha cha cha
> cha cha cha cha
> His father he made just one mistake—   cha cha cha cha
> cha cha cha cha
> Underestimate how much heat they could take
> Uh-oh, Icarus
> Uh-oh, what a guy
> Soaring and climbing,
> But he fly too high.

When Charles brought his finished wings onstage, there were gasps from the cast. Robin applauded. Kosher, who was in the audience, crept slowly toward the stage as if checking out a mirage. Sasha sat in his customary seat three rows back and tried not to look. The silk shimmered and the sequins reflected the lights, making the theater look like a disco. Sections of the fabric were covered with a thick paint that looked like wax. Long, delicate rainbow-colored fringe caught the wind when the wings moved up and down. The most amazing aspect of the wings was their size. They were as wide as they could be and still fit in the theater. As Charles soared above the audience, his wings would completely fill the space over their heads. He'd designed the fringe to burn in colors and sparks.

"You better see if they work with the pulley," Sasha said. "Otherwise we just have Florenz Ziegfeld."

A few cast members laughed good-naturedly. I was stung. I looked at Charles, but he was already absorbed in conversation with Kosher.

"Clear the theater," Kosher called out.

"Be back for a ten o'clock *dress rehearsal*," Bruce shouted. "Oh sure!" Reeva shouted. "I'll be at the bar on the corner. Call me."

"Rikki Nelson, you come with me." It was Sasha's voice. It sounded authoritative and cold. I slumped toward him. But he laughed and poked his fingers into my sides.

"You're like a little Catholic schoolgirl sometimes," he said. "So naive. So afraid of the devil."

Then he told me we were going to work together and finally I would learn exactly what I was to do. When we reached his room, he placed me on a mat, sat down on his mattress, and began to read from a book of myths. In his slow, exaggerated storytelling tone, Sasha read to me about Zeus, Athena, Apollo, Artemis, Narcissus, Hera, Dionysus, Poseidon, Icarus, and all the other characters that appeared in the show. I knew them already, and I knew their stories better than I knew fairy tales about the Three Little Pigs or Red Riding Hood or Jack and the Beanstalk. Yet Sasha droned on. It was as if he were soothing himself to sleep. He didn't lift his eyes to see how I responded. The next thing I knew, I woke in a darkened room. The clock said 9:50. I dashed down the hall and stairway and ran into the theater. I looked around me in disbelief. The seats were filled with people. I ran up the steps of the stage and discovered the whole company behind the curtain lying on their backs as still as corpses. They were all in costume and masks. I started to panic. I told myself to bend down and see if anyone was breathing. They're meditating, I told myself. I heard the murmuring of the overcrowded house outside. I saw a hideous old man with a knotted great mane and beard, a humped back, and rotting hands staring out the side of the curtain. He watched the people with a cool interest. Suddenly he swung around and caught me with his round marble eyes. His nose was like the rotted beak of a sick bird, and his lips were reptilian. I shrieked.

He leaped forward and grabbed me.

"Rikki," he said with a laugh. It was Sasha. He pulled me close to his matted chest and patted my head. My heart was pounding.

"I'm s'posed to be your grandfather," Sasha said. "Not a creature from the lagoon." I dared to steal another glance at his horrible face, but now it was more elderly and kindly despite its scales and ugly features. I still didn't love the eyes.

"Go get dressed," Sasha said. "I'll hold the curtain for you." I didn't want to ask what he would've done if I'd slept through the whole night. I lifted my feet carefully as I stepped over the members of the company, who continued to lie on the floor motionless. Charles was hidden at his back table applying the wig for his Narcissus routine. He motioned at the bodies. "Aren't they like something out of a spaceship?" he said to me. "I mean, don't they look like they're being frozen for the next century?"

Then he turned to one of his closets and pulled out a delicate dress made from hundreds of rags. Real leaves and acorns were sewn into the fabric, as well as rings of Indian corn and clay beads. The dress fit perfectly. Charles took a brush and spread a soft brown dirt on my face as if it were rouge. He darkened my eyes and wove leaves and soft branches in my hair. Sasha came up behind him and, for a moment, my body tensed. But Sasha took Charles by the shoulders and, in spite of the difficulty that both their masks and costumes presented, the brothers kissed each other on the lips. It was a very long kiss, and although it was passionate, their lips pushed with such force, it was violent too.

"*Merde,*" Charles said to Sasha.

"Yes, *merde,*" Sasha said. And he walked back to peek through the curtain.

"In case you're wondering who all those people are," Charles said to me, "I don't know."

It must've been midnight by the time we began, but the audience waited patiently. The next night was supposed to be our opening, and the actors complained to Sasha about the people. "You wanted a rehearsal," he shrugged. "I keep my word." The first half hour of the run-through went well despite confusion about the order. Some gods went on before they were supposed to, and once two gods entered at the same time. But the actors seemed to be delighted by the accidents. My main job, which was to observe and react, required no acting. Sasha, as the Myth Man, usually picked me up and carried me to different spots on the stage. Then he'd set me down and a god would torture, tease, or instruct me. Midway through the show, after Reeva's warrior Hippolyta, Charles entered in a plain red jumpsuit with a flesh-colored mask. His hair was in neat curls and he fidgeted like a young boy. Sasha as the old Myth Man brought on the glittering wings, and I heard the audience gasp as Charles leaped with exuberance when the Myth Man invited him to fly. Sasha carefully attached the wings to Charles. I didn't catch the moment when he clipped him to the pulley, though I was standing right next to them. The lights dimmed, and a bright circle of torches began to revolve above the balcony. It was like the Fourth of July, or the KKK firing up a cross. A bright spotlight hit Charles as he ascended in slow motion over the heads of the audience. There were cheers. I stood onstage and watched Charles weighted by his ten- or fifteen-foot wings soaring toward the fire. Mustafa pushed on a wooden box filled with sand. Drums rolled. The torches began to crisscross and jump up and down as Charles reached them. The patterns were frantic, hungry, and evil. The speed of the flames gave the fire a greedy, human character. Charles let out the long eerie cries that Robin had composed in Bruce's Latin text. Kosher cranked the pulley, and Charles plummeted toward the stage with the fringe of his wings glowing in the colored spotlight. But something about the speed of his movement must've caused the heat of the glowing threads to break into flame. By the time Charles reached the darkened stage, his wings were completely on fire. The sleeves and collar of his jumpsuit had ignited too. He was supposed to finish his song and then collapse into the sand, but I knew he was only halfway through the lament. His whole costume was going up in flames. I looked out at the audience, and they were fascinated—as if Charles's incineration were a part of the show. I turned my head and saw that Sasha was not moving. He was staring at the flaming wings and their wild shadows as if he were watching an extremely beautiful accident—an improvisation he didn't want to stop. Robin sat by the gong and chimes, accompanying Charles. She glanced up nervously several times for a cue from Sasha, but none came. Kosher's back was turned. He was busy setting props for the next scene. I looked again at Sasha. The brighter the flames rose, the more he seemed to be frozen in a state of awe. The wings were now totally engulfed in orange-blue angry flames, the sequins melting off like drops of blood. The whole back of Charles's jumpsuit was beginning to smoke. His eyes were closed, and he was singing in Latin.

"Charles," I said. "You're on fire."

Charles opened his eyes. He appeared confused.

"Charles," I repeated. *"You're on fire."*

I reached into the sandbox and started throwing fistfuls of sand at him, but it didn't do any good. At that point, Charles whipped his head behind him, stopped singing, and screamed, but he was unable to move. His panic broke Sasha out of his trance, and he ran onto the stage, threw Charles into the sand pit, lay on top of him. Kosher barreled onstage and threw himself onto Sasha like a football tackle. Robin paused for a minute, rose half up, and then sat down again and began playing a breathtaking wild solo of bells and drums. The audience stirred a bit, but since they were watching experimental theater, they weren't clear about whether they were witnessing an actual catastrophe or a symbolic interruption of life interrupting theater. The show continued, and Randy Paul drove Charles to St. Vincent's emergency room.

Late that night I was called to the pay phone, and I heard Charles's voice say he thought he and I were a better team than Anne Bancroft and Patty Duke in *The Miracle Worker*. I was too sleepy to say much. So much time had passed since I'd talked, I was unable to sound out full sentences.

"When, home, burn man?" I asked.

"Tomorrow, back, teepee, ours, Ring-Ding," Charles replied.

"No pain," I replied.

"No pain in Spain," Charles said. "Love you, weirdo."

"Weirdo," I answered. We hung up.

Other than that, it wasn't until late the next day, when Sasha and the company gathered for rehearsal and critique, that anyone realized that I'd talked out loud. Sasha asked me to say his name and he hugged me. Then I began carrying on excited, odd, jagged conversations full of meaningless poetry and broken words. Everyone wanted a try at talking to me and there was a competition to see who could translate my nonsense quicker. Later, when a journalist asked me how I'd rediscovered "the will to speak," I left it open by saying I really didn't remember. That way, Sasha could use the event for whatever grants, private funding, or publicity he needed.

SUBTITLES IN BRAILLE

CHAPTER 10

We left for Europe a year later than planned. A *New York Times* critic had slipped into the "open demonstration" of *The Myth Man* and wrote a full-page article the following day entitled "Genius Haunts a Westside Warehouse." Charles, his back a volcano of blisters and craters, said that if the review had been for a Broadway show, we could all retire to our yachts off the coasts of Capri. He suggested we print T-shirts lithographed with Sasha's face and my body. He thought we should open a concession stand and sell Myth Man mugs and toothbrushes, Myth Man posters and banners, and Myth Man dolls with tunics, accessories, and masks.

"I also want to design a Rikki Nelson Miracle Girl Doll," Charles said. "And sell it in a limited edition."

"Charles, Charles, you're stupid," I chanted.

"*No*, I mean it," he said. "You pull a little ring and nothing happens. She is silent. You keep pulling the ring and you get nothing. It's like a lottery. One day you pull the ring and she says

"Charles, you're on fire," or "Fourscore and Seven-Elevens sell Ring-Dings."

"Charles, Charles, kla do flong," I chanted. My verbal skills were unsteady and often lagged behind my thoughts. The doctors said it was a form of temporary aphasia and I'd teach myself to speak my thoughts over time. I loved constructing odd sounds and songs, and Sasha immediately incorporated them into the show. He never asked me what anything meant. "There is a purity to it," he explained to the rest of the actors.

Charles was as pleased with my transformation as anyone else, but he was suspicious of my chanting and odd syntax. He accused me of faking it to please Sasha and he may have been right. I could think in sentences, but I didn't seem to be able to translate full thoughts into speech.

Sasha used our extra months in New York to rehearse *The Myth Man* for the first time. He was concentrated and calm. He worked every detail of our movements, listened to every sound, and spent hours on each lighting cue. Most of the company thought that our twelve-hour rehearsals were unnecessary since the show was already sold out weeks in advance, but Sasha explained that he didn't want the force of our work dragged down by popular opinion. He didn't want us falling into habits dictated by the predictable laughs or silences of the audience. He said that now, more than ever, it was our job to be like priests who conducted rituals every night. We were scholars searching for buried truths in ancient archetypes. Reeva protested. She said Sasha's schedule broke every union rule in the country and even religions called for days of rest. She threatened to expose his "overseer" behavior to the paper. He grudgingly gave Sundays off. He glared at us on Mondays as if we'd squandered the gifts he'd given us during the work week. He sneered when he overheard conversations about Thai restaurants or Laundromats or movie houses.

One Sunday, Charles and I were resting quietly in our room. Charles was sprawled out on his bed reading a book of poems by Rilke. I was watching *101 Dalmatians* on View-Master plastic binoculars Charles bought for me. The only sound was the *whirrr* and *click* as I pushed the square plastic button and changed to the next colorful frame.

"Tell me when you get to the part where they get stolen," Charles begged me. "I love that part."

There was a knock, and the next thing I knew, Sasha was standing at the foot of Charles's bed. He was all arms. His head bobbed up and down. He seemed lonely and ill at ease.

"Sit down and join the Christian Science Reading Room," Charles said.

Sasha stood up straight and took in a breath. The fair skin on his neck and cheeks was blotchy.

"Listen, Charles," Sasha said. "The box office should eventually cover the payroll with all the sold-out houses. And there are foundations swooping around like vultures promising grants—but right now . . ."

"Yes," said Charles.

Sasha stopped clumsily and looked away from Charles with embarrassment.

"I said 'Yes,' " Charles repeated. "Don't even bother thinking about it. I'll arrange to cover whatever is needed until . . . whenever. . . ."

"This has got to stop sometime," Sasha said. He seemed relieved and depressed.

"It'll stop when it stops," Charles said lightly. He'd laid aside his Rilke and was holding up a cardboard circle of Disney slides toward the sun. He was trying to decide which story to give me next.

"What's that?" Sasha asked.

"*Fantasia.*"

"How can she appreciate it without the music?" asked Sasha.

"I'll put on Ornette Coleman and Gracie Slick later," answered Charles.

Sasha didn't know how to leave. He fidgeted.

"It's surreal isn't it?" He smiled. "They line around the block as if for the Beatles. People wait for autographs outside the stage door.

Don't they realize we're all wearing masks? It's pathetic in a way."

Charles sat up and clapped his hands once. "I think it's *wonderful*," he said.

"So . . ." Sasha shrugged.

"Do you have the budget with you?" Charles asked.

"Of course," Sasha answered.

"And there's adequate expenses for you?"

"I want nothing," Sasha said quietly.

"I'll add your salary." Charles sighed as if they'd been through this before.

Sasha handed Charles a single sheet of graph paper. Numbers were scribbled in Sasha's tiny handwriting.

Charles glanced at it and then folded it neatly like origami paper. "I'll go over it later and have my accountant draw up the checks tomorrow."

Sasha bit the knuckles of his right hand and walked hesitantly toward the door.

"Why is it always like this?" he asked Charles.

Charles groaned. "Like what?"

"Why must I come groveling—like your son for his allowance?" Sasha said.

"Sasha . . ."

"No, really—why *once* can't you approach me—volunteer—anticipate the need—*offer* your assistance? Why do you make me ask? Apply to you with my little budgets?"

Charles put his hands on his hips. He seemed aggravated, but also amused. "You're *impossible*," he said to Sasha. "If I came to you first, you'd accuse me of intruding."

Sasha's face was pale, his mouth set.

"I don't think so, Charles. I think you know how hard it is to fund this work. I think you know what a chore it is to ask the rich to take me on like a hobby or a fashionable toy. You know how bad I am at these things. You won't just open an account for me because you enjoy my discomfort. It gives you a way of still controlling me. It makes you feel like you own a portion of my soul. It's not enough for you to design and act—you have to blackmail too."

Charles shook his head. "Let's not do this," he said. He still sounded amused. "You're being absurd. It's all the excitement."

"You *won't* infantilize me much longer," Sasha said proudly. He drew himself up to his full height. "I'm sorry Rikki had to hear this."

When he had gone, Charles turned to me and said, "Now, that's an example of damned if you do, damned if you don't, and damned every way in between."

"I guess so," I said, but I wasn't completely sure. I was too aware of Charles's smile. He made no effort to hide his pleasure. He hummed a quiet, unrecognizable tune. Then again, he was probably stoned.

For all the acclaim Sasha achieved in the underground, the daily papers gave most of their attention to "the long-awaited return to the stage of the eccentric but brilliant Charles Solomon." The journalists referred to his triumphs on Broadway and then his disappearance from the theater. They described his movements, his looks, the sound of his voice. They compared his work in the past with his current performance as Narcissus, Adonis, and Icarus. They wrote as if he'd invented his characters. Sasha retaliated by cultivating interviews. His picture appeared in magazines and papers looking like a surprised Afghan hound. (The headlines said "Volotny Reinvents Theater," "Volotny Creates Magic Out of Myth." Robin told me that several years ago Sasha changed his name from Stephen Solomon to emphasize his love of the Russian theater. Charles said it was because he didn't want to be Jewish.) Charles refused to talk to the press out of deference to Sasha but it only made him seem more mysterious and desirable. I couldn't tell if he had any feelings about all the attention. He preferred to take me to the Natural History Museum and stare at the reptiles and bones. I preferred the stuffed gorillas, but Charles insisted that lizards knew more.

"Like what?" I asked.

"They know how to reincarnate," Charles said. "into Tony Lama boots and handbags. We're looking at a prehistoric Bendel's." He seemed sincerely tired of show business and fame.

"When this circus is over," he told me, "I'm going to begin serious study to be a monk or a priest. I just haven't zeroed in on the religion yet."

At night after the show, Charles often left the warehouse with groups of men who looked as if they were dressed for Halloween. One night I was awakened by quiet laughs and saw a dark-haired woman in a green chiffon evening gown seated on Charles's bed. A short, stocky greaser with tight blue jeans and a ripped T-shirt sat next to him. They were holding a spoon over a candle and circling the round part of the spoon slowly over the flame.

"Just this once," I heard the woman whisper. I heard the greaser laugh. He said something mocking in Spanish or Greek. I was too tired to sit up and let them know I was awake. The next morning Charles was asleep under his quilt in his white Indian nightshirt. His mouth was open and his hand was lying palm up on his forehead. I thought I'd dreamed it, but the inside of his arm had tiny purple punctures that looked like vampire bites.

Randy Paul now worked full time for Sasha. She organized and documented his ideas and rehearsal techniques for a volume of something called the *Tulane Drama Review. TDR* was devoting a whole volume to Sasha and *The Myth Man.* Randy Paul cut her hair to shoulder length, but continued to wear brocaded Romanian blouses and knee-length dark skirts. Her tights were always slightly twisted and her high-heeled boots came to her ankles and tied up the front. Charles said she looked like the president of the Sylvia Plath Literary Club at Brandeis, but Sasha seemed genuinely delighted by her. Robin told Charles that Randy Paul was Sasha's intellectual twin. They talked for hours about classical drama and third world ritual. Randy Paul worked very hard to set up public relations for Sasha so the students, thinkers, and arts advocates in New York could get the benefit of his ideas. She did her best to make friends with the actors too, although Sasha told her that he didn't want any publicity focused on them. That kind of easy ego gratification would interfere with their performances. Randy Paul complimented and name-dropped with the actors so she could obtain information she brought back to Sasha. The actors didn't know what she was doing and kept hoping she'd set up interviews. But Randy Paul believed in Sasha's doctrines completely and wanted nothing to get in the way of his brilliant rules of work. Becoming his spy seemed to be her way of expressing her romantic love for him. Reeva disappeared several times a week for auditions. She was up for a bus and truck tour of *Hair* and a national commercial for Ragú spaghetti sauce. Bruce was quietly working on a popular musical adaptation of *Antigone* with the producers of *The Fantasticks*. Juno had been approached to star in a proposed Broadway musical based on *Nanook of the North*. Mustafa was building sets for a children's theater in Central Park. Even Kosher had received a letter from some investors in Japan, asking him if he was interested in starting an avant-garde Bunraku theater based on what he'd learned in New York. Robin became well acquainted with the alternative music crowd in New York and jammed with several jazz and pop stars. She sang backup or improvisational vocals at the Bitter End and Bottom Line late at night on the weekends.

One Saturday night after the show I was approached by a frizzy-haired, breathless, overweight lady named Ellen Baum to record my chants for National Public Radio. She wore a sweatshirt with a hood and army pants. I shrugged and said yes.

The next afternoon she bounced into my room with a skinny hippie who carried a huge tape recorder and a microphone. He had a fuzzy beard and tiny eyes. He scowled at the walls and ceiling while placing me in a corner of the room for the right "echo." He called to Ellen Baum to go ahead and she made some introduction in a mellow monotone about the new emphasis in music, poetry, and theater on sound rather than meaning. She referred to my years of silence. She said I was bringing messages from a part of the brain that was preverbal. She said I came from a world where silence had its own language. I was already beyond serious baby talk and was talking in simple sentences, so when Ellen Baum introduced me, I had to fake my old way of gibbering.

> *Chixi kai tiki ti*
> *Bo bo dom dom bader yee*
> *O wok ancha fangla tam*

121

Sliter anto xi paforn
Sleep sun fire wings yes
The water sand sad stone
See dance laugh fish swan
Lizard love McDonald's be quiet.

After fifteen verses or so, I stopped. Ellen Baum sat silently with her head bowed. The skinny hippie clicked off the tape machine and said, "Jeez." Ellen Baum sprung up and enveloped me in a hard, emotional embrace. Then she wrote down her telephone number and said I could come for dinner anytime. I'd changed her whole way of listening. I knew Charles would be disappointed in me. He told me that he never wanted me pulling cheap scams on people with my good looks or vulnerable eyes. He'd lived his life that way and, if nothing else, he wanted me to learn to have compassion for gullible people. "Or," he had said, "you have to earn more than a hundred bucks for the gig."

Several months into our sold-out run, Sasha called an early morning meeting. It was strange to be invited to his room; but on a freezing morning in the last days of winter, we rushed to be with him. Many of the interns had never been in Sasha's room and stood at attention as if they'd entered a palace. I sat on the floor next to a wall and looked for a dirty sock or other evidence that he was human. The room was washed, waxed, impeccable, and, if anything, emptier than before. Sasha stood before us in a powder-blue kimono. He was holding a cup of coffee. Randy Paul stood next to him. Robin sat on the floor behind her, cross-legged and mammoth in a Mideastern robe. Her face was bloated a bit, and she distractedly twirled her hair on her forefinger. There was a Japanese screen pulled forward to cover the contents of the rest of the space. We were all squeezed together by the door.

Sasha smiled grimly.

"Well," he said. "You see it is really very simple. I am not an agent. I am not a rock-and-roll manager. I am not a dramatic coach for second-rate actors to abuse my techniques in meaningless off-Broadway and Broadway shows. Our work is not an Equity showcase for the commercial vultures to swoop down and take whomever and whatever they please for their hypocritical enterprises. And I hoped that you would not be tempted by the lure of financial gain. I never dreamed you'd compromise yourselves for the indulgence of monetary recognition or empty material rewards. But you've surprised me. None of you is as special as I thought. You've turned our whole work into a Forty-second Street arcade."

The group was silent. They weren't prepared for the surprise attack. Stunned by Sasha's flood of words, it took a moment for the meaning to sink in.

"So what do you want?" Bruce asked.

Sasha sipped his coffee. His silence accused every one of us.

"Me? I don't want anything," Sasha said. "It's what *you* want. If you want to continue your artistic adultery, that's your choice. But don't think your indulgences go unnoticed. Your concentration is off. Like all addicts, your movements have lost impulse and inspiration. You are distracted and listless. I tried to fill you with a certain spirit, and now you are empty.

Mustafa cleared his throat. "So we'll rehearse more," he said.

Sasha shook his head. "No, no. I will not waste my time working with people who no longer value my work. It's no big deal. It happens all the time."

By now, each actor in the company was, in turn, guilty, anxious, confused, and frustrated. Randy Paul smirked with righteousness.

"Either you discontinue your secret little attempts at Western superstardom, or I'm canceling the whole project—the tour—and dissolving this company—immediately."

"You don't own us, Sasha," Reeva lashed out.

"Exactly," Sasha agreed. "And I won't order you around like mindless slaves. But I don't have to work in conditions that jeopardize everything I believe in."

"What do you believe in this week?" Charles asked.

"Loyalty," Sasha said coldly. "If this was a sport, the coach would never allow you to play on his team while negotiating with the opponent. If it was war, it would be unthinkable to fight for both sides."

"No one's deserting you," Robin said.

"I'm asking you to think about what you want to do," Sasha went on, ignoring her. "In a way, to ask yourselves who you want to be. If our work no longer fits into your plans, then I will be almost relieved to end it all now. Perhaps you'll miss the parties and the sycophants—but you'll find substitutes."

"Give us a little credit," said Bruce.

"You must all decide," said Sasha, "because I'm not going to let one or two of you quit and then try to continue as if the project is whole. Who would be next? I can't work in an atmosphere of blackmail. Either you all come to some . . . conclusion, or the theater goes black . . . tonight."

The meeting disbanded. I could hear the actors cursing Sasha and arguing with each other. I heard Charles say "insane possessiveness" and someone else mumbled that Sasha was "jealous" and "hypocritical." I stayed behind to see if Sasha might have an extra word for me. I also wanted to study Randy Paul. Sasha smiled at me.

"You could always live with Charles if you're worried," he said. "He knows so many people in commercials and modeling, even television."

"You could say what you mean, for once," I told him. "You're mad at me because of the radio show."

Sasha blushed. "I'm *hurt* by you," he said. "But it's much deeper than the radio show."

"No, it isn't deeper," I said. "You're mad because of the radio."

Sasha smiled slightly. "Maybe," he admitted.

I pointed to Randy Paul. "She's a spy," I said to Sasha.

Randy Paul tried to grin, but she blinked and wrinkled her nose instead.

"She's unnecessary," I told him.

Sasha laughed. Randy Paul pretended to laugh with him.

"She's my friend," Sasha said. "Are you jealous?"

"No, I am not jealous." I said to Sasha. "*You* are jealous. You think if I sang on the radio show, someone will take me away from you."

"Rikki Nelson," Sasha said, his face now grim, "you've already let a stupid producer, Ellen Baum, take you away from me."

"Don't be stupid, Sasha," I said. "I am not taken, and I will not be took."

I turned and left his room.

As usual I couldn't trace the lines of communication within the company or the methods in which messages were delivered to Sasha. We performed that night, so I figured people had somehow given their lives, as he requested. I knew that the actors would be willing to die for Sasha because it was only for the moment. They were experts in rebirth. There would be other lives, other requests to die, and they'd take each one as it came. As Charles sang (to the tune of "Strawberry Fields Forever"):

> *Nothing is real*
> *Nothing to get hung out about*
> *Extraordinarily futile*
> *Endeavors.*

Ten days later, the *Myth Man* company traveled by a charter jet to Amsterdam, Holland. Kosher drove a U-Haul truck to Kennedy Airport hours before and supervised the packing of every single one of his puppets and masks. Charles went along to assist in packing the costumes, but he met a flight crew that had just disembarked a TWA flier from Bali and wandered off with the stewards and stewardesses. He wanted to examine the fabric and relics they'd brought back, as well as share in the unique blends of opium, grass, and hashish the flight crew smuggled from the Indonesian islands. As a result, he missed the flight; but he'd missed so many flights over so many years that Sasha had automatically included an extra ticket for him that departed twenty-four hours later. In fact, Charles preferred to travel to Europe alone. He told me that transatlantic flights were like amusement park rides, only much more civilized. "Everyone must sit down, and they don't carry huge stuffed animals and helium-filled balloons." But Charles wanted to hear each person's story on a flight and share the excitement of visiting a new country in a different time zone where to be an American was to be "despised, capitalistized, worshiped, and revered." Charles said the talks with fellow passengers were so personal and intimate that it was like "beauty parlor heaven."

I'd been left behind and wasn't allowed to join the group until weeks after they'd left. No one had been able to locate my birth certificate. Without a birth certificate, the State Department wouldn't issue a passport. I found myself living in a town house on the Upper East Side with Sasha's benefactor, Mrs. Preston DeVane. She had two grown children, both in college somewhere in New England, and that seemed to give her the credentials to take care of me. As it turned out, I didn't mind Mrs. Preston DeVane. At first she seemed extremely nervous and fragile. She drifted through the three floors of her town house as if she couldn't decide where to flick the ashes off her Virginia Slims cigarette. The town house was very beautiful. She'd decorated it in the colors and patterns of the Southwest. And she collected Indian sculpture and jewelry. She had cabinets full of kachina dolls and turquoise and silver, leather rattles and peace pipes. Feathered circular leather webs hung over every bed. She told me these were "dream catchers." They helped sift out the bad spirits from the good and keep them from entering your dreams and turning them into nightmares. She had masks, puppets, costumes, and headdresses hung on her exposed brick walls and knew the names of the tribes and rituals for each of her artifacts. In every bedroom and sitting room was a small fireplace surrounded by drums, fat wooden flutes, and turquoise-colored fetish bowls. The fetish bowls were ceramic pots filled with corn and beads. Each one cleansed the spirit of the room and could make spells.

Although Mrs. Preston DeVane knew a great deal, she was, at first, very timid and apologetic. She was equally hesitant with her servants, a Mexican maid named Chira; a cook, Alphonsa; and a West Indian chauffeur, Pierre. She spoke hesitantly to them, as if she felt guilty being their employer. I learned from Chira, a doughy Chicana in her fifties, that Mrs. Preston DeVane's husband had walked out on her very recently and she had to take pills to keep from crying all the time. I expected that I would do nothing but count the days until Jonah or my mother filled out the forms which gave formal permission for me to travel through Europe with Sasha. My mother was holding out for some money or a plane ticket, and Jonah was directing a production of *Finian's Rainbow* at an old-age home outside Ocean City, New Jersey. Neither returned phone calls or telegrams. Mrs. Preston DeVane swore to Sasha she had the situation under control, but when I first moved in with her, I was terrified that I'd become a prisoner of the Upper East Side and would never see the group again.

Mrs. Preston DeVane also had framed pictures on every coffee table, bedside table, and mantel of the same Indian woman with a red dot on her forehead and crossed eyes. Mrs. Preston DeVane nervously explained to me that this was Banachoy Krimnada, her guru, who ran an ashram in upstate New York. Chira explained to me that Mrs. Preston DeVane had suffered breast cancer several years back, and it was Banachoy Krimnada's nutritional diet and meditation "regimen" that cured the cancer completely. Mrs. DeVane's devotion to the ashram after that was very strong, and one of the central reasons for the departure of Mr. Preston DeVane. Men don't like flat-chested women, Chira told me; and businessmen are bored by the search for the Godhead.

Once I was privy to these facts, my vision of Mrs. Preston DeVane and Sasha riding each other in the storage closet became more ornate and frightening. I imagined craters in her chest filled with corn and beads, or sometimes I saw her shirtless before Sasha with two circular portraits of cross-eyed Banachoy Krimnada framed in silver where her breasts had been. I began to devise ways of trying to catch Mrs. Preston DeVane naked, but she never seemed to undress. I think she took long baths in the early hours of the morning while the servants and I slept. Breasts, at that time, were becoming a personal fascination to me. The absence of breasts was as exciting to me as the variety of sizes, colors, and shapes I'd imagined when I looked at Robin or Juno or when I'd seen Reeva naked as Venus. Though barely eleven years old, I'd begun to develop enough for

Robin to stare at my chest one night and clap her hands together in what seemed to be an expression of wonder. She ran off to find Charles. Charles examined me clinically, not touching me, but making me turn around and freeze in several angles. Then he told me I had two Hershey's kisses growing on my chest and he couldn't handle the fact that soon he'd have to be giving out questionnaires and conducting background checks on the boys lined up outside the door. One day, he and Robin took me to a friend's lingerie shop on Christopher Street, and she dug around all her negligees, garter belts, and see-through panties and came up with a ridiculous white training bra with a pink bow on it. Charles fitted it to me, and Robin acted as if we were in the middle of some tribal coming-of-age ritual. I preferred to wear boys' sleeveless undershirts.

Mrs. Preston DeVane relaxed with me after a few days, and she turned out to be much different than I'd expected. She was bluntly honest, curious, and a library of gossip. After five, when cocktail hour started, Chira, Alphonsa, Mrs. Preston DeVane, and I would lie around on the oversized southwestern pillows and share a pitcher of sangria. Mrs. DeVane loved to laugh and encouraged anyone who could come up with a nasty enough story to get her going. Her laugh was quiet and she held three fingers in front of her lips so as not to exhibit bad manners, but her rail-thin body would shake, and her pale blue eyes teared with pleasure.

"You must listen to Sasha every minute, darling," she said to me one night. "He is the absolute *hope* for the theater. He has the vision of a shaman. Unfortunately, he also has the personality of a snake."

Then she laughed in her quiet way and told us about the time she was lovers with the chief of all the master drummers in Nigeria.

"I actually had to call him *Chief.* I felt like I was talking to a German Shepherd. He could drum, though. He could speak real poetry on his drums."

She took a gulp of sangria and laughed in delicate snorts. "That *wasn't* why he was crowned Chief, however. He must've had the longest schlong in the African continent. The first time I saw it, I saw my life passing before my eyes."

Chira and Alphonsa gasped and attempted, with drunken twitches and ticks of their eyes, to remind Mrs. Preston DeVane that they were Catholics and I was a child.

"Oh, really, now," Mrs. Preston DeVane scolded her maid and her cook. "You two would be much better off if you were less repressed. As far as I'm concerned, the Holy Trinity is just another dirty story of incest, homosexual lust, and three boys in search of a fun party. And Jesus is just one of those passive-aggressive rock-and-role types whom women lust to possess. They build all kinds of fantasies around him because he simply is too neurotic to make a serious commitment."

I thought Chira and Alphonsa would quit Mrs. DeVane's service right then, but obviously this wasn't a new theme. They talked about the seven stations of the cross as seven possible positions for intercourse, and suddenly a wild bantering about Easter and resurrection became a discussion about how many erections their husbands and boyfriends could have per night.

"Emilio," Chira groaned, "he never gets completely soft. Thirty years and I still go to bed every night with an oily dipstick in my face."

Alphonsa, who was only thirty but very fat and sluggish, groaned. "I always get the Explorer's Club. 'Oh, baby, let me lose myself in you. Baby, let me get buried in you. Let me crawl inside you and touch every inch of your big, dark cave. Oh, honey, I want to die in your huge ocean.' "

Mrs. Preston DeVane sighed. "Well, Mr. DeVane," she said demurely, "was not a fan of long-distance running. He was a sprinter. He liked to dash short distances and head for the showers with his medal."

The women laughed, drank, and woozily toasted each other.

"What about you, Rikki Nelson?" Mrs. Preston DeVane asked. Chira and Alphonsa glanced at their mistress and each other with guilt and surprise.

"It's simple," I lied. "I am a virgin."

"Of course you are, dear," Mrs. Preston DeVane said encouragingly. "And you stick to your guns. Don't touch the stuff."

Mrs. Preston DeVane gestured toward Alphonsa and Chira. They had begun to nod out on each other's shoulders, leaning back on their pillows.

"They are real heroes, Rikki Nelson," Mrs. Preston DeVane said. "Escaped from fascist governments, witness to their families slaughtered, learning new languages, customs, going from being the queens of their own households to live-in servants in mine. What does our Sasha know about the Chiras and Alphonsas of this world?"

Mrs. Preston DeVane gave me a kind, bleary smile and lit up a Virginia Slim.

"I think he knows," I said doubtfully. "He says he makes his theater to wake up everybody."

"It doesn't matter." Mrs. Preston DeVane sighed. "I've already pledged a million dollars toward the development of his next play. Do you know what it's about?"

"I only know *The Myth Man*," I said.

"Yes, well, one doesn't like to be insensitive or crude in these patron-artist situations. But he hasn't really explained his ideas to me. I don't have a clue what the new piece will be about."

"He probably doesn't know," I said.

"Hah, hah," Mrs. Preston DeVane laughed in loud syllables. "Hah, hah."

Chira and Alphonsa stirred and each turned a bit on her pillows.

Mrs. Preston DeVane put a finger to her lips and then lay back quietly on her chair, a happy smile on her face, and closed her eyes. Her cigarette burned to its filter in her outstretched hand.

During the days when she was much more nervous and fragile, I took a certain interest in following her as she skittishly passed from room to room, up and down stairways, and in and out of hallways. At first she didn't seem to notice I was there, but eventually she began talking to me, or rather she talked and muttered and I was there to witness the words without reply.

"My guru says every object you own takes its place in your spirit. As if you can build cabinets in your soul. So I've tried to purchase objects that are ancient and crafted by the wise and religious. But it's *their* holiness that lives in all these masks and drums—not mine. Sasha once said to me that I am not a seeker, but a shopper. He said it lovingly, but it stung. I can't seem to open up. Even this house (I completely redid it after I got rid of Preston) has walls. The antique locks on the doors make it an extremely attractive fortress. My guru says houses are built by those who need to protect themselves from the dangers of the inside, not the outside. I offered to donate the house to the ashram as a New York office, but Banachoy Krimnada refused, saying that until I learned to become free of my terrors, I would carry these walls with me wherever I went. Sasha understands my agony. He knows what it's like to stand on the outside and watch yourself trip and fall through the darkness. I introduced him to Banachoy Krimnada, and it was as if they'd shared the womb. The light that emanated from the two of them rendered me speechless and I thought, if only I could hear what they weren't saying.

Mrs. Preston Devane sobbed dryly. "Sometimes I think I'm too old to trade in my habits and desires for the unknown."

When she took her tiny red pills, she didn't wander and mutter. She dressed in matching gabardine pleated skirts and suit jackets and went off into the city with her chauffeur. She was on the board of UNICEF, Asia House, Arts International, the Preservation of Native American Culture Society, the African Relief Society, CARE, and the New York Philharmonic; and she was a principal stockholder in Philip Morris Company and Revlon. "it's all very charitable—this third world promotion," she said gaily, "but when these people revolt, I'll still be the first one they chop into hamburger."

Once I saw her long gray limo parked out front of the town house. The passenger door was open an inch or two and the light in the back was on. Steel drum music was blasting from the tape player, and the fumes coming out of the crack in the door were unmistakable. I tried to peek in without being seen, and I saw Mrs. Preston DeVane and her chauffeur sprawled out on the wide leather seat passing the biggest, fattest joint I'd ever seen. She caught my eye and grinned at me. Her eyeballs were wide and red. She pointed to the joint.

"It's called a spliff," she said. "It comes from the islands." The chauffeur, wearing only his uniform pants, scratched his bare chest and nodded dreamily with closed eyes. I wanted to tell Charles. I knew he'd laugh his head off. I'd received a dozen fresh tulips from him in a refrigerated cardboard box. There was a card inside with a windmill. It said:

> They eat their french fries here with mayonnaise.
> The people are *wonderful,* even though they speak as if they've got something caught in their throat.
> Sasha is happily demolishing a theater while waiting for you.
> The producer had to be shot with a tranquilizer gun.
> I have found us a magical hotel. My life is nothing but clogs and cheese without you.
>
> Charles

I didn't want to push Mrs. Preston DeVane, but she was very aware of my fear that I'd never be allowed to join my "family" in Amsterdam. She assured me that she had every available "connection" working on it and informed me that my mother was a "petulant, conniving bitch" and that Jonah was a "sot." She did her best to comfort me by taking me to the Metropolitan Museum, the ballet, art movies at the Carnegie Hall cinema, F.A.O. Schwarz, and the Cloisters for a serious and indecipherable meditation on the unicorn tapestries. One night we had a special dinner on the floor of the terra-cotta, glass-encased patio of the town house, and Alphonsa cooked up some kind of corn mush and venison. She prepared vegetables that looked like the organs of a dissected frog. There was a special guest that evening. He was a man in his thirties who must've been six-foot-five or over. He had unnaturally black hair and unnaturally dark skin and dark blue eyes. His ears and nose were pierced and he wore so many layers of thick silver and turquoise jewelry, I thought his skin would bruise. His deerskin shirt glowed with beaded fringe and animals embroidered in multicolored threads. He wore skin-tight faded blue jeans and scuffed cowboy boots with three-inch heels. When he smiled, his teeth were bright and even. He looked like a movie star.

"This is Journey," Mrs. Preston DeVane said proudly. "He's of the Cherokee, Navajo, and Hopi people, and I wanted you to meet. I had a long talk with Sasha and told him in no uncertain terms that it was a crime that he didn't have a Native American shaman in your group. Journey's flying to join Sasha tomorrow."

"Hi," said Journey. *"Ska tawi gni atayni."*

I nodded at him, but I was suspicious. What if he was traveling to Europe to take my place?

"We're also celebrating," Mrs. Preston DeVane said quickly. "Your papers are finally in order, Rikki Nelson. I will receive them tomorrow and have you on a plane by the end of the week."

I jumped up from the floor and hugged Mrs. Preston DeVane, who patted my back and sighed.

Journey lifted a glass of corn liquor and said, "Here's to collaboration. The dove and the raven share the sky. The dove is white so the raven may be black. The raven is the hunter so the dove may bring the branch of peace."

Mrs. Preston DeVane drunkenly lifted her glass. I stayed curled next to her. I didn't know why, but her friend Journey reminded me of a TV game show host.

"Journey has published the most intriguing book," Mrs. Preston DeVane said. She wasn't talking to anyone in particular. "It's called *The Spiritual Tourist's Guide to Hidden Hotels.*"

" 'Hotels' is a metaphor," said Journey.

"Journey lists all the dates, times, and locations of secret Native American rituals," Mrs. Preston DeVane explained.

"How can he do that if they're supposed to be secret?" I asked.

Journey stood up slowly. His jewelry made him sound like wind chimes. He was so huge, it strained my neck to look up at him. His hands were spotted like a palomino and lighter than his face. He smiled with his teeth again. His eyes were glass. Perhaps he was stoned.

"I am one of the leaders of the Native American Action Council, the NAAC. For me, politics is sacred and the sacred is politics. White

America must experience the beauty of our people so they will stop robbing us of our land and demeaning our heritage. We are not worthless alcoholics, we are high priests from the hills of the coyote and the nests of the eagle. We represent the rocks and cactus and can document the language of the stars."

"Here, here," said Mrs. Preston DeVane softly. She was so drunk, she was staring intently at a square of terra-cotta on the floor as if it were rotating. "Won't Sasha die over this man?" she asked.

I wasn't sure. Journey was still standing, sweating profusely. His dripping face actually seemed to dissolve like clay. It was like putty; I looked for another, more solid face underneath. He also breathed heavily, trembled slightly as if he had a heart condition or was much older than his blue-black hair made him seem. He stood there like an oversized Disney version of an animated Indian. He spooked me. He didn't seem to have emotions. I thought perhaps very evolved shamans simply wore human bodies and stored their souls some-where else. For whatever reason, I excused myself and went to bed. I said I was too tired to hear a story from Journey about the turtle, the snail, and the dead butterfly.

Later that night I awoke to a shaking beneath me. My eyes adjusted and I saw that the white canopy over my bed was rocking. The whole house seemed to fill with a *boom boom boom.* The sound wasn't loud, but jingled the chandeliers and caused the china in the oak cabinets to vibrate. I wondered why Chira or Alphonsa weren't yelling in Spanish, running after me, or why there were no sirens filling the sky for an air raid or earthquake. The house was dark, and I could see the flicker of candles coming from the patio. I assumed the electricity had blown. As I approached the patio, the *boom boom boom* got louder, and I saw Mrs. Preston DeVane and Journey both stark naked, surrounded by a circle of candles. Journey was sitting, and his mammoth hand held a mallet with a leather head. He was pounding one of Mrs. Preston DeVane's drums and quietly whining a chant that sounded like an imitation of the kind you hear Indians do on old western movies. His eyes were closed and he sounded out of breath. His whole body was painted in streaks of multicolored paint. Mrs. Preston DeVane was dancing around him, inside the circle. She had a cigarette in one hand and was drawing lines and Xs and circles on herself with the other. She lazily hopped from one leg to the other and sometimes spread out her arms like a bird and swooped down and sang, "Eeeeee." I saw the scars on her chest. They were outlined in red and orange paint. As Journey speeded up his drumming, she bent backward from the waist and did a version of the Limbo dance where you hop under a stick at birthday parties. Journey whinnied and called out the names of some animals. "Mouse! Woodchuck! Bear! Horse!" Now he reminded me of the guest Indian on a Saturday morning children's show. I didn't want to get caught, so I went back to bed and forced myself to fall asleep in my vibrating room.

When I woke the next morning, Journey had already left for the airport. Chira was mopping the patio, cursing in Spanish. Mrs. Preston DeVane slept through the day.

I was due to leave in three days. I thought I'd be relieved, but I felt uneasy instead. I had a hard time imagining the airplane. I'd seen pictures of airplanes, of course, and advertisements with stewardesses serving unrecognizable sections of orange-colored chickens tucked into square plastic plates, but the actual idea of sitting in a chair in a tube shooting across the ocean didn't seem logical, and I began to lose sleep and look out my window suspiciously at the sky. I wasn't afraid of crashing. I was afraid of catching on fire. I kept seeing Charles's wings igniting as he slid down the pulley. I envisioned Sasha watching off to one side, not able to or willing to rescue him. I imagined the plane plummeting over the city of Amsterdam and Sasha standing on a rooftop with binoculars. I tearfully began to make up stories in which Mrs. Preston DeVane would decide, for my own good, to adopt me. And she'd adamantly insist that I remain in the States and attend a proper boarding school upstate near her ashram. I didn't talk to her about any of this, of course. I had no trouble hiding my fears. My work with Sasha taught me never to impose my moods on the lives of others. Secretly, I lived each moment like a terrified martyr condemned to burn at the stake. I was bitter. There would be no redemption. Only flames, loneliness, and ashes.

The day before my departure, Mrs. Preston DeVane gaily proposed we have a "ladies' lunch." I dressed in a Pollyanna velvet-and-lace pinafore Charles had sewn for me, dug out some anklets and a pair of patent leather Mary Janes. Mrs. Preston DeVane, in a gray one-piece silk dress, gold circle pin, and matching mink coat and hat, took me to the Russian Tea Room. I wanted to cry because I'd never be able to go to such a glamorous restaurant again after my impending death, but I smiled as best I could and decided to ask her questions I'd never dare to ask if there was a chance I would live.

"How did you meet Sasha?" I asked her after she ordered me borscht and fruit-filled blintz.

She sipped on her White Russian and nodded. "Ah, yes." She smiled dreamily. "Well, it's complicated and yet very simple. My ex-husband, Preston, used to invest in Broadway shows. Someone convinced him, God knows who, to put money in Charles's last show. Sort of as a joke on Preston, you see, because Charles was, well, you know, *weird,* and Preston, my God—Yale, the Air Force, Harvard Business School, WASP—you name it.

"I thought he'd have a *stroke* when he saw the show. *I* adored it. Pure genius. But Preston thought he'd be *indicted* for pornography or perversion. Then the show ended up making a fortune—I mean, a *fortune.* I suppose you know how filthy rich Charles is? Anyway, Preston felt obliged to attend one of those affairs—for investors and artists. Well, he and Charles got to talking and Preston fell *in love.* I don't mean sexually, of course, though I wish he had, might've loosened him up a bit, but I mean he and Charles became fast friends. Charles has this *uncanny* sense for business, given that he's a total flake, and he *knows* so many subjects. The man is encyclopedic. But then, so's his broker."

Mrs. Preston DeVane was known at the Russian Tea Room. They brought her White Russians without her having to ask. I was happy to absorb her tumble of words without having to think of the doomed TWA Flight 763 to Amsterdam.

"So, my darling," she went on, "Charles joined us for dinner, went to hockey games, and now and then confided about some of his real estate purchases to Preston. In the meantime, he and I became very close. He redid my hair color, advised me on wardrobe, escorted me to rock-and-roll benefits, introduced me to Greenwich Village, and taught me how to roll a joint. When Preston left me for a girl about your age, Charles was right there. I know he and Preston have remained friends, but Charles absolutely nurtured me. I was hideously depressed; and although I volunteered for every charity on the Eastern Seaboard, I was absolutely, totally trapped in the drama of the useless, middle-aged woman set out to pasture. Charles suggested I come to the theater and stuff envelopes. I thought he was crazy, but he must have been psychic. He told me his younger brother Sasha was an odd bird, but he was doing the most important work—possibly in all modern theater. Charles himself was giving up Broadway and movie roles left and right to work with him. When I arrived at the theater and Sasha and I looked at each other, I was stunned. I knew him. This is a cliché, I suppose, but Sasha and I have always known each other. He has a true destiny and I'm very lucky to be a part of it. He never asked for money, and I certainly didn't want to be the old, horny bag who pays for sex and satori. So I waited a long time, until I saw it made no difference. Now I've set up a trust, exclusively to fund the next work after *The Myth Man,* and I know I've bought myself a few acres in heaven."

I was drowsy from the rich food and the continuous drone of her drunken praises of Sasha. I wanted to pretend I didn't know him, so I wouldn't have to fly to perform with him. To my surprise, Mrs. Preston DeVane suddenly leaned forward and spoke to me in a confidential tone.

"Sometimes he wonders if you wouldn't be better settling with a nice family and meeting children your own age. I could arrange that, you know. He's asked me if I thought he was stealing your childhood."

"Tell me what's good about childhood," I asked her.

Mrs. Preston DeVane lit a cigarette, tapped a long fingernail on the table, and look up thoughtfully.

"Well," she started slowly, "there are toys, I guess, and games.

There are secrets with friends; and if you happen to be lucky, there's unconditional love."

"I have all that," I said.

Mrs. Preston DeVane nodded her head. "And yet you've been so glum since we fixed your departure. It's as if I'm sending you to a prison camp. I thought maybe you didn't want to do the work anymore. And Sasha told me not to force you—"

"It's not that," I said quickly.

"I didn't think so," Mrs. Preston DeVane said, relieved. "He *adores* you. Your life is any child's dream."

I stared down at the table. I figured I'd tell her.

"I don't know how the plane works. I don't think it will," I said. My teeth started to chatter. Tears came to my eyes. "I don't want to fall from the sky and catch on fire."

Mrs. Preston DeVane lifted one of her blond eyebrows, smiled, and reached across the table with her tiny hand. Her skin was cool and dry.

"Would you like me to fly with you?" she asked kindly.

"No, thank you," I said. She was too delicate to influence the balance of a falling plane.

Mrs. Preston DeVane withdrew her hand and fumbled around in her suede purse.

"Many people are afraid to fly," she said mildly. "But look at me. I've been around the world and back many times and *I've* survived."

"You and I are different," I said. My teeth were chattering so hard I was afraid the fancy waiters would hear them.

Mrs. Preston DeVane pulled out a bottle of pills from her bag and shook them playfully.

"My philosophy is, if neither meditation nor prayer, religious chant nor trance dance does the trick, get stoned."

She broke off a tiny piece of a blue pill and made me take it right there. Within minutes I was grinning and telling her I'd caught her with Journey.

"Oh, my," she said with mock concern. "Well, be sure when you describe the scene to Charles, you make it very, very dirty. Otherwise, he won't be impressed."

She called some expert child psychiatrist and got me my own bottle of pills, kept me lightly stoned for the next twenty-four hours, and drove me to the airport in her limousine. We sat in a special TWA lounge, and she ordered me an orange juice. She pulled a tiny bottle of vodka from her bag and poured a couple drops of vodka into my orange juice. The orange juice made my throat hot, and my head was warm and fuzzy. She slipped me a couple of tiny little bottles and told me to put them in the Gucci travel bag she had bought me. She must've called ahead, because we didn't have to be inspected or stopped at immigration, and she got to walk me right to the plane. Despite the fact that I was stoned and drunk, my hands began to sweat when I looked at the round walls and ceiling close above me and the thick, tiny windows that never opened. Mrs. Preston DeVane took a couple of the stewardesses aside and spoke quietly to them. I mistrusted their sympathetic cheerfulness. Sasha often said that there was a rhythm to real emotions, just like in music. People who just grinned and laughed too much were either fools or had Buddha nature. These ladies didn't seem to be very Buddhist.

Mrs. Preston DeVane squatted down and threw her arms around me in a rough, loving embrace. She squeezed me as if to give me courage. I started to cry.

"Sure you don't want me to stick around?" she said. "I can always shop, and I'm the world's best groupie."

"No, thank you, ma'am," I said. "But thank you for everything."

"Next time you see me, call me Willie," she said. She smelled of vodka and Chanel No. 5.

I was crying into her bony shoulder. I think she understood that I was upset about more than the cold metal capsule with its beaming executioners. As odd as my time had been with Mrs. Preston DeVane, she was an older lady who'd been kind and funny. I'd slept in a soft bed with a white canopy. She'd let me run free around all her magic objects, and she'd treated me like one of the "girls."

"You're my pal," she said to me. Then she stood up, dabbed her eyes with a lipstick-blotted Kleenex, and ducked out past the stewardesses, who slammed the thick metal door behind her. I reached into my Gucci bag and felt for my tiny vodka bottle. I uncapped my pill container and slid two pills into my mouth. I swigged them down with the vodka and didn't wake up until we were flying over the ocean and Michael Caine, in a brown shirt and khaki pants, was standing on a fragile rope bridge which was swinging perilously over a bottomless gorge. My eyes were barely open when one of the stewardesses rushed over to me.

"We were very worried about you," she said. She wasn't smiling. "We couldn't wake you."

I tried to answer or bring her into focus. Sean Connery and Michael Caine were laughing over the bottomless gorge as Indians and a dark-haired woman in a sari watched in horror.

"Would you like to eat?" the stewardess asked. I didn't want to tell her, but her nervous energy was jeopardizing the balance of the airplane. Also, I couldn't talk. My brain was in a different time signature from my mouth.

"Are you ill?" asked the stewardess.

I had a picture in my mind of Charles, his wings on fire, plummeting on the cable pulley over the audience. I began to sweat. I imagined Sasha, in a black jumpsuit, sneaking into the theater and carefully and quickly altering Kosher's perfectly designed mechanics. Then I saw a different image—Sasha and Kosher in a quiet conference with each other and, later, in the moment that Charles descended from the balcony, Sasha giving Kosher a slight smile, barely nodding his head. Kosher blinked once. No. It wasn't possible. Then I saw TWA Flight 763 to Amsterdam pointing its cold nose toward the sun and flapping past the planets toward its fiery arms. Mrs. Preston "Willie" DeVane's swooping her painted arms in the circle of candles. The plane would catch fire and free-fall into a bottomless gorge, and I was on fire and Charles was in flames and Willie DeVane was melting. Sasha floated past, riding on Randy Paul's back. He watched. He grinned.

"Little girl," I heard the stewardess say. "Are you ill?" I managed to shake my head no and she left. I reached into the Gucci bag for the pills—I snuck two more into my palm. I guzzled them down with several drops from the tiny bottle of vodka poured into a plastic glass of orange juice the stewardess had left on a nearby armrest.

When I woke up, a steward was carrying me down an escalator in the Amsterdam airport. I saw duty-free shops and signposts in English and Dutch. He brought me to a clean white room where there were several policemen and immigration officials. The steward sat me in a chair and left. It was hard work to sit up in the chair and keep my eyes open. My stomach was burning. The six or seven men in varied uniforms were speaking rapidly in Dutch. One was on the phone. Another was speaking into some kind of small box that gave off static and answered back.

One of the men turned to me and spoke slowly in an accent that sounded like he was gargling. He had a red mustache, bald head, and a skinny, tired body.

"Who gave you the vodka, Miss Nelson?" he asked gently.

"I stole it from where I lived," I heard myself say.

"Did any employee of TWA or immigration of JFK Airport give you the vodka, Miss Nelson?"

It took me a moment to realize that this was not a different question, but really the same one as before.

"No." I tried to sound honest, but I didn't know what was going on, and the burning acidic sensation in my stomach was moving up to my chest and throat.

"Do you often steal liquor, little girl?" the man asked. Now he sounded angry.

"Just this time," I replied. It was true.

"Do you often steal?" he barked.

One of the other uniformed men said something to him in Dutch, and my interrogator took a deep breath as if to calm down.

"Those pills are from an American psychiatrist. Why do you have them?"

"I was scared to fly," I said.

"You are not seeing a doctor for other reasons?" He was holding up the bottle.

"What other reasons?" I asked him. I began to feel like I was going to pass out.

Just then, yet another uniformed man brought Charles into the room. He was dressed in a beautiful embroidered shirt with puffy sleeves, cutoff blue jeans, and white high-topped sneakers. His looks seemed to aggravate my interrogator even more. Charles looked at me with glee.

"Perhaps you do drugs, Miss Nelson. Perhaps you are a thief. A truant. Perhaps you are violent."

"Oh, for God's sake," Charles said loudly. He spoke harshly to the whole room of uniformed men in fluent Dutch. I could see they weren't impressed with him. I stood up unsteadily and grabbed the trash can next to the desk. I started throwing up in it. Charles pulled my hair back, put his hand on my forehead, and kept talking.

I lifted my head long enough to see my interrogator talking on the phone. Then he handed it to the man in uniform. While he spoke to whomever Charles had told them to call, I kept throwing up. I heard the second man mumble into the phone in a prissy, offended tone; but soon he stopped. The next time he spoke, his voice was slightly defensive—then apologetic. He hung up the phone, said a few short words to my interrogator, and then nodded toward Charles and me.

Charles gave me a glass of water and washed me off. Then he briskly led me out of the airport. I don't remember much. We stopped at a few shiny white garbage cans so Charles could lift me up and I could heave into them. By the time we reached his car, my stomach was emptied out. I was drowsy, thick, and light-headed. The car was a tiny gray bug with only two seats and three wheels. It looked like a circus vehicle. Charles strapped me in and drove very carefully, staring straight ahead.

"I'm really surprised at you, Rikki Nelson," he said in a mocking, grave tone. "I thought you would mix your booze and pills better than this."

I was trying hard to stay awake. I couldn't answer.

"Do you know how inconvenient it would be if you'd overdosed? You're the only reason I came. I mean, I had plenty of offers for fairly interesting porno movies and obscure plays. I might've done some Shakespeare in mime. I thought we had a deal."

I was too spent to say anything but "Wasn't" and "We do."

Charles kept his eyes on the dull gray road.

"I'm sure Willie DeVane wouldn't have given you those pills and vodka if she'd known you planned to abuse her corruption of you."

I hung my head. "It was me," I said. "I was afraid in the plane."

"Well, I'd wish I'd known," Charles said. "I would've flown right over and flown back with you. Me and my wings."

Then Charles made a quiet sound. A short intake of the breath. His eyes widened for a moment.

"Oh," he said. He reached over with his right hand and pushed the hair from my face.

"I think you'd better sleep this off," he said. "Luckily, Sasha's in some secret meeting today on a hidden houseboat. With an Indonesian puppet master or a Balinese prince or something. I can take you somewhere special . . . an AA meeting conducted in Dutch and German."

I don't know whether Charles said any more than that. I sank into a sick, dreamless sleep.

After we performed in Amsterdam, our show became what Charles called "the buzz of Europe." Sasha had been invited by the American consulate and the minister of fine arts in France to meet with the number one director in Europe, Jacob Avon. He flew to Paris early, leaving Robin to pack for him and Bruce to dole out our travel expenses. On the train from Brussels to Paris, Bruce told everyone that Jacob Avon had been imprisoned in Poland for five years because of his work and had accepted permanent asylum in Paris. He was best known for taking the librettos of Gilbert and Sullivan operettas, translating them into Polish, and designing confrontational agitprop happenings out of them. His signature work was a redoing of *The Mikado* as a bloody, ferocious antiwar spectacle. He'd recently resurrected *The Pirates of Penzance* as a controversial anti–big business audience participation piece. His pirates dressed in suits and ties, kidnapped members of the audience, and tied them to chairs in the boardroom. The modern major general was chief stockholder and chairman of the board. The audience members, with machine guns at their heads, were forced to vote against any money toward education or housing for the poor. The women were all dressed as secretaries and served coffee throughout the show, but wouldn't allow anyone to drink it. A scandalous S&M sex scene between the chairman and the wife of a visiting American investor was the talk of France. It took place on the conference table to a translated reinterpretation of "Poor Wandering One." Another controversial aspect of Jacob Avon's work was that he had a loudspeaker built into every set and shouted nasty critiques of his actors' mistakes as they performed. Sometimes he'd stop a scene in the middle and restage it from the loudspeaker. Jacob Avon had received numerous death threats over the years, a fact Sasha envied and admired, but Charles said half the threats were from his wife and other actors in his company. Nonetheless, the French adored him and treated him as if he were an artistic saint. They gave him anything he wanted. He was a rude, monastic director and never granted interviews. The fact that he wanted to meet Sasha was an honor for all of us.

The French government had just purchased, at Jacob Avon's request, an abandoned meat market. It was a block long and two blocks wide and came complete with step-in freezers. Rusty cleavers and hooks hung from the ceiling. The purchase included three flatbed trucks which had been used to transport live cows from the farmlands. The market and trucks were to be Avon's official theater. He wanted it exactly as it was. He didn't even want it washed or swept. When Sasha and Jacob Avon met, Robin said they got along like father and son. Jacob Avon offered to hand over his theater for *The Myth Man.* Sasha took Kosher along to impress the esteemed director with the purity and commitment of his vision and to measure the meat market for our sets. Charles wasn't invited because he believed Jacob Avon's actors behaved like "zombies" and that the use of the loudspeaker system in performances was "creative as the Third Reich."

We got off the train from Amsterdam and were herded immediately into the meat market. We saw a hunched old man with a thick broken nose and no lips scowling at us. One of his black-brown eyes wandered. Sasha stood next to him, looking like a proud son. The old man shuffled hesitantly up to Reeva.

"Would you be so kind as to hang upside down from a hook?"
He asked in a thick accent. Reeva glared at Sasha, who nodded his
head. Reeva dropped one leg in the round part of a rusty, blood-
stained hook and hung, as if from a trapeze. Jacob Avon took out
a tiny notebook and scribbled for over fifteen minutes. Then he ran
out of the market. Reeva didn't move. "I may as well just hang here
till we open," she said. "It's gotta be better than the hotels Sasha
books us in."

Kosher convinced Sasha to abandon the idea of staging *The Myth
Man* in Jacob Avon's theater. He said the ceiling was too low, the
trucks cumbersome, and the overall atmosphere "too violent." But
I knew the smell made him sick. Kosher only ate meat cooked well
done in sizzling oil and hated the smell of sweat and dirty feet. He
was constantly washing himself.

We were staying in the Hotel Welcome. It was a cheap pension with
linoleum floors near Notre Dame. The beds were made up with
damp, stained sheets. Our room tilted so badly that Charles could
roll a coin from his bed to mine. "Too bad we didn't bring a sled,"
he said cheerfully. Despite our success, our salaries remained very
low and when Reeva or Mustafa complained, Sasha told them that
every bit of extra money was being deposited in a fund toward the
creation of the next piece. Bruce, as stage manager, was the one who
handed out the money, and he kept meticulous records of advances
and loans. He confided in Charles that Journey, the newest member
of the group, who had yet to perform or attend one rehearsal, was
at the top of the list for borrowing funds. Journey's publisher had
scheduled lectures at several small universities. He was to give a
speech entitled "The Oppression of Native Americans in Contem-
porary America." We also heard him giving "private" healing work-
shops in his room to groups of French students and writers.

"So what does he need all this money for?" Bruce asked Charles.

"Skin and hair treatments at Chanel—I'm *sure* of it," Charles
answered. "Call me a racist, but when he fades, he looks like Troy
Donahue."

"It sounds like a dog is tied up," Reeva said of the yipping and wailing in Journey's workshops. "How'd he set up business so fast?"

"He hands out pamphlets on the steps of the schools," Charles said. "He's a closet Krishna boy."

I loved payday. I always reveled in the texture of the clean white envelope with my name neatly printed on it. Bruce knew my pleasure and teased me. He always held it slightly out of my grasp.

"Say your prayers?" he asked me.

I'd nod.

"Clean your plate?"

Exasperated, I'd nod.

"Study your conjugations?" (Bruce was teaching me Latin.)

"Bruce!" I'd groan and jump for my money.

"A junior capitalist. A future Republican," he'd say with mock despair, and hand me the envelope.

The large paper francs fascinated me. They looked like play money. In Europe, as in America, I handed my salary over to Charles. He'd take on a proper air and meticulously divide the cash. A certain portion of it Charles tucked away. He said it was to be my "mad money." "This is for college, travel, or bartending school when you're older," he explained. "A woman should know she can be independent." He told me he was also adding money of his own to my "fund" so I could buy a pearl necklace when I was sixty, but I never bothered to sneak a look in his drawers or papers to find out how much I'd saved. I didn't care and Charles was adamant that I never borrow from my savings. His money managing was the only evidence I saw of what Willie DeVane had called Charles's "tight ass." Whatever leftover money I had he let me spend on dolls, books, or clothes. Charles supplied the junk food and numerous postcards, key chains, T-shirts, and socks he wouldn't let me buy myself.

The actors in the company loved Paris. Many of them set out on private adventures or met up with old friends. Bruce roamed the galleries and bookstores and sat in cafés reading by himself. Christoph was a different man. He lived with his wife and six children from past marriages and lovers. She'd been a model and had a thin, sculptured face, wide eyes, and arrogant laughter. Christoph attended university rallies in his free time. He went from café to café talking French politics and joined up with a group of older radicals whom he described to Charles as poets with writer's block, out-of-work actors, university professors, and philosophers who'd been dismissed for their opinions. They were unshaven, shaggy-haired young men who chain-smoked, drank a lot, and always seemed to be suffering. They suffered out loud in long, rambling monologues. Reeva and one of these friends, Alain, fell in love. Alain always had his eyes on Reeva's body. Reeva stroked his cheek and tried to get him to smile. At first Bruce joined the group, but when he saw Alain and Reeva draped over each other's chairs, he retreated to the bookstores.

"I'm a waiting man," Bruce told me. "I'm waiting for Reeva to realize I'm alive. I'm waiting for Sasha to stage one of my plays. I'm waiting to find out what I want to be when I grow up. I'm so good at waiting, people hire me to wait at bus stops for them."

Alain and Reeva argued a great deal in French. Their fights started out jokingly, but then she'd slap him, throw water or wine in his face, and storm out, leaving him sitting. Christoph's "gang" liked to move from café to café, and Reeva walked out of six or seven of them. Most mornings, however, I'd see Reeva and Christoph walking hand in hand, nuzzling, laughing, punching each other, and purchasing bouquets of tulips off the vendors by the Seine.

Robin was staying with a group of dancers she'd known from her many visits to France. She said they were "dear friends." They dressed in clogs, leg warmers, capes, and exotic velvet hats. They rented a beat-up carriage house with a gate and a garden. They all slept together in a loft bed that was as long as one wall of the house. Robin slumped at a wood table in the garden, drinking wine from the bottle. She sang strange improvised songs while her friends leaped, lurched, twisted, fell to the ground, and wound their muscular legs around each other. Then they'd roll from corner to corner in a "glom," separate in slow motion, and start doing push-ups. As beautiful-looking as Robin's friends were, I didn't enjoy watching them dance. Even when Robin told me they were preparing for a world tour, I wasn't very impressed. It seemed like fake dancing. Robin explained to me that their dance was all about exploring shapes and tactile improvisation.

"The body is one shape by itself—another shape when it attaches onto another body. It's like cells or the notes in harmony. . . ." she told me.

Robin's speech was almost always slurred and her face was puffy and eyes circled with dark half-moons from too much wine. I became her confidante. She began to question her career, her too tall, muscular body, and her love for Sasha. She told me she had sleeping pills that the dancers had given her. She told me she wanted to go to "some other place in the cosmos." Day after day she sat at that table while the dancers made shapes at her feet, drinking, singing, reading the *I Ching*, or throwing tarot cards. I decided to summon Charles. Something was happening to Robin that I didn't understand. When Charles saw her, he checked her into an expensive hotel on the Left Bank. Her suite had velvet walls and a king-size bed. He brought me along.

"Every time you meet up with these kids, you fall apart," Charles reminded her. "It's the booze, the pills, and the sexual square dance."

Robin looked nervously at me.

"You went to Catholic school," Charles said. "You almost joined a convent. You can't possibly sleep with eleven different boys and girls every night. You love Sasha, fool that you are. True, he's completely abandoned you for meat hooks and grinders, but a package deal won't fix it."

Robin gave him a melancholy smile. She embraced Charles and then lay down on the king-size bed. Charles emptied out her bag and took the pills. Robin stayed at the hotel for the entire Paris engagement. Charles told the dancers she was writing a symphony and needed to be celibate and sober.

———

Charles was unusually calm in Paris. He spent most of the hiatus in our crooked room. He sketched costumes and strung tiny clay beads on threads. He designed necklaces and earrings for the whole company. He was absorbed in a book about the Aborigines in New Guinea and masks they made from mud. The only time he went out was to take me sightseeing. We took the elevator to the top of the Eiffel Tower and traipsed through the Louvre. He sang to me inside the stained-glass walls of Chartres and danced me through the bushy-headed trees of the Tuileries. We bought cold quiche from *pâtisseries* and ate it on our beds. He bought me a designer baseball shirt at Le Drugstore and we shared a hamburger, fried chicken, and french fries at Joe Allen's. The restaurant was located on a dark, busy harbor. We strolled across wobbly decks, taking in the fishing boats, sailboats, and small yachts. "My ship has sails that are made of silk," Charles sang. He was very peaceful, focused, and generous. Paris seemed to be a second home to him. He was fluent in French, understood the Metro, and talked cheerfully to cabdrivers and shopkeepers. He avoided conversations with hip-looking artists or writers in cafés. We walked along the Seine and he leafed through antique book illustrations, wrapped in tissues, displayed by vendors alongside the postcards and posters of famous paintings. Charles seemed determined to be a tourist. He made no effort to locate old friends. He was the only one in the group who wasn't involved with some gang of intense bohemians. One day when we were sitting in a hidden garden behind an old stone museum, I asked Charles why he wasn't visiting friends. He closed his eyes for a moment and then sighed.

"I lived here so many times, little one. I had a real life here. The people I knew have changed or left. So the friends I've decided to visit are places. Motherhood has settled me down. I'm getting old."

"Where's Sasha staying?" I asked. "Why don't we see him?"

"How to explain this, Pussycat?" he mused. "Sasha is staying in the very richest section of Paris in an elegant apartment. He is being taken care of by two old friends who drive him everywhere, throw dinner parties for him, and introduce him to opera stars, ballet dancers, and men and women who have dollar signs instead of middle initials. Our friends fix him brunch, do his laundry, and listen to his plans for the future. They have two championship brown poodles named Pablo and Vincent."

"What are the friends' names?" I asked.

"Lena and Monique," Charles answered. "They're women."

"Will Sasha get crazy like Robin?"

"Oh, no, this is very different," Charles said.

"Why can't we visit?" I asked. "They're your friends too."

"Sasha wants them for himself," Charles replied. "He wants everything for himself right now."

"Do you like these women?" I asked.

"Very much. I admired them tremendously before they became Sasha's full-time cheerleaders . . . they were brilliant and hilarious. Very daring—for rich people. But now . . ." Charles shrugged.

"Why does Sasha have to have so many slaves?" I asked.

Charles shook his curls and pursed his lips. He blew air out, making a trumpet sound.

"It's his way of making sure people like him. I guess if people leave flowers at his door and wash his feet and hang upside down from meat hooks, he can be pretty sure they won't leave him."

"They could say good-bye anyway," I said.

Charles tilted his head downward and his spectacles slipped to the edge of his nose. He squinted at me and bounced up and down on the old park bench.

"Is that so? May I quote you, Miss Rikki Nelson?" Charles must've said something to Sasha, because within days he announced he wanted to have an outing with his "family."

Charles, Sasha, Robin, and I traveled a long distance on the Metro to a suburb outside Paris. We ended up at the biggest flea market I'd ever seen. There were rows and rows of booths with green awnings. One section stank of raw meats. Another large section gave off the tart smell of vegetables and herbs. Another stank of fish. We hurried past the food and ended up in a forest of blue jeans and army jackets and plaid shirts. Sasha stopped for a moment to admire a pair of faded overalls. Charles put his arm around Sasha's neck and playfully pushed him along.

"I want to be a farmer," Sasha complained.

Charles led us to a corner of the market where several booths displayed a wide variety of antique clothes in brushed denim, silks, velvets, and patterned and quilted cotton. The sellers were mostly country women who sat behind the tables bent over tiny electric heaters or little stoves. They barely looked at us. There were a few American hippies who greeted us with nods and meaningless laughter. Robin dug through the clothes hungrily, holding up velvet dresses and capes, long flowered skirts, shawls, and peasant blouses. Sasha made faces of horror at several of the selections and she shrugged and put them back. Charles, meanwhile, was measuring a pair of black Persian pants with a low crotch and thin legs against Sasha.

"I look like I'm going riding with the Shah," Sasha said.

"You *look*," Charles said, "like a beautiful poet."

"I don't want to be exotic," Sasha insisted. "Now is not the time."

Charles groaned, kept the pants for himself, and helped Sasha pick out a simple outfit. Sasha enjoyed modeling a pair of faded tight-fitting blue jeans for his brother, who searched out a collarless white shirt and an embroidered silk vest.

"I don't look like a Flamenco dancer?" Sasha asked.

Charles growled through his teeth. "I hate shopping with you," he said. "It's like taking your grandmother to the cosmetics counter at Bonwit's. Will I get a rash? Do I look cheap?"

Sasha laughed and patted Charles on the back. "But I *only* trust you," he said. "You have the eye. You must help me to look right."

Robin was at a booth counting her francs with unusual difficulty. She had a tall pile of clothes that a country woman was folding piece by piece, while eyeing Robin's money hungrily.

"Watch," Charles whispered to me.

Suddenly Robin thrust her money in her pocket, threw her hands up in the air, and started to walk away.

"No, no, no," she said loudly. "It's too much. What, am I crazy? To spend a week's salary? I could get this stuff for half the money in the States."

The seller's face fell. Then her eyes narrowed. She signaled Robin with her hand. "Lady, lady!"

Robin reluctantly returned to the booth. The seller held up one of the shawls and quoted a price. Robin stared at the shawl a long time, unable to decide. The woman yanked a velvet jacket from the pile and put it with the shawl. She offered a price for the two of them. Robin pulled a flowered skirt from the pile and added it on. The woman started yelling. Robin yelled back.

After several minutes of fighting, Robin walked away again. "I don't know why you people try to cheat innocent tourists," Robin shouted in broken French. "It's a crime."

Robin strutted toward us. Her face was red and she was breathing hard. "I don't need new clothes anyway."

Sasha shook his head. Charles led us forward. Robin stopped every now and then to compare similar clothes in other booths. Suddenly a little boy, younger than me, tugged at Robin's large embroidered bag that hung from her shoulder.

"Lady," he said, "my mother wants to talk to you."

Robin promenaded like a queen down the central aisle of the market.

"She's a master. She practically caused a riot in Damascus," Charles said under his breath. We watched from a distance as Robin and the seller bickered over each item. The woman started crying noisily. Robin cried too. Finally they reached a settlement. Both became instantly cheerful, admiring the clothes as the seller and other women folded each item in old newspapers and tissue paper. Robin laid out the cash.

"You'd think she was a Jew," Sasha said with a sigh.

"I beg your pardon?" Charles coughed.

"It's just a metaphor," Sasha said.

"So is 'You stink like a nigger,' " Charles replied. "And besides, I seem to remember going to your bar mitzvah, before you converted. Did you formally convert? I can't remember."

"Let's not have a scene from the civil rights movement." Sasha smiled. "I never discriminate, not in theater nor in bed. Besides, I want to buy Rikki Nelson a present."

Robin joined us, holding the package up in triumph.

Sasha's smile turned to a scowl. "I don't know why you torment those merchants," he said righteously. "They are poor country people."

"Bargaining is a sport," Robin said guiltily. "Everyone does it."

"Why don't you just pay them what they ask?" Sasha went on peevishly. "You can afford it."

"She was charging me at least double what any other customer would pay," Robin said defensively.

"But you are *double* any other woman," Sasha said, and pinched Robin's bottom under her flowing skirt and long blouse.

Charles took my hand lightly in his and swung it back and forth. "Isn't love wonderful?" he said.

I noticed that many of the sellers and buyers in the French marketplace were stealing glimpses at Sasha and Charles. The two brothers were blond and tall as basketball players and they strode around like dancers. At one point Sasha leaned down and lifted me into his arms.

"You can have anything you want in this market," he said. Robin's jealous smile was a grimace.

"I'd like a watch," I said.

"A watch!" Sasha exclaimed.

"A watch!" Charles repeated.

We dashed toward the booths with broken and new, stolen and secondhand jewelry. The sellers were mostly Mideastern men who jabbered in rapid Arabic, whistled, grunted, and chuckled while I checked out their displays. The choice seemed overwhelming. I didn't want to pick anything too expensive, and I wanted to find a watch that pleased both Charles and Sasha. I saw a delicate silver watch with a soft silver band. Each side of the band had a small heart made of tiny rubies. I didn't know if it was cheap or expensive. It just seemed very feminine to me. And it glittered.

"I don't think there's really anything," I said.

Sasha looked crestfallen. "Are you sure?" he said.

I could see the silver and rubies from the side as I nodded at Sasha. Robin shifted her weight, yawned, and leaned against the jewelry table.

"I don't think I want a watch," I said.

"I have to pee," Robin interrupted. "Before we take that epic Metro ride back."

"We all should," said Charles.

"Are you sure?" Sasha repeated to me. He still seemed very disappointed. I didn't want to take anything from him. I didn't want debts or to owe him favors.

"Not today," I said. "On days like today I don't need presents."

Sasha's face lit up. He bent down and kissed both my cheeks.

"Saved by a cliché," sang Charles.

Robin rushed me toward a dirty café across the square from the market.

"Sorry, Pussycat," she huffed, "but my teeth are floating."

The café was dark and a few workers sat at the bar. They commented among themselves when Robin and I entered. Robin disappeared behind a door which said wc. I felt unaccountably homesick. I wished I were in the warehouse by the river. I wanted to watch a tugboat hauling a freighter on the dirty water and to stare at the ugly New Jersey lights.

"You better go," Robin said, "but hold your nose."

I gagged when I got inside the WC. There was no toilet, just some holes in the floor. I had to squat over the holes and stretch my underpants out so as not to miss. The WC stank of wine and the holes were partially clogged with feces. The toilet paper was as coarse as a paper towel.

"You look a little green," Robin said to me when I returned. "Are you okay?"

"That place stank," I said.

"I'll never understand why folks can't just clean up their loos," she said with a sigh, "or why I can't clean up my life." We were rushing toward the subway stop where we were to meet Sasha and Charles.

"That's not an equation," I told Robin.

"Oh, yes, it is," she replied sadly.

"By the way," she said, and yanked me into a doorway as if she were going to kiss me. She reached down into her bag and pulled out the silver watch with the rubies.

"I lifted it." She grinned. "I saw your eyes."

I embraced her with phony enthusiasm and she laughed and squeezed me. I could never wear it. The rubies and silver sparkled in my hand and I experienced the lonely drifting that had overcome me before. I feared I'd be left alone in the market and be taken home by a poor, strict Catholic family. I'd be forced to eat calves' brains and use putrid bathrooms for the rest of my life.

We all dozed on the long Metro ride home and I awoke stiff, hungry, and glad to be far away from that foreign village where no one lived but only hovered, stared, and sold.

That night a chocolate-brown Mercedes pulled up in front of the Hotel Welcome. Charles dressed me in a royal-blue velvet shirt that came to my knees, a black satin vest, tights, and brand-new blue alligator cowboy boots. He told me he knew where I was going and he wanted heads to turn when I entered the room. He reminded me that I was almost twelve and French girls my age were already publishing their memoirs about affairs with racing car drivers. When I asked him why he wasn't coming, he sighed and said once again that he was too old.

The Mercedes was driven by a woman in a fur coat who looked like a middle-aged version of a sullen fashion model. She had large eyes with heavy lids, a small nose, and full pouting lips. Her hair was dark and long and draped over one eye. She'd flick it back with a dramatic move of her head. She was introduced to me as Lena. The woman in the passenger seat was tiny and thin, but moved in bursts of giddiness and high energy. Her hair was silver gray and her blue eyes were huge, pale, and watery. She had a straight nose, thin lips, and very crooked teeth, but she was nonetheless extremely attractive and warm. She wore an oversized man's wool coat. She was Monique. Sasha was squeezed in between the two of them and Monique made jokes in French about punishing him with the gear shift.

I was surprised to see Reeva, Alain, Bruce, Juno, Mustafa, and Christoph crowded into the back. Robin wasn't with them. Bruce

155

patted his knees and I climbed in. The Mercedes floated soundlessly through Paris. The city seemed holier at night. The monuments glowed and looked serene, silent, and warm. I began to think that the bossy, nervous French people moved too fast and spoiled their own city. We arrived at a district in Paris called Pigalle that was rough and colorful. It could've been a set for a cheap movie on gangsters and casinos. The neighborhood seemed painted and flat as a cardboard. The neons blinked on and off like a discount version of Times Square.

Sasha turned around and squeezed my knee. "A night on the town," he said.

Lena said something in French about corrupting me. Her voice was low and gravelly.

Bruce said, "Oy, I wish."

Sasha laughed and turned to Monique. "She has a wisdom that comes from being mute for so long," he said. Monique turned around and winked at me.

Reeva leaned into my face and lifted one eyebrow. "Do yoooo hahve JuJu?" she growled. She smelled of sweet brandy. Alain sulked and looked out the window.

We got out at Le Club. Bruce whispered that it was one of the classiest spots in Pigalle. Elegant waiters in white tuxedos led us to our table, which was in the center of the floor. The tables rose in tiers overlooking a large stage with a round dance floor.

When we were seated, Monique patted my shoulder and said, "This used to be an ice-skating rink, you know. Many famous acts played here. There was a famous couple, oh fuck, their names I don't remember, but they had this specialty, a spin? It was quite truly miraculous. You remember, Lena?"

"Of course I remember." Lena laughed. "Who forgets such things?"

"Well, it was amazing to watch. The man, he holds the woman by her arms and she puts her legs out straight and they spin and spin some more. They are like a top."

"I remember this," Sasha said. "You can have a glass of wine tonight if you want, Rikki Nelson."

"This is a story *tres* unique," Monique said. "So listen, darling—
one night. The whole audience is full, like this tonight, as a wedding
cake crowded with people, no? And the skaters are doing their act
and they spin and they spin faster and faster and he's holding her
arms and her legs are out and zzeeee who knows why—"

"Who knows anything?" Lena shrugged.

"He loses his grip." Monique takes in a gasp of air. "*N'est-ce
pas?* Understand? He *lets go of* the woman and she goes zee zee
right through the audience, like, what is it? The Revenge of the
Electric Saw."

"*The Texas Chainsaw Massacre*," said Bruce.

"Yes *exactly*," said Monique.

Lena whispered something gently in Monique's ear. Monique
nodded and bit her lip with her crooked upper teeth.

"Do I scare you darling? Is this *too* unpleasant?"

"No, I like it," I said. Sasha grinned. Monique slapped me five.

"Well, *okay*," she said. "So I wasn't here, but I read about it."

"We all did." Lena sighed. "For weeks and weeks."

Monique took in another breath and leaned over the table toward
me. "Do you know that one man was actually capitulated?"

Lena put her hand on Monique and let out a chesty dark laugh.
"Decapitated," she corrected. "The man, his head—" She put her
finger to her throat and made a quick slice from left to right.

"Yes," said Monique, "and some woman lost her hand and someone else half his scalp *zoom* like in an Indian war. I don't remember
now, but I think maybe *six* or *seven* people had to go to hospital."
Monique had pretty much related what she had to say. She stared
at me with the wide eyes of a storyteller who'd finished a grizzly
ghost story.

"What happened to the woman?" I asked.

Monique blinked and slapped her head. "The *skater*, but of
course—you see the wall behind us? Up up up all the way in the
back where the projector is?"

I turned around.

"Yes," I said.

"Poom, right through the wall. Like a jigsaw."

"*Power* saw," Bruce said with a laugh.

"*No.* Chainsaw," Monique corrected. "No . . ."

"Power drill?" Bruce tried.

"That's it! That's it! Zzzzz! A power drill. They had to take the whole wall out with her stuck right in it."

"Is this *true?*" I asked Monique.

"I swear to Christ. I swear to God. How could I invent such a thing?"

Sasha was laughing hard. He had wiped his eyes with his napkin. "It's true. It's true," he said. "It's legend."

"Then why are you laughing?" I accused him.

Monique blushed. She sat up straight and smiled. "He thinks I'm hilarious," she said.

"Oh, I've got to pee," Sasha said. He jumped up from the table and walked across the dance floor. I saw several customers look up and point him out. He was recognized. Our show had been in the Paris papers every day for weeks.

As soon as he was out of sight Lena turned to me. "So, how is the *other* 'Papa'—Charles?" she asked casually.

"He's reading," I answered cautiously. She blinked like a cat, then touched Monique's hand. Monique leaned in with interest.

"Charles is reading," Lena repeated.

Monique made an angry sound and shook her head. "These competitions," she said. "The both of them. Jealous. Jealous. Just like their mother. And their *aunt.* Insane. Absolutely insane. American psychology. It champions such behavior. Poo!"

Lena shushed her. Sasha was on his way back to the table.

"Everyone is looking at me," he said with delight. "And I have done *nothing.* Paris is desperate." Monique and Lena exchanged a glance. Wine was disappearing from bottles so fast I didn't even see it poured into glasses. Bleary-eyed, Sasha insisted on switching to vodka. Bruce was feeding me sips from his glass.

"The trick is always to stay more sober than everyone else," Bruce said drunkenly. "But I can't remember why."

Alain and Reeva were entangled, kissing and rubbing each other. They liked to make out in public. Charles once told me that the more people liked to carry on for strangers, the less they did at home.

The house went dark and chaotic; spotlights crossed and circled the tiny stage area at the edge of the dance floor. A crackly loudspeaker announced something in French I couldn't understand and then disco music blared from tinny loudspeakers. Monique held her ears. Reeva started dancing in her seat. The small, shiny curtain opened and a group of women in sequined hot pants, white leather boots, and glittery halter tops did a Motown slide and die out onto the stage. The audience cheered. The music became a French version of the Temptations' "Ain't Too Proud to Beg" and the women lip-synched to the voices on the tape. Each woman was heavily made up, wore thick false eyelashes and lipstick. There were about twelve of them onstage. Some were quite beautiful. Some were old and fat. There was one who was clearly odd. She danced only in profile with her short Judy Garland haircut, a hooked nose, and a long neck. She flapped her long, gawky arms and wore a melancholic, birdlike expression despite the strong, lively beat of the Motown sound.

Monique glanced over at me nervously and winked. Lena kept rhythm with her manicured fingernails on the table. Sasha quickly became restless and stared down at the table as he consumed his vodka.

It took until the second solo—a heartfelt, lip-synched version of "My Funny Valentine"—for me to realize that the women were men.

"This is a drag show," I informed Bruce. He nodded.

"Very high class. Comes from a long tradition. It's considered a serious entertainment. Most of these women—men—have been at it for years. Their characters are famous."

One of the heavier performers was lip-synching what Bruce said were Sophie Tucker jokes in French to buzzing background music. The audience applauded and laughed. I stole a glance over at Monique and Lena and suddenly I couldn't figure out whether they were men or women. Sasha, with his long, golden hair and delicate hands, confused me too.

The gawky, hook-nosed woman strode out to a tall stool, sat

down, put one long bony hand on her rather flat chest, and began to sing to a tape of Edith Piaf. The audience went wild. I felt sad and very drawn to the dark figure under the small spotlight. Her hands went into fists, she closed her eyes, she stood with her feet apart, and it seemed like she wanted to tear herself right down the middle for the crowd. When she was done, about half the customers stood up and screamed. The heavy disco music crackled on and the rest of the women entered in cheap toddler outfits—spangled diapers, tiny satin tutus, black leather bonnets. They carried bottles as phalluses. They did a porno vaudeville interpretation to "Yes Sir, That's My Baby." They finished, bowed as a group, got different audience members to "feed" each one her bottle. Then they pranced off. The French voice announced the time of the next show. The restaurant began to empty out.

Lena shrugged. "It is more for the tourists now—certainly than it was ten years ago."

"Probably the tourists have changed," Bruce said. "They want broader strokes—immediate glitz."

"Exactly," said Monique.

"I really enjoyed it," Juno said shyly.

Sasha was staring morosely at the empty stage.

"You hated it, Sasha?" Lena asked.

Sasha smiled sadly. "No," he said. "I rather like it decadent and cheap. No pretense of art."

Everyone nodded in agreement.

"And, of course," Sasha went on, "I was thinking of Charles."

Lena and Monique looked uncomfortable.

"Yeah. He's s'posed to be *the* master of drag in the States," Reeva said to Alain. "But he won't do it now. I wish I could've caught his shows."

"His early shows," Bruce said, "are *legend.*"

"But that's not what I'm thinking about," Sasha said apologetically.

The table went silent.

"The first time . . . you probably don't know this . . . was here." Sasha sighed.

Lena nodded. "When he was a junior in high school, Charles decided to forsake sunny California and become an American Field Service student."

"Charles?" Bruce laughed.

"Yeah, well, we were quite middle class, you know." Sasha smiled. "And Charles took a year in Paris. He loved the French fashion designs and the art and the drama . . . he *wanted* to be French."

"That's when I met him," Lena said. "He was living with the family of one of my girlfriends."

Girlfriends. I examined Lena hazily. So Lena was a girl. Unless she meant the type of girls she took to the movies if she was a boy.

"I was furious, of course, that he'd dare to do something without me." Sasha grinned.

"But you know he'd begun acting strangely that year"—Sasha's voice became mysterious—"withdrawn and secretive—so really I was rather hoping he'd pull himself together."

"What was the matter?" Bruce asked.

"A restlessness." Sasha sighed. "I didn't understand or tolerate it well. Of course, I had no idea about its *source*."

Sasha's drunkenness was making him lose track of his own story. He stared off and I thought he was finished. No one else at the table knew what to do either. After a long pause, Sasha continued.

"At first we got letters full of good tourist observations and bright comparisons between American and French high schools," Sasha said.

"He was so popular," Lena offered. "Like a god."

"But then the letters stopped and his family reported he rarely slept at home. He'd stopped attending school. For some misguided reason, my parents decided I should be the one to bring Charles home.

"It was like a mystery book. Every place I showed up—he'd just left. I wrote him notes and postcards with the name of my hotel on it—but he never got them, or refused to acknowledge them."

"You were staying at a *hotel?*" Bruce said incredulously. "But you were like fourteen years old."

161

"Thirteen." Sasha nodded. "But deprived of the usual immaturity. Always the little soldier."

"Wow," Bruce said.

I was suspicious of Sasha's story.

"Anyway, thanks to Charles, my search led me to the Paris Opera, the ballet, the Sorbonne, the back alleys of the Left Bank, where I met craftsmen, poets . . . Charles had been adopted by the elite of Paris culture. He was . . . a wunderkind—a divine mascot. But no one would reveal where he was and what he was doing. He wanted to stay in Paris and be left alone. I was hurt, really—I couldn't believe he would abandon me. We were like *twins*."

"It wasn't you," Lena said. "It had nothing to do with you."

"Finally," Sasha said, "this rather remarkable woman took pity on me."

"Madame Alice Cardon." Lena smiled.

"She must've weighed three hundred pounds and talked in a voice like her vocal chords had been sliced by a razor."

"Cigarettes and the booze," Lena agreed.

"She held weekly salons in the style of Gertrude Stein and knew all the people who were protecting Charles. He'd showed up at her salon once or twice in the company of a man who was writing a biography of Robert Graves. She told me she didn't approve of family members interfering with each others' lives and that I should go home and play soccer or surf or whatever little boys did."

Reeva let out a laugh and then covered her mouth.

"Yes, it's true," Sasha said. "But I refused to listen to Madame Cardon and argued quite bitterly with her. No one meant more to me than my older brother and I wasn't about to let him leave my life without an explanation. After a while she began to respect me and promised she'd help me find Charles—but the rest would be between him and me."

"Madame Cardon died last year at—what—ninety?" Monique said. "To the end, Charles and Sasha were her 'twins.' "

"I didn't attend her funeral," Sasha said morosely. "How was it?"

"Not as dramatic as you'd think," Lena said sadly. "Not bad—

162

as these things go—a few old poets reciting—a string quartet—but most of her protégés are dead or out of the country."

I wanted to scream with boredom. I reached for Bruce's wineglass. He put his hand over the top and I hit it. He pulled his hand away to see if I'd broken skin.

"Amazon," he whispered.

"Should I finish this?" Sasha suddenly asked. "I don't know why I began."

"Absolutely," said Bruce. "You never talk about yourself."

Lena and Monique exchanged a sardonic look.

"Well—Madame Cardon had a car pick me up at her hotel and the car brought me here. The place was more chic, in a way. It was not about tourists but catered to the intelligentsia and the poor painters and artists, who ran up obscene tabs. Rich patrons took care of all the debts. It gave them a sense of the exotic.

"Anyway, I was led to where Madame Cardon was holding court at a table in the back. The maître d' brought me a ginger ale with a cherry. When the lights went down, I saw a show not so different from tonight except there was a guest soloist. This absolutely stunning teenage girl stepped into the spotlight. She was dressed modestly in a white blouse and pleated skirt. She began to sing a cappella without lip-synching. She sang "Little Lamb"—you know that song from *Gypsy*? Just a simple, sentimental child's ballad to a lamb. The voice was pure and heartbreaking. The girl was riveting and the place went wild. I mean, weeping and screaming." Sasha began to croon,

> *Little lamb,*
> *Little lamb,*
> *I wonder how old I am.*

"Such innocence." Sasha sighed. "Such natural, pure beauty and talent. I screamed myself hoarse. My hands tingled from pounding the table. This young girl was very shy and she was visibly shaken by the audience response. She blushed and ran off the stage. I know this is hard to believe, but I didn't 'get' the whole evening. I didn't understand why Madame Cardon had brought me there. But I desperately wanted to meet this girl—because—well, I'd sort of fallen in love with her, and besides—my young theatrical self was too stung by her talent to let her go.

"Madame Cardon arranged for me to go backstage. I was led to the dressing room and I pulled back the curtain (they didn't have doors then). I saw the girl—she was just as lovely close up as she'd been under the lights. She was sitting on the lap of a man in his thirties. He looked like he was costumed to be a sailor in a musical revue—but I guess those were his clothes. A vest but no shirt. Chains, bracelets, tattoos. Tight leather pants, heavy boots. He was rough and handsome. He was kissing the girl rather violently. I imagined myself as that man. Only . . . I wouldn't have violated her beauty with a kiss. I longed for her, but I wouldn't have touched her, even with a fingertip. She opened her eyes for a moment and jumped from the man's lap. It was then I saw it was Charles."

The table was silent.

"What did you do?" Bruce asked.

Sasha smiled and gestured helplessly. "Nothing," he said. "I turned around, took a cab to my hotel, and left for California the next day. I told my parents Charles was taking acting and singing classes and was sorry he had scared them. He followed me home three days later, and we never said a word about it."

"Never?" Reeva asked.

"No, not even now. But the odd thing was that for years I remained madly in love with that girl—the girl I saw onstage. It was terribly confusing."

I squinted through Lena's smoke and the low lights at Sasha's unfocused expression. He was never careless. I wondered why he chose to tell his story now.

Sasha caught me looking at him and turned his attention quickly to Reeva and to Bruce.

"Of course—you—*know* if he'd just *told* me about the—problem—the gay thing—or whatever. I wouldn't have thought less of him. We all have mortal weaknesses, perversions, shortcomings."

"Why's it a shortcoming?" Bruce asked. "Why isn't it just what it is?"

Lena was looking down at the tablecloth now, slowly moving her head from side to side.

"This is an old argument." she sighed.

"No, no argument," said Sasha. "Just an opinion. *I'm* of the opinion that the more elevated form of sex is between man and woman. I see the other as an indulgence, like my vodka, or someone else's morphine. As a way of life, I believe it interferes with growth—it stunts spiritual awakening. Why? Because you are fucking yourself—so it's no different than masturbation."

Alain awoke from his stupor.

"Men fuck women—that's our destiny and our curse."

"Stop," Lena commanded. And Sasha and Alain immediately obeyed. It was clear Sasha had provoked her as much as he dared.

"There's much mythic and theological evidence to prove to the contrary," Monique said. "In fact, all that matters, ultimately, Sasha, is who you love."

"Homosexuality is not about love," Sasha said. His eyes were half closed from the vodka. "It's watch me while I watch myself loving myself. Love is the tension between two opposite creations of nature."

"*Merde,*" Lena hissed, and threw a thick wad of francs on the table. "You are a brilliant idiot, Sasha. An inspired fascist."

"Do you want to sleep at the house of your lesbian friends?" Monique asked. "Or shall we find you a fraternity house?"

Sasha grinned at Monique and Lena. He was completely unruffled. "You ladies deserve to be lesbians," he said. "There's no man on earth good enough for you."

"Except you." Lena sighed.

"Yes *me,*" Sasha said with a laugh, "but the two of you would kill me."

"Yes," Monique said, and she poked him in his ribs with her index finger. "We just might."

The conversation had genuinely gone above my head. I preferred to close my eyes and think of the dark sad birdwoman and a beautiful blond little girl singing "Little Lamb" in harmony. If Sasha was trying to diminish Charles in my eyes, it didn't work. It was a little hard to imagine him kissing a sailor, but it didn't matter. Sex was no more than an overactive sport to me, rather ugly, useless, and, ultimately, ridiculous to watch. Alain and Reeva started swallowing each other's tongues again, and they looked like they were cleaning each other's teeth. My decision was not to think any further about sex and to never be in a position where I'd be forced to do it again. I gave Sasha what I thought was a very superior, adult smirk, but he turned from me, stared at the stage, and lifted the back of his hand to each eye where either there were tears or he hoped there would be tears.

"With this kind of expectation," Christoph said, "it doesn't matter if we perform like shit." He was leading a pack of us along the boulevard so we could see the lines of people spiraling along the sidewalk waiting for tickets. Christoph seemed to wrinkle more each day. His growth of beard never got too long, but shadowed his face. His hair didn't cover his ears, but his cowlick stood straight up and he hunched over as if in constant pain. The press and word of mouth, Christoph said, had immortalized Sasha and deified Charles and turned the whole group into holy beings. Christoph was being offered six or seven leading roles in movies and TV. But more important, he'd been named the assistant minister of culture.

"*Careeris resurrectus est,*" Charles said.

One unfortunate outcome of our success was that Alain and Reeva were battling more frequently and with greater violence. He was slapping and punching her in public and he called her a capitalist superstar and a superficial bitch. She scratched at him with her new French manicure and called him "a lazy, jealous fuck." One night, at an outdoor café, Alain threw a glass at her so hard that her chair tipped over. Reeva cried out and Mustafa and Bruce jumped on Alain. They punched him and kicked his ribs.

"Animal!" Mustafa shouted.

"Abusive pig!" Bruce cursed.

Reeva drew herself up off the cement. She was weeping.

"Stop!" she screamed. Her voice was shrill. "Stop, damn it. I'm pregnant. I'm *pregnant!* Stop killing him!"

Everyone froze and looked at Reeva. Alain appeared to be the most surprised of all. He lifted his head. His mouth hung open. His lips were swollen and red. Blood trickled from his nose. One eye was swollen shut. Reeva turned to him and smiled apologetically. She shrugged. Alain lay back down on the ground with Bruce and Mustafa standing over him. Then he dragged himself to a kneeling position and finally stood up straight. He looked at Reeva the whole time. When he'd regained his balance, he lifted her up in his arms and carried her away from us down the street, making drunken circles and laughing.

"This is unreal," Bruce said. "From start to finish, none of this shit happened. I'm in Westchester studying law at night school. During the day I work in my father's goddamn retail furniture warehouse. None of this has fucking happened."

Christoph took us to an old wooden bar hidden off an alley between two shops on a cobblestone street near the Sorbonne. The floors were covered with sawdust and the booths were large and smelled dirty vinyl and sour beer. The bartenders and clientele talked loudly so they could hear each other over the soccer game on the radio. The workers and students cheered loudly when Christoph entered the room. He ducked, lit a cigarette, and smiled. He'd already been slightly famous in France playing an alcoholic police detective on a TV series. Now, as assistant minister of culture, he was promising to champion the problems of the common man in the arts. His appointment led to a rash of interviews where he credited his work with Sasha as opening up his psyche with a vision of the "uplifting of all mankind through art." I found this odd, since he only had one small scene in *The Myth Man*. He played Orpheus digging through the rubble of a cave constructed from planks and stones and dirt. He had no lines—he just dug for his love with his bare hands. He would scream at Sasha in French, demanding long, intense explanations of his part, wanting Sasha to give him deeper and deeper motivation. He got splinters and scrapes all over his body as he wildly dug and thrashed in the hole of the cave. He raged that he was being abused. Charles said the need for motivation usually meant an actor wanted a bigger part. I never heard Sasha promise Christoph anything. He laughed at him and hugged him. He criticized Christoph's acting and told him he looked like he was doing a blue jeans commercial or a perfume ad. "So romantic, Christoph. Existential, full of psychological angst."

Christoph's style of acting never changed or fit in with the rest of the company, but he and Sasha often went drinking together. They discussed French cinema and revolution. Sasha seemed both sad and relieved when Christoph decided to quit the company. There were no threats or condemnations. Sasha said he was proud of Christoph and was delighted he'd found a vocation better suited to his "Charles Aznavour temperament."

"Christoph's going to help him fund the next project," Charles had said, "and he's going to count on Christoph to buy him a bigger theater than Jacob Avon. Just wait."

Charles, Reeva, Robin, Mustafa, Juno, and I sat in an oversized booth at the messy workingman's bar. I watched Christoph make the rounds of beat-up tables, filled with students, laborers, enlightened truck drivers, professors, merchants, artists, and radicals shaking hands, hugging and kissing old friends and people he didn't know but treated like "comrades." When he joined us at the booth his brown eyes shone with satisfaction and booze. He slipped in next to me and messed my hair affectionately.

"This is really a time historic," he said. His French accent was more pronounced now that he was assistant minister. "I think I will commission the Ballet de Paris to do a piece about plumbers, electricians, and bricklayers. What do you think, Charles? The corps shall get a grant and perform it in construction sights all over the country."

"Absolutely," Charles said with phony intensity, "and then you should do 'cleaning ladies, busboys, dishwashers and sewage'—think of the possibilities."

"Think of it." Christoph nodded.

His thin wife with the auburn hair swung into the bar. She had a toddler on her hip. She kissed Christoph on the top of his head. He didn't look up. Suddenly his mood changed radically, or he looked as if he wanted her to notice that life was complicated for a man like him. He stared intently at his bottle as if he were alone and miserable. Christoph's wife didn't mind being ignored. She said something sarcastic in French and walked over to a boisterous table of rumpled-looking men in army jackets accompanied by ladies in black leotards, long tight skirts, and combat boots.

Reeva copied Christoph's switch into melodrama. She followed Christoph's wife with curious, tearful eyes, concentrating on the sleeping baby. Her hands rested on her belly. She smiled with a far away expression in her eyes. Alain had completely disappeared after her announcement and Reeva refused to talk about him or listen to his name. She took a sip of her orange juice.

"Maybe I should get an abortion," she said.

"Probably a good idea," Bruce said hopefully.

"But I don't think I can kill," Reeva said.

"I will miss you as individuals, yes—very much," Christoph said, not looking up. "As a theatrical little community, much less so. Our company was built for the purpose of demonstrating one man's vision. He is brilliant, charismatic—yes, even visionary—but a pharaoh nonetheless. This is not community. And our individuality is diminished when we work as a group. We are anonymous drones. Anonymity is essential for the liberation of an oppressed society—but it is dangerous when used to promote the ego of an autocrat."

"It's not *killing*," Bruce said to Reeva. "Think of how your life would change if you didn't do it."

"I don't think I can have a baby and perform," Reeva said. "I don't want to do anything but dance."

"Case closed," said Bruce.

"I could learn," Reeva said, her voice cracking slightly, "some kind of craft. I could teach."

"Get drunk and shut up," Charles said to Christoph. "We're here to celebrate your coronation. What I want to know is how many people have to be assassinated before you inherit the presidency of France."

Christoph grinned.

"Charles probably knows a good doctor," Bruce said.

"I'm sure Lena can help you," Charles said to Reeva.

"Lena's a dyke," Reeva snapped.

"A dyke with three grown kids," Charles said calmly. "And even dykes go to doctors."

I turned around and watched Christoph's wife. She was nursing the rather large toddler and talking sharply to a woman next to her in a dark cape and thick silver earrings.

"Babies are so free." Reeva sighed.

"Mothers are such slaves in France," Charles said. "Here's Lena's number if you want it."

Reeva started to cry. "Don't *push* me," she snapped. She wiped her eyes with the bottom of the tablecloth. "When will she be home?"

"After five," Charles said. "Let's toast Christoph." We all raised our glasses and tears came to Christoph's eyes. No one said anything. We just drank.

Meanwhile, Christoph's dry cool hand was on my bare thigh as it had been the whole night. He moved it up and down, squeezed my thigh, and worked his fingers under my tight denim skirt. He reached toward my underpants and the space between my legs. He pinched the inside of my thighs and tried to touch me with a couple of fingers, but he couldn't quite reach. Since this was a good-bye party, I didn't want to cause trouble. I squirmed and tried to push him off, but he wouldn't let go. I made a sudden move with my chair away from the table and Christoph nearly fell over. I tried to walk gracefully to the ladies' room. I pulled up my skirt and pulled down my panties and washed myself.

When I returned to our table, Christoph had moved to the table next to ours. He sat with an obese man in a T-shirt and a bow tie, greasy hair to the shoulders and spectacles. There was a woman in a Central American serape with long silver hair and enormous hooped earrings. There was also a nervous young man in a suit and thin tie. He had a thick book in an ancient language and didn't stop reading. Christoph stood up and clinked on a glass with a spoon. The bar became quiet.

"To my comrades in *The Myth Man*," Christoph shouted in English. "May they light up all of Europe with the genius of their hearts." The customers shouted and silverware banged against glasses.

"Yes," he went on, "I hope they will survive without me." There was laughter and derisive-sounding shouts all over the room. Robin, who was quite drunk, heaved her large body so she could stand on the bench of the booth.

"To the new assistant minister of cultural affairs," Robin called out. "May all his affairs be cultural!"

There was hooting and braying and Christoph bowed. He looked at me again and winked.

"I guess I'll get the abortion," Reeva said. "But I'm going to die of guilt afterwards."

"Why?" Robin asked. "Who needs another unhappy, fucked-up child on this earth?"

"You know what Sasha said when I told him? He said, 'Have the baby. *Please* have the baby.' He'd adopt it himself." I was stung. Robin's face turned red. She was drunk.

"That stupid *fuck,*" Robin screamed. "I've been begging to have his baby for years, and he said the world was too decadent and violent for any child of his. And he didn't want me to miss rehearsals or shows. He wanted me fully concentrated on the work. The lying fuck. He just hates my chromosomes."

"I haven't seen enough of Paris yet," Charles yelled, "and I'm bored. Bored!"

Before I knew it, Charles was leading about twenty scraggly patrons from the bar up and down the Eiffel Tower to the Tour Jordan, down the Champs-Elysées, through the revolving doors of Le Drug-store, and in and out of the trees of the Bois de Boulogne. Then he rushed us to the Tomb of Napoleon and we bowed. He led Gregorian chants in Notre Dame and sneaked us backstage at the Paris Opera to try on the heavy, elaborate costumes. Each of the twenty-odd followers had to give a short reading along the Seine, but only from French tabloids. Then Charles led army maneuvers at the Bastille; directed an absurd fashion show outside the square, ultramodern Pierre Cardin building; improvised poetry, extemporaneous monologues, and silent prayer at the graves of Rembrandt, Mozart, and others buried in a tiny cemetery; and finished off by maneuvering a takeover of several large round tables at a restaurant called La Coupole, where flaming baked Alaska was served to every participant. We'd gathered followers at each stop of Charles's tour. By the time we hit La Coupole, there must've been over forty excited, noisy people. We'd been hopping in and out of the Metro and taxis, running, flagging buses, hitching with tourists late into the evening. Charles's "entourage" (as he called them) was overtired and full of crazy energy.

The party ended as the mob deliriously cheered the baked Alaska desserts, which were made of fiery meringue and ice cream. They floated along on the waiter's trays toward the overcrowded tables. I was sitting on Charles's lap, half asleep.

"Look at the flotilla," he said to me. "There's chocolate ice cream under those flaming sails." Then he leaned over and whispered to me, "See how beautiful fire can be, little one? It's not always a weapon or the burning of wings."

I ate some baked Alaska. The meringue disappeared in my mouth as if I'd inhaled sweet breaths. The chocolate was thick and rich and had a raspberry aftertaste. It was cold in my mouth and hot in my throat. I ate only a little and fell asleep on Charles's chest.

I dreamed that I was on the stage of the Paris Opera. I had a wig of curls piled high on my head and a heavy Victorian hat covered with fake roses and little birds. My sleeves were a puffy silk gold material and my camisole was laced tight around my breasts. I was singing an aria in a language that I was making up as I went along.

I seemed to be faking the whole aria, since I knew nothing about opera. The audience was full of men and women in tuxedos and gowns, and Mozart stood directly in front of me conducting. Mozart was the boy in the bar who'd never stopped reading. In my dream he never looked up from his score, but simply moved his baton. This was odd because there wasn't any orchestra. I was singing totally alone and I knew that armed guards and fascist generals lined the back, the theater was completely occupied, the balconies were sealed off. I realized that my life depended on the skill of my singing. I looked down and saw that I was naked from the waist down. I had only two long blond hairs on my vagina and my thighs were skinny and the veins showed through the pale skin like purple webs.

Charles woke me up. He was smiling.

"You were singing in your sleep," he said, and squeezed me gently. Then he whispered in my ear. "You also had your hand between your legs. Are we entering a new phase here? I thought only boys did that."

I was mortified. "Did anybody see?" I asked.

Charles signaled with his eyes toward the tablecloth. He'd pulled the end of it over my lap.

"You may want to avoid napping in department stores and public parks until you pass through this phase," Charles said.

"I'm sorry," I said.

"Sorry?" Charles replied. "There are too many sorrys in this world. In India alone millions of women walk around in sorrys. Your brain is overcrowded with sorrys."

Charles saw that I was still ashamed.

"Listen," he whispered. "Think of how wonderful a plant must feel when it invites itself over for a quiet meal of pollen and flies, puts on some Bach, and really gets into photosynthesis. If we could make babies with ourselves, we wouldn't end up with problems like Reeva."

"You're stoned, Charles," I said.

"Actually, I'm not," he said. "I'm just a happy boy out for a date with my favorite sex maniac." I slugged him.

Suddenly there was clamor at the front door of the restaurant.

Bruce ran in, red-faced, out of breath, and made his way over to our tables. Sasha was right behind him, and it seemed like he was trying to smile, but his expression turned peevish and his hands went behind his back like a silent general. His eyes squinted. Most of the customers at La Coupole quieted down and were looking at Sasha. But it was Bruce who spoke.

"Does anyone care that it's four A.M. and we have two shows tomorrow?" he shouted. "Is anyone besides me going to take some responsibility? Fuck you. Fuck all of you. We also have a taping for French TV and Kosher and I are *not* going to do all the setting up." Bruce looked back and shrugged at Sasha, and Sasha nodded approvingly at Bruce. "This isn't a vacation, folks," Bruce went on reluctantly. "Have some respect for others, for the show—I mean really—I like fun too, but . . ."

As his words sank in, everyone in the company suddenly reacted at once, leaping up, pushing toward the door, tossing handfuls of money at the headwaiter. Charles stood me up, but stayed seated. "Damn," he said. "I had one last stop. There's a new enormous outdoor sculpture that's made from all these different metals. I thought we could do a tribute to Olatunji on it."

"Why not tomorrow?" Bruce asked. He was obviously trying to be more of a disciplinarian than he was used to.

"The moment passes," Charles said sadly. He stood slowly and joined the other actors as we moved with Bruce and Sasha toward the door.

I heard Christoph's voice shouting behind me. He remained behind at a table crowded with fans. "Ride, champions! Ride into the sunset! You carry the banner of greatness! Bring myth and beauty to your audience. I love you. When the revolution comes, I will burn down the theater, your puppets, and your masks, but I will carry your naked bodies into the free world."

Charles shouted back, "Good-bye you two-faced mediocre actor. You have all it takes to be a great president. A big mouth. An empty head. And a weakness for young girls!"

Sasha patted Charles approvingly on the back and the two of them watched as Bruce put me in a cab. Then they went off together, arms linked like schoolboys. I was glad they were going to drum on the sculpture Charles had discovered. I didn't want any right moments to pass for him. My cabdriver wore shades and sang loud and tried to sound black. I sank way down in my seat and sat on my hands the whole way back to the hotel.

The night before *The Myth Man* left Paris, the president of France hosted a formal sit-down dinner and dance in Sasha's honor. Charles said that the guests would be dukes, duchesses, barons, shipping magnates, the United States diplomatic corps, famous fashion and perfume designers, the owners of vast stretches of real estate, philanthropists, and wealthy merchants and military officials from all over the world. The women wore long black gowns and the men white or black morning coats.

"We're in a comic book," Bruce said.

In contrast, each member of the group modeled his or her own version of formal wear. Kosher came in a white silk kimono. Robin wore a blue, sequined, strapless go-go dress. Juno wore a floor-length deerskin coat with fringe beads. Journey was dressed almost identically, except his jacket was shorter and beneath it he wore a bright red cowboy shirt. His fringe pants and high-heeled cowboy boots made him look like a cowboy. Mustafa squeezed into a tight three-piece seersucker suit and draped a muslin robe over it. It was the first time I saw him in a white and black Arabic headdress. Reeva limped in on his arm, stopping every few steps to regain strength. She was stunning in several swatches of bright-colored material wound around her body and beads and jewels woven into her long braids. She was working hard on a lonely, grief-stricken appearance. Her lips were tight and her smile was meant to be courageous. I could tell she was enjoying her sadness. Bruce rented a madras tuxedo jacket, polka-dot bow tie and striped cummerbund, pale blue dress pants, and he kept on his white high tops. Charles pulled out a white tuxedo jacket with tails and sequined lapels. He wore matching white pants and white tap shoes. "I feel like a maître d'," he said. Sasha sat at the dais with the president, Lena and Monique,

175

and other dignitaries. He was beautiful in his smooth, clean, perfectly fitted formal dress coat, ascot, and cummerbund.

The dinner dance took place in the restored ballroom of an ancient castle a half hour outside Paris. Each performer from *The Myth Man* company was seated at a different table so we'd be mixed in with the other guests. The tables were spread out in a semicircle to allow room for a dance floor. A full chamber orchestra played Muzak-style jazz quietly at the far end of the hall.

There were name tags at our place mats and little bags of favors. I rummaged through my bag and found a miniature mask, a tiny doll modeled after one of the gods (mine was Zeus), a silk scarf by Chanel with LE HOMME MYTH inscribed on it, a tiny tape with drumming music on it, a white-and-gold-embossed program, and a note from Sasha in French saying something about theater being a joint occasion for audience and performers to share space and exchange energy. Later on, Charles told me that each guest had paid between five thousand and fifty thousand American dollars for a seat at the dinner and all the money was going toward our next show.

The dinner consisted of five courses sped in and out by expertly choreographed waiters in formal white jackets. They brought a parade of tiny little shapes of odd-colored glazes, gelatins, balls rolled in pancakes, and scoops of mashed foods in green, yellow, and purple. None of the food was recognizable to me, and so I ate very little. The man on my left wore a burgundy uniform and a monocle. He admonished my eating.

"Too tin," he said in a low voice. "Too tin. She must be eat."

I noticed that the man sitting next to Robin was talking to her down the front of her dress. He had a fat, bald head and wide, wet lips that looked like an incision. His tux pulled around his belly and his fat hands had a diamond ring on each pinky. His large wife was blond and square and looked as if she'd been flattened out. She concentrated on the food and wine and never looked at her husband as he leaned closer and closer to Robin's bosom. Finally, drunk and aggravated, Robin pulled down the top of her gown and exposed her breasts.

"Is this what you're looking for?" she asked the man.

176

The fat man turned scarlet and sat straight in his chair. He dug hungrily with his spoon into the lime-caramel custard that must've been dessert. No one else at the table glanced over at Robin or said a word. She finished her dinner with her breasts fully exposed. She finally covered herself when the orchestra made a signal that the speeches were to begin.

The president of France thanked everyone for coming and spoke at great length about the genius of Sasha and all that he'd given France over the years. I didn't understand the French, but the tone and pauses were familiar. Then Christoph, acting very adult and mannered, announced, in English, that the government was pledging one million dollars toward Sasha's next project. A woman got up and in a high, nasal voice chattered speedily. I believe she was thanking the committee who'd put the evening together. Finally, Lena, who was introduced as the new minister of women's affairs, spoke briefly about art as an inspiration and healer in painful times. Then she introduced Sasha.

Sasha appeared to be on edge. His face was long and tense. His eyes flitted back and forth. His skin was pale and broken out in red spots. He took a long moment before he spoke. The colonel sitting next to me decided to translate Sasha's French into my ear. He smelled of fish and scallions and there was a whistling sound in his nose when he inhaled.

"Thank you," Sasha said. "There is such love in this room, you help us remember why we do what we do. Do I sound ungrateful if I say to you that the best work should be done without any good wishes, in abject poverty, in a basement without light? Because . . . we must do what we do, not for patrons or audience, not even for ourselves, but we must do what we do to find out why we do theater. So, although I am grateful, I would suggest that all of us must throw away our titles of patron, artist, benefactor, creator, minister, even president, and conduct this search together. When we ask what is theater, we are really asking, how do we live? Why do we live the way we do? Can we recapture the freshness and purity and unbound energy of a baby's first cry, or the leap of a dolphin out of the water? What does it mean to be fully alive? How can we take full advantage of this curse, this privilege of life? This is what the theater must find out. We are scientists for the spirit, and our work is not to entertain, but to research and find the buried possibilities of human awareness. Thank you for your good food, kindness, little gifts, and generous pledges, but most of all, thank you for joining the search."

Journey leaped to his feet, gave a whistle, and started chanting. Little by little, the entire dinner party rose and clapped somewhat unevenly for Sasha. He didn't smile, but stayed at the podium stunned and embarrassed. The reception wasn't enthusiastic enough. He couldn't figure out why. Then he realized his patrons were awe-struck, even frightened. He broke into a relieved, boyish smile and pulled at his hair with his hands. Then he waved across the room at the conductor. The orchestra exploded into a fast-paced fox-trot. I was surprised to see Sasha leap off the dais and head in my direction. He nodded at me and pulled me toward the dance floor.

"I don't know how to do this," I said.

He walked me to the music. "I don't either," he whispered. "We'll just make something up."

A long time passed. He led my feet in odd, fragmented squares and shuffles. He dipped me and spun me. The whole dinner party was watching. We were the bride and groom. The guests beamed. Little by little, other dancers trickled to the floor.

"I did a flop up there, didn't I?" Sasha asked happily.

"No," I said. "You expect too much."

He smiled and hugged me to him. "I want to tell you a secret, Pussycat. But don't tell anyone. Not even Charles." I gave him a look of reproach.

"I have raised altogether almost four million dollars for the next stage of our work," he whispered in my ear.

"Everybody knows that, Sasha," I said.

"Shhh." He jerked me a little.

"That's not it. That's not it," he said.

We danced in silence.

"I have half my funding, but I have nothing else," he said, laughing quietly. "I can't write. I can't think. I don't know what to do next and I don't know why to do it."

"Maybe you should rest," I suggested.

He kissed my forehead and danced me to the section of the floor that was empty of dancers. The music ended and he applauded enthusiastically. A ballad with a tinny saxophone solo began to play. He led me to another section of the dance floor and put his hands on my shoulder. We danced around the perimeter of the circle. He acted as if he were being pursued.

"Rest can't solve this problem," Sasha whispered. His voice had a joking quality to it, but his hands were cold. "I think and think and the only thing I am sure of . . . is that . . . theater is useless. Even the greatest theater is absolutely useless. It's all pretend. It has no real effect on our lives or how we live our lives. It doesn't change us or make us different. Suddenly I have the funds to do whatever I wish and I realize that there is nothing worth doing." Sasha dipped me and walked me across the floor in tangolike strides.

"I may have to stop completely," he said. "Or do something so terrifyingly different that it would be like jumping off a cliff."

"Don't worry," I said. "You always know what to do."

"Don't comfort me with such easy words," Sasha moaned. "I *don't* know. My mind is an empty space. I keep waiting for images or sounds. But it stays empty. I look inward and I stare at nothingness. I'm haunted by the failure of theater to change my soiled spirit."

"But you're the best, Sasha," I said. His dancing and talking were beginning to disorient me. I kept stepping on his feet.

He shook his head sadly and then smiled as if we were sharing his joke.

"You love me," he said. "That's why I can't lie to you. I can't betray your love. All this bloated praise and hysteria only makes the hypocrisy seem worse. I may just give back the money and go to the mountains."

I didn't know how to reply. Sasha's hands became clammy and stuck to my shoulders. He was deathly pale and he danced as if he had no strength in his legs and he wanted me to carry him. The orchestra stopped for a breath and then broke into a stiff, square jitterbug.

"Don't tell the others," Sasha warned me. "Especially Charles."

Suddenly a voice crackled over a cheap-sounding loudspeaker. It was screeching commands in a thick, heavy language. A group of thirty or so naked people burst into the ballroom. They were smeared with pig's blood and filth. They banged on pots and pans and hopped and wiggled with grotesque movements. They formed a circle around the president of France. They sang "I am the very model of a modern major general" in Polish and then one of them led a fat hog into the ballroom. The hog was dressed in a military coat and hat. The loudspeaker screeched at them and they separated and took the dancing couples hostage. The orchestra continued to play the jitterbug.

"Decadence," the group screamed in English. A naked woman with the word THEATER written on her body in blood kissed the military hog on the lips. Sasha's and my captor forced us to our knees. The man was bearded and hairy and stank of sweat and sour blood. He made the sign of the cross in front of us and started reciting the Lord's Prayer, accenting it with loud belches and snorts.

Sasha sighed. "This is so boring," he said in a low voice. "Even the so-called revolutionaries have nothing new to be furious about. Jacob Avon is jealous I got so much money. Listen, he can have it. Success is nothing but a deadly burden of guilt and expectation. The wisest man is the abject failure who wanders penniless and friendless, wanting nothing from this world."

"So make something bad," I said to Sasha. "Write a huge flop."

His laughter consisted of short sobs and gasps. "If only it was possible, my little flea," he said. "But I am a prisoner of my own talent." Our captor grunted and rubbed his muddy hands on Sasha's white coat and my dress.

"This is Broadway," Sasha hissed at him. "Ten-million-dollar farts from fully subsidized assholes." Our captor spit at Sasha, and Sasha laughed and applauded.

The invaders left as quickly as they came. The rich guests murmured quietly among themselves and wiped spots of blood and dirt off each other with napkins dipped into bubbling water provided with apologies by the caterers. The guests were titillated and amused.

The president wore an expression like a tolerant father. Sasha led me back to my seat next to the man with the monocle and kissed me long and gently on the forehead. Then he left the room. I dozed in and out for the rest of the party, until Charles woke me with a shake. He grabbed my wrist and pulled me to my feet. The ballroom suddenly had a thick cloud of smoke. The members of the party were rushing toward the exits. Charles said Jacob Avon's people had set the castle on fire, but I wasn't sure. I imagined that the final moment of guerrilla theater could have been staged by Sasha.

The tour was long and I lost track of time and the languages and landscapes of individual countries. We traveled through Italy, Greece, Sicily, and crisscrossed to festivals in Geneva, Copenhagen, Oslo, and Tunis. Sasha was gone. The summer season was when awards were announced in America and he flew home to win a special *Village Voice* Obie award, a citation from the New York Outer Critics, a Best Director award from the Drama Desk Committee, a certificate of honor from the classics society of the State University of New York, and a special Tony award. He also had to fly to several colleges such as Yale, Oberlin, USC, Juilliard, and Purchase University to receive honorary doctorates as well as deliver two commencement addresses. He gave speeches entitled "Theatre and the Future" at Carnegie-Mellon University and "The Archetypes of Inspiration" at Sarah Lawrence College. He also said he was taking time to do in-depth research on our next show, which would begin rehearsals when he joined us at the Avignon Festival in the South of France. I was relieved to hear him talk about our future so confidently, but I wondered if he was lying to the company or if he'd really found the inspiration he'd been mourning.

He left the company's rehearsal schedule under Bruce's command and told us that we should consider Bruce and no one else as an extension of his spirit. As soon as he was gone, however, Bruce turned all the responsibilities over to Charles, and no one complained or questioned the transition. Charles enlisted Kosher to do tai chi with us every day and Reeva, now that she was healed, led grueling dance workshops. Robin taught us scat singing and Mustafa had us doing calisthenics. Juno told strange and funny stories that we acted out as she chanted. Charles stayed in whatever theater we were at all day, every day and rehearsed tiny details of the scenes with the actors. He corrected moves that had become sloppy and asked Bruce to go over the stories of each character so the meaning would be fresh and clear. Under Charles's direction, the company became more enthusiastic than they'd been in months and the performances were precise and full of spirit. He was a much more attentive director than Sasha and never insulted the actors. In several countries he suggested we improvise a second show (to be done at midnight) to give audiences a sense of magic and keep our imaginations alive. One night in Frankfurt we did *Hansel and Gretel* with two children from the audience being led on the terrifying, comic journey through a park, and Charles supplied cookies for the thousand people gathered outdoors in the real forestlike environment he'd chosen for the adventure. In Geneva he gave us an outline for a midnight version of *The Pied Piper* and Kosher led two thousand or so people up the side of a mountain playing shakuhachi by candlelight. With Charles directing, the company was committed and at ease. The audience and critical response was always positive. Several times we were written about on the front pages of the press. TV cameras followed us everywhere. Of course Sasha got all the credit and when I asked Charles if that bothered him, he smiled and said, "I keep a list of all the things that are unfair in this world. Someday when I have time, I'll really get pissed. But right now I'm having too good a time."

At the end of the summer, Sasha joined us in Avignon. He was warm and excited to see us. But he appeared spacey and ragged. His eyes were unfocused and he stuttered a bit. He stared into space a great deal or held his hands out and looked at them. He never asked how the tour had gone and no one said a word about Charles's work. Luckily, Randy Paul had been with Sasha in the U.S. documenting his speeches for her book. Sasha announced that, contrary to what he'd said before, we wouldn't start working right away, but ought to take Avignon as a kind of vacation, since we only had three shows in our month-long stay at the festival.

Charles told me not to worry. He said Sasha always died after finishing a show and lived like a dead man unable to answer the riddle which would bring him back to life. Charles said Sasha always gave up the theater until he got the idea for his next show. No one could talk him into believing he'd write anything again. Once, he went so far as to force Charles to plan his funeral and memorial service.

"But doesn't that bother you after all the work you've done?" I asked.

"It's on my list." Charles nodded. "It's number six or seven. I'll scream about it in a couple years."

I was certain Sasha knew that Charles directed the company in his absence. Once or twice I caught him looking at Charles and his spacey eyes turned cold and suspicious. The change lasted as long as a few blinks of his white-blond lashes, but I felt the chill. I felt the dread Sasha had expressed to me in Paris. The theater couldn't save his soul.

Avignon was the perfect size town for me. It reminded me of the villages described in the Hans Christian Andersen fairy tales. It was enclosed by ancient stone walls, and a long arm of rocky shore jutted out into the Rhône. There was a tiny fortress at the end. White birds circled and screeched. I loved to sit watching them. The festival took place all over the ancient part of the town. A cobblestone square the size of a large open field and enclosed by small stone houses served as the center of activities. Outdoor stages were constructed on every corner, decorated with colorful sets and flags of each of the participating countries. Huge bright yellow and red banners flew over the square advertising the festival. Performances went on in all the tiny churches, stables, and markets that peeked out from the narrow, winding streets and alleys off the square. Young and old performers, in and out of costume, sat by the old fountains or unrolled sleeping bags on the grassy hills outside the main square, where the famous wall overlooked the sea. The performers treated each other as old friends. They hugged, laughed, and exchanged clothes, jewelry, and stories. A strong hot wind blew constantly in even breaths and surprising gusts. Charles called the wind a "maelstrom." He said the Gypsies claimed the wind made people mad and forced them to do strange things. When the wind blew a certain way, people fell in love for no reason, ate too many sweets, and remembered songs they hadn't sung since they were children. When it blew another way, the sane people became moody, sneaky, criminal, and everything you tried to do turned out disastrously.

The company shared a large villa, tucked into the side of a mossy hill. It must've been a wealthy person's mansion at one time. It was made from old stones. The roof had wooden shingles. It was three stories high with five or six large, airy rooms on the second and third floors and a bedroom for a "mad aunt" (Charles said) in the steeple-shaped attic. The ceilings were low with old, cracked beams and the first floor had several odd-shaped sitting rooms. The kitchen was a large open space with a cracked wooden counter. Antique copper pots hung from the low beams. The stoves were so old that Charles said we should all tie our hair in buns and bake bread from flour grown from wheat planted in the garden.

Every room that faced the river had tall French windows the width of a whole wall, that opened by pushing old wooden shutter doors. The windows spilled out onto small stone and iron terraces with cheap fold-up chairs and card tables. From my windows I could see the stone fortress and the Rhône. Charles and I were on the third floor of the villa. We had an open, breezy room with nothing but two beds, a dresser, and a ceiling fan. There were faded spots where paintings had hung, but the mustard walls were bare. Charles pushed my bed toward the open windows which led to our terrace. He said that Avignon had stars I'd want to watch before I fell asleep. And on certain days the colors of the light and sky were more varied and subtle than Charles's wooden box of thread and buttons.

At first everyone was cheerful and active in Avignon. Even Kosher

184

stood out on his terrace day and night doing tai chi and grinning at the actors who were having jam and bread on the stone porch below. Sasha lay quietly on a deck chair set on our grassy yard overlooking the sea. He held what seemed to be a book written in French on his lap, but didn't read. He slept. The only time he rose from the chair was to take his dinner in his room and to go to sleep at night. Robin stayed beside him reading a thick book out loud. It was an English-Sanskrit dictionary. Neither of them spoke the language but seemed to draw great pleasure from learning the sounds. Robin was content and cautious. She rarely had Sasha to herself, and she acted as if she was afraid to disturb her unexpected good fortune by talking or making sudden moves. Charles said she thought she could hold Sasha to his deck chair with good behavior. Obedience was glue for her. Her passivity was a method of Catholic voodoo to keep him there until death.

Charles treated the Avignon Festival as "the greatest thing since Coney Island." He knew many of the experimental theater artists, craftsmen, and musicians from all over the world. During the day he introduced me to jugglers, fire eaters, clowns, jewelry makers, leather workers, puppeteers, a troupe of Renaissance musicians and Dada performers and hippies. We watched a group that looked like Japanese Beatles rehearsing rock and roll to a slide show of mushroom bombs and photos of Hiroshima. I met some belly dancers who performed traditional rituals with veils and finger cymbals to the Supremes, translated into German. I met some flamenco dancers and a rowdy group of Gypsies who were working together on performing fragments of Garcia Lorca using flamenco and American tap dance. We went to a puppet show in a black tent. Only twelve people at a time were allowed in. The puppets were realistic faces painted on papier-mâché heads the size of the puppeteer's fingertips. And he'd made tiny wigs and hats and costumes for his fingers. The show was eerie, and it was performed in complete silence except when a puppet hit a tiny gong the size of a quarter. The puppets weren't bright-colored children's puppets and there were no fairy tales or slapstick. Each tiny character kept changing from man to woman to animal to monster. Charles explained to me that the miniature epic had been inspired by a midnight cult movie called *El Topo* and a book about a shaman called *The Teachings of Don Juan.* He said everybody was into journeys these days. Charles said if he ever made a show he'd call it *Sitting at Home with a Beer.* Next to our *Myth Man,* the puppet show was the most popular offering at the festival. The lines outside the tent stretched across the town square. Waiting for tickets had become an event in itself. People sat pleasantly day after day sharing loaves of heavy bread, bean sprouts, apples, and cheese, and singing folk songs. Vendors passed out free ice cream. Clowns distracted them with balloon animals and tricks on stilts.

Charles knew the puppeteer very well. They hugged and kissed after his show. He was a young man in his early twenties with a black crew cut and dark eyes with long lashes. His nose was thin and straight. His teeth pushed his upper lip forward. He was small, thin, and dressed in a black shirt and black jeans. He was elfish and lithe. Charles said he was "a Houdini." When I met him I was surprised to hear that his high-pitched voice had a sweet southern drawl. He laughed easily. He took Charles and me by the arm to his workshop and showed us all the miniature chairs, mirrors, beds, staircases, mountains, lakes, dresses, hats, and instruments he was making for his "people." He and Charles referred to each little puppet by its first name. The puppeteer's name was Peter and I liked the way he looked directly at Charles and teased him. They seemed to have known each other for a long time and cared about each other in a gentle, casual way. At one point Peter thanked Charles for bringing him to Avignon and Charles gently put a finger to Peter's lips and said to please keep his "producer trip" a secret. Peter laughed and rolled his eyes. His skin was white as clown face, but healthy and clear. He was smooth all over. He had no stubble on his chin or fuzz on his hands or chest. He had the eyes of a man, he was half boy. He seemed to believe his puppets were real living creatures, but he wasn't crazy. He made fun of his stardom. He called his puppets "the girls" and enjoyed complaining about their endless demands. I liked Peter and smiled to let him know it. He fixed a stare on me that was both affectionate and curious.

"Baba has given you a loved one," he said to Charles.

"Baba black sheep," Charles replied. "Baba's his guru," Charles explained to me. "Peter must share Baba with me whether I want him or not."

"Miss Rikki Nelson is a beautiful child, son," Peter said, ignoring Charles. "A Victorian waif with balls. Baba has finally given you a sister reason to leave the brotherness of self-punishment."

"That means that he likes you," Charles said, turning to me. "We always have to translate Peter's *nesses* and *isms*. He likes to make everything a noun. It goes along with his believing that couches and hot plates have souls."

"Can we come back?" I asked Charles. "This is where I want to come every day."

"Well, I want you to swim," Charles said, "but we can visit Peter when he is not performing Tom Thumb does Ingmar Bergman."

Peter winked at me, worked his way into a black velvet robe, and began carefully placing puppets on his fingers for his next show.

"I'd like you to come back as much as God will allow," Peter said.

"Are you referring to God, Baba, or Sasha?" Charles asked.

Peter grinned. "I'm referring to whomever's at the controlness of your innerisms."

Charles was gone every night. I figured he went to Peter, and it was a calming thought. He'd tuck me in and tell me some ridiculous story, lie down until he thought I was asleep, and then sneak out our door. He always returned at dawn and didn't even bother to get into bed. He'd change his clothes, tiptoe onto the terrace, and play the recorder. I loved the sound of the recorder during those early hours and I was soothed by the simple, playful melodies he made up. The hot winds were affecting him, and he was making Avignon magical for me and restful for everyone else. Sasha staged our performances outside near the walls of the city for the thousands who visited the festival. The reception was loving and strong, but we weren't icons. We were one of many great experiments. The lack of pressure helped to sustain the sleepy nature of our vacation hours. After staging the show, Sasha returned to his deck chair, Kosher to his balcony, Robin to her book, and Charles and I sought out more characters and adventures along the windy, ancient streets of the village.

One morning I woke up with the hot sun on my face. I realized I'd slept through the dawn and it was late. Charles was not playing his tunes on the balcony. I heard loud voices from the patio. I heard Sasha laughing and talking rapidly. I heard forced reactions from Robin and, for the first time in days, I recognized several other voices from the company. It was clear they were entertaining someone and that the lazy rhythm of the vacation had transformed into nervous, excited energy. There was one voice I couldn't quite place. The woman had a throaty, slow way of talking and a loud, coarse laugh. I crept to the railing on the balcony and looked down. I saw my mother sitting in Sasha's deck chair. She was wearing a one-piece bathing suit with the straps undone and part of her breasts exposed. Her hair was white blond and hung in a page boy to her shoulders. She sat with a drink in one hand and a cigarette in the other. She looked a little like Sandra Dee or Angie Dickinson. I wanted to shout down to her from the balcony and wave and then run down the three flights of steps onto the patio and into her arms. But I couldn't embarrass myself. Instead I took a half hour trying to pick out the proper shorts and T-shirt and settled on a denim sundress that felt too clumsy and square.

When I walked onto the patio, everyone looked up at me with confused expressions and overly bright grins. The whole company was sitting around my mother on chairs. Charles was off on the grass nearby stringing beads. He lay on his stomach. My mother didn't get up from Sasha's deck chair. She held out her arms, her glass in one hand and a cigarette in the other.

"Precious!" she cried.

She'd never called me Precious in my life. But I walked to her and she embraced me. She smelled of hair spray, tanning lotion, gin, and nicotine. Her arms were strong and she seemed nervous. When she let me go, I tried to help her out by not staring at her. I focused on my feet. They seemed big and flat compared to my mother's high-arched graceful feet with the bright red pedicure. There was a long silence. And then Sasha clapped his hands and said in a thick, undefinable accent, "Surprise, huh?"

I tried to catch a glance from Charles, but he was now lying on his back matching beads and tying knots. My mother slid over on the deck chair and patted a small space for me to join her. There really wasn't any room for me and the edge of the wood cut uncomfortably into my thighs.

"Just don't block the sun, honey," my mother said. "I was just telling these fabulous people that if anyone had told me that I was gonna travel with my Rikki Nelson around the world, I'd recommend he go dry out somewhere."

Everyone laughed indulgently at my mother's attempt at humor. I winced. She punched me playfully. It was meant to be affectionate, but I had to struggle to keep my balance on the chair.

"Well, let's hear ya talk!" she said loudly. "When I started readin' all those columns 'bout that ingenuous babble of yours, I almost bust a gut. All those rich folks comin' in for the Early Bird Special was treating me like ah was damn near a celebrity myself."

I couldn't think of a thing to say. I wanted to ask, *Are you still a whore?* but I thought that might get us off on the wrong foot. Finally I decided on the old party line.

"Sasha saved me," I said.

Sasha, fascinated by this reunion, bit his lower lip and nodded his head slowly and watched my mother carefully. She'd put her drink on the patio and flicked a cigarette butt onto the grass. She began applying cream to her legs in long, seductive strokes. Her eyes teared a bit and her thick eyeliner ran just enough to give her harsh beauty the look of a clown.

"Hearin' that little voice frees me from the bondage of a mother tormented by the weight of worry and guilt." She glanced up at the group while she picked the cream from inside her nails.

"You know, I didn't believe in God much," she said. "But I do find myself leaning towards the spiritual side of things again. Right before I caught the bus to Miami, I saw a white egret with one teeny-tiny little baby and I don't know if I prayed or what, but I saw it as a sign. I asked that egret to help me do right by my baby here."

"Many cultures look to animals for guidance," Sasha said encouragingly.

My mother clucked her tongue and returned Sasha's interested stare. "You are all so smart," she said. "I'm just gonna have to carry an *Encyclopedia Britannica* strapped to my belly to keep up with all these weird facts you all know."

Suddenly Charles started spinning on the grass and humming an odd out-of-tune series of notes through his nose.

"What the *hell* is that?" my mother asked.

"That's Charles," I answered quickly. "He's my nanny."

"Your *what?*" my mother snapped.

"A playful phrase," Sasha assured her.

"Well, in Florida nannies are either illegal Cubans or niggers who can't do nothin' else."

Reeva bristled.

"Facts is facts, ma'am," my mother said to Reeva. "And if I state facts, it doesn't mean I approve of 'em. I'm a hostess in a restaurant for folks who have nothin' to do but wait to die. I have no uppity illusions."

"Mommy paints," I found myself saying, and didn't know why.

"Really?" Robin gushed. "What sort of style?" My mother stared past Robin indifferently. She delivered her answer to Bruce.

"Landscapes, but nothing that'll show up in a gallery or such. I do it to ease the tension and make an extra buck."

"You should paint here," Sasha said. "The colors of the earth change by the hour and even by the minute. Many great painters lived outside on the hillsides for days at a time trying to capture the light."

"Well, personally I need a bed." My mother smiled. Then she scowled. "Is that guy just gonna keep spinning until he drills a hole to China or what?"

"We all do it," Robin explained. "It's a way of finding our center. It's a very valuable exercise for concentration and balance."

"Well, don't try to teach me," my mother said with distaste. "I'm prone to vertigo. I'd never taken an overseas flight before and there were times, I swear, I broke into a cold sweat. I thought the plane was flying upside down."

"Maybe it was," Sasha said.

My mother laughed too loudly for too long. Then she yawned. "You kids are too much. Hippies with brains and money. Rikki Nelson coulda done a lot worse. A lot worse. I said to this lawyer boyfriend of mine—" she glanced at Sasha, "well, not a boyfriend —a wishful thinker, I said to him, before we get all messy in courts with judges, et cetera, et cetera, I wanted to see for myself. . . ."

A chill went through me.

"That was a generous and wise decision," Sasha said with a tone that combined sympathy and seriousness. "I can understand how a mother could go mad over the loss of a child and just take action without any thought."

My mother's eyes welled with tears. Tiny sobs shook her full breasts, which were now nearly fully exposed over the top of her bathing suit. She wiped at her mascara with her knuckles.

"She was stolen from me, but you all weren't the criminals. When I catch the bastard who did it, I'll hang him by his fingernails."

She must need money, I thought. Or she's bored. I couldn't believe she really wanted me. I stood up.

"You waited too long," I said. "You didn't care."

My mother fastened the straps of her bathing suit and blinked slowly and shook her platinum hair.

"Rikki Nelson, we will not have ourselves a psychodrama in front of your nice friends," she said to me. "Ten-year-old girls don't know everything."

"I'm eleven," I said.

"Well, for *your* information," my mother retorted, "*I* was in jail. Thanks to your friend Jonah and his doctor friends."

My mother stood with drunken pride. Her body was heavier than I remembered, but her stomach was flat and her legs looked strong in her spike-heeled slippers.

Sasha watched, fascinated.

"I don't believe I can walk to my hotel in these damn shoes," she said.

"Bruce will drive you," Sasha said. Bruce bolted to attention.

"I have a beautiful room overlooking some kind of wall with cannons and bitty windows," my mother said.

"The fortress," Robin volunteered.

"It's too small for us both," my mother said to me. "But if a bigger one opens up, you can move in with me."

I said nothing.

Charles was still spinning.

"Tell that boy that if he hits oil, I want a cut," my mother said to Sasha. She gave me her cheek. I kissed it.

"*Love* the dress," said my mother. And she reached out and took Bruce's arm.

My mother invited the company to dinner at the most expensive restaurant in Avignon. I was embarrassed because I knew it was a tourist trap. The Festival Jardin had stucco walls painted with a tacky mural of a miniature Avignon. The floor was painted blue and was supposed to be the ocean. The tables and booths were designed to be sailing vessels. Nets and shells covered the ceilings. The waiters and waitresses dressed in medieval attire and spoke English. The menus unrolled like ancient scrolls and the selections were what Charles called Anglo-Franco. He said dishes like tournedos, beef bourguignonne, and quiche were the chicken chow mein and egg rolls of French cooking. My mother insisted we order one of everything and pass the dishes around our schooner-shaped table. When the wine steward came to the table, my mother said to him, "Honey, what's something old and sexy, but not with all that crud around the top?" Then she told him that the silver tasting cup he wore around his neck was "adorable" and asked where she could purchase one.

"Good Lord, freedom makes me sassy." My mother laughed. "Please excuse my lack of intercontinental manners. You all must think I'm ignorant white trash."

"I find it very refreshing," Sasha said. He continued to study her with calm fascination.

"How long were you in jail?" Reeva asked. My mother looked at Sasha.

"I was a call girl. There's no use denying it. My poor Rikki Nelson knew it, didn't you, darling?"

I nodded despite the fact that I hadn't known what she was by name.

"Very upper class." My mother puffed nervously on a cigarette. "I mostly serviced those poor old men in the Florida retirement communities. A lot of 'em were impotent with their wives and they needed to know that their engines weren't permanently stalled."

"So you were performing a charitable service," Robin said kindly.

"No, honey. I was just a cheap whore like any other. I had some younger clients—contractors, construction, landlords. I supplied drugs for their pleasure too. When I got busted, the list of charges was as long as a grocery list for an A-rab family at the A&P."

"So how long were you in for?" Bruce asked.

"I liked it so much the first time, I went back," my mother said. She didn't seem to want to answer Bruce. "And then it became my favorite resort. I went back three more times after that."

Charles was playing light drum patterns with his fingers on the tabletop. He attempted to smile at my mother.

"Maybe Rikki Nelson doesn't need to know all this," he said.

My mother turned to him. Her heavy cat eyes took him in scornfully.

"Women need the truth to grow, Mr. Spinning Top. Women are poisoned from the time they are children by lies. My daughter has to know where I started and how I changed. If she is to come live with me after this tour, she needs to know I won't be saying X when I mean Y."

Charles shrugged. "In certain instances I don't see the advantage in telling a child all the raw facts."

"I bet you don't, Mr. Hoity Toit," my mother said.

"Did you paint in jail?" Robin interrupted.

Once again my mother appealed to Sasha.

"Have you ever worked with an actor who was not born to it, had no talent and no desire?"

Sasha took a great deal of time to consider the question.

"Yes, I have, in fact several times," he replied.

"And what was sticking up the guy's butt? What was the problem?"

Sasha leaned forward and touched my mother's face like a blind man, as if he were sensing the source of her feelings.

"That is a *very* complex question. But I would say fear. Fear of taking risks. Fear of growing. Fear of losing oneself. Of failure. Of the total reconstruction of one's inner life."

Charles sighed audibly.

"Well, that's me, all right," my mother said. "I had no talent as a mother. I had no instinct. And honey, just the idea of it made me puke. But now I'm gonna ride into the sunset with my daughter here and we're gonna have one hell of a happy ending."

No one said a word.

At the end of the meal, my mother scanned the check and whistled loudly. "Do you realize I could buy a membership to a fitness club with what this cost?"

"Let me pay," Charles said quietly.

My mother ignored him and reached into her bag. With shaky hands she brought out fistfuls of crumpled francs and piled them in front of Bruce.

"You're the Jew," she said. "I bet you sure can count. But don't you go and steal none of it."

I pulled at my fingers in tension and embarrassment. But Bruce just made a face at my mother and popped one of the balls of francs into his mouth.

"We *eat* money, lady, we don't steal it."

My mother licked her lips and blew Bruce a smoky kiss. I was surprised he tolerated her. I didn't understand why everyone was paying her homage. She was rude and gross. Clumsy and dishonest. I became more and more quiet and allowed myself to sink back into the familiar silence that had kept me out of trouble in the past.

I don't know when the dinner and drinking finally ended. Someone carried me to my room. I woke up shortly after I was dropped unceremoniously onto my bed. The moonlight came through the large balcony doors and created bright streaks, angles, and shadows on the walls and ceiling. Charles lay on his bed, his arms pointed at the ceiling, trying to make shadow creatures with his hands. I watched as one hand creature ate the fingers of his other hand. It was a slow, terrible slaughter. I laughed out loud.

"Welcome to the animal kingdom," Charles said. "This is an outdoor safari ride where you can watch from your Jeep. At this moment our rare collection of bunnies, puppies, guppies, chicklets, and lambs are being devoured by their parents."

He dropped his arms to the bed and groaned.

"My mother's a pig, isn't she?" I said.

Charles thought a moment.

"She's more like a character Tennessee Williams had the good sense to cut from one of his plays." He curled onto his side, drew his legs up, and smiled at me.

"Who's Tennessee Williams?" I asked.

"A *wonderful* playwright, pussycat. He managed to make exquisite poetry out of ruined lives, and squeeze love from even the most wretched families. I'll put him on your reading list for when you're fifteen. No need to depress you now."

"There's no love in *my* family," I said. "None. Absolutely."

"You can't be so sure," Charles said. "The heart is like a lasagna, layers of ground beef, cheese, noodles, tomato sauce. Sometimes a noodle will spring a leak and the cheese mixes with the ground beef. The heart is not a neatly cooked pump. It leaks too. I have no idea what I just said."

"I hate her," I said to Charles impatiently. "And I don't know why someone doesn't just tell her to shut up."

Charles sat up for a moment, looked as if he were going to get off the bed, and then collapsed again. I laughed. I realized I hadn't laughed since my mother arrived.

"It's like this, Pussycat," Charles explained. "There's not one single person on this entire earth that doesn't have some kind of . . . thing . . . about his mother. This group is a pretty raggedy gang of motherless children, no? So then here comes this lady who's a card-carrying mother! No matter who she really is. She's got all the credentials—the womb that gave birth and the child in proximity. So everybody's just falling all over themselves to get some kind of hit off this licensed mother."

"But she's a *terrible* mother," I said. "Don't they see that?"

Charles sighed. "This is going to be hard to understand, Pussycat—but I'll give it a shot. The *worse* the mother—the more nasty, insulting, alcoholic, and selfish—the more *attractive* she becomes to a gang like ours. They want to win her over or something—expose her hidden sweetness. It's like PCP or cocaine cut with speed. The more awful the drug, the deeper the addiction."

I didn't understand Charles at all. Now he was flat on his back and his legs were straight up in the air and he was rolling an imaginary log on his feet.

"Charles," I said to him. "How come you haven't fallen for her?"

"Well, I had a perfectly nice mother," Charles said softly. "She was gorgeous and hilarious and kind. And except for a few heartbreaking incidents, she and I were friends until she died. Therefore I'm not looking for understudies. And secondly, Rikki Nelson, it would do you well to remember that *I* am your real mother, your mother fucker, and your mother of invention. So it's easy, you see, to spot an imposter."

I smiled. I felt protected and relieved. As I dozed off, I watched Charles's legs extended from his flattened-out position on the bed. He had a love scene going between his feet. The left foot kept making passes at the right. But the right was very shy and kept backing away.

I was only alone with my mother during one afternoon. The rest of the time we ignored each other. She seemed delighted to lead the group on tourist excursions through medieval ruins and to lighthouses, nightclubs, and restaurants with bilingual menus. I didn't want it to happen, but one day she grabbed me by the arm after lunch and said, "Let's go shopping."

My mother wasn't interested in any of the jugglers or clowns. She sped past the afternoon outdoor performances of masked dancers and foreign street theaters.

"I will not buy any of that hippie-dippy stuff in those markets, Rikki Nelson," she said firmly. "And I don't want you to either. They lie about the sizes and it looks like they all shared the same ball of yarn to embroider those ugly necklines and sleeves. Plus you can't tell if any of that stuff is really new. It could be crawling with bugs from God knows what hellhole in some backwards country."

We ended up on a street in the modern part of Avignon that could've been a commercial district in any small city in the U.S. My mother led us into a leather and denim store and began pushing messily through the racks of clothes. Now and then she'd yank a skirt or a jacket off its hanger and press it against herself. Finally she settled on a leather miniskirt and a short leather vest with fringe.

"Whaddya think?" she asked me.

"It's okay," I said.

She disappeared into a dressing room and, after what seemed like an hour, burst through the curtains.

"Ta-da!" she sang. The skirt was skin tight and the vest, without a shirt, showed her bra in the arm holes.

"I love it," she said to me. "Do you love it?"

I stared at her, afraid to contradict her or make her angry. Although she had a full, tight body, the outfit hit her in all the wrong places and made her thighs look too big and her arms appear pale and dry.

"You're pretty," I said lamely.

She rushed forward and embraced me. I could smell her sweat, her perfume, the thick odor of nicotine, and sweet liquor. She repulsed me.

"I knew it'd work out with us," she said.

When she returned the second time from the dressing room, she headed for the salesman behind the register, but then stopped.

"Well, what about you?" she asked. "Want some blue jeans or something? It's my treat."

I wondered where she'd gotten all the money she'd been spending lately.

"No, thank you," I said. "I'm fine."

My mother's face darkened. "Little Miss Prissiness," she said mockingly. "You sure are a serious girl. I don't believe I've ever seen you smile." She moved closer to me as if to get a better look. My heart sped up.

"Hit your lips with the forefinger and third finger. Keep 'em together and just—smack—like this," she said. She tapped her own closed mouth with two of her fingers and their long bright-red nails. Her mouth went into a grimacing smile. "Go on, try it," she insisted.

I hit myself with my two fingers in the middle of my lips and made myself smile.

"*See*," my mother said triumphantly. "Never fails. The photographer at the restaurant uses it on all the glum old biddies when he takes those cheapo portraits. You know, to send north? Charges an arm and a leg too. And extra for the cardboard frames."

I tapped my mouth again and forced a second smile to please her. I thought it might get us home sooner. My mother paid for her outfit after trying to bargain down the price. She berated the salesman for not speaking better English when Avignon was clearly a "tourist town."

"These French think they're God's gift to the world," she said to me. She was speeding through the streets again.

"Let's get us a drink in one of those outdoor doodads," my mother proposed.

We ended up in a huge semicircular café in the center of the modern sector of the town. My mother decided that she wanted to sit inside because the service would be quicker. She ordered a glass of wine and I asked for a Coke. We sat in silence. She took out a compact, examined herself, and reapplied her makeup.

"Your friends are a riot," she said to me. "I can't say I'm all that interested in that show you all are doing, but I like that Sasha. He's a classy guy. I was ready to haul the whole theater into the courts on kidnapping charges, but Sasha flew me over here and said I ought to see for myself. Gave me a walloping per diem too."

"They didn't kidnap me," I said. "Jonah brought me to them."

"Jonah," she said. "If I could find Jonah, I'd make him pay back but good. You don't know what he did. You'll never know what he did."

My mother put her hand on mine.

"You are really set up, Rikki Nelson, and I don't have to think you suffered waiting for me all these years. It's a relief beyond relief."

"I'm happy," I said.

"Well, you should be," my mother said. "And I can tell that I'm gonna learn a lot from being with you on the rest of this here tour."

The waiter brought our drinks. My mother immediately ordered a second glass of wine. I felt so sickened by the idea of her staying with us that I couldn't touch the Coke.

"There's something I have to be perfectly blunt about," my mother said. "I've told Sasha I don't want you associating with that Charles creep anymore. I've ordered him out of your room and you're not to speak to him 'cept if the play or somethin' calls for it. And I don't want you ever alone with him."

I gripped my hands to the side of my chair and didn't move. "Why?"

My mother pulled her chair back as if about to get up, but she was stretching out her legs for comfort.

"Well, you're probably too young to understand, but that 'man,' if you want to call him that, does things that aren't natural. He's a sick person. I don't want you to be influenced by his dirty way of life. Also, you're starting to develop a little. I can tell you got some curves and buds, Rikki Nelson, and it's wrongful for you to be shar-ing a room with a grown man, even *if* he despises women. Sasha agrees with me, of course. I pointed out to him that this Charles person was probably talented but abnormal and, well, to be blunt, I've seen my share of women who had his same disease in jail. They weren't women. They were men without . . . well, the *instrument*. They were mean and strange as any circus freaks I've ever seen. Short haircuts, flannel shirts, struttin' and growlin' and comin' on to you. A disgrace. There should be a hospital or an island for creeps like them and this Charles. I want you to learn sex right."

"You're lying," I said to my mother.

She blinked her eyes, shocked. Her mouth opened slightly.

"You just don't like him because he sees through you," I said. "He knows what you are."

199

My mother slapped me. She bit her lip and slapped me again.

"Now, you listen to me, Rikki Nelson. I'm not some radical, left-wing theater type with my drugs and long hair and astrologist sayings. I'm your rightful mother and you'll respect me. I know a sicko when I see one and I can just imagine what sort of games he's been playing with you in his dresses and his wigs."

I stood up. "You're a horrible person," I said.

"*Sit down,*" my mother shouted. Her voice was so loud that half the café turned to watch us. My mother gritted her teeth.

"I can see you've been lacking discipline," she said. "It's good I came before you got too old and grew into a wild animal."

I shook with rage. I stood holding the back of my chair because I was afraid I might scream or break her glass. I was spiraling backward through time.

"The hot winds have turned evil," I shouted. "You've brought a spell."

My mother wiped the sweat off her upper lip with her napkin. "Well, if this ain't proof, I don't know what is," she said calmly. "You're a certified mental case. Maybe I'll just take you straight home after all."

Charles would've said that I went to the B side of my good-girl 45 record. That's what he said when I had a rare violent temper tantrum. Part of my body floated—disconnected and calm. It watched quietly as I threw my full glass of Coca-Cola in my mother's heavily made-up face. Then I flung the chair on the floor and took off. I raced through the winding, colorful carnival of Avignon until I reached our villa. I ran up the three flights of stairs and dashed into Charles's and my room.

His side of the room was completely bare. He'd packed and left. There was no sign for me, no note, no secret signal. Even the smell of incense was gone.

I stood in the middle of the floor and started to scream. The sound ripped at my throat and sent sharp pains through my stomach. I couldn't stop. I didn't want to. The silence would be killing. I began to rip at my hair and pounded at myself with my fists. Suddenly two strong hands grabbed mine. A voice said, "Shhh, shhh, breathe. Do as I say. Breathe." It was a voice I never disobeyed.

"Easy, little one," said Sasha. "Easy. Come back from this, now. It's a nightmare. Nothing's as bad as what you're dreaming."

I pretended to relax. I settled stiffly into his clean, bony arms and chest. I tried to cry, but I couldn't.

"That's better. Now the poison is flowing out."

After a while he sat on the floor cross-legged and gestured for me to do the same. His pale gray eyes held me with pity.

"Your face is as red as a tomato, little one. I ought to pluck you and eat you." There was no trace of an accent in Sasha's voice.

"You are quite remarkable." He smiled. "Screaming like a newborn infant fighting her way into this world."

"I don't care," I said.

Sasha smiled again. There was nothing condescending about his manner. "Yes, you do. You care too much. You've settled into this life of leisure and play. Like all of us, you've forgotten the difficulty of our work and you don't want to experience any more pain or struggle."

I glared at him.

"The only way to grow is to accept change," Sasha said. "Even if it's for the worse. You can't know where the frightening turn in the road is going to take you later on. You just have to keep walking."

I was not in the mood for Sasha's mystic poetry. I hid my face behind my hands.

"You took away Charles," I said. "You listened to my stupid lying mother and you fired Charles."

"I need to see your face, little one," he said.

We were having a tug-of-war.

"I need to see your face," he repeated. I lowered my hands and looked at him coldly. Sasha was still smiling at me. He didn't seem concerned.

"Your mother is coarse. And she's clearly uninterested in the cultural finery of our lives. She'd rather watch TV than see our work. And she challenges all the artsy, refined choices we've made in our clothes, our food, our wine, even our discussions. But there's a reason she forced her way into our lives. We've become self-satisfied. She's very real."

"I don't care what you think," I told Sasha. "She's just a bossy bitch. I want Charles."

"Charles isn't *fired*, little one," Sasha said with a laugh. "He's staying in town. Your mother is, after all, legally your mother. And you are maturing physically and mentally. Even Charles agrees that the old roommate situation might not be healthy anymore."

"Charles *said* that?" I asked.

Sasha took a moment to consider. "Charles knows, regardless of what he thinks."

"You're giving me back to her," I concluded. "After you promised I'd be yours. . . ."

Sasha shrugged. His eyes teared slightly. "Even broken promises are lessons. You learn that there's no exchange between two human beings that can't be destroyed by larger forces. It's the arbitrary nature of our existence, little one. This is your first death."

I felt like I was becoming invisible, disappearing into the light of the bare room. His tone became more desperate.

"Listen to me." He shook me by my shoulders. "Don't hide from me. I brought your mother here as an effort to keep you. I had every intention of fighting for you. In court, behind the scenes, with money, lawyers." He smiled. "Sicilian hit men. . . . You must realize how much I love you. This is the way I can *keep you*."

I nodded reluctantly. Sasha became melancholy and a bit dreamy.

"I think your mother is here to upset the whole balance of our lives. To bring us out of our lethargy and this plateau of repetition. Rehearsal, performance, dinner, travel. We've become superficial and boring. We've had no obstacles or real challenges until now."

I couldn't believe Sasha was so stupid.

"I realize," Sasha went on, "that the bond between mother and child is somehow utterly pure and sacred, and it's against nature to break it up. I want what's right for you. The protective instincts one's blood mother feels are ferocious and uncompromising. She wants you to have a real childhood. You should grow up as a young woman with many possibilities, not just theater."

"She doesn't care about anyone but herself," I said. "And you are using her to hurt Charles."

202

Sasha smiled. He was enjoying our conversation. "That's not true," he said. "Where does a little girl learn such devious thinking? Your mother may drink too much and say the wrong things, but she wants you back again, with a sincere longing. And I have no reason on earth to hurt my brother. I love him as she loves you."

My teeth chattered. My hands were cold. Sasha was lying and I was helpless.

"So I'm leaving?" I asked.

Sasha smiled again and shook his head. "Certainly not now. I told you I want to *keep* you. We have a whole month until the end of the tour. After that . . ." Sasha stared off; his eyes lost their focus. Then he yawned and stretched his long arms.

"None of us knows. Right? I have to create a whole new piece. The way I feel, it could take years. I want you to grow up, Rikki Nelson, without the odd unpredictability of this. . . . You've already seen too much too soon. Your mother demands that you have some time as a little girl. I can't disagree."

I felt devastated, but Sasha had managed to intrigue me with images of junior high school, art classes, chasing turtles in the bay, and reading the comics in the *Miami Herald*. He saw my thoughts immediately.

"That's why you're my girl," he said. "You listen from your soul. You and I have a very special connection. And I can be sometimes cold and clumsy in my judgments. But you are innocence and perfection to me. If I struggle, it's to try to give you the best life possible. I want you to be the person I have loved with the fewest mistakes. I can't keep you safe, but I can try to breathe the best of life into you. Like a lifeguard saving a drowning child. Real love is an emergency and the decisions have to be quick and vehement. God help me if I am wrong."

I needed sleep to drown out the warring voices in my head. I couldn't move. Sasha left me and I tried to imagine what Charles would say.

Foul play. Foul play. Kill the umpire, his voice echoed in my imagination. *You're being sold a bill of goods,* he warned me. *You're at a garage sale of two greedy eighty-five-year-old spinsters whose twenty-eight cats shit on all the merchandise. Smell it before you buy it.*

I must've stayed in my room for two or three days without leaving. Now and then I heard someone carefully check on me, but I couldn't rouse myself to see who it was. When I couldn't avoid wakefulness any longer, I lay in bed with my eyes closed. I didn't know in which direction I was lying. My feet seemed to be where my head had been. The bed felt as if it had moved to the opposite wall. I anxiously sat up, opened my eyes, and, although it was dark, I could make out that everything was relatively in place. It was late at night and, believing that the darkness would shield me, I inched my way off the bed. My mouth tasted thick and bitter. My hair was matted and sweaty. I summoned the courage to walk sideways to the shower and ran a light trickle over my head without removing my clothes. Reaching under my dress, I rubbed my body with a dry cake of soap and rushed out of the stall. I brushed my teeth without looking in the mirror. I decided to check the evil wind to see if it had changed. I carefully made my way to the balcony. I sat on the stone floor and stared through the iron railing into the cloudy night.

Before long I heard quiet laughter. I saw two figures stumble onto the patio. I realized that the drunken dancing shadows were my mother and Sasha. As they came into focus, I watched my mother throw her arms around Sasha and kiss him. She licked his lips and bit him. He laughed with pain and brought his hand up to his mouth. He laughed again and yanked at my mother's hair, pulled her to him, and bit back. She placed her hands on his bottom and pulled him roughly to her. Then she spanked him and he grabbed her hips and roughly pinched her. My mother took Sasha by the belt of his pants and pulled him to the deck chair. He followed her, stumbling and grinning. My mother sat heavily down on the deck chair and Sasha attempted to dive next to her, but she forced him to keep standing. He didn't resist. My mother began to stroke his legs and jerkily lifted up his Indian shirt and sucked on his stomach with wide wet kisses. Sasha let his hands hang and stood with his head tilted slightly back like a man asleep on the Metro. My mother untied the string on Sasha's pants and yanked them to his knees with one quick move. From my view, I could only see Sasha's smooth muscular cheeks contracting into rocks. I put my hand between my legs. My mother was bobbing back and forth like a bird with a long neck. Her shoulders moved forward and back like a Jew in prayer. The faster she moved, the more Sasha's bottom looked like the face of a mountain, and the rest of his body was frozen in stillness. At one point, my mother pulled back and looked up at him. She wiped her mouth with her fist.

"Well, teacher," she asked, "is this experimental theater or Chekhov?"

"Shakespeare," Sasha answered, and he grabbed her by her hair and yanked her forward again.

My mother's head and hands were hidden, but she was speeding up. She was like a train opening up on a flat stretch of track. I tightened my legs around my hand. My mother was wearing the outfit she'd bought with me and she was sitting with her legs spread apart so the leather miniskirt rode up her thighs. As she bent over, the full shape of her breasts was exposed. They were soft, white fruits. My mother's praying and bobbing and climbing became more frantic. Sasha's whole body was turning to rock but he stayed in an upright standing position. It was as if the blood had left his veins. He was dried bone. White and beautiful. Suddenly both of them gasped. It was like they'd killed each other. The solution pleased and scared me. But then I saw my mother smile nastily at Sasha and take a swig from a drink. Then she spat the drink on the grass. She leaned back on the deck chair and pulled her miniskirt all the way up to her hips. Sasha stepped out of his pants. He lowered himself onto the deck chair on top of my mother and tried to kiss her, but she turned her head. She caught Sasha off guard and pushed him off the deck chair onto his knees. Then she thrust her hips into his face. He turned his head. They both laughed, but my mother seemed to be in pain. She kept lifting her hips toward Sasha's face and he'd crawl back a step on the patio floor.

"What's the problem?" my mother snapped. "You're not like your brother, are you?"

Sasha sprung up, sat on her, nearly collapsing the chair, and slapped her. With pale, rigid arms he ripped at her discount fringe vest. My mother looked startled. And just then her focus fell on me.

She pushed at Sasha and pulled down her skirt. I tried to duck, but couldn't gather my senses fast enough to escape.

"What the *hell* do you think you're doing?" my mother yelled. "This has nothin' whatever to do with you."

Sasha's back was to me. He didn't turn around. He hardly twitched. My mother kept shouting while she straightened her hair. "This is for grown-ups, Rikki Nelson, and it's none of your damn business. You are positively strange. I'm exhausted. I'm takin' you home."

I quickly searched through my room and grabbed the few franc notes I found. I stuffed them into the embroidered shoulder bag Charles had made me, dashed down the stairs and out the heavy wood front door of the villa. I followed the winding road from the villa into the main square of the old village of Avignon. Despite the late hour, the midnight performances, demonstrations, and work-shops still had audiences. The square was lit by gasoline torches and the atmosphere seemed secretive and festive like Halloween. I told myself I could learn French and live in Avignon year round. I could hide there. I watched a man eat fire while he recited a monologue. I recognized the words "flame, fire, love . . ." I bought myself a sticky Italian ice, but had no stomach for it and let it fall on the ground. On a distant stage, a group of performers in white masks and white robes were hoisting an enormous cross that was scribbled with graffiti. A puppet in a business suit was attached to the cross and he bled dollar signs. On another platform a troupe of naked dancers jumped, spun, jerked, and fell to the ground in rigid, dis-torted poses. Somewhere else a man in a baggy suit was playing a saxophone.

I began to see all the images at once. I was light-headed and sick to my stomach. I needed to sit down, but I didn't want to be noticed. I went to a small stone fountain and soaked myself in the freezing water as I stared at the coins glistening at the bottom. I didn't have any coins for wishes. The reflection of the torches in the fountain's pool reminded me of Sasha's story about the moth who was so in love with the flame of a candle that he flew into it and disintegrated from his love. I had no love left in me, but the idea of burning to ashes seemed appealing. I wandered, crying out loud, for what seemed like hours. Then I recognized Peter's tent. The line in front of the entrance was as long as it had been the day Charles had taken me there. People sat amiably on sleeping bags and shared wine and sandwiches. I was too tired to stand up anymore. I slipped through the flap and crouched at the edge of the floor while Peter, dressed in his black velvet robe, introduced his finger puppets over a large black candle. I lowered my head onto my hands and breathed in the darkness and relative safety. I don't know if I blacked out or fell asleep, but suddenly I felt a hand on my shoulder. I looked up into Peter's round curious eyes and he smiled at me. The tent was deserted and Peter's small stage was covered with a dropcloth. His puppets were asleep in shoe boxes for the night. The black candle burned and in its flame Peter's pale, smooth face was as white as an angel or a vampire. I recoiled from him.

Peter squatted down and handed me a very tiny puppet. It was a bright-colored parrot made from papier-mâché and cotton. It fit perfectly on my forefinger.

"This is Sue," Peter said quietly. "Sue's a little ornery. She chews furniture and bites on occasion, but she's loyal as they come. The only thing she knows how to say is 'Fuck this—you motherfucker.' But you can teach her more words if you are in a state of wantness."

Peter dragged me to my feet and gathered up his shoe boxes. "Shhh," he said to me. "These divas need their sleepisms. And if they don't get it, it's hell to get them to perform."

He led me out of the tent and through the square.

"Everybody feels like they ought to be complete *weirdness* after dark," Peter said. "But darkness is contrast. That's when you can see shapes, lines, and expressions the most clearly."

I thought about my mother and Sasha. A sob broke from my throat.

"From what I understand," Peter drawled, "you all have been havin' 'bout as much fun as pignesses being led to slaughterisms."

We walked out of the main square and down one of the narrow, winding streets. We ended up in a very ancient section of Avignon with flickering street lamps and tiny stone buildings. The street seemed to be in miniature, exactly like Peter's work. We stopped at an inn that was only two stories tall. Each small window had faded blue shutters and flower boxes with swirls painted on. Peter opened the blue wooden door with a heavy brass key. There was an office off to one side and a small sitting room across the hall. There was a steep stone stairway that led to a landing. We tiptoed up the stairs. Peter gestured that we should sit on the landing.

"Talk quietly," Peter warned. "My landlady's a bulldogissima. She looks like one too. Her face is all folds and her lower jaw sticks out with extreme teethness." He showed me. I wanted to smile.

"Can I ask you a question?" Peter asked.

I averted my eyes.

"What would you think if I told you that Charles and I were like a boyfriend and girlfriend—only there's no girlfriend because we're both boys?"

I felt very weary. "I'm tired of sex," I said. "I don't care about sex. It's ugly."

"No, it's not," Peter whispered. "Not if you care for someone. It's like dancing inside your partner."

"Charles is a good dancer," I informed Peter. "Why can't Charles talk to me?"

"I think he thinks that you might think he's a fellow with cowardess," Peter said.

"Charles doesn't care what people think," I said.

"He cares what *you* think," Peter said.

"I think this is stupid," I said.

"This is a lot of thinking." Peter sighed.

"Really stupid," I repeated. I started to cry. "My mother ruined everything."

"That's what mothers do," Peter said.

"You sound like Charles." I sniffled. "Why didn't he stay? Why did he leave me?"

Peter folded his hands. He sat up straight.

"That's complicated. Boys like Charles and me, we can never be sure, or safe from what . . ."

I noticed Peter had abandoned his *nesses* and *isms*.

"Safe from *what?*" I asked.

"Like we said before," Peter said, "what people will think."

"Because you hug and kiss and touch each other?" I exclaimed. "How stupid!"

"I thought you'd think that," Peter said.

"Stop saying *think,*" I shouted, and shoved him.

Peter stood up. "Shhh," he warned me, "the bulldogissima."

He found another heavy key and unlocked a raw wooden door off the landing. Peter let me in and then turned around and went back downstairs. The room was lit with candles. Incense burned. The ceiling was so low, I could almost touch it with my hand. The room was all gray wood with thick beams and rusty tools hung on the walls. There was a mattress on the floor covered with a single white quilt. Charles lay on top of the quilt, one arm covering his eyes. He was fully dressed in patched jeans and a soft Indian shirt. His feet were dirty as if he'd been walking barefoot. I crawled onto the bed and he put his arm down and leaned his head at a weird angle against the wall. He reached for my hand and stroked the parrot puppet with his finger.

"Hello, Sue," he said.

Charles's eyes were red and swollen. His face was lined with tension. He'd been crying.

"I don't care," I said.

Tears filled Charles's eyes. His nose looked sore and red. He wiped it on his sleeve.

"I do." He shaped the words very slowly, opening his mouth wide, but making no sound.

"My mother's a pig. You said so yourself." I didn't understand why he was so frightened and sad.

Charles slid his head and neck a bit higher against the wall. "Yes, but legally, you see, she *is* your mother. She can do anything. Pick your wardrobe. Bring court action against me. Tie your shoes. Have me put in prison."

I didn't believe him. "For what?"

"Pussycat. It's complicated. And for once, it's a history I don't want to share with you. I'll just say that in many places men who like men are considered dangerous."

"There's no way my mother could arrest you," I said. "*She's* the one who's been in jail."

Charles plopped down on the bed again.

He growled. Then he moaned. Then he whistled. "This is Sasha's way of passing the time when he can't write," Charles said. "He conducts experiments with human sexuality and agony."

"You mean like the way he was with my mother tonight?" I asked.

Charles flung his hand over and grabbed mine. He squeezed his eyes shut.

"I don't want to hear this," he said.

I started to cry.

"And Sasha's making me go home with her. Nobody's stopping it. Nobody cares." I realized I sounded insufferably whiny, but I was beyond living up to people's standards of conduct—even Charles's.

Charles sat up. He let go of my hand and stretched his arms over his head with his fingers intertwined. His joints cracked. He looked like a bird. He shook his curls.

"I think I'd better pick another time to fall apart." He yawned.

"I don't understand." I wept. "I don't understand anything."

Charles leaned forward and brushed the tears from my eyes, nose, and chin. "A lot of this is about Sasha and me," he said. "You're the pickle in the middle and your mother is the invited guest performer. If it wasn't so diabolical, I'd applaud its inventiveness."

"*Ness, ness,*" I said.

"Yes. Peter." Charles smiled. "And you can stop whining now."

"He's better than Sasha," I said as confidently as possible.

Charles stood up and his head slammed into the ceiling. He bent over and howled in pain. He stamped his feet and clutched his head in his hands. Then abruptly he stopped.

"There," he said. "I'm thinking clearer. I'm three inches shorter and the top of my head has been pushed into my neck."

I started to cry again.

"Stop, stop," Charles said gently. "There's always a sliver in the linen. Into every fife a little Spain gets rained. There's always tempura. Look, look, look to the Rimbaud."

Charles began to throw clothes into his embroidered bag—the

one that matched mine. "Rikki Nelson, listen to me, if you could go anywhere in the world, where would you go?"

I didn't have to think about it.

"California," I said. "I'd like to see Disneyland, Sea World, and a ghost town and a movie studio."

Charles squealed with laughter.

"Okay," he said. "Let's kidnap each other and steal across the ocean on a freighter. Are you ready?"

Charles led me down the stairs and we stopped at the sitting room across from the inn's office. Peter sat cross-legged on the floor sewing a miniature priest's costume for one of his puppets. He'd cut the white collar out of a straw.

Charles knelt down next to Peter and spoke softly to him in French. Peter nodded and smiled. He looked up at me and gave me the okay sign. Peter and Charles embraced each other and kissed each other on both cheeks. Neither appeared to be upset.

"What about Peter?" I asked Charles. We were rushing toward the train station. It was nearly dawn.

"Peter has to work," Charles said. "Don't worry."

"What about *our* work?" I asked guiltily.

Charles stopped and knelt down on one knee.

"There's no work right now. Sasha sees this mess with your mother as very important and interesting for his research. If a raven dive-bombed an infant's crib, he'd find that interesting too. I don't happen to agree."

"I don't agree either," I said.

"Good." Charles smiled. "Then let's be disagreeable."

Charles bought two train tickets to Paris with a stop in Nice.

"I want to take you swimming," he said, "and buy you some overpriced outfits." We left the interior of the train station and headed toward the tracks. Charles suddenly stopped and I skidded into his back and held on. Sasha and my mother were sitting on the stone bench next to the outer wall of the old station. My mother was almost hidden behind her pile of matching blue suitcases. I don't know whether she saw me or not. She turned her back and lit a cigarette. Sasha rose slowly from the bench and walked toward Charles.

"You look like hell," Sasha said. He leaned around Charles to catch a glimpse of me, but I evaded him by burying my face in Charles's shirt.

"Are you going somewhere?" Charles asked.

"No," Sasha replied. He gestured vaguely in the direction of my mother. "She decided it was best."

"Mmmm." Charles nodded. "Sort of like the cease-fire after the country's been leveled, all the men executed, the women raped, and the children starved to death."

"That's a little extreme." Sasha smiled. "Where are you two going?"

"Away," Charles replied. "Where a man's ability to be a good mother isn't judged by the boys he sleeps with."

"That could be difficult," Sasha said.

"Well, you would think that," Charles said. "You're homophobic."

"What's homophobic?" I asked. My head was still lodged in Charles's shirt.

"Can you breathe in there, Pussycat?" Sasha asked.

"It's like hemophiliac. Hemophiliacs bleed too much," Charles said. "Homophobics hate too much."

"I hate nothing," Sasha said. "I do not hate."

Charles's voice became edgy. "Yes, but you enjoy witnessing the hate you provoke in others. Why do you waste your talents orchestrating disasters?"

"I think I'm learning," Sasha said slowly, "that the depravity I claim to see in others is really in me. The work I tell others to do on their weaknesses is the work I must do on myself. And the pain I cause with my manipulations and judgments is only half what I would feel if I dared to judge myself."

"Well spoke," Charles said. "You could run for orifice." He patted Sasha on the back.

The train whistled from a faraway point and Charles put his arm around me and steered us away from the tracks. "I don't think we like this train," he said loudly. "We'll have to wait till the next train."

"Charles, what are you doing?" I cried.

"We can't take *that* train," he said. "You want to be on a Freudian symbol with your mother?"

I looked over my shoulder at the approaching train. My mother stood up and brushed her denim miniskirt, pulled down her halter top. Without directing her eyes in our direction, she called out to me.

"Rikki Nelson, come here."

I refused to move.

"I'm not gonna *take* you, girl. Come *here*."

I slid sideways toward where she stood, making sure I was close to the wall so she couldn't drag me on the train. My mother stood with her hands on her hips, tapping her foot impatiently.

"Come *here*," she repeated.

I refused to move from the pillar I'd hid behind, so my mother stomped forward.

"Are you a mental case or what?" She turned for a moment to check that her luggage was being hauled off the platform onto the train. A porter was busy with the heavy suitcases.

"*Garçon! Garçon!* Whatever you are, be careful with that stuff."

She leaned over to me and thrust a powdery cheek toward my lips. I kissed her lightly. She batted her eyes at me. I think she meant to be funny. I didn't smile.

"Go back to the hotel and take a bath," she whispered. "Put some powder under your arms, okay?"

Her eyes teared. She dug around in the straw bag she was carrying.

"Here, I bought you this." She sniffed. She handed me a key chain made of a large coin. The village of Avignon was etched onto the coin and the block letters said AVIGNON FESTIVAL. I held my mother's hand, pretending to examine the present. Her hand was golden from the sun and smooth from the creams she used. Her long red fingernails were as silent and graceful as five of Peter's puppets wearing bright red hoods. My mother gently pulled her hand away and rushed in small, quick steps toward the train. She wore very high heels, and for the first time, I noticed her ankles were just a little thick and her calves muscular, but stubby. The conductor helped her up the stairs to the train and she began to talk to him about her luggage. I couldn't hear the whole conversation.

I turned around and saw Sasha and Charles leaning against the station wall like two teenage boys. If it wasn't for Charles's curls and spectacles and Sasha's shoulder-length mane, they could've been mirror images. They talked secretly to each other with identical frowns. They gestured in tandem. Charles took a few steps toward me and put his arm through mine. I handed him the key chain.

"Lovely," he said. I expected him to make a snide comment, but instead he found one of my pockets and tucked the key chain carefully inside. Then Sasha caught my other arm and we took long unison strides like Dorothy, the Scarecrow, and Tinman.

"I'll be glad when we leave here," Sasha said. "It's just as the Gypsies say. The winds seduce you and then make you totally mad."

"Three or four years ago a belly dance company was performing," Charles mused. "You remember the ladies from Suriname who danced to Janis Joplin."

"Very well," Sasha said.

"Well, their boa constrictor got loose and strangled several dogs and a child before they shot it with a sleeping bullet," Charles said. "The Suriname belly dancers offered to destroy the snake, but the villagers said absolutely not—it wasn't the snake, it was the winds. I tend to think it was the snake."

"I don't want you to leave," Sasha said plaintively. "The success we've experienced hasn't made me free. I am facing a wall. I can't get over it. How can my work go on without the two of you?"

Charles remained silent. After a while he said, "There's another train to Paris at four."

Sasha bent his head, forcing Charles and me to slow down with him.

"It can't end like this," Sasha murmured. "If it ends like this, then my whole work is a failure."

"Why are we suddenly so important?" Charles said. "How can we be responsible for twenty-five years of your life?"

"We're all responsible for each other," Sasha said plaintively.

"Today we are," Charles replied. "Were we yesterday? You've always had such a convenient memory."

Charles and I remained silent.

"Allow me to be sorry, Charles," Sasha said. "I've certainly allowed you your tantrums. Stay with me until I break through this wall. I knew who I was. I knew what theater was. Now I know nothing."

"You'll figure it out, bro," Charles said gently. "You always do."

"The theater is no longer the answer for me." Sasha sighed. "It's like a death."

Charles reached past my shoulder and patted Sasha on his head.

"What about Rikki Nelson?" Charles asked. "She may be short, but she's a person."

Sasha spoke as if I weren't there. "I'm ashamed to have her look at me. I'm terrified to face her."

"Well, she's right here listening to this whole opera and she wants to go to California," Charles said. We were close to the villa and I could barely walk. All I wanted to do was lie down.

"Then she should go," Sasha said with a sigh. "You both go."

"I'm too tired right now," I said to Charles. "I have to nap."

"Rikki Nelson seems to think the future of the theater and the redemption of your damaged soul can wait until after a nap," Charles said to Sasha. Sasha lifted his head and quickened his pace. Charles and I had to adjust our speed to keep up with him.

"I'm going to be celibate," Sasha said. "I'm going to go back to doing the Tibetan prostrations and yoga breathing and eating properly. I intend to isolate myself and read extensively on shamanism. I'm going to practice silence for five hours each day. I'll only sleep at fifteen-minute intervals. No more interviews, restaurants, or superficial conversations. I'm going to practice the most painful stretching and muscle-building exercises. I'm going to take steaming hot baths until I sweat out all my past influences, the corruptive forces and the temptations that led me off the path. I'll reduce myself to a shell of nothingness and then I'll listen to the silence as if I'm deaf. I'll live in the darkness as if I'm blind. I'll wait in the emptiness to see what grows in me."

"Sounds like fun," said Charles. "But don't forget to make an outline."

We approached the villa. I was actually relieved to see the wide French windows of my room. The whole *Myth Man* company was out on the patio. Kosher led them in a clear slow series of tai chi poses. They seemed light and careless as the birds that flew over the harbor. Each step flowed with the precision and unity of one person.

Once inside the villa, I climbed, exhausted, to my room and went directly to the balcony where I'd seen Sasha and my mother grabbing, hitting, and holding each other the night before. Kosher and the actors looked so clean and peaceful. There was no trace of the battle I'd witnessed. If Sasha or my mother had bled, the blood had been washed away. The air was free of haze. There were no ghosts lurking behind the thick old trees. Charles joined in on the tai chi and he looked like a man who was breathing in spite of having a serious illness in his heart. His arms and legs were light, but he was gasping. Slowly, his breath evened out and he became one of them. The hot winds had turned on us and made us mad, but the memory of evil was already beginning to fade. I heard Sasha's flat, sharp steps move slowly on the stone stairs. The sound didn't echo but disappeared bit by bit. The sky was striped with orange, blue, and gray clouds. It was wide and open and still. No wind rushed across the tops of the trees. Only a gentle breeze. As I watched the actors, I became afraid the river would rise up and become a sea that would devour all of Avignon. Vertigo caused me to step back and reach for my bed. I needed to sleep. I reached into my pocket and touched the key chain my mother left with me. I lay down on the bed and closed my eyes. I felt the edge of the metal coin digging into my side. It pinched, causing a very slight discomfort. I didn't have the energy to change positions or take the key chain from my pocket. I fell asleep to the silence of the tai chi, with the cool light coming through the French windows and the hard metal of the key chain pressing, like a long fingernail, into my ribs.

EXPERIMENTAL THEATER IN THE JUNGLE

CHAPTER 11

XI. *Please state, in a short paragraph, the general scope of work your non-profit institution intends to accomplish. Do not exceed the given space or include cover letters.*

After a combination of objective observation and serious personal inquiry, I have come to the conclusion that the whole system of Western arts as we know it has decayed to the point where it has become irrelevant and decadent. We separate painting from life. We separate theater from the activities of daily life. We sell music as a commodity. We dress dancers in leotards and isolate them on platforms to be viewed like clothes on a rack. Western art forms have fallen to a level where they are expected to "distract," "inform," or tell the "author's" story. Even the most so-called daring works are nothing but veiled "entertainment." We who attend artistic events are treated to nothing more than a parade of egos. I wish to remove my company from the narcissism of this atmosphere and attempt to create a kind of performance which isn't performance at all. I want to merge life and art. I want to discover a part of the world where men and women still combine their daily activities with artistic, spiritual exercises and take my group to live among them. I've chosen the Amazon because the jungle itself is full of rhythms, colors, and sounds which can teach us about the purest act of nonperformance—the art of being. I have had my associate, Randy Paul, an executive at PBS, research the third world for tribes with a rich ritual life that remains untouched by Western influence. Several tribes of the southern Amazon remain relatively undisturbed by tourism or exploitation of the rich environment. They would be perfect partners for an intense six-month exchange with my international company of performers. We hope to teach nothing. Only to learn. We won't imitate customs or falsely convert to their ways. We will absorb this atmosphere. I guarantee no "buyable" result. I want my group to come away with a deeper understanding of the sources of arts. We have to get back to the place where art is a natural extension of the journey between birth and death. I hope we can experience the mystery of the unknown.

XII.   *Please demonstrate a breakdown of your monetary needs without showing specific costs. You will attach a detailed budget under separate cover as prepared by your business manager.*

1. Salaries for fifteen actors. I cannot ask them to abandon their responsibilities at home, although I will encourage them to use as little money as possible during this phase of our work.
2. Salaries and equipment for Ms. Randy Paul. Ms. Paul has her master's degree from Yale, has been a journalist

with *TDR* and the *Village Voice,* and has published numerous essays. She will direct all documentation of the trip on film, and keep detailed notes as well. We have agreed that, once we have established the appropriate contact with the Indian population, documentary footage of our successes and failures with them could prove to be invaluable to our learning process as well as that of others who choose to work in this fashion. Furthermore, a sensitively shot documentary will fulfill your requirements of "developing a form which will demonstrate the process of your work to the public." We will need an added amount for Ms. Paul's small film crew and equipment.

3. We intend to employ an experienced, environmentally sensitive tour guide company to assist us in our initial trek through the jungle. We expect this company to provide the equipment and knowledge of jungle travel to get us to the village areas we have chosen. We see them as flexible guides who will be properly tolerant, if not enthusiastic, about the nature of this experiment. They will supply:

A. 7 Land Rovers.

B. A truck.

C. Cooking and kitchen equipment.

D. Medical equipment. We will bring a certified medic or nurse, but intend to rely on the wisdom of our Indian hosts for whatever doctoring we require.

E. Emergency radio equipment, which will enable us to communicate with a central office in a nearby village.

F. 30 tents and sleeping bags.

G. Proper water supplies as well as maps to natural waterfalls, streams, etc.

H. Mosquito nets and any other protective devices needed to shield us from the insect life of the jungle.

I. Weapons for protection if necessary.*

4. We intend to put a substantial amount of equity aside to use as compensation or to purchase the proper kind of symbolic compensation for the Indians we'll encounter, in return for our camping on their land. We don't expect these people to participate in the exchange with us for free. We do not want to repeat the mistakes of past imperialist occupiers by corrupting an innocent culture with unneeded material distractions, but we want to be of use if special medical treatments are needed, or if, say, the Indians want a play park for their children or want to dig a well. Peter Hyde points out bartering, exchanging dances for dances, poetry for poetry and song for song is the purest form of economic trade. But we must be prepared for any unexpected requests which, when filled, will help the Indians trust us more fully.

5. Rent and salaries for the Myth Man office in New York so it can function while we travel.

6. Plane tickets, inoculations, visas, and any governmental or border taxes.

7. Hotel and per diem for all company members before and after our entrance into the jungle. We've been advised to spend a week in a civilized city to become acclimated to the time change and to attend the special preparatory classes administered by Tropical Treks, Inc.

8. Contingencies: Insurance and travel expenses for part-

---

* As we adapt more and more to Amazon customs, we intend to become less and less reliant on the services of the tour company crew. We will, however, utilize the tour guides' expertise especially since South and Central America have been fraught with civil war. After a while I hope the tour guides will become a part of our global village. We plan to employ Tropical Treks, a reliable tourist company which specializes in adventures and independent clients. Their company is recognized by the International Tourist Association and serves groups interested in jungle exploration from Puerto Rico to Africa to Central and South America. They have also driven many well-known journalists and U.N. and government inspectors into war zones.

time participants. (Meaning: evaluators from the foundations, poets and artists from the region, spouses and lovers.)

9. Any possible theatrical devices—set pieces, costuming, paint, or tools.

10. Emergency equipment: The rental of a helicopter service in case of injury. The hiring of a security force if we, by chance, accidentally enter a war zone.

XIII.   *If you intend this to be a matching grant, please list the other donors, foundations and corporations who have expressed interest or who have already donated funds toward your project.*

1. The Preston DeVane Foundation	$1,000,000.00
2. The Rockefeller Fund	250,000.00
3. The Brazilian Government	300,000.00
4. The Argentine Government	100,000.00
5. Anonymous—Saudi Arabia	100,000.00
6. Anonymous—Minister of Culture—Jordan	50,000.00
7. The French Government— Minister of Culture	1,000,000.00
8. Mobil for International Arts	150,000.00
9. The Charles Solomon Fund—Seed Money	250,000.00
10. Dow Looks to the Future	50,000.00
11. The America del Sur Alliance	10,000.00
12. Exxon Salutes Central America Fund	100,000.00
13. Coca-Cola del Sur	300,000.00

XIV.   *What is the estimated overall cost for your administrative needs and the execution of the project you described in paragraph XI?*

$7,500,000.00 after taxes. This is a large sum, but not when you consider that we are trying to create a village and a way of life.

XV. *As stated in the guidelines (26) you will be including a resume or curriculum vitae under separate cover. Please list in this box any publications about or relative to your organization as a whole or essays, articles or books you have published.*

1. *Travels with the Myth Man*—Hawk Press—essays by Randy Paul
2. *Masks, Puppetry and Silence*—*Tulane Drama Review*
3. *The Visual World of Sasha Volotny: Collected Articles*—NYU Press
4. *She Was Silent*—Nancy Duchess and Wendell Cates—Grove Press
5. *The Healing Powers of the Myth Man: Ancient Trickster Rituals*—Black Sparrow Press—Introduction by Sasha Volotny
6. *Journey*—Red Rock Press (Philosophy and Indian lore)
7. *Myth Men: The Directors of a New Theater*—reviewed by A. E. Hart—Grove Press
8. *The Magical Theater of Sasha Volotny*—TCG Press—Cover article

XVI. *Please list no more than ten names of individuals who you feel can give us a fair recommendation and sponsorship for your work as well as an intelligent evaluation of your past accomplishments.*

1. Archbishop Theodore B. Raphael—Los Angeles, California
2. Rebbe Abraham Jacob Gellman—New York City
3. Swami Sri Chilam Avinay—Madras, India
4. Joe Elk Morgan—Elder—Sedona, Arizona, Hopi Nation
5. Chief Ine Dala—Uruba Nation—Ife, Nigeria
6. Thadeus Kremmel—Director, Rotterdam Opera
7. Richmond Killigan—Theater critic and journalist—Harvard University

8. Lady Stephanie Durgess—Historian, archaeologist, & anthropologist—Oxford University
9. Rok Mok—Nationally recognized street storyteller and children's advocate, U.S.A.
10. Muhammad Ben Hagin—Muezzin and High Priest— Jamaica, Queens, New York.

We will include, under separate cover, the most current reviews of our international tour and a few choice letters from audience members.

XVII. *In a paragraph, please state what you intend to accomplish during the period of time you have outlined in cover letter 2B.*

I have no expectations and no goals. To enter into this situation with any sort of specific show in mind would violate the whole meaning of the process.

XVIII. *Please use this space to inform the Foundation of any facts which might not have been covered by the questions on the applications or the separate materials you are submitting under separate cover.*

Even the dreams of the sleeper
can be invaded
by the wish to dream.
It is when the warrior
is empty of hunger
that his prey
crosses his path.
                          Cherokee Poem

E.S. says to talk to Sasha about trying to bring Indians back to U.S. for N.Y.–California Latino Festival.—M.K.

J.M. is concerned about directing too much funding towards global oriented work and not concentrating enough on separate races, i.e. the Didgereedoo Band from New Guinea, Clog Dancers from Appalachia, Carlos' Rhumba Theater. Let's be careful not to bleed our funds towards foreign projects. Might be accused of racism in U.S. Make sure when we announce Sasha's grant, we precede it with grants to East L.A., Harbor of Southside of Chicago, etc.

Do we give the whole million at once or half for the first three months and half after observation in the jungle? Who's going to be our on site observer? The Bank of Brazil can facilitate the disbursement of funds with minimum administrative costs.—E.L.

Sasha has to allow a little publicity on this. Can't give money to a vacuum.—P.T.

Military in Brazil is expected to begin another offensive against radicals and guerrillas and dissident tribes in the jungle. The timing of this grant is perfect. We'll be creating a neutral "spiritual" force that's on neither side of the fence. Must emphasize that this work is apolitical.—C.B.

226

CHAPTER 12

I'd never seen wild parrots before, lined up on the branches of trees the way crows line up on a telephone wire. And sometimes six-foot iguanas crossed our leafy path like raccoons on a highway. Curtains of thin leaves hung from the trees like the long plaited hair of black women and sometimes the webs of the vines became so thick we had to stop the Land Rovers and our guides took out machetes to cut their way through. Whole tribes of butterflies rested on bushes like flowers. It startled me when they suddenly took flight. During the first miles of our trip, the sky was still visible, but as we drove farther and farther on the muddy trails, the trees seemed to lean in and join arms with each other, blocking out pure sunlight and letting in only bright thin strands. As our Land Rovers crawled along the narrow, muddy paths, I understood why our guides said the jungle was a cathedral. The green ceiling curved over us like praying hands. I was assigned to the second Land Rover with Bruce, Charles, Robin, and Surni, a new actor from Bali. His face was round and his eyes bulged like on a mask. He had a wide grin and a high mischievous way of laughing. He barely spoke English, but nodded incessantly as if he were understanding every conversation, even when no one was talking. Our driver was a British thug named Chetter, whom Bruce was sure was a mercenary. Chetter chain-smoked and rolled his own cigarettes, and drove with a heavy hand on the gears. He dominated the conversation whenever he could and liked to scare me with stories of poisonous snakes and insects and odd, gory sights he'd seen in his work. He had a short beard and a long ponytail. When he talked, he swiveled around to focus on us. I was sure we'd slide off the dug-up road into a mass of vines or pile of sticky plants. By the end of the first week I'd grown used to Chetter's driving, but some of his stories bothered me. I was excited, but on edge because Sasha had decided we'd travel without any specific destination. It was like being inside a dream, not knowing when you'd wake up, nervous whether the images would remain beautiful and strange or turn into a nightmare. Sasha was buoyant and loving when we set off from the Ramada Inn in São Paulo.

"It's simple," he said to the group. "The less we know, the more we can be surprised. I want all of us to wake up, to gasp, to live a real adventure!"

Chetter turned out to be a boozy, rather morbid guide. He had an encyclopedic knowledge of the foliage as well as the animal life of the jungle. But by the end of the first week of bumping along the uneven roads and trails, he changed his monologues to grisly war stories and would turn with a leer to check out our reactions.

One such story he told on our first day in the jungle. "Once the military, you know, they told a bunch of Indians that they was gonna relocate them to a brand-new village. Soldiers came and gathered up the whole lot. Old men, women, children, and loaded 'em on one of those pesticide planes. Took 'em up in the air, flew a bit farther in, you know—then opened up the trap and dropped the whole bunch like human bombs onto another village. It was hailing corpses. The folks got impaled on trees, stuck upside down in mud, blew apart in the air. Heads, hands, and feet was falling from the sky onto the thatched rooves of this other village. It was a warning, mind you. Military didn't want the Indians having no sympathy with rebels. Didn't matter, though. Eventually the military sent in special forces and burned the second village to the ground."

"Can't you just keep telling us the names of the plants?" Bruce asked. "I'm pretty up-to-date on the slaughter in Central and South America."

Chetter laughed and Surni giggled. Robin kept wiping the sweat off her forehead with towelettes. Charles leaned over the side of the Land Rover.

"Stop, stop, stop!" Charles yelled.

Chetter growled and crunched on the brake. We all fell forward.

"Gonna hold up the caravan," Chetter said to Charles. "Rule number one—don't fuck with the caravan."

"One second," Charles said. He waded into the knot of jungle on the side of our primitive road.

"You should fucking be wearing socks," Chetter called out. "You're fresh meat for the snakes and spiders."

Charles advanced like a hunter. He bent his long body over, picked up a bright-colored feather, inched slightly forward, and clamped his hands over something. The horns from the five Land Rovers behind us started to blare. Charles leaped back to his seat.

"Thanks," he said to Chetter.

"You damn hippie." Chetter grinned. "When we get farther in, I can't let you be a Boy Scout."

Charles uncovered his hand and showed me a tiny green iguana with an orange belly.

"What shall we name it?" Charles asked.

"Tarzan," Bruce offered.

"It's a girl," I said.

"Then she's Jane," Charles said. "Sit, Jane. Lie down, Jane. Fetch." Robin and Surni laughed. I noticed that Robin's clothes were soaked with sweat. She looked like she'd just come out of a shower. She'd taken to pouring her canteen over her head.

"Careful with that, darlin'," Chetter said. "Once we get deeper in, even boilin' the river water doesn't do a bit of good. It's full of nasty parasites. Save your requisitions."

The lead Land Rover was called the Control. Sasha, Kosher, Randy

Paul, and a Finnish documentary cameraman hired by PBS sat crowded in the back. The cameraman's name was JoJo and Sasha said he had years of experience filming in jungles, wars, underwater, and in deserts. He, Sasha, and Randy Paul talked about the camera's relationship to nature. Kosher slid down as far as he could in his seat. He wore a gauze mask and a safari hat from which hung a veil of mosquito netting. Charles said he looked like a combination of Ben Casey, M.D., and Katharine Hepburn in *The African Queen*. Kosher was terrified of bugs and germs. He believed Japanese blood had no immune system for any sickness south of the equator. The Tropical Treks crew tried to assure him that they'd taken several tours of Japanese businessmen straight to the Amazon in search of a location for luxury hotels and condos, but Kosher didn't believe them. The driver of the Control Land Rover was a huge bearlike man named Klerck with a thick brown beard, short-cropped hair, and watery blue eyes. He must've been six-foot-five and he always had a bottle of Dos Equis in one hand. He was quiet and droll and enjoyed being the designated leader. He like to brag about the rich men whom he'd led into the jungle. Mostly he watched us with a drunken, mocking leer. Bruce was convinced that Klerck was not only a mercenary, but CIA as well.

"I *know* it," Bruce kept saying. "He kills people with electrical cords and his bare hands."

Sasha sat next to Klerck in the passenger seat dressed in khaki Bermudas, a white T-shirt, and a safari hat the group had given him as a present. I'd never seen him so excited. He constantly turned around and waved to us. During lunch breaks, when we'd stop and the crew passed out plastic packages of tea, sandwiches, and potato chips, Sasha visited each Land Rover and said over and over, "This is *fantastic*. It's primal. Never in a *thousand* years could you paint these colors. The quality of noise is unique. Have you noticed those moments of sudden silence? It's like all of nature stops and then *boom*, it starts up again."

"I think this is Sasha's way of having a vacation," Charles said. "When we were kids he loved watching Rat Pack and jungle movies. I don't know why he didn't just buy us all tickets to Hawaii and rent himself a Land Rover." But Charles smiled lovingly at Sasha as he watched him run from jeep to jeep, grabbing Reeva and making her touch a flower or yanking at Juno and Bruce and telling them they had to look at a certain spear of light.

The other Land Rovers in the caravan were driven by the members of the Tropical Treks crew: the cook, the mechanic, and the "med." They hauled the heavy equipment from the jeeps to the improvised campsites, packed and unpacked our cooking gear, and acted as gofers for Klerck and Chetter. Their Land Rovers held the rest of the actors, the PBS documentary assistant director and sound men, and one very old wrinkled creature who wore madras trousers, no shirt, and went barefoot. The old man hopped on when we arrived at the jungle and had been introduced to us as King. Klerck said he would be our translator in case we ran into any people who spoke rare Indian languages. King's milky eyes often had an amused, lecherous expression. His leathery skin was a mask of scars and tattoos. Short white hairs prickled from the top of his head, and when he grinned or scowled, his eyes disappeared into the folds of his face. When he opened his mouth, two or three reddish brown teeth stuck out unevenly from brown gums. His body, though slightly hunched, was lean and muscular. Pictures of suns and moons covered his arms and bare chest. They were raised mosaics —a combination of more tattooing and scars. King never spoke, but he was always first in the food lines and took cigarettes, chocolates, and gum from the Tropical Treks guides as if he were an animal they were taming by the technique of positive rewards. Bruce was infuriated by what he called the condescending attitude the Tropical Treks had toward a "minority individual." Bruce said they treated King as if he had no intelligence or spirit. But King had no use for conversations with Bruce about the jungle, Mayan mythology, or the fascist brutality of military regimes. King just grinned at him, waiting for a cigarette, a Certs, and he loved orange Tic Tacs. If he was lucky, Robin donated one of her coveted, melted-down miniature Snickers bars. Sasha adored King and he told several of us that he was a perfect example of pure decadence and animal spirituality. Several evenings, Sasha tried to get King to dance or sing ancient

Mayan rituals and King would make up a few hops or twists, a yodel, or a toothless, indecipherable story. Sasha knew he was faking, but showered the old man with food and smokes anyway.

The traveling company was so large that Charles called it the Cecil B. DeMille Bus and Truck Tour—I never counted, it was like a circus train of fully loaded vehicles to get us through the jungle. It took eight months in New York after the end of our European tour for Mrs. Preston DeVane, Charles, and Sasha to finish raising enough funds for the number of people Sasha wanted to take.

Charles said that when Sasha finally decided where his work was to go next he wanted nothing less than to settle a village of his own in the wilderness. "He developed a pilgrim complex," Charles said. "His new goal was to reinvent Thanksgiving." Sasha believed that once his new village found its identity, rituals, songs, and dances, he could create a whole new life for the group. We would be unencumbered by the habits, rules, and temptations of Western culture. But the company, happy to be back in New York after the *Myth Man* tour, had resisted at first. During a long meeting at the warehouse, Reeva said it was just a white man trying to imitate what blacks and Indians had been forced to do from the beginning of time. What was the luxury of being a refugee? Bruce said it was cultural pirating. Mustafa said it sounded like it would be boring as hell and too much lifting and building. And there were other complaints. Kosher worried about the effect of the dampness on his puppets. "Go to desert," he said, "much better." Charles stuck up for Sasha. "Hey, it's a free trip to the land of sambas," he said. "It's exotic. Think of the postcards you can write." Robin pointed out that actors from all over the world traveled to New York on the chance that they could participate in a workshop with Sasha. Some kids just arrived at his door, hoping. We were lucky to be included in his plans. Time and again Sasha asked the group if any one of them was happy with their love life, their daily regimen, the future of their careers, their families, or their individual spiritual and moral growth. I was surprised to see that each actor admitted to being isolated and adrift. Journey was the only one who claimed to have found "a peace deeper than contentment." He told Sasha he had, as a shaman, found a way to be as light as the butterfly in the air and as grounded as the coyote on earth. He said he'd be honored to join hands with his Spanish forefathers. Sasha looked at Journey and burst into laughter. Journey's eyes clouded behind his wide movie-star smile. Sasha hugged him. "I am laughing at myself," he said. And Journey joined in with his loud, long bass. The meeting lasted sixteen or seventeen hours, but by the end, everyone agreed to take the trip with an "open and positive heart," as Sasha insisted. Charles said the proposed documentary "didn't hurt the struggle to give up our lives to the unknown," but I noticed that Sasha's gentleness and enthusiasm erased a lot of the disappointment that there'd be no show in New York and no real performing for a long time. For me there wasn't any decision to make. Charles and Sasha were a team again. Where they went, I followed. They were my home.

After a fourteen-hour plane ride to São Paulo, Brazil, we checked into the Ramada Inn for rest and orientation. Sasha asked that the group not go exploring or dancing. We'd need all our energy for the months ahead. No one disobeyed. Even Charles stayed still. He said São Paulo looked like Detroit and the outdoor samba clubs and voodoo were too hard to find without some major research in the all-night cafés.

The "Trekkies," as Bruce called them, gave us an orientation lecture in the Ramada ballroom. We were assigned sleeping bags and canteens, taught how to pitch a tent, showed slides of poisonous snakes and plants, and shown the code that the guides used on the horns of their Land Rovers to alert the caravan. One beep was stop. Two beeps meant lunchtime. Three beeps was the signal for campsite, unpack the gear. A long, sustained tone meant emergency, wait for Control. Two long tones meant the emergency was over. Sasha asked if it was necessary to communicate in such a blaring, obvious way, but Klerck told Sasha the jungle was no joke. He also said we must never venture anywhere away from the Land Rovers alone. The jungle swallowed lost travelers. Sasha quietly confided in the group that he thought the guides were rather gloomy and anal. We'd find our own way, he promised, and if we really kept in tune with each other, no one would need these hysterical horns.

The next day we set out on anonymous, dreary highways that turned into dirt roads. After a week of fifteen-hour days, we came to the mouth of a wall of knitted trees and tangled vines. Before we entered the jungle, Sasha had us stand in a straight line and stare at "the door of our most mysterious theater." The Tropical Treks, Inc., staff stood behind us and smirked.

At the outset of our journey, Sasha and Klerck had argued over the number of passengers per jeep. Klerck complained that we were exceeding the recommended weight for the tires. We would be crowding bodies onto small seats in a dangerously hot climate. Sasha explained that a bit of discomfort was nothing to the strong, healthy bodies of his people. This wasn't a tourist expedition. They also disagreed about how much gear should be packed in the Land Rovers and truck. Kosher insisted on bringing his puppets. Charles added some masks and costumes. Mustafa thought a load of tools would come in handy. Randy Paul needed lights, tripods, cords, a generator, and other heavy items to guarantee the best work from JoJo. Klerck sneered at Sasha as if he were going to be glad to watch him sink into quicksand with all his unnecessary luxuries. Charles said the two of them were clearly in a power struggle for Chief of the Motorized Village.

We drove from dawn to dusk. We crawled along on rutted, muddy trails. We covered very little territory, but the hours passed quickly. Charles, Robin, and Bruce traded songs from musical comedies, folk, and rock-and-roll albums. Bruce imitated Aleister Crowley and invented classic jungle tales starring Beaver Cleaver and Mary Tyler Moore.

"This week," he mumbled in a low, dull drone, "Mary tries to seduce Beaver with some fresh-squeezed papaya juice, but Beaver, overwhelmed by the spiders crawling in his soup-bowl haircut, falls backward onto a cactus and, thus impaled, waits for Wally to return from collecting slugs by the rivah."

When we ran out of games like Concentration and mimicking Jimi Hendrix and Barbra Streisand, Chetter was always ready with an anecdote about Kenya or India or the Southern Pacific. Someone was always being tortured or maimed. Whole populations wiped out. He talked about rape, slaughter, earthquakes, and high tides.

We stopped only for lunch and several "pee breaks." Our orders were to eat from our box lunches standing up. And the women were instructed to try not to squat too low while peeing. Klerck said that poison ivy was like a mosquito bite compared to the rashes and skin fungus you could get from some of the foliage in the jungle.

Early on, the cook and the med, two rangy, rather towering, and muscular women in their early thirties, lectured the whole company on the proper positions for defecation in the out-of-doors. They demonstrated how much we should bend our knees and lean forward. They used a large pair of bikini bottoms to show how far forward or backward we should pull our underpants, hand clenched around the crotch, in order to avoid spraying them by accident. The cook and the med were accustomed to rich, adventure-seeking tourists and hadn't encountered actors before. They weren't prepared for the giddy humor that exploded into a graphic song-and-dance improvisation by Charles, Robin, Reeva, and Bruce during the question-and-answer period. The improvised song included a harmonized honky-tonk chorus:

> *Do we defecate to the west?*
> *Do we defecate to the easties?*
> *Do we defecate for inspection?*
> *Initial each puddle and engrave each feces?*
>
> *If we fall into the brambles and bushes,*
> *Will our private parts explode?*
> *Will our breasts melt to blotches,*

Things crawl from our crotches,
Each time we drop a load?

The cook and the med took the dramatic interpretation on their lecture as an insult and decided that these travelers were a group of stupid, disrespectful brats, incapable of respecting the rules of jungle travel. From then on, they withdrew from the group at mealtimes, keeping to themselves, gossiping with disgusted expressions. Charles said they probably hated all the tourists they worked with, despised the men like Klerck and Chetter who were their bosses, and basically disapproved of everything but mysteries by Ruth Rendell. They were the only members of Tropical Treks, Inc., who kept meticulous written records to turn in to the office at the end of the tour. Bruce called them "The Squealer Sisters—Misses Cinched and Pinched."

The roads were so rough that our bodies got knocked around against the seats in front and the door handles on the side. We all had bruises. We'd been told to be sure to go to a dentist before we left so there'd be no problem with loose cavities or cracked teeth. Reeva and Robin and Juno complained that their breasts hurt. Charles made them jogging bras out of stretchy vines and ripped-up Hawaiian Bermuda shorts. As the days passed, most of the group took on a tattered, sweaty look. T-shirts no longer matched shorts. Socks were different colors. Hats and bandannas lost their shape. And except for the Tropical Treks crew and Sasha, who maintained his crisp safari look, the group's clothing was quite mad. Charles called us a "cargo cult." He said the cargo was "remainders from a President's Day sale at Loehmann's."

Journey rode in the fourth Land Rover with Mustafa and several members of Randy Paul's film crew. Mustafa reported that Journey was sitting stiff and silent, his mouth fixed in a terrified grin. After several days inside the jungle, he'd begun to shake his head all the time, the way a horse swings his muzzle to get rid of a fly. Journey kept blowing air out of his lips. As the days passed, Mustafa told Sasha that Journey periodically would stick his forefingers in his ears and scream "*Cha!*" at the top of his lungs. Every time a bird flew overhead or an animal crossed the road, he closed his eyes and mumbled. Once he wedged himself down on the floor of the Land Rover and wept. By the end of our second week in the jungle, Mustafa reported that Journey had taken to pulling down his cotton pants and showing his circumcised penis to anyone who came near him. "All right," he'd growl. "I'm not an Indian, okay? I'm not an Indian. I was born in Miami. My father's a high school science teacher, but that doesn't mean I have to die." All night long we'd hear him talking to himself. "I can't see the sky. Where's the fucking sky? I can't get out of here. There's no stars."

One night Klerck and Sasha and Chetter had a long meeting and decided to send Journey home. We were still in close enough proximity to public campsites that Klerck could radio a Tropical Treks guide who was on his way back from another tour and arrange a rendezvous. Journey was packed into the mechanic's jeep and they set out. He never said good-bye. Now he wore two pairs of sunglasses and Sasha's safari hat and sat with a sleeping bag pulled up to his chin. He kept swatting at the air. As they drove away, we heard him shouting, "Don't take me deeper. No executions. Don't dispose of me. No suffocations. Get me out of here. I need a window. Get me to a hotel room." All of us stood in a clump watching him go. Randy Paul shook her head no when JoJo lifted his camera.

"So much for our shaman," Charles said.

"I liked him," Sasha replied. "I always knew he was a phony, but I didn't care. His phoniness was so thorough, it fascinated me. It never occurred to me that he was mad. And he had such interesting hair." Sasha turned to Charles. "I think this is a premonition," he said quietly.

"Oh, no," Charles said. "Don't get into that. Journey was certified. He could've been Lady Godiva as easily as he was a shaman."

"No," Sasha said. "It's changing. It's turning. Our little vacation is soon to transform into a real test of our spirit. This is what I hoped for. Disorientation. Withdrawal from our daily comforts and defenses. The jungle's about to declare war."

Charles put his hand on Sasha's arm. "Please," he pleaded. "You've been so unusually cheerful." Sasha removed Charles's hand from his arm and walked toward the Control Land Rover. Charles made no move to follow him.

After that, Sasha instructed Klerck to take us on a less picturesque route so we could travel through the remains of small villages that had been burned to the ground. "Bloody secret wars," Chetter said. "All these fucking, half-assed wars in America del sur. No named oppressor. No named enemy. No named cause." Bruce said Chetter didn't disapprove of the nameless wars for their violence, just for their lack of definition. "You blow the head off one of 'em," Chetter said, "and you find out you just killed your squadron leader. How the hell are you s'posed to know?"

We usually camped in the ashes of the villages because they pro-vided a breathing space from the relentless web of the jungle. We camped behind the Land Rovers to be safe from "any little skir-mishes we might accidentally run into," Klerck told us. For the first few weeks, camping had been easy. We pitched our tents, laid out our mosquito netting and sleeping bags, and let the Tropical Treks people do the rest. But several days after Journey left, and the at-mosphere of the jungle became more menacing, Sasha decided to make our nightly routine a disciplined exercise. Sasha said it was a meditation on the act of basic survival. We were each assigned very specific chores. Sasha called us together. He'd sketched out an elaborate rotating chart for our jobs. The chart was as detailed and meticulous as his paintings for the sets he'd created for *The Myth Man*.

"From now on, how you load and unload a truck or wash a dish is much more a part of your growth as an actor than interpreting a monologue by Shakespeare," Sasha announced. "And it requires that you relinquish your egotistical notions about menial labor versus the artist's crafts. I think these tiny chores are the most important exercises you'll have ever undertaken in your work with me." Sasha proudly handed his plan to Klerck.

Klerck and Chetter exchanged a look of disbelief. They'd been hauling, digging, and lifting their whole lives and they found it hard to believe that Sasha was making chores religious and artistic. Then, half laughing and yet nervous to be in the spotlight, they took turns reading out the chore rotation in slightly shaky voices.

We were each to do the same chores for a week, then switch with someone else indicated on the chart. Mustafa and Chetter unpacked canvas cots and mosquito netting. Surni was to help Klerck convert several of the seats in the Land Rovers to "beds" for squeamish campers. Robin was assigned to assist the surly cook. Bruce's job was to ration water and keep track of the food. I passed out dishes and silverware. Reeva set up chairs around the designated eating area. Klerck always made the bonfire. Kosher was to string a primitive set of tiny lights to the generator to illuminate the pitch-black campsite. Only after he'd accomplished his chore was he allowed to unpack his puppets, examine every inch of them, rewrap them, and load them back onto the Land Rover. Other jobs, such as serving food and washing and drying dishes and clothes, would rotate daily according to Sasha's chart, which Charles called the astro-illogical wheel.

Sasha, eager but calm, took it upon himself to dig the latrine and garbage pit and fill in the holes the next morning. Randy Paul voluntarily assisted him, even though she had her share of work supervising and directing the work of her film crew. "How can I film what I don't know?" she said to Sasha. Chetter clearly disliked Randy Paul. He referred to her as "one of those superior types—all book learning and no common sense. Likes her close-ups of graves and mutilations but won't bother with a healthy soldier 'less she can paint him as some bloody criminal." Almost everyone on the excursion shared Chetter's dislike of Randy. Bruce cursed the way she hung on Sasha, wrote articles about him, planned her documentary about him, doted on him, and reported back to him any behavior she considered subversive. Her thin, overserious face with its overbite, long stringy black hair, and graduate-school clothes were only a cover for a character Bruce called Snitch the Bitch. Even her own film crew moved especially slowly simply to goad her. Only the cameraman, JoJo, took her seriously. He was the kind of man who stayed completely by himself, taking apart and cleaning his camera as if it were a rifle. Most of the time when he wasn't shooting, he slept.

Charles pranced through the campsite with his brand-new Canon camera. He snapped pictures of each actor at his or her job. He said he was going to publish a book and call it *Fresh Air Camp for the Rich and Famous*. Bruce informed him that soon there'd be a warrant out for his arrest and Charles said, "Good, good, as long as the penitentiary's in the U.S. with cool cement walls." One night the actors ganged up on him and stole his camera. But a few days later he got it back after he promised he'd take no more pictures at the latrine or at dawn.

Sasha decided to assign Charles a permanent job and Charles told Sasha and Klerck he refused to do it. He'd been ordered to rope off the campsite. The barrier would prevent any stray children in the area who might smell the fire or food from invading the campsite. Sooner or later they'd start begging, Chetter said. "Then we should feed them," Charles replied. "Isn't that one reason we're here?"

"They're worse than mosquitoes," Klerck said. "You can't swat them away. Then they come back with two or three brothers, sisters, or cousins."

Chetter explained that the rope created a boundary that the children would immediately recognize from the secret wars and hidden armies. They'd learned if they crossed the military borders made with barbed wire, they'd be shot on sight.

"I don't understand," Charles said. "I thought we were here to join with these people, not make ourselves generals."

Klerck told Sasha that as we got deeper, we could expect two hundred to three hundred orphaned children a night. And they'd descend like locusts. They were vandals. They stole. They'd been living in the jungle without supervision for so long they were animals.

"We could work with them," Charles said to Sasha, "make it a part of the improvisation of this trip."

Sasha seemed undecided. "I understand your anger," he said. "But I want to do what's right in a bigger sense. I'm not sure that we're here to undo the cruelties that a people have done to themselves. To observe, to understand, yes. But I'm not sure it's right to intervene with an existing human ecology. Besides, losing our food and valuables is not a part of the improvisation of this trip," Sasha said sadly. "We have to be as ruthless as any tribe that wants to survive. The poor children are obviously already wounded and infected by the Western poisons we're trying to escape. If we are to start from zero, Charles, that means that even our so-called 'good works' take us backward into a superior, somewhat imperialist way of thinking."

"But I wrote those grants for you," Charles argued, "and you said you wanted to make an exchange. Who could need it more than children? We don't know why they're orphans or whether they're Eastern or Western. We could *give* them something."

"We said exchange. Not charity. Never charity, and not at our expense," Sasha insisted. "We're not UNICEF. We can't solve the consequences of decades of civil wars we know nothing about. We're on our way to build a community, and when I discover how that community is to be run, perhaps we'll also discover the correct nature of charity in the jungle. Maybe we'll even build a school—"

Charles let out a laugh as if he couldn't believe what he was hearing. He stalked away.

"No old games!" Sasha shouted after him. I could see he was trying to keep his temper. "No old mutinies! Even protest is a habit. Give me the chance you promised."

I watched Sasha and Charles carefully from then on. I promised the jungle I'd toss my ego and submit to its ways if they just wouldn't fight. I tried to read every flicker in each of their eyes. I listened to the pitch and rhythm of each exchange. During the eight months we'd spent in New York after the tour, they'd been inseparable. Charles put together the budget for Sasha and helped him plan every aspect of the excursion. I was there when he told Willie DeVane he'd decided it was the only way to free Sasha of the familiar writer's block that made him cry out loud in the mornings, drink vodka through the night, and make lists of friends and enemies while trying to decide whether to kill himself.

"You'll get away from European influences," Charles kept saying. "You'll forget the pressure for a while. We'll go somewhere where the land and people will tell you stories. Then something will come to you. It always does."

Sasha chose the Amazon because it was so foreign to him. Charles found Tropical Treks, Inc., and then Sasha recited his proposal out loud and Charles put it into written form and figured out the whole budget. They spent their days and nights together laying the groundwork for the journey. When the money was completely raised and the practicalities had been attended to, Charles had left Sasha alone to do whatever casting and creative work he needed. I thought their problems had dissolved into mutual respect and collaboration.

Seeing Charles's dismay, Bruce now found a time to approach Sasha about the children. "Play is a kind of neutral with kids, Sasha. Every culture has a form of play. Couldn't I hang out with the kids and see what jazzes them? I won't impose anything, I'll just hang out. It might give them a breather from the shit they've been going through."

"In Europe and the U.S. play was a form of communication," Sasha replied. "Most Western children understood your warped humor." Sasha smiled sadly at Bruce. "Isn't it a little condescending to imagine that these children can be relieved by games or one piece of bread?"

Bruce kicked the dirt at Sasha's feet and turned away. "Why the *hell* am I asking your permission?" he said loudly. "When the hell do I think you have that kind of power over me?"

"Despite your big mouth, you are a loyal man, and you want this experiment to be a success," Sasha answered kindly. "And I appreciate it. I appreciate your struggle. And Charles's struggle. I myself am very uncomfortable. But every time one of us does whatever he pleases, we are in danger of anarchy. You are not an anarchist at heart. The love of unity is deep within you. You are a loving man."

Bruce blushed and softened. He shrugged. "Run for Senate in your next life, Sasha," he said.

"You know I'm here to free myself from old habits," Sasha said. "Otherwise you would've been the first to turn around."

Flattered, Bruce wandered away. He looked like he didn't know where to go.

I'd expected jungle children to be in brown rags with bloody bare feet holding out rusty tin cups for begging. I was surprised when the first gathering of children looked as if they'd bought their clothes at a mall. There were perhaps fifteen of them ranging in age from toddlers to young adolescents. Many of the boys wore brightly colored polyester pants and sleeveless basketball undershirts with big faded numbers. Several boys had no shirts at all. Their pants were muddy and ripped. Some boys went barefoot. Others wore thick, oversized combat boots or men's dress shoes without laces. Others had floppy sneakers, Nikes or Adidas that were often mismatched. A few boys sported gaudy Hawaiian shirts and oversized Bermuda shorts. Most of the boys had short-cropped hair or were shaved bald. The girls wore cheap blue jeans and short-sleeved blouses, or pastel-colored dresses with tight skirts and sleeveless tops. Some wore mini-skirts and halter tops with sandals, thongs, cheap plastic Mary Janes, or went shoeless. The girls had many different hairstyles. Some had wavy page boys, others tied their hair into tight buns. A few of the girls' hair was chopped unevenly to mimic the look of a British rock star. Many of the girls wore gold crosses around their necks and had ribbons, barrettes, coins, and cloth flowers stuck in their hair.

The "scavengers" would've looked like any kids hanging around a McDonald's except their faces and limbs were covered with scrapes; red, infected sores; and thick, swollen scars. Their lips were blistered and bloody. Flies sat unmoving on the eyes of the toddlers like false eyelashes. And all of them were a shade or two darker than their normal color because dried mud was smeared over their skin. I remember one filthy girl with a swollen eye and rotten teeth who carried a hot-pink plastic Mickey Mouse purse on her wrist. And a couple of beat-up-looking boys shared a baby-blue children's plastic radio which was completely gutted. The wires, screws, and batteries were a rusty blue from mold.

The first nights out, the number of kids only grew to a few dozen kids who stayed far from the camp. At the end of our third week in the jungle, we were far enough away from national police stations or regular tourist encampments that the children emerged in buzzing masses from their hiding places in the jungle. Chetter said they knew about us from the time we'd entered the jungle and had been slowly gathering. They came silently from all directions and stood several feet from Charles's barriers. They didn't beg or reach out. They stood in a clump with the toddlers up front and stared into the eyes of anyone who dared to look at them. They never sat down or changed positions. Bruce said he felt like we were being visited by the "Children of the Damned." Reeva became self-conscious and short-tempered. She told Sasha she felt like she was in some "goddamn aquarium." Juno stayed away, hidden in the back of a Land Rover, and Mustafa waved his fat fist at them and cursed them. He threw a blanket over his head and ate by flashlight. He began to walk around with the Tropical Treks cotton blanket covering him, looking, as Charles said, "like a ghost at a kindergarten Halloween party." I knew that Charles walked silently among the children late at night when he thought the encampment was asleep. He didn't do much. He touched them, spread some ointment on sores, and handed out Tic Tacs. One night I saw Sasha sitting up in his sleeping bag watching Charles. There was such anger in his tight features that I had to close my eyes for fear of what might happen. But he said nothing.

The Tropical Treks guides were the only ones who seemed at ease with the growing crowds of children. They talked loudly and drunkenly. They tried to teach our company, in a condescending series of talks, how to behave. They let us know that we weren't the only tourists with "bleeding hearts."

"Don't think of them as people," Klerck advised us one night. "Watch." He threw a piece of bread into the still life of the little muddy faces and suddenly we heard squeals and screams. The mass came to life as the children dived toward the piece of bread and swarmed on each other. The children viciously attacked each other with bites, fists, rocks, and sharp sticks. Whichever child ended up with the bread scaled up the nearest tree. The rest stood below, chanting and helplessly shaking the tree.

"Why did you do that?" Charles asked angrily.

"Had to show you." Klerck smiled. "Once and for all, you got to learn why we don't want you givin' them anything. Situations like these, you got to understand, have their own rules. It's too bad in a way. But that's how it is."

Bruce and Charles decided that the rules were too dictatorial. Charles was tired of sneaking. They stepped over the barrier and walked slowly toward the children. I stood close to the rope and watched. Very gradually, Charles transformed himself from the beautiful blond "tourist-man" to one of the children.

He imitated the sunken posture, the empty stare, the occasional scratch. Little by little he began to make fun of several of the boys and girls by staring into space, swelling his lip with his tongue, pressing his nose flat, drooling at the toddlers. By the time he and Bruce reached down to the ground and covered themselves with dirty mud, the children knew they could laugh. Charles threw a piece of bread the size of a quarter into the air and he and Bruce fought for it, beating each other up with slapstick punches and kicks. The children were squealing with laughter. Then Charles pointed to the camp and began doing really nasty imitations of the snobby British crew and several of the actors. Bruce stuck out his belly and scolded Charles as if he were Klerck. He encouraged the children to join them. Most were too detached and exhausted, but a few rushed to be next to Charles and Bruce and joined in. They marched around with Klerck's imperial, drunken posture. Then Charles modulated the phony English words into more joyous syllables and began to improvise silly songs. He incorporated the sounds of animals, rain, thunder, and insects. The children had begun to trust Charles and Bruce and were slugging them affectionately and trying to sing along.

Suddenly there was a boom and a loud snap and a flood of light.

The children froze, shocked, as JoJo rushed forward with his camera aimed toward the singers. The children stopped playing with Charles, covered their faces, dived for the ground, and hid. For a moment I thought they'd run away. Charles whirled around, grabbed JoJo, and tried to stop him, but JoJo knocked him with the camera and Charles lost his balance and fell to the ground. The children reappeared slowly and then ran forward in a mass. They began to shove each other and fight to get close to JoJo's lens. Suddenly they were flashing wide, phony, toothless smiles.

"TV," they cried. And several waved at the camera, fixed their hair, and stuck out their chests. "TV! TV! TV!"

Charles crawled under the barrier, got back on his feet, and stormed toward Randy Paul and Sasha.

"Cut off those fucking lights," he shouted. "Get the fucking camera out of those kids' faces."

Randy Paul blinked her froglike eyes at Charles impassively. "Sasha agreed that this could be invaluable footage."

The children became wilder as JoJo panned their violent swarm. "TV! TV!" they shrieked. "TV! TV! TV!"

Sasha sat stiffly in a canvas chair. He turned his back to all the action.

"Get those lights off," Charles said breathlessly. "This isn't the *Ted Mack Hour* or a Jerry Lewis telethon. Those kids were trusting me. You fucked it up."

Sasha's mind appeared to be far away. He stared at his long hands and shook his head in despair. "I don't like watching a mob scene any more than you," he said.

"But I thought you wanted to help these children. If we have footage of their turmoil, we can show it on television."

"You created the turmoil," Charles shouted. "Turn around in your chair."

Sasha angled his head slightly toward Charles. He smiled distantly. "You're angry when I won't let you do what you want and you're angry when I help you. Why am I starting to think you're using these children to challenge my authority, make my decisions seem ludicrous?"

"We were just having *fun*," Charles shouted. "Why is everything a big symbol?"

"Because, unfortunately, everything is," Sasha said. "That's the way it is with us. I'd like us to have a cleaner line of communication. I thought we were headed in that way, but you simply can't be direct. Maybe incidents like this will help us. Maybe that's partly what this trip is about. We watch each other make mistakes."

Sasha smiled, got up, and walked very slowly toward Randy Paul. He moved as if he'd just woken up from a deep sleep. For a moment Charles stayed where he was, silent and confused. Then he let out a frustrated yodel sound, but no one could hear it because of the din from the children chanting, "TV. TV. TV." They were hissing, spitting, and cursing each other as they fought to get close to the camera.

I was standing by the rope watching both sides of the action when Chetter yanked me back. The overexcited children had gone out of control as they rushed back and forth following the camera. They were closing in on the rope barrier. Suddenly the flood of light slammed off. We were in darkness except for the bonfire. Klerck, Chetter, and Mustafa stood at the rope with metal pipes. They lifted them in the air. The children sank back into the darkness.

"Jesus Christ," Bruce shouted. "Why don't you just zap them with napalm and save yourselves the trouble?"

"They'll be back," Klerck said mildly. "And thanks to your games, their number will be doubled." The three men lowered their pipes and went back to the Control Land Rover to drink beer and play cards.

"Stupid children," Mustafa mumbled under his blanket. "Children of communists. You see where communism gets you?"

"I want to call a meeting," Sasha said.

Several minutes later, the *Myth Man* company, the film crew, JoJo, Randy Paul, and the staff of Tropical Treks, Inc., sat in an awkward circle improvised from chairs, rolled-up sleeping bags, and duffles. Kosher practically had to be pried from inside the truck. He was wearing a full-length flannel nightshirt, thick Japanese slippers, a veil of mosquito netting, gauze mask, and gloves.

"Greta Garbo," Robin said. I couldn't tell if Kosher smiled under his gauze or not.

"Watch for snakes, now," Klerck said pompously, "and scorpions too. They love the darkness and the fire, small tight spaces and sweat."

Several people adjusted their feet and shook out the bottom of their jackets. Sasha sat at the center of the circle wearing nothing more than khaki pants, a T-shirt, and open-toed sandals. Charles squatted next to him in shorts and a fishnet undershirt. He was sifting the ashes on the ground with his bare fingers. He looked tired.

"I won't go on and on as you might expect me to," Sasha said. "It's just that you must understand that in an unknown environment as dangerous as the jungle we cannot function as a democracy or a hippie collective."

"Bloody right," said Klerck.

"I may be incompetent and at times I may seem insensitive, but I am the leader. You have to do as I say. I didn't realize that I would have to enforce rules or even make up rules when we started out, but the jungle dictates not simply the images of our dreams, but the form and structure of our community. What I have learned is that democracy is impossible in a foreign, potentially hostile environment. That must be why every tribe had its chiefs. I don't claim to be your chief, but I see now that I must be the absolute last word on your behavior. And you must do as I ask you even if I make mistakes from time to time or seem unreasonable. I will do the best I can with intuition and meditation to guide our journey in the right direction."

Klerck and Chetter bristled.

"And, of course, I will be acting on the advice of the Tropical Treks people," Sasha added, "but the final decisions will be mine." Sasha paused and looked at Charles, Bruce, and Reeva. "If you want to vote for another leader, we should do it now." The circle stayed quiet for several moments.

"What happens if we disobey?" Bruce asked. "Are you planning to build a community prison?"

"Yeah," Reeva said. "You gonna put us in a cage and haul us behind the Land Rovers like circus animals?"

"This isn't a government," Sasha said, "and I am not the SS. You are all allowed to state your opinions, of course. I will listen. I respect and care about all of you. But your peril is my peril. Your pain is my pain. Your lives are my life. And your injury or deaths would dim my soul." Sasha rose from his chair, signaled with his head to Randy Paul. She nodded to JoJo to turn off the camera. The three of them walked away from the meeting.

"Well." Robin sighed. "Ballanchine is supposed to be a tyrant too."

"I hate this," Charles half cried. "Just hate it. Rikki, I'm sorry. We should've gone to Disneyland."

"Disneyland." Surni, the Balinese actor, grinned and clapped his hands. "Disneyland! Disneyland!" He practically sang the sounds. "Want to get some job, Bali pavilion there. Yes? You know someone?"

Charles turned his head, following Sasha's movement away from the fire. His expression showed more concern than anger. Robin wiped her eyes. Chetter rolled his metal pipe uncomfortably in his hands and pretended to concentrate on it. Sasha was standing next to a Land Rover talking directly to JoJo's camera.

"He's just being his old dictatorial self again," Charles said hopefully. "Maybe he's got an idea about a multimedia-live-action show about the birth of a South American dictator. You know, like Chaplin. Only instead of rolling a helium globe, he rolls our heads."

"Don't laugh at me when I say this journey will make us all lovers because I truly believe it will," Sasha was saying to the camera. "Not in the physical sense—you can always screw who you want. But we are deeply dependent on each other for our physical well-being and our sanity. Together we can gain self-knowledge and inspiration from the jungle. If we split apart, we will debilitate each other and the jungle will destroy us."

I felt the presence of the hovering trees and I found it hard to breathe in the close, muggy night. It had been so long since I'd seen the sky. My heart sped up. I slid next to Charles and he pulled me onto his lap and rocked me.

"I wish I'd brought marshmallows for the campfire," he whispered. "I'd teach you how to make a S'more. That's a Hershey bar graham cracker marshmallow sandwich, toasted, melted, gooey—like my brother's brain."

Sasha continued his interview for the camera.

"What I'm trying to say, in the simplest terms, is we must make a profound effort to be sensitive to each other's needs. We must cast aside our vanities and defenses and coexist like a tribe under siege." He reached out to the camera with both hands, palms up. "A disagreement—rather, a *misunderstanding*—like tonight would be a mere rumble in the city. In the jungle it is thunder. It reverberates. If we allow such trivia to go on, the disharmony will endanger our lives. If Klerck or I make rules or issue orders, we do not do so to flaunt our superiority over others. We are doing what we can to guarantee safety and to create an atmosphere which will keep the group healthy and positive so we may thrive on this adventure."

"Bloody right," Klerck said.

"What's our final destination?" Randy Paul asked. This was a rehearsed question. Sasha smiled. His eyes were calm and introspective.

"I don't know," he said. "I wanted an exchange with a tribe untouched by . . . the . . . you know . . . but this is quite different than I expected." He smiled. "We'll just have to find a patch of land and create a community from our own best efforts."

Klerck coughed nervously and looked toward his crew. "He'll last one more week," he muttered drunkenly. "That's when we reach the end of the Land Rover trail. After that it gets too damn uncomfortable for bullshit types like him."

Sasha ignored Klerck and finished his interview. Then he and Randy Paul disappeared. He reappeared moments later carrying a chair to a far corner of the campsite. He placed it carefully in position and sat down again, staring into space. I sensed he was lost, but I believed he'd find the show he wanted and call off our aimless wandering so we could go home and rehearse.

The Tropical Treks crew gathered by the Control Land Rover and spoke low enough that they thought no one would overhear, but my ears were tuned to secrets and I'd become an expert at reading lips.

"I didn't sign up for this tour to join a bloody cult," the cook said to Chetter. She was cleaning her filthy nails with a pocketknife.

"Naw. It's not a cult," Chetter said quietly. "He's a theater type, y'know. Instead of telling us not to blow off at each other, he recites a bit of poetry. I got a cousin who's an actress. She bloody plans her auditions by some bloody tarot card reader. They're airheads."

"Well, it gives me the creeps," said the med. "I think he's got a touch of malaria. Makin' him talk like Winston Churchill. These people aren't balanced right. And I can't believe they drag that poor miserable little girl around with 'em. She's practically a freak!"

I stood hidden by the truck, unseen by them. I wondered if I was a freak. I didn't know what I looked like anymore. I couldn't imagine I'd changed that much. We'd only been gone a month. I wasn't sure. I thought it was a month. I was losing my sense of time. A person could change drastically overnight. I could die within a half hour's time. I could stop breathing after a minute. I began to check my arms and legs to see if I felt my skin and muscle. I was covered with huge bites and scratches. I itched. I bled. I felt pain. I pulled at my hair and felt the yank on my scalp. I hadn't been swallowed by the jungle. I blinked so my eyes wouldn't be glassy like Sasha's. Why was I a freak?

Charles patted me and quickly lifted me into his arms to carry me to Land Rover number two, which he'd fixed up as my "bed and breakfast."

"Are you doing Journey's greatest hits?" he asked.

"Am I a freak? They said I'm a freak," I replied.

"I hope so," Charles said. "Would you want to be a stuffy little girl in some boarding school? Would you want to dress up in a pleated uniform and carry a strap book bag and a field hockey stick?"

"Maybe," I said.

"Don't break your mother's heart." Charles gasped.

Every night Charles tucked me in and sang me to sleep. He knew I was frightened of the starless sky and the sharp scraping sounds of lizard tongues and giant cicadas. He comforted me by listing what he liked about the jungle. He explained that the colors and shapes in the jungle were so well designed, he was beginning to believe in God again. "Think of it as a huge living room with an exotic decor," he whispered. He said the mismatched shapes of the vines and foliage were like the messy hairdos of rockers and dope fiends, hippies and yippies on the Lower East Side of Nature. He'd always adored snakeskin but had no idea that it looked so good on snakes. He liked the way everyone's hair was kinking and frizzing up, their clothes fading and gathering spots and rips, especially his own. He thought the oversized frogs were obscene stand-up comedians, the bats like World War I fighter pilots, and he called the oversized mosquitoes "snowflakes gone bad."

That night, after the incident with the children, I asked Charles if he was angry at Sasha. Charles tucked my sleeping bag right up to my chin and waited to unroll the mosquito net. (I hated the mosquito net. I felt as if I were being packed in a box.)

"My brother is a Phoenix," he said. "He burns himself and everyone else around him to ashes and then, pop, he reappears. He's a fresh new baby bird full of sweetness and gifts. I have faith and that's my fatal flaw. But *Jungle Book*'s the last scene between us. After this trip, it's time for me to get into designing, painting, and writing. I want to protect you on this trip and maybe make it worthy of your memoirs. I plan to spend some real time with Sasha, iron some things out before I leave him for good."

"Does he know?"

"Yes, he does, Pussycat. We had a lot of legal and financial documents to draw up so I could leave the company quickly and painlessly when this is over."

"What about me?"

"At the end of this period, you'll be free to be in his shows and to take part in my meaningless life. It's not a courtroom like *Perry Mason*, Pussycat. You won't have to choose."

I turned on my side and saw Sasha sitting dead-still in the same chair, back straight, his eyes wide open but focused inward.

"I guess that's a good thing," I said. "I'm tired of problems."

"We're all tired of problems," Charles said. "Even our problems are tired of problems."

"Don't leave me tonight," I said tearfully. I saw him reach for the mosquito netting.

"Sh-sh-sh," Charles said. "Pretend we're on a movie set shooting a remake of *The African Queen*. You're Kate Hepburn and I'm the piano." Charles started to sing weird jazz runs using the syllable "Plink plink plink. . . ."

I fell asleep as I did every night, free-falling from darkness into waves of light and the pictures of dreams. They were all scored to the rhythm of Charles's breathing, and even after he'd left my side, I inhaled and exhaled as he taught me, so I wouldn't give in to my terror of being closed inside, the net above my head and the leaf web that shut out the sky.

The next few days the caravan moved quietly through the jungle. The trail began to disappear and the guides had to stop the Land Rovers frequently to get out and chop vines with their machetes and dig up plants with their shovels. The tension from the jungle made our company obedient and childlike. We slept and ate in the Land Rovers, since camping seemed impossible.

"We're on the verge of losing control of our environment," Sasha announced happily. "This is something I've never experienced before. We'll have to bargain with the elements in much the same way as primitive man. This is what I'd hoped for."

"Let's feed the rubber trees some freeze-dried scrambled eggs," Bruce suggested. Sasha looked past him.

On the fourth day we came upon the remains of a large village that had been burned to the ground. The skeletons of a few huts stuck up from the ground. The earth was black and there were some human and animal bones half buried in the ashes. Robin led me from the area while Charles and Kosher collected the bones with horror and admiration. But both had the idea of incorporating the skulls and bones into masks and costumes. The group watched silently. JoJo filmed it. Sasha sat in a Land Rover watching the group's reaction. Robin and I played gin in the truck, but we both could see. Afterward we set up camp. No one wanted supper and we all went to bed early.

I awoke, as I always feared I would, in the dead of night. At first there was nothing but solid blackness and I stifled an urge to call out. I was sweating and I lay stiff under the sleeping bag. The fire had burned to embers, but they were blurry streaks. The tiny lamps were out. There was nothing for my eyes to adjust to. The darkness remained solid and impenetrable. I felt the air throbbing. It was an eerie, steady throb that seemed to rise from the earth. Then I realized I was hearing voices all around me whispering over and over, barely audible, whispering and chanting, "TV. TV. TV. TV." I tried to sit up, but in my panic I couldn't punch through the mosquito netting. I thought I'd suck it in and suffocate. I lay back down and yanked it out of my mouth. Finally I pulled the sticky veil off my head. When my eyes adjusted to the darkness, I could see the faint silhouette of hundreds and hundreds of children surrounding the camp. Their bodies didn't move, but I kept hearing the sound "TV. TV. TV. TV" as it rose and spread back into the jungle for what seemed like miles. I watched as several large bodies dashed around the camp. I heard quiet voices, the slamming of doors, and saw the bodies run toward the barriers surrounding the camp. Then came a variety of new sounds. Pops, sizzles, bangs. I saw sparks and gray smoke. The crowds of children backed away silently. I heard dragging and quiet moaning. More pops and bangs. More rustling. Small feet running, dragging. More whimpering and moaning. The throbbing had stopped. Now there was only a buzz of crying in the distance and the soft swish of vines and branches being brushed against, stepped on, dragged forward. The large silhouettes retreated calmly to hidden places in the campsite. I crawled deep down under my sleeping bag and breathed my own sour smells. When I awoke at dawn, I couldn't open my left eye. A bite had swollen it shut. My upper lip felt itchy and heavy too.

There was a grim, hushed meeting taking place in the center of the camp. Chairs circled the ashes of the previous night's early bonfire. Sasha, Randy Paul, Reeva, Juno, Chetter, Klerck, Robin, and Bruce sat holding dirty coffee cups. They leaned in from the edge of their chairs as if examining a chessboard. Charles stood behind Sasha on one leg like a flamingo. He was chewing on a stick. He was sharing it with the ancient translator, King, whom I hadn't seen for days. King was drinking a bottle of Yoo-Hoo and seemed completely disinterested in the meeting.

"These could be my people," Reeva was saying. She was weeping. "How could you do it?"

Juno's pudgy hands were clutched in tight little fists. "This is how you people have always treated Native Americans," she said quietly. "We're target practice for the white explorer."

"Hardly," Klerck said drolly. "There must've been five hundred of those buggers surrounding us last night, ladies. Scavengers, all of them. The odds were, shall we say, a bit uncomfortable. It's part of our contract to protect you."

"You shot into an innocent crowd of children," Reeva sobbed. "*Children.*"

"It was a warning," Chetter said impatiently. "If we hadn't scared them off, we'd have a thousand by tonight. And you've not seen what they can do to a campsite."

"I'd like to take responsibility for this," Randy Paul said. "This is entirely my fault."

"I probably made them feel welcome," Charles said. "I must've given them the idea we were civilized and friendly."

Klerck glared at Charles. "That's not the point," he said. "They wouldn't stay satisfied with a simple game or two. They're fucking rabid."

"Wild animals," said the cook. "Roaming in packs. Whole armies of 'em."

"If it makes you feel any better, we've been through this before," said Chetter. "Sasha told us not to act on past experience, but we've had to do this kind of thing more and more. That's why we've been considering phasing out this part of the tour."

"Yes indeed." The cook sighed. "It breaks your heart."

"But you may have killed some of them," Reeva sobbed. "You may have murdered children who carried no weapons and hurt no one."

"Oh, I doubt we did more than scratch a few." Klerck sighed. "We're all pretty fair shots, you know."

"I heard moaning," Juno said.

"Bullets make nasty scratches," Chetter said. "But they fake it, you know, just to get you to step into the mob of 'em."

"How can you be sure?" Robin spoke. Her tone was overly rational and conciliatory. She kept glancing at Sasha. Her hand was on his bony knee. "You fired into the pitch-dark into a group of five hundred children. Can you guarantee us no one was killed?"

"What if someone was?" the cook snapped. "What can we do? Invite a thousand of 'em for dinner and let 'em riot and steal and take off with all our provisions?"

"We've got our instructions," Klerck said. "The governments of these areas want those children discouraged. It's bad for development and tourism and it gives the good Indians a lousy name. You think *we're* rough, you should see what the tribes do to their own people!"

"Oh, I'm sure they're torturers," Bruce snapped. "After all, they're just savages."

Sasha cleared his throat and folded his hands under his chin in a prayerful position. "How can a discussion undo what happened?" Sasha said quietly. "It's tragic and unfortunate, and it's beyond our understanding. I'm appalled. But I can't help but feel that from the moment Charles began his little plays with those children, we were killing them."

"We just sang and laughed," Charles said helplessly.

"Yes, I know." Sasha smiled sadly. "But a song and a dance are promises we can't keep. You open up the possibility of hope where there is no hope. This is fascinating because, in a way, generosity becomes more cruel than selfishness. I told you this trip would challenge all our values. Our goodness is worthless. Goodness becomes evil."

"Hey, then let's just get some guns and finish off the little motherfuckers," Bruce snapped. "We'll win the Nobel Peace Prize."

"Don't be simplistic," Sasha said.

"It's always me." Charles sighed. "I hand out Tic Tacs and destroy the third world."

"The pain of this experience is a gift," Sasha said. "We should use it to examine our habitual reactions to life and recognize that we know absolutely nothing about good and evil."

"What about those kids?" Reeva asked. "What if they need help? What if they're off bleeding somewhere?"

"I don't know," Sasha said. He was silent for a long time. "I imagine they've developed an organic form of survival and healing. But I just don't know."

Sasha got up slowly and walked with Robin to the Control Land Rover. He stood straight and proud, but all his clothes were soaked with sweat.

As he walked off, Mustafa applauded. "Allah be praised," Mustafa said. "There goes a man's man."

"This can't be what he wanted, is it?" asked Chetter. "What's he looking for anyway?"

"He's not looking for anything," Randy Paul said with authority. "And there's nothing he wants or doesn't want."

"What about dead children?" Bruce asked. "Where does that fit into this search for the fucking sameness of opposites and the mystical nothingness of everything?"

"Dead children are everywhere, babe," Klerck said. "In all these third world countries, they're the first to go. You got to kiss off sentiment."

"Man, I'd like to get me in a plane and drop a couple tons of condoms on these countries," Chetter said. "Now, *that* would be humanitarian."

"Hello, Joe Palooka!" Charles said loudly, and the group turned and looked at me.

"The girl's got a whopper," Chetter said. "And a fat lip."

"Shoot her," Juno said bitterly. "She's defective."

I broke into a run. Reeva darted after me and led me back. She squeezed my arm reassuringly. The whole group focused on me. I hated being a child.

"We're safe from her." Reeva winked at Charles. "She's got some boobs. Her waist is thinning out. She's a young woman now. She won't harm us."

I lowered my head in shame. I didn't want the whole company knowing the changes in my body. I was already aware that my period was due and didn't know how I'd handle it in the jungle. My first had come while we were on tour in Rome, and Robin, Reeva, and Juno took me to an Italian bistro and toasted me. They taught me about tampons, Kotex, cramps, bloat, and PMS. When Charles heard what had happened, he told me he was going to build a hut and keep me outside until the "cursed visitor" went on her way. Now, he said, I could have babies and to be careful of sperm floating in bathwater. The meeting split up slowly, but I stood still, holding myself tight, pulling in my stomach and trying not to cross one leg in front of the other to hold in the imaginary flow.

I was afraid I'd start bleeding right there in the camp and the blood would flow onto the ground and make a conspicuous puddle in the ashes. Even as we set out in our Land Rovers later that morning, I was afraid of my own blood. As Chetter ground the gears and forced us through the mud and vines onto the trail, I saw the leaves of plants and trees covered with dried blood from the night before. I blushed and closed my eyes with shame as if it were mine.

For the next few nights we stayed close to our vehicles. No large fires were lit and no loud conversation took place. The whole caravan began to stink of unwashed bodies and clothes, half-eaten food, and the sour, thick smells of the jungle. The foliage had become so thick, we made little progress. And then one hazy, oppressive morning as we were crawling along in the caravan, Klerck began to blast the horn of the Control Land Rover. Chetter quickly began to lay his forearm on his jeep's horn, making long, sustained blares. One by one the other vehicles joined the noisy honking until we sounded like a traffic jam in midtown Manhattan.

"What's happening?" Robin shouted. She was sitting in the passenger seat in the front.

"We're about a half mile from what we call Wheel's End Village," Chetter yelled. "It's where the jeep trail finishes, where most of the tours turn around."

A half hour later we could see a vast clearing. Tents, tepees, and thatched huts were scattered haphazardly between rusty gas pumps and odd-shaped canvas booths. A hand-painted sign labeled each booth. One said COFFEE FRESH PICKED. Another said SOUVENIRS AND POSTCARDS. Another, POLAROIDS, MAPS, GUIDES. There were two stands which displayed small, medium, and large bottles of green, murky fluid. The sign said ESSENCE OF JUNGLE ENERGY. A row of five Portosans were lined up by the side of the road as we drove into the village.

"Don't get your hopes up," Chetter said. "Nothing works and everything's filthy."

The caravan picked up more energy and speed than it had in weeks. The Land Rovers slid and tottered perilously as the crew kept honking their horns, whistling and shouting to each other. "Ay! Hey! All right! Ay! Hey!" Their good spirits were contagious and I felt a surge of relief as if we were arriving at a small city or as if our ordeal were coming to an end. There was no basis for my hopefulness, but the others in the company seemed to be experiencing the same lightness. Charles stood up in the Land Rover and pulled out his binoculars. I could see Mustafa running alongside his vehicle and Reeva was sitting on the front of her Land Rover like a statue on the bow of a ship.

The caravan sped into the huge clearing. It was the size of several football fields. Tepees, dome-shaped tents, and tightly packed mud huts were crowded into a semicircle like a wagon train. Rickety wooden showers and a primitive general store were a part of the constellation. "A global ghost town," Charles said. The rest of the area spread out into a very wide, flat stretch of tarmac that looked like an airstrip. Odd symbols were painted on the homemade runway in bright yellow, orange, and red Day-Glo paint, and there seemed to be several altars lined up on either side of the wide runway. The altars stood like arcades at Coney Island and they spilled over with prizes and toys. Metal and glass wind chimes, large glass crystals, the insides of clocks and radios, stained glass, and bizarre-looking rag dolls dressed vaguely like American astronauts with clay helmets and cotton jumpsuits were some of the offerings I managed to see. I noticed that the roofs of the tepees, tents, and huts were covered with the same kind of paraphernalia and the trees in the surrounding forest jangled with glass, metal, and clay bells. "Oh, my," Charles said, "I think I've died and been sent to a boutique."

Little by little, the people who inhabited this "village" straggled out to greet us. Each adult had the same wide-eyed cheerfulness and there was something overly sweet about them, like the actors who do bad children's theater. They hugged the crew from Tropical Treks and nodded to the company as if they'd known they were coming. I was surprised to see that the village housed white, black, and Asian hippies in their twenties and thirties. Only a few children ran around and one or two dark-skinned Indians sat by the wooden stores chewing and staring into space. The "villagers" wore bright purple drawstring pants and matching blouses. They all had a bald spot where a circle had been shaved on the top of their heads. They offered us beers and cornbread—the first bottle and slice for free—and a small, mousy woman with a completely shaved head stepped forward, bent from the knee, and said, "Do you care to join us in a chant? It's really cool."

Sasha politely interrupted her and requested to meet their "chief." A tall, thin man with a full beard and hair down to his waist pointed toward the jungle and shook his head.

"He lives and meditates in the main receptor house," the man said. "He probably won't come out until the moment arrives."

Klerck excused himself and said he wanted to speak to the Tropical Treks caravan privately. The villagers smiled with great understanding and floated off toward their shops and chores. (Each house seemed to have a vegetable garden and a tiny aviary of exotic birds and lizards.)

"Look," Klerck said, "you can shower here. Buy souvenirs and stock up on provisions, but be careful."

"What exactly is the religion of this tribe?" Sasha asked.

"Ain't no religion," said Chetter. "They've all come here sort of in bits and spurts and over the years. Ask 'em yourselves. You'll get a kick out of it. Too bad they had to indulge themselves in other businesses."

"They deal drugs and sell high-powered arms to the guerrillas and turn around and report on guerrilla movements to the government," Klerck said. "They've made this here airstrip according to their 'beliefs,' but the planes that go in and out of here ain't exactly carrying holy water. Any one of you buys drugs or arms, it's Tropical Treks' responsibility to turn you over to the army. Penalty's death, you know."

"I don't think we have too many criminals here," Sasha said mildly. "We will use our time exploring, buying souvenirs, and resting. I want my company to exchange with the villagers. Besides, I need time to find out where the footpaths lead and where we should go next in our journey. We ought to have a consultation with a local guide."

Several members of the Tropical Treks team looked at each other with alarm. They were exhausted and dirty and had expected to be going home soon. Reeva groaned. Kosher shuffled back to the truck. I felt my expectations sink, and exhaustion and dread took me over once again.

"This is the last stop covered by the Tropical Treks contract, Sasha," Klerck said coldly. "I've made no provision for any further manpower, insurance—"

"You and Chetter and I will meet privately," Sasha interrupted. "I'd like your people to continue with us. Meanwhile, I'd like my actors to study this village and try to fit in as well as possible. We share common ground with all peoples, whether they are holy shamans or desperate souls selling weapons of destruction."

Villagers opened up their booths a few at a time. The dark-skinned Indians with jet-black hair disappeared from their chairs into the jungle. The village sellers gave us identical smiles. Their skin was smooth and not at all wrinkled from their years in the outdoors. They didn't push their goods on us, but smiled in a friendly, detached manner. They worked slowly. A heavyset woman with dirty blond hair in purple bell-bottoms and a tie-dyed T-shirt laid out bottles of handmade creams, and oils and envelopes filled with herbs. When she leaned over, I could see that the bald spot on her head was painted with intricately overlapping purple Jewish stars. An older man with silver sideburns and a goatee set out books printed in colored ink on the bark of trees. The titles read *No Accident*, *He Who Waits*, and *The Reddiness Chart*.

"What kind of religion is this?" Bruce asked.

The man tore off a button of a mushroom, chewed it like gum, and laughed. "Hardly a religion," he said. He spoke in a Brooklyn accent. "Two things at play here. One—nuclear holocaust. It's coming. It's a definite. And this spot is a scientifically proven haven. Bomb won't reach here, northern Canada, or some isolated spots in New Zealand."

"What's the second thing?" Reeva asked, but the man wandered off and joined several other men who were sweeping down the airstrip with strange motorized machines that looked like the tiny cars with rollers that slid around ice-skating rinks. These little cars had wet brushes attached. Other men ran alongside and applied fresh coats of iridescent paint.

Robin introduced herself to a white-haired woman who showed us several trays of herbal mixes that she said cured fevers, rashes, colds, heart disease, and even certain forms of cancer.

"Western medicine is barbaric," the woman said.

"I'm Robin." Robin grinned.

"Oh," the woman said. She had a thick German accent. "We relinquished our names long ago. We believe they will give us their names when they arrive."

"Who?" Charles asked.

"Extraterrestrials," the woman replied casually. "We've all seen their ships. Some of us have seen them in bodily form. We're all just waiting for the next step—to go on board—just a kind of get-together."

"Like a mixer," Charles said.

"I suppose so," the woman said, and smiled brightly.

"First, we're waiting for laser communication to let us know they're on their way." She pointed to the bald spot on the top of her head. "We've created this village so they'll know they're welcome. I just hope they get here on time. I have every faith they will, but intergalactic travel is slower these days, what with the pollution our space program is sending into the spheres."

Bruce followed a bald, pudgy woman and asked if he could see some proof of her reported space travel. She laughed affectionately and offered him Jimi Hendrix heroin instead, or, if that didn't appeal, she had some cassettes of the Mamas and the Papas and Ike and Tina Turner live at the Fillmore East. When Robin asked the heavy woman in the flowing robe if she could purchase the healing herbs, the woman told her it would take two years, day and night, to learn how to minister them. But, in the meantime, she had teas and soup mixes and Iranian hashish. When Robin declined, the woman asked her if she needed any pain pills or stay-awake powder. They ended up reading astrological charts together. When Bruce introduced himself to the pudgy woman, she warmly shook his hand, leaned forward, pointed to her tattoo and said, "My name can only be read by laser communication." She sold Bruce a cold beer and offered to take him on a snake hunt. She then offered Bruce a plastic bag of "Essence of Jungle Energy."

"Melt it over fire in a spoon," she said. "You'll get your dreams back, you cynical Jewish lover boy."

Randy Paul and her crew circled the area taking pictures of each hut, tepee, and booth. She hadn't been allowed inside the homes by any of the inhabitants and found she had to negotiate an overall fee even to film the exteriors. A tall, graying, strawberry-haired white woman wrapped in a purple tie-dyed cotton cloth argued with her over money. The woman had the appearance of a healthy New England housewife and yet she went in and out of understanding Randy's English. She only grunted and shook her mane of graying strawberry hair. Sometimes she'd say one or two words over and over. When they finally reached an agreement, she embraced Randy Paul. The woman held her for so long that Randy Paul began to squirm.

"Those of us with skin and bones must learn to crawl into each other, honey." Suddenly she had a southern accent. "When we have our final encounters, the ones who come for us will enter our souls and we're gonna merge with them. They'll talk to us through overtones and refracted pulses of light. They'll take us onto their spacecraft by reducing our flesh and bone to high-pitched tones and radiant beams which will penetrate the earth's magnetic field."

"Could I have some footage of you calling to them?" Randy Paul asked.

"Our life is one big telephone call to the constellations, honey." The woman laughed.

The villagers mostly ignored me. They were too busy selling themselves and their goods to the actors and the film crew. They never tired of smiling and demonstrating whatever they had. Many offered to go find "anything for good price, low price, on sale for discount." One young man in a cotton cape and purple burlap pants was sent off to purchase a case of Dos Equis for Klerck and a box of bullets. I heard one girl in her twenties offer herself to Mustafa, and when he laughed, she added her mother, sister, and three aunts. The girl was a beautiful half Indian, half Asian who believed she'd be chosen to conceive the first intergalactic baby. The girl told Mustafa she knew how they made love in outer space—that an alien had entered her through the tattoo on her head and when he came, she poured crystals out her eyes. Mustafa began to discuss the idea of being taught space sex by her, but Reeva and Juno dragged him away. The girl followed them for a few yards and told them that aliens made love thousands at a time, with one singing sex organ, which was a metallic gong-shaped planet bigger than Saturn and all its rings.

"These poor people," Reeva said. "They have a sickness in the brain. They're doing a live version of a comic book."

"I don't know," said Juno. "They have a lot more hope than I do right now."

Later, I saw Mustafa behind a hut making a deal with three Indians. They'd soundlessly reappeared from the jungle surrounding the village. Mustafa mimed something with his hands. It looked as if he was describing a fish he'd caught. The Indians watched intently and then ran off, talked quietly to several of the villagers, and returned almost immediately with a heavy machine gun. Mustafa examined it suspiciously, aimed it, and, in a disgusted gesture, gave it back to the Indian men. They ran off again and returned just as quickly dragging five or six other choices.

All of us, at one time or another, lined up, half numb, at the outdoor showers. You paid a dollar, pulled a cord, and a bucket of cold water dumped over on you. It was a dollar a bucket, so it took between five and ten dollars to wash and rinse yourself properly. An old woman in a purple housedress with a path shaved down the middle of her hair sat cross-legged in the dirt to collect the money, charging extra to rub a foul-smelling cream onto the skin. She clipped fingernails and toenails and offered to heal athlete's foot, give haircuts, massage sore muscles, read palms, or restore healthy skin with some "Essence of Jungle Energy Tea" for a scale of prices she recited like a waiter listing specials each time a new customer stepped into the shower.

"This is like a mikvah," Bruce said.

"What's a mikvah?" I asked him.

"It's Jewish—Orthodox." Bruce smiled. "It's where you go after you've had your period to cleanse yourself for your husband. 'When any woman makes a running issue out of her flesh she is unclean.' Leviticus—very sexist, but relaxing from what I hear." Bruce seemed to be speeding. When he smiled, he gritted his teeth.

He chose to have his palm read after his shower. The old lady in charge stared at his hand for a long time.

"You will get what you want," she said in a smooth, breathy voice.

"You have a strong midwestern accent," Bruce did his own imitation of a psychic. "Let me guess: Indiana."

"The United States won't survive," the woman said, smiling. "It will fall into the fiery center of the globe. This is one of only three places the bomb will forget. So let's get back to your fortune."

"Okay." Bruce shrugged. "How 'bout telling me when the bomb's gonna drop so I can pack up my tennis gear?"

The old woman stared at Bruce's palm and smiled patiently. "The palm restricts itself to your little adventures," she said. "Not the events of the spheres."

"No problem. No problem," Bruce said. "Give me what you got."

"You will get what you want," the woman repeated. "But first you have to know what you want." She stared for several more moments, touching his hand affectionately.

"You must be very careful on the highway. Make sure your doors are tightly shut. A man was driving at a high speed, his door flung open, he fell out—a terrible thing."

"Wasn't he wearing his seat belt?" Bruce asked. He laughed nervously.

"Yes, but not tight enough," the old lady said. "He slid through and was dragged. A terrible thing. No skin left."

Bruce jumped up and pointed his finger at the old lady. "That's just rude!" he said. "You should stick to tall dark strangers and long lives."

The old lady closed her eyes, shook her strange hair, and laughed. Bruce was annoyed.

"God, I should've taken that job stage-managing *The Fantasticks*," he growled. He was speaking rapidly and combing his wet curls back again and again with his fingers. "I haven't had a normal conversation since this shit started. I'm cracking up. I'm really on the verge!"

Kosher actually removed his layers of clothes and allowed a strong, tanned Asian man to rub him down with some muddy-looking cream, but he kept the gauze over his mouth and refused to remove his Japanese socks.

"You stink of fear," the man said. "You invite sickness and accident with your smell. The insects and animals know this smell. They feast on it. They laugh at chickenshits like you." Kosher grunted in pain and quickly struggled free of the man, put on his clothes, and ran toward the truck.

I caught up with Robin and Charles. They were wandering through the village and quietly bickering.

"I don't need a baby-sitter," Charles said.

"Why can't I just walk with you?" Robin asked.

"You're a terrible liar," Charles replied. "It's all those years in the convent."

Robin's face reddened. "Sasha didn't want you to be alone," Robin admitted.

"Sasha's afraid I'm going to join up with a drug gang," Charles said, "or stay here and wait for UFOs." He whirled around to me and tweaked my nose.

"Are you with the CIA?" he asked me.

"No, I want to sell you my sister," I said.

Charles smiled. "I think this place is what Times Square must've been like. Before Columbus landed," he said. "I wish I knew what was going on. Where are we going next, Rikki Nelson? Heaven, Hell, or Hoboken?"

Charles collected whatever tiny statues and feathers and buttons struck his fancy. Many of the villagers found his tall, lithe, dancing body irresistible. He skipped and turned from place to place and they followed and held out objects of all kinds. Charles listened to every offer they made and examined all their broken, worthless souvenirs. Robin looked around for any interesting clothes or ritual garments. None of the clothes were "authentic" and most had spots or rips. We tried to find a snack, but the fruits were overripe and the candy bars stale.

We were passing the time, wondering when Sasha would tell us what he intended to do. He'd disappeared with Klerck in one of the jeeps and had been gone for the entire day. The light was nearly fading from the sky when suddenly we heard a booming, frightening sound from above, a roar that vibrated through the earth. I covered my ears. Charles pulled me to the ground and covered me with his body. I thought it was the army raiding the village for guns and drugs. I looked up and saw a giant prehistoric grasshopper. Its round glass head loomed over the tree tops and its wings buzzed over its head. It bobbed up and down and began to lower itself onto an empty section of the clearing. The villagers were unafraid. They laughed and clapped and ran toward it.

"A helicopter," Charles shouted over the metallic noise. "Well, why not? Why not a fucking submarine too? And a couple of commuter trains and destroyers?"

The blades of the helicopter slowed down. Once the blades were still, the door slid open and Sasha and Klerck jumped out. They were followed by a tiny, thin, copper-skinned man in a Hawaiian shirt and cutoff blue jeans. He had the face and gestures of a small boy, but he was balding on top and there were bags under his eyes. He wore a necklace of tiny wooden beads around his neck. After he jumped from the helicopter to the ground, there was a moment of inaction, then a ramp was lowered from the door of the helicopter and a black man in a neat khaki outfit helped maneuver a wheelchair down to the ground. I didn't recognize the woman at first. She was very ill. Her face was gray and her hair had almost all fallen out. Then I realized it was Mrs. Preston DeVane. Charles, Robin, and I ran toward her. Sasha was beaming.

"My geniuses," she cooed, accepting kisses and embraces from all of us. Her bones stuck out sharply under her translucent skin. "And are you learning from the mystique of the Amazon? I've been here countless times, you know. It never ceases to humble me."

None of us said anything about her condition, but I was very distressed and found myself staring at her scalp.

"Come over here," she ordered me, and looked me in the eyes. "This is my cancer," she told me. "The doctors have quoted the most gloomy statistics. But I'm sure all those nice dead people didn't have my money."

"How did you get here?" Robin asked.

"Oh, there's some ghastly little hidden military base around here somewhere," Mrs. DeVane whispered. "They have an airstrip of sorts. You can charter a Lear from São Paulo and a 'tourist' helicopter to here if you're corporate enough."

Charles slipped behind Mrs. Preston DeVane's wheelchair. The black man in khaki moved to stop him, but Mrs. DeVane waved reassuringly to the nurse.

"That's Moki, a kind of witch doctor intern from Haiti," she told Charles. "He's a lovely nurse, but hopeless when it comes to voodoo. I think he's a vegetarian. I should send him home."

"Good friends are the best source of true healing," Robin said.

"I suppose." Mrs. Preston DeVane sighed. "If your good friends are Nobel Prize winners in oncology. Anyway, I've tried apricot pits and visualization, vitamins, coffee enemas, acupuncture, meditation, dancing the 'Freddie'—you name it. I thought I'd give the Amazon a try and, if nothing else, see how my geniuses were doing."

Charles wheeled Mrs. Preston DeVane toward Sasha and the tiny man. The villagers were gathered around the man, waiting patiently to hug and kiss him. The light was leaving our small square of sky. I tried not to give in to my horror of the darkness.

"Is Mickey Rooney over there the leader of Santa's village?" Charles asked. Mrs. Preston DeVane chuckled. Her small laugh was raspy and full of phlegm. She paled and closed her eyes.

"It's spread to my damn lungs," she said. "And to my bones too." Then she smiled her glamorous forties movie star smile at Charles.

"Yes, dear, he is the mayor of the district. Nothing very mystical. He reports to the governor and so on. Collects profits from the criminals and then arrests them, takes bribes to free them, and then blackmails them so they can keep themselves out of prison. A very powerful little criminal from Iowa, who's wanted all over the U.S. and believes in UFOs. I'm surprised he's still alive. But if you're going to work in this part of the country, he has to be paid off. He rules over these schizophrenic stargazers and uses them as his army."

Villagers from all the huts and tepees and stores continued to gather around the little man and Sasha. Klerck and Chetter were off to one side arguing bitterly with the cook, the med, and the rest of their crew. There was no official greeting between the tiny mayor and his citizens. They just stepped forward and meticulously counted out American, German, and Brazilian money into his hands. As each villager handed over his earnings, the little man put his palm to the villager's forehead and with a strength that was surprising pushed the person over backward. Each villager landed so hard on the ground, I thought he'd break something. But everyone seemed fine, though a bit dazed.

"Not exactly John Lindsay," Charles said.

A man with a red beard began blowing strange sounds through a cardboard mailing tube. The heavy woman banged on a frying pan and aluminum pot with a drum mallet. The rest of the village began to breathe "Whooo" in high, airy, out-of-tune voices. The sky was almost completely dark. A few of the ancient ladies lit Sterno pots and placed them in the center of a circle. The lights and camera popped on. A group of women holding dim flashlights began to dance what Charles said was a combination of "I'm an Indian Too" from Peter Pan and the Hokey Pokey. Each woman paused directly in front of JoJo's camera, rolled her eyes back into her head, and stuck her tongue out. Then the men followed with a different circle dance. Their arms were linked and they hopped up and down.

"I told you this place was Orthodox," Bruce said.

"They're doing it for us. Give it a chance," Robin said.

The women crossed in a diagonal. Their elbows flapped up and down and their heads bobbed back and forth like geese. Finally the whole village formed a circle around Mrs. Preston DeVane. She sat in her wheelchair smoking one of Klerck's hand-rolled cigarettes. She smiled brightly and waved at the hopping and stomping villagers as if she were Queen Elizabeth visiting one of her colonies.

"This is completely bogus," she sang through her teeth.

The speed of the drums picked up and the circle of villagers began to shake and shimmy and whine through their noses.

" 'Bali Hai will call you,' " Mrs. Preston DeVane crooned.

"The jungle is making her drunk," Robin said to Charles.

"Yes," Charles agreed. "The jungle, the music, the fine company, and the gin she brought from home."

Charles hopped on one foot into the circle and did a jitterbug while holding Mrs. Preston DeVane's free hand. This was followed by a series of playful entrances by the actors. Even Kosher, in his nightdress and hat, managed to execute a perfect handstand on the arms of Mrs. DeVane's wheelchair.

I stepped tentatively into the circle. She opened her arms to me. I ran toward her and leaned down to kiss her. Her arms were bony around my back. She patted her lap and I sat on her, keeping most of my weight on my feet.

"Your hair is matted," she said. "I'd like to give it a good brushing. Isn't this fun? How are you doing?"

"I think this is s'posed to be a ceremony," I said. "I don't know if we should talk."

"Oh, darling, I've seen *tons* of them," she said. "Now tell me the gossip." The pounding and chanting was getting faster and faster. I heard shrill whistles and moaning. The villagers' dancing seemed to be getting more frantic.

"Kosher's scared of germs," I said. "The Tropical Treks people hate us. And Sasha has writer's block. He's behaving oddly."

"Sasha always has writer's block," said Mrs. DeVane. "But he won't have it for long. He knows his grant money can't last forever. And when has he behaved normally?"

The circle began to snake in like a square dance. I hugged Mrs. Preston DeVane and made my way back to Charles and Robin. I looked for Sasha, but he'd disappeared.

The tiny mayor entered the circle and stood very still. He had a Day-Glo Magic Marker in his hand. He walked casually over to Mrs. Preston DeVane and held the Magic Marker in the air like he was making a salute. The villagers linked arms and forced us to join in their circle. They closed in on the little mayor and Mrs. Preston DeVane. They lifted their arms as if playing London Bridge and at that moment the mayor forced Mrs. DeVane's head forward and drew a circle on her scalp with his bright purple marker.

Then a woman handed him a bottle of green, mossy-looking liquid that had a "Jungle Energy" label on it, and he poured it all over Mrs. Preston DeVane in her wheelchair. The ooze dripped down her face, but she barely noticed. She was half dozing. The villagers went into a frantic dance in which their arms reached out toward the sky, they grabbed at the stars, and pulled them into their bodies.

Then the circle broke and all the villagers got on their knees in straight lines and sat perfectly still. They looked up at their small patch of sky. They bowed their heads and showed the sky their tattoos. They stayed there unmoving. Reeva started to laugh nervously. Mustafa jumped up and strutted toward the Land Rovers. Nobody else moved. The square of villagers was like a field of statues. Sasha had reappeared and walked quickly over to the center of the square next to Mrs. Preston DeVane's wheelchair. He nodded toward Moki, the Haitian nurse.

"Get a towel," he said.

Moki moved instantly and returned with a white cotton towel. Sasha took it from him and rubbed the sleeping woman's hair and face.

"I feel as if I lay down in a wad of gum," she said woozily. "And what the hell is on my head? Are we going to Electric Ladyland, Sasha?"

"Take her to her cot in the chopper," Sasha ordered Moki.

"Absolutely not," Mrs. Preston DeVane snapped. She sat up and ran her fingers over her greenish strands of hair. "I am now a full member of your tour."

Sasha grinned. He signaled for our company to meet at the Land Rovers. The square of villagers had not moved.

"Don't mind them," Mrs. DeVane said to me. "They're waiting. They'll just sit there for a few hours. They think the aliens will come sooner if they build up waiting points. Sort of like Green Stamps."

The anxious actors immediately took squatting and sitting positions around one vehicle. The Tropical Treks people stayed defiantly in the background at first. Klerck and Chetter, however, took a few steps toward the rest of us and then joined the group. The cook and med reluctantly made an effort to follow. They stood on the periphery.

"Well, I'll be," Charles whispered. He wriggled his eyebrows in the direction of the Tropical Treks crew. "Look how they've joined us in our search. Sasha must've paid them off good."

Sasha sat on one of the backs of a seat. It was a metal throne.
"Well, now." he clapped his hands together. "Tonight we have seen
a bunch of fake zealots doing really bad trance dancing for the tourists. Who knows if these people are mentally ill or if they've been
infected by the poisonous elements of the jungle? But who are we
to criticize, anyway? None of us has been in tune with ourselves. I
include myself, above all—in fact I blame myself."

JoJo's camera clicked on.

"All this corruption and decadence is fascinating because it was
born of the contradictions within this jungle. This brilliant, un-
friendly jungle seems to snatch the very souls from human beings.
Mine included."

Sasha smiled and widened his eyes in amazement.

"We couldn't have known the challenge we would encounter
when we started out, but it's been a real test. Can we create anything
beautiful and sustaining in this place that hates the human heart?
Our combined spirit would have to be extraordinarily powerful to
conquer the malevolence that surrounds us. It seems to me that the
jungle has defeated all the other human beings who have tried to
invade its territory. How can we possibly fare any better? I want to
find out how to live with this honorable monster. I want to defeat
it in the battle of our souls. I hope we can create radiance out of
this darkness. I've been insensitive to the people I love the most. I
expected you to change overnight into total ascetics giving up every
glimmer of desire and your past habits. I spat on your wishes to
perform, to be the very creatures I've encouraged you to be. I was,
as the psychologists say, projecting. I wanted you to make me pure.
Now all I can do is ask you to understand that my actions were not
badly intended. I just despise a theater made from the wish to please,
to feed human weaknesses, to placate the consciences of our decay-
ing audience. Can we try one more time? Can I ask you to help me
write a new show and let me tell you what it will be about? It will
be about us. A group entering the jungle, trying to make a new life,
a new set of rituals and rules, a purer way of life. Our successes and
failures. Our individual and collective experiences will become the
content of this show. Including my successes and failures in being

your 'chief,' so to speak. Including the loneliness and discomfort of our efforts. Including the obvious comedy . . ."

"So Randy Paul is gonna make a documentary about us trying to create a society which is ultimately going to become the model for a documentary-drama-comedy that we'll perform on our stage?" asked Bruce. He was shifting his body impatiently and rubbing his knees with the heels of his hands.

Sasha folded his arms and laughed quietly. "Bruce must always have his lists and dictionary definitions," Sasha said. "Well, good for him. Yes, that's it. But you know it can't work unless we really try very hard to create a day-to-day world we believe in. Belief doesn't come easily, but I want to try. I don't want to end up like these poor, sick people. At least if we fail, we know we can create something quite remarkable by making a new kind of theater out of our failures." Sasha clapped his hands together. His eyes were bright and his neck colored with red blotches. "So here is our plan, my 'villagers.' We shall begin on the walking trails tomorrow and travel for several days. Eventually we shall come to the remains of yet another Indian village that was abandoned and burned to the ground during a war, or by guerrillas, or the military. No one really knows. This grim nothingness will be our home. Klerck and Chetter have generously agreed to lead us. We have made an arrangement to leave our Land Rovers and heavy baggage in a hidden area near enough to Wheel's End so they can be closely guarded. We will take only the barest necessities. None of our usual performance gear."

Kosher raised his hand. "Not possibre," he said.

Sasha grinned at Kosher as if he were a child. "Kosher, we've made certain that the U.S. government will enforce the *strictest* punishment if our property is violated."

"Not possibre," Kosher repeated.

Sasha's face reddened. He had no patience for interference. "Okay." Sasha shrugged. "You can bring the puppets along, but they will weigh on you eventually, I promise."

Kosher left the meeting.

"Why are we going to another death scene? What will we do?"

Reeva asked. Her voice had a peevish tone which Sasha didn't seem to hear.

His gray eyes remained wide with excitement. "We're going to build our own village, with primitive tools and the materials of the land. You'll design your own dwellings and help each other make temporary homes out of nothing but the land. Then we will build a temple. A church. A longhouse. Call it what you want. But we will create walls, a floor, and a ceiling. I don't know whether we'll worship or pray or create performances, but it will be our living monument. We'll fill it with hard work and real faith. If we build it as one person and toil with concentration and dignity, we'll leave behind a positive consequence to this journey of despair." Sasha looked into the camera. "Maybe it is nothing more than another theater, but it is *our* architecture of hope. When we get home we will make a show about building our village and making this monument. We will live this journey for real and, like many cultures, we'll share the gods and customs we discover with audiences."

Sasha rushed off to talk to Klerck and Chetter. The rest of the group split off and found areas to sleep. No one commented. No one said a word to each other. Charles seemed relieved. He shook his curls and did a little dance with his long fingers in front of his eyes. The only voice which came through the heavy air was Mrs. Preston DeVane's. She coughed heavily for a while. Then she pounded on the arm of her wheelchair with her hand.

"Here, here," she said. "I'm all for it. Count me in."

As we set out before dawn the next morning, I craned my neck toward Wheel's End Village. The villagers still knelt, backs straight, tattoos facing the sky in their square of symmetrical lines. Their formation hadn't altered. They barely moved.

"I hope we don't end up like them," I said to Charles.

"No way," he replied. "I look terrible in purple."

CHAPTER 13

I didn't know why the birds seemed to have disappeared. I'd stopped hearing the indignant screeches of the small birds or high-pitched cross fire of the parrots which we had gotten used to. The farther we walked, the more muffled the sound and light became. Even my breathing got quieter. Sometimes I'd stop and hit myself in the chest just to make sure the air was still moving around. The jungle thickened, but the foliage looked ill. The leaves of plants turned brown, with holes gnawed in what used to be green, shiny skin. The trees began to thin like Mrs. Preston DeVane's chemically poisoned head of hair. The vines took over. They were white and sticky and they seemed to strangle the life around them. Klerck, Chetter, and Mustafa led the way, crouching low as if this new dying jungle were a live enemy. They cleared the trail with vicious strokes of their machetes. The colors of the ceiling were now a muddy dull green and brown. When it rained, it wasn't cleansing, but steamy. The vines wound tightly around our ankles. There was lots of falling and tripping; there were sore knees, sprained wrists. The trunks and thick branches of the trees twisted out into the middle of the trail, covered with oversized growths which looked like living mushrooms. Sometimes it seemed that the trees reached out and grabbed at me and tried to suck me in. A net of vines obscured the sky entirely. Sometimes the vines came down so low, we had to bend from the waist to make our way through. The footpaths were barely discernible. It was a maze. Klerck pretended to be sure of his direction. He ripped at vines with his bare hands and pointed toward the ground. Once or twice I saw his neck redden with the fear and embarrassment of having totally lost his way, but he never admitted it. He kept on. Sasha followed him. Mustafa followed Sasha. Chetter, Charles, Robin, Bruce, and I tried to keep near the front, and the others, in changing combinations, tried to keep up or sat on the ground, defeated by exhaustion. Then we'd all stop, barely able to take a breath and too anxious in the eerie silence to rest. Moments later, unable to bear the inactivity, we'd move on.

Walking twenty steps could be an hour's worth of work. The med, cook, and mechanic from Tropical Treks, Inc., hated the exertion and complained quite loudly to each other that this wasn't what they'd come for and they didn't care about the "fucking bonus." They called Sasha a blind idiot. Kosher—dressed in layers of protective jackets and pants (including gardening gloves and a beekeeper's hat), had looped a thick rope around his upper chest and shoulders and dragged two heavy coffinlike boxes filled with his puppets. (Charles said he looked like he worked in a radioactive nuclear plant.) The ordeal must've been excruciating even for Kosher. But he never complained. Sometimes Charles or Bruce or Robin tried to help him, but he snapped at them irritably and told them he was fine. He looked like the photos of priests in Italian village festivals who dragged heavy crosses at Easter time. He was always several steps behind at the rear of the line and kept company with Moki, the Haitian nurse, who lovingly pushed Mrs. Preston DeVane along in her wheelchair. Moki was a very devoted, straightforward kind of man who kept trying to tell Mrs. DeVane that she was "without a brain and killing yourself good." Mrs. Preston DeVane drank her gin, endured the constant bumps against her frail bones, and affectionately told Moki to shut up. She said it was "dull to die in a hospital bed attached to pinball machines surrounded by rich dilettantes." Charles wove a wig for her out of dead flowers and vines and she wore it proudly over her balding head.

The bright flowers had long ago disappeared, and mossy rocks began to appear in their place. We didn't know how long we traveled because Chetter's watch was soaked from the muggy atmosphere and had stopped working. We didn't really sleep at night, but lay down for a couple hours and then moved on ahead. I stopped trying to count days, since day and night were almost the same. Now and then there was a small wet wind or a brief downpour, but for the most part we fought our way through a continuous wall of dense air. The climate was ripe for insects and no amount of repellent or lotion seemed to discourage them. And the flies didn't take off when I tried to swat them away. Slimy snakes and tiny brown lizards crawled and slithered past our boots, filling me with nausea, and if I didn't concentrate, I'd start telling myself stories about death, slugs, worms, and maggots. I was amazed at the high spirits of most of the actors, including Charles. No matter what Sasha did or how angry they were, they always seemed to forget and bounce back. They liked the challenge of the trek because they saw every discomfort as material for their big show in New York. They trudged along, each carrying Tropical Treks–issue backpacks filled with provisions and tools. Charles called us the "Trapped Family Singers." Everyone seemed to have found a second wind and passed the time teasing each other, performing for Mrs. Preston DeVane, and accepting imaginary Tony and Academy awards for the biggest mosquito bites. The troupe members showed their bruises to JoJo's camera and talked to Randy Paul's tape recorder.

Reeva said, "Can't you see this as a dance? The pushing, falling? Being tangled? Breaking free?"

Robin stared cautiously into JoJo's lens and said, "We don't know anything right now. It's a powerful, terrifying, and exhilarating state to be in."

Mustafa, loaded down with several bags and a belt of tools around his waist, said, "Maybe you make me movie star. I keep carrying this shit I be Mr. Universe."

I was mystified by the extreme change in mood. Finally I realized that they were all either very drunk or stoned. Bruce was undoubtedly their source. He would periodically duck behind a tree and emerge pale, smiling, slow, and off balance. I hadn't realized how much hashish, cocaine, and speed, the promise of a show, and a movie could rev them up. In their heads they were buzzing, rehearsing, hearing applause, and sleeping in their New York beds. I didn't feel the same excitement. My whole body was shaking and miserable with fatigue, dampness, and bites. I didn't want to relive those moments for an audience or even in my most private memories. I wanted cool, uninterrupted sleep. My only comfort was Charles. He never let me become too isolated or cranky. He'd always show up by my side with an unexpected bracelet woven from vines or a piece of dried apple. "Mother's here," he'd say. Sometimes he'd lift me and carry me on his back so I could rest.

When we finally arrived at the ruined village, the earth and trees were coal-black. There weren't any skeletons or burned-down huts. There wasn't a hint of the people who'd lived there. It was eerie. There had been a large stream, but now it was nothing but a bed full of slimy rocks. I felt like we were in the palm of a filthy fist. Klerck, whose main pleasure came from giving orders and slashing at vines, assigned us each a knife, portable shovel, or machete. After a restless few hours of silence on our sleeping bags, we did what we could to dig the rocks out of the ashes, but after a while we begged to stop. We were weak from hunger. We each had a small amount of provisions in our backpacks and there were bags of freeze-dried foods in the boxes the stronger travelers carried. Sasha had said we would try to learn to live off the land. Klerck thought this was a riot and I realized he'd agreed to come along simply to watch Sasha fail. I'm sure he and Chetter had been promised enormous bonuses too. Chetter seemed to care about us in his crude way and was always checking up on Reeva. Klerck had his eye on Robin. I don't know whether he liked her because she was Sasha's woman or because they were both so big. She shared his booze. The heavy drinking brought out the acne and bumpy quality of Klerck's skin and he walked more and more like a bear balancing on his hind legs.

Our first night was spent with some of us crowded into the two large tents we'd carried, and others outside shut like caterpillars into special waterproof sleeping bags that left only the face uncovered. Kosher slept in the coffins with his puppets and Moki worked on Mrs. Preston DeVane's wheelchair so it leaned backward into a kind of hospital bed. There was a lot of laughter because everyone was so close and I could smell liquor and grass and sweat. Charles kept his arm around me in our tent and Robin snored on the other side. At one point I awoke to see Sasha leaning into the tent, staring at the mob of us laid out in sleeping bags. He whispered something inaudible and raised his hands, touched his forehead, and fell to one knee. Then he left.

The next day Sasha announced that we would begin to build houses for our village. He divided us into teams. I was assigned to Mustafa and Juno. Juno wanted an igloo. Mustafa, who was already drunk by the end of breakfast, chopped down several flexible baby trees. He stuck the thicker ends in the ground, tied them together at the top with strong twine, and told Juno and me to weave vines all around it. "Think of it as weaving a big basket," Juno said. I circled the skinny frame so many times with long muddy vines I got lightheaded. The process took hours, but when we were done, we had a kind of rickety igloo or tepee.

"Praise Allah," Mustafa said. He'd taken to wearing his filthy cotton blanket over his head again and was speaking more in Arabic than in English. My muscles hurt from pulling at the vines and my hands were blistered. Juno was greedily moving her backpack inside her new home and Mustafa was scaring me, so I went to find Charles.

Charles and Kosher found four strong trees at the edge of the clearing that almost made a square. They built two wide hammocks out of twine and canvas and then constructed a thick lean-to over them covered with leaves on each side. They reinforced the leaves with vines and mud and Charles made pillows by stuffing moss into socks which were too filthy or torn to salvage. The hammocks could serve as a bed for at least four people if you lay on top, or they could be the roof of a lean-to if you wanted to crawl underneath.

"This will hold us till winter comes," Charles said. He looked exhausted. He lifted me up onto one of the hammocks and lay down beside me. His skin was wet and hot. We slept through dinner and I awoke soaked and hungry. Charles pulled a bag of Fritos and a melted Nestlé's Crunch from his backpack and we shared the food in silence. Then we fell asleep again and I awoke to solid darkness. I lay rigid until the gray-green light made it safe for me to crawl off the hammock to the privacy of the latrine outside the camp.

Each of the groups built shelters of one kind or another. After several slow, timeless days the company began having "open houses" in which they took each other on tours. The campsite reminded me of a wet beach covered with ugly, crumbling sand castles, but the designers were proud of their work. They talked about plumbing, decorating, mortgages, and barbecues. My favorite dwelling was Reeva and Chetter's. They made four walls out of empty beer cans, used paper cups, Tropical Treks food wrappers and boxes, mud and rocks collected from the dead stream, and any junk they begged from the film crew, who'd brought a healthy stash of soda and candy. Inside was a pile of rubber leaves three feet deep which made a soft bed for their sleeping bags.

Sasha inspected the housing, with JoJo and Randy Paul following him. He was sweating and constantly pulling at his hair with his hands. His smile was bright, but his clothes were soaked. Sometimes he'd touch a "house" with his hands and close his eyes. Or he'd lean his forehead against the dwelling and whisper something. Once he caught me staring at him and he knelt down in front of me and took my hands.

"In many cultures, little one, dwellings are blessed by priests," he said. "I want to recognize this hard work and pray that these walls protect all of you. A good director should be a shaman. Not like our poor Journey. But a real shaman. I'm going to try very hard to take care of all of you." Then Sasha stood up and clapped his hands. The company automatically gathered around him. They seemed relieved to have some central focus.

"I think we can stay here now. Don't you think?" Sasha said. "I think we've made a home. Who knows? Maybe we can live here."

Bruce was hugging himself and swaying forward and back a bit as if he were in a trance. His eyes were yellow and his tongue was coated. "You've got to be kidding, Sasha, right? I mean, you've got to be kidding."

"He doesn't know if he's kidding or not, darling," said Willie DeVane drowsily. "But he'll soon figure it out. He thinks there's a big stadium audience out there watchin' all this. He thinks when the applause comes, you'll all wake up in New York. Someone ought to tell him the reality. Gently, of course. All geniuses get lost in their own poetry."

Sasha smiled uneasily. "Our cynic and our saint," he said toward the sleeping woman. "The witch of Sasha's village."

Charles had strung a woven rooftop of vines from four poles over Willie DeVane, but she barely had the strength to look up. She mostly dozed in her wheelchair, Moki kneeling beside her on the black, burned ground.

"Sasha," I said anxiously. "When do we go home?"

"Don't think about that now," he said. "You of all people should relish these moments. What a childhood. You'll be able to use this the rest of your life."

"If she ever stops paying off her shrink," Bruce said with a sigh.

By the end of the week, we'd half cleared a large space of jungle for the foundation of the temple. Klerck and Chetter lit gasoline torches and set fire to all the remaining foliage. It smelled rancid, like rotten food, and burned slowly with low flames and oily smoke. I imagined iguanas and snakes burning in the flames. The smoke barely lifted and settled in around us like black fog.

"I gather Sasha's village isn't devoted to ecology," Charles said, and faked a short fainting spell.

282

The smoke caused Willie DeVane to cough so deep and long that Moki picked her up and carried her into the jungle. When he returned, she was limp in his arms. "Not good," he said tearfully. "Not good." Charles helped lay her down on Reeva and Chetter's bed. I lay by her side holding her small manicured hand. She opened her eyes and smiled at me.

"Get the fuck out of here, darling," she said. She dozed off again.

I don't know if it was the smoke or the endless repetition of shoveling ash and swatting at vines, but one day I completely lost sense of time. I no longer could count how many days we'd inhabited our "village." I could barely tell morning from evening. I slept at odd hours without planning to and I worked like a laborer when I was awake. The jungle, for some reason, seemed dark and lifeless all the time. I knew I was twelve or thirteen years old, but my age didn't seem to matter either. I felt as if I'd grown as old as Willie DeVane and that we were all old and living in a graveyard underneath tombstones, unable to dig out.

But Sasha became younger and envigorated. He was rail-thin and moved quickly and nervously. He read a program he'd designed for our "new community." Tai chi with Kosher. Dance with Reeva. Calisthenics with Chetter. The cook, med, and mechanic stood off to one side and laughed at the troupe of sick and exhausted performers stumbling through stoned versions of athletic exercises. They'd stopped trying to participate in anything. Robin cooked our meals out of the provisions we'd brought and whatever edible fruits, vegetables, and plants we scavenged from the surrounding area. The food was awful. Everyone was losing weight. Most of us had diarhhea. When Reeva complained, Sasha stroked her matted, filthy hair and said, "You are losing the past. When you're clean, new food will sustain you."

"Man is supposed to be the smartest animal," Sasha told the camera. "But the jungle, with all its elements combined, is much smarter than man. I'm not here to fight the jungle. You can't *win over* a creation this wily and magnificent. I want the jungle to be my teacher."

"Do you think of yourself as a shaman?" Randy Paul asked Sasha. Sasha thought for a long time. He smiled.

"Not yet. Not yet," he said. "I have much to experience and learn. But these people, who have come this far with me, need a special guide to help them interpret this dark new world of ours. I hope I can be that person. I hope I can teach myself to be whatever our version of a chief or shaman will be. Some days I feel myself filling with a light that could radiate and open up this whole godforsaken place. Other days I feel as if I'm drowning. It's like this jungle has pinned my soul to the ground and is strangling me. But that's the classic battle, isn't it? There's no story of enlightenment that doesn't bring the seeker near to death. I'm willing to fight. I am exalted by the powers I might gain if I win."

"Do you want the jungle to transform your theatrical power into true magical power?" Randy Paul asked.

Sasha stared at his palms for a long time. "I've always hoped they'd be one and the same," he said. "Most serious artists see no difference."

"Out of film," JoJo announced.

"Good timing." Sasha smiled mysteriously at Randy Paul, who smiled with the exact same expression back at him.

Sasha, Kosher, and Charles spent every day designing Sasha's temple. After our exhausted exercises, several hours each day were spent rummaging in the dense forest for the right building materials. We were told what kinds of rock, mud, twigs, dead wood, leaves, and vines to search for. I don't know how many days we were sent out collecting, but I enjoyed this part of the work. If I was lucky, I'd see an iguana or a bright red spider. I liked pulling in rolls of vine like yarn or fishing line. I felt powerful with my machete. Once, when I was collecting chips of rocks for the temple's foundation, I saw movement against a tree that was netted in vines. I looked closer and recognized Reeva's sleek brown back. She was leaning against Chetter. He held the back of her thighs and lifted her.

"You are goddamn beautiful," he said. His breath was short and raspy.

"Then get me out of here," Reeva whispered.

Another time I caught Klerck and Robin lying on a bed of rock.

"Something could bite us," Robin was saying.

"It's so goddamn uncomfortable," Klerck moaned. "Goddamn I wish I could find one fucking way to lie down here without something jabbing my ass."

Another time I saw Bruce leaning against a tree. He had a vine wound around his arm and he was injecting himself. Juno ran up to him and slapped him. Then she kissed him and they rocked in each other's arms.

I couldn't wait to go out for materials. At a group meeting I volunteered to collect more rocks.

"Making friends with the jungle?" Charles grinned.

I nodded.

"It's pretty," I lied.

"Do you see God out there, Rikki?" Charles teased. Sasha listened with great interest.

"I want to," I lied. "Sometimes I see things that God has touched." Tears came to Sasha's eyes.

"Mostly, I'd like to catch a snake." I shrugged.

"Well, remember," Klerck broke in with his usual imperiousness, "some of them are deadly. I mean deadly poisonous."

"I wouldn't really grab one," I answered him with disdain.

Klerck turned his back, confused. Sasha crouched to take hold of my shoulder. He stared at me. I lowered my eyes.

"Do you know how this trip can change the rest of your life?" he asked.

"I know you've said it will, Sasha," I answered.

"But do you have any vision of how different the rest of your life can be?"

"I don't know what the rest of my life is going to be," I said to Sasha.

"That's the point," Sasha said. "I am helping you start over right here. You are my whole future. I have very special dreams for us."

Sasha kissed me on my forehead and walked away. I tried to smile at Charles, but he was watching Sasha and frowning. Then he took a joint out of his pocket and disappeared into the jungle.

We tried to live hour to hour, from rain shower to silence, from buzz of insects to tepid breeze. When the latrine got filled, we burned it, stinking up the camp. When the garbage overflowed, we sorted out what was useful for the temple and what we should destroy. I tried to measure how long we'd been staying in the camp by the dirt accumulated on our bodies. Charles kept trying to find a stream and wanted to rig a shower somehow using the water that ran off the leaves after a rain, but he hadn't succeeded. He was sleepy a lot. We were all losing energy. Mustafa did a great deal of heavy labor. He no longer grinned his stupid good-natured smile at anyone. He wore his blanket and took his hammering very seriously. He was the one who hauled the heaviest rocks from the bed of the empty stream. He used a smaller rock as a hammer to smash chips of other rocks and wouldn't let anyone near it. He counted out loud every time his rock hit a nail. He only took breaks to fall to the ground and pray to Allah (which he did constantly). Mustafa had never been religious in his life and no one knew he was Muslim. Bruce couldn't exactly tell, but he didn't think Mustafa was praying in Arabic, and God only knew which way Mecca was. Sasha told the group that Mustafa's response to the work was exactly the kind of unexpected change that he'd hoped for. Mustafa stared straight ahead while Sasha was talking and, as soon as he was done, went back to dragging heavy rock after rock to the temple. One day, while Mustafa was on his knees praying, Robin tiptoed past, a short distance from him.

"Whore of Satan," he hissed, not looking at her. "Whore of Satan, Satan's child."

I don't know whether it was the fires, the hammering, or our attempts at singing that attracted them, but one day a straggly group of children gathered outside our clearing. They looked very different from the children we'd encountered before. They were either half-clothed or naked this time and they were thin as skeletons. Some of them had large running sores on their bodies, some were blind, and many seemed to be delirious or mad. Yet they were more animated than the children we'd seen at the other campsites. They laughed quietly and mumbled among themselves. Their noise became a constant as the days passed and their number grew.

Sasha instructed Kosher and Bruce to put up a barrier between us and them.

"Oh, no need for that," Klerck said casually. "These ones are mad as little hatters. They just stare."

"That's unbearable," Robin said.

"Yeah, bad luck," Klerck continued in his offhand way. "Only thing we need to worry about at this point is if they're carrying some kind of plague."

"Well, we'll be carrying our own soon," the med shouted angrily, standing with her arms folded in her usual distant spot at the edge of the group.

Mustafa was already up on his feet and started to work on what appeared to be a stone wall.

"We're going to be walled in?" Charles said. "In the middle of the Amazon jungle?"

"We need privacy. Every culture has a right to privacy." Sasha's whole bottom lip was split from a cold sore. His skin was broken out in a rash. His eyes looked tearful. "Our temple is only a skeleton," he said impatiently, "and I want privacy for our work to go faster. And I don't want sickness."

Bruce was shivering. He pointed toward Willie DeVane's empty wheelchair. She had not left the bed of rubber leaves in a very long time. Charles took extra care to fortify the walls around her. ("I'm your Peter Pan and you're my Wendy," he'd sung to her, but she barely blinked her eyes to answer.)

"Well, I think you got it anyway," Bruce said. "Willie's plenty sick and you let her stay in mosquito city."

"Hers is a different kind of sickness," Sasha said. "Her mind is clear. She carries no doubt. She was poisoned by her lifestyle and has set herself free. We must rid ourselves of suspicion and self-doubt."

"That's no plague," sneered Klerck. "We're talking plague." He did his bear dance toward Robin.

Mustafa was moving incredibly fast. There was something scary about the way he was piling up rocks and mumbling to himself. Kosher, Reeva, Robin, and Bruce reluctantly assisted him. Now and then he prayed. He'd look up at the children, curse them, and laugh as he speedily piled rocks, incorporating beer cans and cardboard boxes when they were in his path. He didn't stop until several days later, when he'd completed a wall about three feet high around the perimeter of our land. The children were shut out, but we could all see their heads and hands peeking above the barrier. It was strange.

Most of the actors talked of leaving, but no one could abandon Sasha, so they concentrated on little else but the day Sasha's temple would be built. This would be the sign of liberation to them. They whispered to each other that if the building could be completed, he'd have his chance to call the search a success and we could go home. Our food supply was running low and we were forced to share soggy canned goods and bags of dried fruit. The water in the tanks and canteens we'd all carried was, despite strict rations, very nearly depleted. There were only the filthy cups and bottles filled with rain water. We weren't allowed to wash. Juno had a fever and Bruce developed a blistering rash all over his body. His skin was yellow and he had bad stomach pains. The med refused to go near either of them. She was afraid whatever they had was contagious and she had terrible diarrhea herself. Willie DeVane was in a coma and Moki wouldn't let anyone touch her. Robin stole some aspirin from the med's kit for Juno and aloe oil for Bruce's rash. Robin rubbed the oil onto Bruce. Different actors were exploding into tantrums. They'd explode without warning, often without an immediate reason, and then sink into an exhausted or melancholy silence.

"You know what's really bizarre?" Bruce panted. "We didn't go down in a plane crash or tip over in a sailboat. We chose this. We actually chose this. If he's making a play, let him write it on a pad with a pen. I don't want to be a fucking guinea pig anymore.

"I am a Jew separated from my telephone," Bruce sobbed. "I am a Yale graduate who is a failure at being a junkie. I studied the classics and playwriting to come to the jungle and be a construction worker."

"You've got a fever," Robin soothed. "It makes everything seem worse."

Sasha emerged from the temple, walked over to Bruce, knelt down, and took him in his arms. Then he pushed him away and stared at him. His gaze turned cold. Bruce seemed afraid. Sasha continued to stare. The camera clicked on.

"What kind of superficial game do you think I'm playing?" Sasha said. "This is not rehearsal! You are not an experiment. We are past such things. We live and suffer here for real. We must abandon thoughts of going home. *This* is our haven and I'm going to help you rise from your lethargy and doubt and *contribute* to our life here." Sasha turned and quickly walked away.

"Is he fucking totally crazy or not?" Bruce sniffed. "I can't tell, man. I can't tell what's real."

"Exactly." Robin nodded. She'd lost about fifteen pounds and looked sturdy and energetic despite the dark circles beneath her eyes. She smiled all the time as if she knew something I doubted she really knew.

Time passed and the temple began to take shape. It might've been ten days or two weeks. Time wasn't moving and Willie DeVane wasn't waking up. As long as she slept, there was a numbness in me that was pierced by attacks of dread that she might die. And I felt an odd uneasiness as I watched the temple rise. Something seemed to change in Sasha with each stage of its completion. He became more excited and grand about every detail. He worked himself and the other actors as if we were in our old warehouse constructing a set. I saw Charles try to calm him.

"Go easy, cowboy," Charles said quietly.

Sasha turned on him. "Go 'easy'?" he snapped. "Do you think we're on Broadway? We are making a *real* mythology. This theater is *real*."

"This is a bad sandbox," Charles said, and walked away.

Sasha stared after him. Then he squinted his eyes and mouthed three words: "You are destruction."

The foundation was made of stones and mud. The walls were constructed out of different-sized trees tied tightly together with vines and rope. The spaces in between were packed with mud and stone and leaves and twigs that looked like a mosaic. A quilted kind of net was draped over the ceiling—Reeva and Juno, Kosher and Charles had spent hour after hour weaving the intricate fabric. Thin saplings were crisscrossed under the net to hold it up. The work distracted and soothed the mounting discomfort and restlessness of the actors and crew. There were moments everyone seemed proud of it. I heard Chetter marveling that it was nearly a three-thousand-square-foot structure. Charles told me he thought it looked like a combination of a Swiss chalet, a Polynesian restaurant, and a *huppah*. Even as the company grew more and more exhausted, homesick, and disoriented, they were all amazed by what they were accomplishing with their bare hands. I found their ability to forget their misery to be amazing and repugnant.

"Let's face it," Bruce said. "It's a great story for a show if we live to perform it."

Charles squealed with laughter. "It's useless," he shouted. "It's absolutely useless. And I'm getting old and growing a hump on my back. Why don't we leave Archbishop Sasha here and go worship in a church of our choice in New York City?"

But no one made a move to escape, not even Charles. They were all waiting for Sasha to come up with something miraculous, the way he always had. I guess they believed that the more awful each moment of our survival became, the greater the creative reward from Sasha. I even sensed that they wanted him to see them suffer and then sacrifice themselves to his dream, to appreciate their cuts and sores and fevers. I can't imagine what the film crew was thinking, but I knew Sasha and Randy Paul had long intellectual arguments with them in French, English, and German. They quoted poets and talked about Fassbinder and Werner Herzog and drank whiskey until we could hear their shouts and laughter all over our village.

The cook kept saying she'd have Klerck's head when they returned to London. She was always writing her observations and checking off how many Tropical Treks rules of the road he'd broken. But she and the med were too stunned and exhausted to make the hike back to Wheel's End Village on their own. "This is a goddamned concentration camp," the med muttered as she walked around. She wore large mirrored sunglasses that were shattered on both sides and she looked like a clown.

Anytime Sasha took a moment from the temple or his conferences to smile or wink at me, I wanted to appear hopeful like the others. And he seemed to sense when my terrors got the best of me because many times I'd find him standing behind me, staring. He'd take my hand and lead me to the door of the rickety temple and say, "Of anyone, *anyone*, this is for you. You are the child and you'll carry what we've done here inside you forever. You'll always have some of this and some of me inside you and it will make you different from anyone else." In those moments I felt Sasha was keeping a great secret and that he intended to reveal it only to me. He'd put his long forefinger up to his temple and place his other hand on his chest. "Stay pure inside," he'd whisper.

Sometimes Sasha sat absolutely still for hours watching the temple take shape. When the structure was as secure as it could be, Mustafa squatted down next to one of the walls and leaned his head against it as if listening. He rarely left that spot from then on, except to pray. Sasha called him "my gargoyle by the gate."

The med told him she thought Mustafa was having a breakdown.

"We're all having breakdowns," Sasha said, grinning as the camera closed in on them. "That's the goal. Like a muscle. You have to break it down with incredible pain to build a new and stronger tool. Why should we stay the way we are if we are weak and defective?"

There were times when the group was as irritable as I'd ever seen them. Robin looked sexy with her fifteen-pound weight loss, but she felt stinging pains in her knees when she walked or bent over. Bruce's rash got infected, his fever grew worse, and he wasn't sleeping at all. Reeva strained her back while lifting rocks and had cold sores inside her mouth. I suffered from diarrhea and hallucinations, and I worried all the time about Willie. My joints ached and it was hard to swallow. All of us had blisters and splinters and sore muscles, scrapes, and large red bites that turned purple and green.

One night Reeva and Bruce got into a discussion about civil rights. Reeva didn't believe nonviolent protests would do the trick and Bruce believed in the teachings of Martin Luther King. It ended with Reeva throwing a precious packet of powdered juice in Bruce's face and calling him a worthless junkie. Robin screamed at Reeva for wasting community property on her political opinions. Juno yelled at Robin that she was so desperate that she had to sleep with Klerck to get back at Sasha. Charles sneered at Juno and asked her when was the last time she had lifted her sickly hand to do anything. Klerck called Charles a condescending swish. Kosher told me to stop being a nosy little girl with no manners or respect. I said at least I didn't have to bring my damn puppets everywhere I went. Mustafa called out that we were all instruments of Satan. Then Moki came out of Willie DeVane's hut, his smooth black cheeks streaked with tears, and told us she was dead. He bowed his head and started to cry. Charles motioned toward Willie's tent with helpless outstretched arms and opened his mouth as if to scream. Then the whole group scrambled and crawled together and everyone started sobbing. I stayed where I was and stared at them. If I could have killed them all then, I would've. I went inside Willie's hut and saw her lying on the bed of leaves. I knelt next to her and lay my head on her bony chest, waiting for her to put her arms around me. I closed my eyes. I wanted to cry. The pain was so brittle in my chest and throat, I thought I'd break apart. I loved Willie. She was a pisser and a flower and sad and generous and rare. I felt a hand stroke my hair.

"Oh, God," he said. "I wish I could bring her back for you, darling. But I don't know how yet. Someday I think I'll know. But right now it's too late. You have to accept that she wanted her spirit to rest in this hell of ours. She believed in me. She believed I'd transform it into gold." I looked up at Sasha. He seemed dry-eyed and peaceful.

"Come, now," he said. "This is just her body. It failed her. But she loved us very much."

Sasha and Moki carried Willie's wrapped body out into the jungle and cremated her. Those were her wishes. Then Sasha put her ashes in an empty gasoline can and disappeared inside the temple. The order was that no one was to follow him until he called for us. Charles draped vines on Willie's wheelchair and he and Robin sang one of Willie's favorite songs, which Charles told me was from *Oklahoma*: "I'm just a girl who cain't say no . . ."

We spent the next days trying to get through the exercises and meditations Sasha called for. He rarely left his temple except to check on us. The construction work seemed to have ended without any miracles or ceremony. He had disappeared behind the beaded curtains Charles designed as a doorway. We stayed in our corroding village. Juno's fever wasn't going away and her skin now had a yellow tinge like Bruce's. The med announced that the whole group was developing symptoms of dehydration, malnutrition, and exhaustion. Robin suggested we collect mushrooms and plants and experiment with different herbal medicines. The med, in her broken sunglasses and dirty stethoscope, sneered. "Oh, yeah, rare," she said. "Poison'll cure you good. You eat those mushrooms and you'll forget your itches and aches, all right." When Sasha walked among us, his pale eyes burned. He had several nosebleeds. His gums were infected and he seemed restless. His hands had developed a slight tremor. One day Charles gently suggested that perhaps this meant that it was time for the journey to be over. Sasha laughed, hugged Charles, and told him he was kind to be concerned, but he was absolutely completely wrong.

"We will all reach a wall," he said, "and then I will lead us over it. Just like athletes. Just like I always have."

"We've been on the edge for a long time, Sasha," Reeva said. "And I've seen too many walls. This village of yours is not a real village. That temple of yours has our pain in its walls, Sasha. So what are you going to do with it?"

"Maybe I will do nothing. Is that bad?" Sasha asked.

"You've wasted a damn lot of people's good time," Chetter said.

Sasha smiled. He seemed so much more confident than he'd been when Willie died. And his eyes were distant, almost uncaring.

"I really believe that none of you could've lived this long in a hellish wasteland if we hadn't taken this journey. Nor could you have built your own dwellings or scavenged for your own food. We have all been spoiled. We've taken too much for granted. There's nothing so terrible about reliving the experience of man's helplessness against nature."

"I didn't know this was Project Outward Bound," Charles said.

Sasha ignored him.

"We could die here," Bruce said quietly. He could hardly walk anymore.

Sasha was standing. He walked unsteadily toward Bruce and tousled his hair, cupped his chin in his hand like a lover.

"Death means you give up. I'm determined to fight, like Willie, to the end. We haven't been defeated by this jungle yet, and I will not allow you to sabotage my victory. I'm just beginning to find strength I never knew I had. You will too. What is the city, but a Sodom full of distractions from death? All our precious comforts and talents are distractions from death. We die anyway. Here we face death nose to nose and, though I doubt we can win, we can learn to face our mortality and make the absolute most out of the limited equipment God has given us. We have never been so naked or exposed. And we are learning how much we waste and take for granted in the protected, decadent existence of what we so carelessly labeled as our lives."

Sasha seemed mesmerized by his own words. He stared lovingly at the actors, many of whom were dozing or nodding off. Charles was biting his nails, which was something I'd never seen him do before. He reached out one arm like a long wing and pulled me so tightly to him my rib cage hurt. He didn't let go the whole time Sasha droned on as if the words themselves were a wind that might blow me off the ground and Charles had to keep me grounded and safe.

That night, Charles woke me up. His nose was smeared with dirt. His glasses had been cracked several days before. His lips were bloody and dry and his hands were cold. He was totally stoned.

"Kosher's being bad." he grinned. "He says if people don't 'raugh,' they get sicker. I want you to come have some fun. But first . . . serious business."

Charles took me to a corner by Mustafa's three-foot wall and sat me on his lap. We watched Kosher unpacking his puppets from their coffins.

"I want to tell you something," Charles said quietly to me. "Before we left, I put some money in a trust fund for you. The lawyer in L.A. is named Roswell Jacobs. He's in the Beverly Hills phone book. It'll help you live. Also, Peter's last name is Godshaw. Peter has a whole house and an apricot poodle named Miss Pumpkin Ann. She drags her back legs like a cripple if you don't feed her. And she sleeps next to the little puppets and guards them from mice."

"I'm never leaving you," I said. I didn't know why he was telling me all this and I felt like I should forget it as soon as I heard it. Destroy it. Shred it. It would break my head open otherwise.

"I want you to know you're provided for," Charles said. "And pretty soon I want you to go into the temple and tell Sasha you're twelve years old and you don't need to push to the edge of your energy, contract malaria and dysentery, and go insane to know you're alive. Tell him you need to go home. You *must* go home."

"I won't leave you," I repeated. "Forget it, please."

Charles lifted me off his lap.

"Later," he said.

Kosher stood carefully on the rickety wall. He was manipulating one of his most beautiful puppets. A huge fish that swam through water and opened and closed its gills and fins and blinked its eyes.

The children were terrified at first. They didn't take their eyes off the puppet. They nudged each other and huddled, moving closer to each other's bodies. Kosher swung the fish down into the mob. The children let out airy squeals of fright, but they didn't run away. Kosher stepped down off the wall and began dancing through the crowd. The children reached out tentatively to touch the air near the puppet, but didn't come near Kosher.

"Here, guys," Charles said. He lifted up a five-foot multicolored puppet of a dragon, stepped up onto the wall, held his nose like he was about to dive into water, and jumped toward the crowd of children. The dragon had a red sequined tongue which unrolled for at least a foot while the beaded pupils of its eyes zoomed around in crazy circles. Charles maneuvered the bamboo poles under the dragon's body so it waved up and down like a roller coaster. The children weren't afraid of Charles as they had been of Kosher. Charles came off like a golden angel, whereas Kosher was so covered up, he looked like a man who'd been bandaged head to toe after a serious accident. Reeva heard the commotion and joined in, following Charles over the wall and into the crowd with puppets of an old man and woman. These were huge hand puppets fashioned from soft rubber. Their toothless wrinkled faces cursed and spit at each other and their fat hands pinched each other's noses. The children made "Oooh" sounds and their faces began to show delight. I realized the children weren't doomed animals at all and I felt angry and scared on their behalf. I wished I could jump in the middle with a puppet of my own, but Kosher's collection was made up of his oldest and most treasured characters and the group had learned how to manipulate them long before I joined up. (Kosher insisted on bringing them for just such a moment as this. When I asked Charles why Kosher couldn't leave them with the Land Rovers, he told me puppet people like Kosher and Peter couldn't be without their companions for long. Their puppets were a part of them. The puppets had been born from their hands and were as beloved as children.)

Soon the other performers joined, one at a time. Robin, who arrived messy and drunk, dug out an evil-looking sorcerer in a black satin cape with a rhinestone-studded three-cornered hat. The sorcerer stabbed at the air with a sword and jerked his head from side to side. The children backed away when they saw him until one child, a young boy with a blind eye and a distended belly, took up a stick and challenged the sorcerer. A great sword fight began and the child slew the sorcerer. He was a hero. Then Bruce entered the scene with a very dumb pig sculpted from foam. It kept dropping little piglets into Bruce's hand. The performers transformed. Their energy was high and focused. They played with the crowd of children until some got so overexcited they looked like they might faint. Then the performers lowered the puppets and offered to help tend to the sick children, but the children were very protective of each other and those who were still strong stood in front of the sickly ones to guard their friends. No one wanted the puppet show to stop, but Kosher gave a signal and the activity began to wind down. When it seemed time to stop, the actors backed up slowly so as not to startle the children. After they hopped over the wall and put the puppets back in their coffins, they turned around and were startled to see Klerck and Sasha waiting for them. Klerck's eyelids were heavy with disdain. His hands rested on his thick sides. Sasha stood slightly hidden behind him, but I saw his face. He'd lost all color and his features were rigid and drawn. His eyes drooped. His lips were sucked in.

"Well, that was very generous of you," Klerck said with even more than his usual sarcasm. "No doubt you'll give the rest of us cholera, malaria, and God knows what by tomorrow."

"We're all sick anyway," Bruce said. "What the fuck."

The laughing and shrieking of the children began to lower in volume, but we could still hear rapid chatter and imitations of the puppets' voices. That was the sign of a good show.

Mustafa jumped over the top of the wall and walked around it slowly, like a sentry, staring the children down. They backed up and became instantly silent.

Sasha edged himself out from behind Klerck. One hand covered his mouth and his eyes remained unfocused for a long while.

"Performers have to perform," Robin said apologetically. "It's in our blood. And the children . . . they're a part of this jungle, not scavengers like the others."

Randy Paul moved in next to Sasha. He nodded at her. JoJo panned the group as it stood facing its leaders. He zoomed in on Kosher, who was tenderly wrapping and repacking his puppets. Then Kosher turned to Sasha. It was impossible to figure out what he was thinking.

Sasha smiled meekly. He stood hunched over as if his bones had been shattered by a terrible blow.

"If you want to please the children so much, give them the puppets, Kosher," Sasha rasped.

Kosher didn't move.

"Lidicurous," Kosher said. "They know not how to make them arive."

Sasha's voice rose. His eyes were teary. "You've carried them everywhere like a cross. Your vanity is completely tied up in them. It's not like you can't make others. You're using the damn puppets to create a barrier between you and our work. This whole time. You refuse to let go of the past and now, just at the most difficult moment, when we are about to break through our misery to some real discoveries about ourselves, you use the puppets to create cheap, instant gratification. You defy me. You spit on my rules."

"I youl teachah. You not eben glown up yet," Kosher said angrily. "You *know* puppets. Puppets pure! Wood, paint come to rife!"

"Yes, but I want to invent fetishes," Sasha said. "I will be told what and when our rituals will be. I will proclaim a new healing theater. It will come to *me* from my private agony and search. Not *your* old false idols. If you knew how close I was, you wouldn't act the traitor."

Kosher giggled. But it was metallic and empty.

"Aha, so you master now? Sasha?"

Sasha said nothing. He pursed his lips.

"You want make pliests not theatah?" Kosher laughed. "Even pliest make celemony, they weah lobes and mask. They dance in stleets."

"In a dying, antiquated culture. Full of impotent, irrelevant old men," Sasha said. "We are trying to create a new world, not be slaves to the past."

Kosher laughed through his nose. It was a broken, muffled series of sobs. He began to shake his head from side to side. He didn't stop the motion.

"Sasha want to be king," he said. "Theatah isn't enough. Sasha gone mad."

Then he grabbed his puppets two and three at a time and roughly flung them over the wall at the children. The children gathered shyly around the dead cloth, wood, rubber, and plastic objects with their silk and satin dresses and bamboo poles, and stared reverently at them. A long time passed. The children couldn't touch them.

Kosher quietly pulled off his hood and stepped over the wall and out into the crowd of gaping children. He took out a machete and began hacking the puppets to pieces. Several of the children started to cry as Kosher calmly destroyed each puppet until it was nothing but chopped-up parts and rags. Most of the company turned away from the sight. Robin covered her eyes and began to cry.

Bruce attempted to confront Sasha, but Sasha held up his hand and said, "Not now."

He was watching Kosher. He seemed terrified and excited. JoJo shot from a discreet distance.

"No one could act this," Sasha said quietly to Randy Paul. "Don't you see? No one could capture this in a script or even improvisation. Never. It's the agony of giving up everything you know."

"But what's the upside?" Charles shouted. "Where does all this sacrifice get us? Why are you destroying the puppets you love?"

Sasha turned to Charles. His eyes were cold.

"I wouldn't expect you to understand, Charles," he said. "Not in a hundred years."

When Kosher finished wrecking his puppets, he ran into the jungle. The children descended on the broken parts and rags and divided up what they could. Sasha and the company stood for a long time saying and doing nothing.

"That's it," said the cook. "I'm home."

"Me too," the med agreed.

"Leave your supplies," Sasha told them.

"We'll do whatever the fuck we please," the cook said.

"You'll leave the supplies," Klerck growled.

"And I'll issue quite a report to Tropical Treks too," warned the med.

"Fuck 'em, I just quit," said Klerck. "Get going with your 're-ports,' why don't you. You won't make it halfway back."

Sasha raised his hand.

"No, this isn't the way to do it. Not after we've come so far. Try to look into me. . . . Let's discover the alternatives to impatience and pettiness."

I thought he was going to tell us more, but he simply turned around and limped unsteadily toward his temple. We followed.

"Look at this," he said as he walked pointing to the temple. His expression was wild, his face tight. "The answer for all of us waits for me here. I will find the magic to free us all. So soon, so very soon. You know as well as I there's something else waiting for us in this journey. It's up to me to uncover the secret, and when I do . . . there will be light and love and an ecstasy none of us has ever imagined. A purity born out of the shit."

"Sasha, man, enough is enough," said Bruce, but his words were unsure and his dark eyes were more imploring than defiant. "It's okay to blow a gig, man."

Sasha said nothing, but drew himself up very straight in front of the hanging vines of the temple door. The vines jangled with Charles's beads, and the door was inlaid with cut-up tin cans that looked like mother-of-pearl. The whole temple had been ornamented with designs made out of leftover food containers and found objects. Kosher and Charles had done most of the cutting and shaping of the moons, stars, spirals, and hands, mosaics of broken beer bottles and faces carved into the wall of trees. From a distance the edifice looked like a real temple, but not of any specific religion. I was surprised that the members of the company didn't follow Sasha inside. Nor did anyone storm off. It was like a frozen carving of followers receiving blessings from their holy man. Whatever any of them said or threatened or screamed, they never left him. Once again, I felt the urge to kill them all.

Just as Sasha was about to disappear behind the door, I heard a long descending cry. All breathing stopped. I thought the sound had come from me. Charles threw himself in front of me as if shielding me from a bomb blast. Sasha's expression was calm, almost curious. Suddenly Sasha was on the ground, as Randy Paul talked excitedly into her tape recorder and JoJo zoomed in tight.

Kosher had lunged from the jungle like a wolf and he was on top of Sasha. He was holding a knife to Sasha's throat. I couldn't hear what he was saying exactly. Kosher's thick accent made it impossible. I concentrated on the glistening silver blade. I knew how sharp that blade was. The children in the crowd saw the commotion as an opportunity to grab the remaining fragments of puppets, their miniature props, and their ripped costumes. They swarmed a little closer to the wall. Mustafa, reacting to the surging of the mob, quickly fell down onto one knee behind the wall, threw aside his blanket, and pulled out a machine gun. He started shooting. I heard the pops and saw children swat themselves as if bitten by mosquitoes. Several of them fell.

I crouched low and held on. Charles spread his arms and shouted furiously at Randy Paul, keeping his body pressed to mine.

"Get good footage of *that*, you bitch. Make sure you get it." Charles pointed toward Sasha. "He wants real life, okay, he's getting it now."

At that moment I heard what I thought was a loud machine. It was as if a tiny airplane had flown low, by my ear, with its propellers cutting through the night's heat. Charles fell over on his side. I looked down and saw a red flower on his calf. I looked up and saw Mustafa aiming at him.

"You've got to be kidding," Charles said to me. I smiled, but his eyes were closed and his mouth was open and he was breathing hard. He looked so sad.

I grabbed Charles's hands and wrists and rubbed them. Whatever happened, I didn't want him to lose his heat. Robin ran over to us and began to scream. Klerck came pounding from across the clearing like a rhino on a rampage. He tackled Mustafa and beat him until he stopped resisting. The crowd of children had already run off, dragging their dead and wounded behind them. No one tried to help them. Sasha lay still on the ground, Kosher standing over him, panting and talking to himself in Japanese. Sasha's eyes were open and his face was scraped and bloody. The small cuts made him look childlike. He didn't smile, but seemed oddly amused with the shouting, weeping, and chaos. Klerck dug my hand off of Charles's cold wrist. Moki, Chetter, and the med began to work on his bleeding calf. I heard a faint song. Mustafa was rocking back and forth on the dirt, his hands clapping quietly to a beat. He chanted in his weird language. Then he lifted his arms in prayer, and everything went into slow motion for me.

CHAPTER 14

That evening there was no laughter, no fury or weeping, no sounds of gossip or sex. I heard Robin moaning and retching. The curious children were back, humming and whimpering from a distance. Aside from quiet murmurings and the wet sticky wind, sounds seemed disconnected and slow and full of silence.

The film crew, Chetter, and Klerck shared their stash of flat beer. I overheard them comparing deaths they'd witnessed. One of them had seen a volcano cover a town with lava and ash. Another had been in Cambodia and had seen a whole village mowed down like bowling pins. Klerck said he walked into six or seven headless corpses in the Congo during some civil war. We all waited for Sasha. He'd retreated to the temple. Charles was seated in Willie DeVane's wheelchair. His calf was bandaged in rags and yellowish gauze. He saw my face and started moving the wheelchair back and forth to a dance rhythm. Moki sat next to him.

"Would Carmen Miranda do it this way?" Charles said. He looked old.

"We can't judge Sasha's actions now," Robin said gently. Her eyes were so puffy, they were practically shut. Her speech was halting and drunken but she seemed to think her mind was working clearly. "We're in the kind of situation that will look completely different years from today."

"Are we talking biblical—like thousands of years?" Bruce asked wearily. "Or tomorrow? How long do I wait for this to look different?"

"What's the wife of a shaman called?" Charles asked weakly. "A shamaness? A shamanista?"

"Stop! Stop!" Robin cried. She started to dig at the ground with her hands. Her big body was heaving with sobs.

I was alone. I felt the urge to walk. I didn't trust my eyes or ears. I stole one of Charles's joints and smoked it too fast. I decided if I kept my mind in chaos there'd be no need for opinions. Opinions seemed to cause death in the jungle.

I heard a *click click click*—a call. I saw Kosher sitting on the farthest corner of the wall. I was afraid of him, but I answered his call anyway. His head was bare, so he looked less crazy. He was busily carving something. His thick callused hands moved so fast that his knife sang. His face was very wrinkled. I'd not noticed his age before. His upper lids drooped over his eyes. His surgical mask was around his neck. His lips were one long line. I realized he was at least fifty-five or sixty years old.

"So," he said to me. "What's new?"

I tried to smile. I winced. I bit my lip.

Kosher stopped carving. He realized I was keeping a distance. He squatted on the wall and shook his head with wonder.

"You scaled of me?" he cried. "Oh, no! No! Nevah!"

I managed a smile.

"If I wanted to muldel Sasha, I faster than a frying burret. More powelful than a rocamotive."

Kosher giggled. He started carving again.

"No, no—nothing rike it. Enough is enough. Even too much rove is bad. Too much royarty. Too rike Japan—clazy!"

Kosher frowned.

"He hurts people. I terr him to stop. He misused teaching. He say I am aflaid. Yes, I am. So what? A wise man knows when to tlemble. I terr him. Sasha, you no know how to tlemble."

Kosher stopped carving. He bowed his head.

"It is all make-berieve. Evlything Amelican theatah people do—make-berieve. Evelything. Sasha want leal rife. Why don't quit and rive leal rife?

"So," he said. "I go. I go to Tokyo. Do cheap theatah. Audience. Puppets. Mask."

I reached out and touched his arm. He patted my hand and grinned.

"You think I'm not so bad?"

I didn't let go of his arm. Kosher wiped his eyes with the sleeve of his army jacket.

"You fibber," he giggled. "You hated me. I was a mean old master."

"I don't care," I said. "You're my teacher."

"Bely rong way to billage," Kosher said. "Hericopter come to billage. Challes wants you to come with me."

I withdrew from Kosher. I couldn't leave Charles. He was my mother, my nanny, my whole family. "Why doesn't he go with you?" I asked.

"Challes a beautiful soul." Kosher sighed. "Rike a rong piece of silk—all sunright. Sasha brack caves under ocean. No sun. Yin and yang. Can't exist without the other."

I grabbed Kosher again. The muscles in his forearm were as hard as the wooden rods of his puppets.

"Challes demand Sasha you go with us," Kosher said softly. "Sasha says no—you his cleation." Kosher looked at me. "Like God he make you. Did you know that?"

I shrugged. "They fight about everything. I'm just one more thing."

Kosher squinted. He shook his head back and forth. "Not a stupid girl," he said.

He went back to finishing his carving. I couldn't make out exactly what he was up to.

"Okeydokey," he said happily.

He handed me a tiny straw basket the size of a cup. It had a perfectly woven straw lid. I lifted up the lid and there were twenty or so intricate wooden figures. They were miniature stick dolls with tiny wigs and faces. Each had a different costume.

"Tlouble dolls," Kosher explained. "Evelytime you have plobrem, you whisper it to one of them. He do what he can. Don't use one too much, though, he get tired. Put under head at sreep. Will also catch bad dleams."

I embraced Kosher.

"Don't show Sasha," he warned me. "Now I must sit arone."

I decided to walk off my confusion and fear. The whole area of our village was still unusually quiet. I guess people were mulling their own yeses and nos. I poked a stick into the stinking pile of ashes that remained from a campfire—The children hadn't managed to take all the remains of Kosher's broken puppets, masks, props, and costumes. The leftover plaster of paris, rubber, and plastic limbs and faces lay scorched from where Klerck had started to burn them—Sasha's orders. I stepped over the wall and as fast as I could finished the joint I'd stolen. Now I noticed a small group of children clustering over where the puppet show had danced among them. When I approached the listless group, each child held out one hand in a beggar's pose. The smallest child had a filthy cloth around his foot and trailed blood as he stepped forward. He'd probably been shot by Mustafa. The begging children moaned a little as they jabbed their outstretched hands in my direction. I stepped out of my clogs, then unzipped my blue jeans and pulled them off. I yanked my T-shirt over my head and slowly eased my underpants down my legs and over my ankles. I held my breasts in my hands and strutted back and forth in front of the children. They lowered their arms and stared, but kept an eye on my discarded clothes. The sight of me really didn't interest them as much as the blue jeans. The littlest child bent down and reached forward for my clogs. I kicked his shoulder lightly with the front of my foot. He fell backward and the other children lunged for me. I struggled free and ran naked toward the clearing. I heard a hiss. I turned around and saw Mustafa standing by a wall of the temple, hands and feet bound. He rolled his eyes upward so they became white and strange. "Daughter of Satan," he whispered. I turned my back to him and, bending from the waist, I mooned him. I was about to run and find Charles when I heard my name spoken from inside the temple.

"Please come inside," Sasha said. His voice was shaking. When I didn't move or answer, his voice became light and happy. "I always intended that you be the first to share this space with me. The moment has arrived. Sometimes after the worst, most destructive storm, the air can be really, really clear for the first time. Would you please come and celebrate with me?"

I had stopped being surprised when the company would come back together again after falling apart. Or when Sasha would quit and return. By now probably no one in our group would be shocked if the dead came back to life. Sasha once told me that every time a coin disappeared from his hand and reappeared behind someone's ear, it was an act of resurrection. How could I possibly get away? How could I even think of betraying him?

I thought the inside of the temple would be bare, but the first thing I saw was a smooth path made of tiny stones from the dead stream. It was outlined by torches. Perhaps they were meant to keep the mosquitoes away, but they flickered, and splashed jumping shadows on the dark walls. Sasha stood at the end of the aisle of torches. He wore a filthy pair of drawstring pants and nothing else. He was rail thin and he'd painted a large sun on his chest. There was a bed behind him up on poles. A quilt of leaves and vines covered the square frame. Candles and sterno cans were set in a semicircle. I didn't have to wonder where all the objects had come from and who had built Sasha's private world. I knew it was Charles.

There were primitive drawings pinned on the walls. They seemed to be sketches of Aztec, Mayan, and African symbols, but I couldn't really tell. A triangle of dead lizards, mud and oils, dried bones, skins, and insects fit inside the semicircle. Sasha soothingly urged me forward. "Don't be afraid." He laughed softly. "It is disgusting at first, I know, but it's no big deal. I'm studying shamanism. These are nothing more than props and good-luck charms."

He reached down and dipped his fingers in a bowl and painted a stripe down the middle of his face with a red liquid. He motioned that I come to him. I remembered I was naked and covered myself with my hands. Sasha held out one of his Indian shirts to me and then tossed it. I grabbed it off the floor and put it on. He turned his head to the right and closed his eyes. His head was shaved so close he looked bald. His thinness accentuated his high cheekbones and beak of a nose. He resembled the Indian on the old American nickel.

He lifted his right hand high up in the air and jerked it, giving the air a slap. Suddenly fire rocketed from it. I jumped.

"Flash paper," Sasha said. "The oldest trick in the book. But what if I could do that without flash paper? What if I had that power?"

I shrugged. He grinned and motioned that I stand next to him. I stepped forward, staring longingly at the soft pile of leaves on his bed.

Sasha reached down and dipped his fingers into the red liquid. It smeared like blood. He painted a stripe on each of my cheeks.

"Now we're twins," he said playfully.

He lifted the shirt and began to paint circles around my breasts. I thought of Willie DeVane and Journey. I recoiled. He grabbed my hair and wound it around his forearm, reeling me in. I had no choice.

"I want you to be mine," he said gently. "You are not yet fully cynical or destroyed by corrosive doubt. You don't know how to sabotage. You love me and I believe in your future. If you betray me, then nothing has meaning. I may as well die. If I have failed with the others, I want to prove to you how much my actions are motivated by the purest love. A power to love given to me by God. You are my final chance."

308

I felt trapped. He gently lowered the shirt so I was no longer exposed.

"What has you so scared?" Sasha asked. His eyes seemed to take up his whole face. He was examining every inch of me.

"I don't know," I said.

"Sickness comes from doubt." Sasha unwound my hair and held me by my wrists. "Doubt will kill you. Doubt is tearing apart my group. You can help them believe again. You can bring them back to life. You are the spirit of my work. If I love you right, we can teach the others together."

Sasha let go of my wrists. He held out his arms to me. I leaned my head on his bony shoulder and felt my breasts touch his chest.

"No one ever thought you'd speak again," he whispered in my ear. "And I found your voice. No one believes that I am fighting for our souls. You and I can bring radiance back into the world. You'll be the proof that my vision is real."

I couldn't say anything. I knew Kosher and Charles were waiting for me to tell Sasha I had to quit. They wanted to take me away. Sasha pressed me against his feverish skin and I was silenced by his breathing.

"You must believe in me," Sasha repeated. "Our destinies are intertwined like the vines and trees of this jungle. We can't defeat the death of hope without each other. We can become one superior being, more powerful than any theater group, army, or religion. We don't need the Koshers or Charleses of this world."

I shook as he held me tighter. I cried at the images of Charles alone, Bruce and Kosher defeated, and Willie DeVane in a gasoline can.

"All the people in this group, and you most of all, were given a new life by me," Sasha said, and he rocked me back and forth as if to soothe me.

"I can just as easily take it away." His voice was eerie.

I kept very still. I didn't know if he meant he'd fire me or kill me.

I closed my eyes. I felt Sasha lift me gently onto his bed or altar.

(I wasn't sure what it was.) He was so close I could smell the sourness of his skin. His voice was very low.

"Please don't think I'm crazy, little Rikki Nelson." He laughed. His voice sounded almost normal. "All of this I can explain, make as simple as a fairy tale for you, my little blond-haired darling."

My eyes were shut tight, but I lifted my arms as he pulled his shirt over my head. Once again I was naked. I felt the leaves under my sore body. They were smooth and cool.

"I want you to relax, little one," Sasha said. "I'm going to tell you a story. Remember how I used to read to you during the *Myth Man* rehearsals?"

I nodded.

"I'm going to tell you the most marvelous fairy tale by the Brothers Grimm." Sasha's voice had become fatherly, but something in its even tone dictated I do exactly as he wanted.

Sasha touched my hair with the tips of his fingers. His lips brushed my ear. I shivered. I opened my eyes.

"No, keep them closed," Sasha said.

He leaned closer to me. I felt his breath on my cheek.

"This story is Sasha," he said. "You will know by this and why I've chosen you to join with me, build the future with me, have my children and be the messenger of my love."

"Sasha," I said, "I'm only twelve."

"Shhh," Sasha whispered. "There are no ages when two people join as one. It transcends time." I tried to understand but I felt younger and more helpless as I faced my agelessness and all the responsibilities it seemed to bring. I tried to concentrate on the idea of a fairy tale. I hoped it would be as illuminating as Sasha promised.

"There's this boy, see, who's born into the world fearing nothing," Sasha began. "And since he fears nothing, he can feel nothing. At first his parents think he is retarded, but he's actually smart. In fact he's a future king, he just cannot feel fear. He sees poverty, death, beautiful women, glorious sunsets, horrendous monsters, but he feels not one iota of fear."

Sasha poured onto his hands some oil that smelled like eucalyptus. He turned me over onto my stomach and began rubbing my back.

"He met villains on dark roads, in forests, in back alleys, and felt nothing. In the face of tigers and lions and crocodiles, he was calm and empty."

I knew I had to respond. I had to care about this story.

"So what did he do?" I asked. Sasha squeezed the back of my neck. I tried to relax, but I trembled.

"He set out on a quest," Sasha said. "He devoted his life to finding fear."

I opened my eyes. I was soothed by his voice and the story. I realized he'd stopped massaging me and was painting something on my back with his fingertips. I could feel his designs reach all the way over my buttocks and thighs, down my calves and the arches of my feet. I felt the sticky liquid dry quickly. My skin was pulled by the dried paint. I wished I could see the colors.

Sasha turned me onto my back and stared down at my body with his calm, gray eyes. I closed my eyes again in shame.

"Now you must look at me," he whispered firmly.

I opened my eyes.

"Do you understand so far?" Sasha smiled. He sat cross-legged. He was very relaxed. He clasped his hands together and crooked his head to one side like a painter. His fingers were caked with the dried blood.

"As you can imagine, the boy set out on a great journey," he continued. "He traveled by land, by sea. He met with a ferocious one-eyed cyclops who tried to decapitate him with an ax. But the boy just sighed and slew the cyclops with his sword. His ship was capsized by an enormous poisonous electrified eel, but the boy just swam into the mouth of the eel and out of the tail. He didn't even feel a shock. He came upon the king's army and slew every soldier, one by one, the whole time sighing and saying to himself, 'I wish I could feel fear.' Finally he came upon the old demented king himself, who said, 'If you will guard my haunted castle, the castle which has killed hundreds of young men, I will give you my daughter's hand in marriage.' And the boy sighed and said, 'Oh, very well.'"

Sasha got up and dipped his fingertips in one of the bowls. His fingers were dripping with blood. He knelt over me and painted circles and triangles on my stomach. He stopped and then decided to paint my whole body in solid stripes of brownish red and a murky green he chose from another bowl.

"For three nights the boy guarded the cold empty castle, with its inexplicable creaks and moans. The first night, he put up with several card-playing, man-eating black cats who tried to slit his throat and tear off his head. Each time he killed one, its corpse multiplied until hundreds of cats were upon him."

Sasha stopped moving and sat rigidly.

"But since he sat very still and showed no fear," he whispered, "they eventually became afraid of him and ran away."

Sasha looked down at me, troubled. I closed my eyes.

"Open your eyes," he whispered. "Painting isn't enough. Not if we are to be as one person." He produced a razor, the kind Kosher used to cut leather. He moved in a flash and slit the skin on one of his cheeks.

I looked up at him. He gazed at me curiously. "I have to make sure you're listening, little one." I saw the glint of the razor in my peripheral vision. I experienced heat in my cheeks but not pain. I saw the blood flowing down his face and felt the warmth on my own. I knew I was not to cry out or let tears come. "We are closer than brothers and sisters." He smiled. "Closer than mothers and sons. We define a new family, but I must steal a few ancient customs to bind us."

"What happened," I said in a tight voice, "to the boy?"

Sasha smiled, nodded, and closed his eyes to find his place in the story.

"The second night," he whispered, "the boy sat on a hard bench to keep himself awake. He was very upset. 'Oh, but I wish I could shudder. If only I could find one thing to make me shudder,' he cried. 'But surely it won't be here.' And he sat lamenting till midnight, when he heard a hideous wail and half a man fell down the chimney. 'Woe ho ho!' said the half man. 'Here comes the other half.' And sure enough the other half of the man fell down the chimney. And the two hideous halves did a disgusting dance until the intestines, heart, lungs, brains, and bones were joined and there was one hideous foul man.

" 'Let me sit on your bench,' said the hideous man. The hideous man tried to push the boy off and when the boy pushed back, hundreds of half men fell through the chimney, and also nine dead-men's legs and two skulls fell, and everyone set out to go bowling."

Sasha grabbed a torch and began to dance, hovering over me on the bed. He moved slowly, doing the half man's dance. He closed his eyes to see his story better. He brought the flames closer and closer to the skin of his stomach. I gritted my teeth, knowing if he burned himself, I would have to be burned too.

"I guess most people," Sasha sang, "would be terrified by the sight of hideous half men using skulls as bowling balls to knock down pins made from dead-men's legs."

"I guess," I said. My eyes didn't leave the torch.

"But the boy didn't shudder," Sasha growled. He brought the torch close to my breasts and stomach and made rapid, tiny circles. The sparks stung me. "And neither would you. You understand fear."

Sasha snuffed the torch in a gourd of water and collapsed next to me on the bed.

"The third night," he went on, "the boy sat down on his bench in the haunted castle and said sadly, 'Oh, but if only I could shudder. I would truly be a man!' When it grew quite late, six tall men came in carrying a coffin. They opened the coffin and beckoned that the boy look in. He bent over and saw his *very own body*."

Sasha lay still. He seemed to stop breathing. I didn't dare touch him. I imagined him suddenly changing shape and coiling and hissing above me like a huge cobra.

"Was he dead?" I asked Sasha. "The boy. Was he dead?"

I was scared of his stillness. He waited such a long time to answer.

"Perhaps," he answered quietly. "I don't really know. But he looked down at himself in the coffin and said, 'Hey, there, lad, you're too young to be lying there like that! Wake up! Wake up!' And he began to slap the corpse awake. The corpse rose and became a huge rotted old man who tried to strangle the boy and tear off his face."

"He wasn't scared of that?" I asked. The story was beginning to disturb me. The dried blood and paint irritated my skin and caused it to be itchy. My cheek was throbbing. I wanted the plot over and done with. If my life was supposed to be over when the story was over, I didn't care.

"He wasn't even scared of death," Sasha said. "He was stronger than death. He wrestled the old man to the ground and lo and behold, the old man became the king, who said, 'What a brave lad you are. You shall now have all my gold, my kingdom, and my daughter.' "

Sasha jumped off the bed, took a drink of some foul-looking water, and removed his drawstring pants. He stood there naked. To my exhausted eyes he seemed like a combination of a skeleton and a clown. I saw his white penis contrasted against his painted body. I turned my head.

"Look at me. My flesh is nothing," he said.

I obeyed. I decided to get the story moving again as fast as possible. Why postpone the ending? "Doesn't he ever shudder?" I asked.

"I'm not finished yet." Sasha laughed. He approached the bed but stood beside it. He stared at me with unwavering interest. He spoke in an odd rhythm. His voice was sweet, like a very small child.

"Though the boy won a kingdom and a bride, he felt he had failed terribly in life because he had not found fear, had not learned to shudder, and therefore could not be a man. After his wedding day he moped and sighed and all he could say was 'I wish I could shudder! I wish I could shudder!' "

Once again Sasha climbed onto the bed. He straddled me, kneeling, and brought his face directly to mine. Our lips nearly touched. He spoke his words right into my mouth.

"When the boy went to sleep," Sasha continued, "his new wife took a look at her husband and said, 'If he wants to shudder, I'll make him shudder. I'll go out to the stream and get a pail of water. And that's just what she did. She pulled the blanket off her sleeping husband and poured the freezing spring water up and down his body. The boy woke and cried, 'Oh, what is this I'm feeling? I'm shuddering!' He truly knew fear. He was a man."

Sasha was examining my face intently to see my reaction to the story.

"Do you understand?" he asked.

"Yes," I lied.

"I knew you would." Sasha closed his eyes and nodded with satisfaction. "You shall be my wife. You shall fetch me the cold water. You will be the source of honesty and purity, and with you I'll always feel who I am."

Sasha shivered.

"Now we must make a covenant," he said. "After today you will be unquestionably mine. Not even Charles shall have you. We will live inside each other where no one can find us or separate us."

Sasha gently spread my arms and legs apart. I was a pinned moth. He looked down at me. Tears mixed with the paint and blood on his cheeks.

I was sinking into a state of detachment. My eyes were open but I could've been blind. The images of Sasha staring at my painted body was projected miles away. I knew what was going to happen, and I knew I wouldn't fight. Sasha lay down on top of me, and I didn't feel his body or his weight. If I was meant to die inside of him I just hoped there'd be something more than darkness. I heard a loud voice but I was too lost to believe it was real.

Charles limped into the aisle of torches. I tried to float upward and call out to him from inside Sasha's body. He stopped for a moment. I knew his eyes had to adjust to the strange firelight. Sasha continued to lie on top of me. He was relaxed as if dreaming.

"What is . . . this . . . your cocktail lounge now, Sasha?" Charles called out. "Where are we? Bali Hai?"

Charles moved forward, dragging his injured leg, pausing with every step. When he got close he stopped. Then he saw me. He put his hand to the side of his head and let out a scream.

"Oh, my God," he said. "Oh, my God. Oh, my God."

He bent his bad leg and hopped toward where Sasha and I lay. I felt his hands reaching for me. They grabbed onto me and pulled. But Sasha remained limp, making it impossible for Charles to free me.

"Get up, you bastard," he shouted at Sasha.

Charles saw the slash on my cheek.

"Get up, Sasha," Charles repeated. This time his voice was harsh with authority.

Sasha turned his head and smiled sadly at Charles. He put his arms under my back and pulled me into him. I was suffocating.

"This is a covenant," he said. "Rikki understands. Once we join together we will be an inseparable force. There's no room for you, Charles. The contract of love is spiritual and binding."

"No, no, no," Charles said. "No philosophy. No spiritualism. No. Just let her go. This is very wrong, little brother. You've lost it."

"You're hardly the one to lecture on morality, Charles," Sasha said gently. "*She* brings me real innocence and love. You have never done anything that wasn't tainted by your vanity and weakness."

Charles was crying and tugging helplessly at me. Sasha had me in a full embrace with his arms and he'd managed to intertwine his legs with mine. It was like a wrestling hold. Charles's bad leg prevented him from using all his strength. He settled for holding my hand. He cried continuously, sobbing quietly.

"You've simply got to let her go," Charles said. "If this is about us now or us in the past, we'll fight between ourselves later. I'm telling you, Sasha, you can't direct human lives like shows. You can't rape because it happens in myths. Let her go now. You're too stretched. Something's cracked."

Sasha smiled and shook his head. I watched the two of them with dull curiosity. The outcome barely mattered.

Suddenly, Charles stood up and grabbed one of the torches and held it over his head.

"That looks beautiful," Sasha said with feeling. "You're like Prometheus trying to steal the gift of life from me, but the vulture got your liver long ago."

"I'm going to set your temple on fire Sasha." Charles wept. "This journey has been a disaster. It's time to go home."

"I just learned more about love than any sonnet or play could ever teach me," Sasha said. "I'm learning to love good and evil equally. *Not* like two blond-haired brothers who look like twins. Who, by loving each other, love only themselves. Not like that, brother. This is a pure love."

"I don't believe that. I don't believe you know what you're doing anymore," Charles said. "I think you're desperately alone and terrified. You're in way over your head."

Charles was crying with his whole body. He tottered so badly I thought he'd fall over.

"Let Rikki go, Sasha," Charles sobbed. "I'm going to ignite this roof. It'll go very fast. You don't want her hurt."

"On the contrary," Sasha said gently. "We can all be like the Phoenix. Our love causes us to burst into flames. Our love will make us rise from the ashes."

Charles didn't answer. He stopped crying. He straightened himself up to meet Sasha's clear gaze. He lifted the torch in slow motion toward the overhanging vines and held it inches away. He began to move the torch a fraction of an inch toward the quilted ceiling. When the torch was at the point when one jerk of his hand could ignite the ceiling, Charles stopped. He and Sasha stared at each other for a long time.

Then, suddenly, I was pushed to the floor. I fell hard.

Sasha was screaming.

"Fuck you!" he shouted at Charles "Fuck you."

Simultaneously, Charles was shouting "Run! Rikki! Run!" and I took off, naked, out of the temple. In my peripheral vision I saw the ceiling begin to spark and smoke.

I ran, gasping, through the hanging vines and realized that the whole company was standing outside the door of the temple. Klerck and Chetter had their arms spread out, to stop anyone who might try to run in. "They'll be out," Klerck growled. Robin threw a huge T-shirt on me and Bruce tried to hold me, but I wriggled free. Randy Paul was shouting at JoJo as he circled the burning temple on his knees, shooting from every angle. The whole temple was smoking. Mustafa was jumping up and down, his wrists and ankles taped.

Klerck pulled him to the ground. Sections of the temple were now engulfed by flames. I could hear Charles and Sasha screaming at each other inside as I ran past the group and leaped over the wall into the jungle. I looked back one more time, I heard the walls crackle and hiss, and I saw them explode into flame. I thought I saw Kosher rush past everyone and run inside, but I wasn't sure. I saw Robin pulling at her hair and rocking back and forth. Perhaps she followed Kosher in. I didn't know. Klerck and Chetter were frantically shoveling dirt and ashes at the structure, trying to douse the flames. I had no idea if Sasha or Charles had gotten out. I almost stopped to see, but I heard Charles's voice inside me, *Run. Run.* There was nothing in my head but those words and my body's need to get away. I didn't want to witness whatever was to come. The air stank of wet fire.

The mob of remaining children took the smoke and flames as a signal to run amok. I watched them scramble over the stone wall in an attempt to loot the empty camp. I watched Chetter and Klerck gun them down. As they fell like toy soldiers, I thought I'd get shot too. I took off and ran deeper into the jungle. I kept running until the silence of distance and heavy air covered the noise from the camp. My feet were raw and bleeding. I stopped and stayed in the silence for a long time. I was freezing and burning. I sat and watched for snakes and iguanas. I vomited water several times. Half awake, I began to dream out loud. After a while, I nearly slept. I fantasized building a tree house and running guns and dope for all the orphans of Central America. I whispered orders to my orphan cavalry.

It was dark beneath the roof of trees. My legs were swelling and itching and aching. One side of my face swelled up and I realized that the deep slash on my cheek was very hot and throbbing from excruciating tenderness. The heat made me dizzy. I remembered Sasha telling me when I was nine the difference between a sleepy little girl and a girl who was meditating. He said that in a sleepy little girl silly dreams took over and time passed easily and lazily with no effort. When a little girl meditated properly, every second took forever. Every vibration and shade of light became a part of the mind and pried open the senses. I was so sleepy and weak, I thought I was dying, and I couldn't see any reason to stop letting the dreams talk to me and become pictures. It was so easy to let go of my body and give in to the panorama of images. I drowned, didn't bother to swat insects or bind the cuts on my feet and ankles. My calves were torn up too, but I didn't care. I thought about Charles in New York, the night his wings caught fire. I saw Charles with the torch in his hand. I didn't know what had happened to him. I stood up. The pain was awful, but I wanted to turn around and find out. I wanted to find out. I imagined facing Sasha. His skin blackened, his eyes surprised and trusting. I knew I couldn't live through another day in Sasha's command. Pain reminded me what returning to the village might mean. Then I imagined Charles burning and I became angry and thought of Sasha being arrested by some powerful international police force. I couldn't specify the nature of his crime, but I knew my courtroom of simple people and real shamans and priests would condemn him. I watched myself testify to the horrified judge. The judge ordered Sasha to be kinder and less fanatic. To take us home and give us dinners, naps, and vacations in Paris. I cried when I realized my dreams were getting me nowhere. I might very well stay in one place and die. Sasha and Charles might've been incinerated in the temple. I couldn't think of a reason to go back, so I just started walking.

The way I went seemed like a mime walk. I went forward, but stayed still. Everything always looked the same. My feet were raw and tender. The swelling in my face and feet pulsed with infection. My vision was blurred. As my steps moved me along the overgrown trail, I realized I'd never seen the luscious jungle of *National Geographic* or Channel 13 documentaries. My jungle was arid, stiff, ungiving. There were scattered children along the way, whimpering from sickness or gunshots, but they didn't even look at me. I was glad. I wouldn't have known how to fight them off or help them. In the beginning I stepped over a couple corpses, dragged off, probably, after Klerck and Chetter's assault. I thought I'd steal from them, but when I put my hands in their pockets, I realized they had nothing. I was ashamed. I became terrified of their ghosts. I began to walk without stopping. I knew if I waited, I'd change my mind.

I just walked. I didn't think about a direction or purpose. Every minute I fought the urge to give up and let myself sleep. In my head, Charles hummed "When Johnny comes marching home again—hurrah—hurrah—" I tried not to think about my death or my future. I just kept walking. I told myself stories.

I remembered a walk my mother and I took when I was six. We were visiting one of her clients in Pittsburgh, and it was my first snow. A real blizzard. She had on a soft black fur coat and a Russian-looking hat. Her gloves were suede and the boots matched. It was snowing with fat white flakes, but the sidewalks were clear. I was bundled in a snowsuit. My boots were made of rubber. We were walking to a restaurant to meet the man for lunch. My mother held my hand and we were proud companions. A car slowed up on the street and honked. I guess the guys were greasers. My mother smiled and waved. They followed us for quite a while. My mother played with them. The one in the passenger seat had a mustache, tiny blue eyes, and crooked white teeth. He held out a can of beer in a soiled strong hand. He asked my mother if she wanted some. She laughed and said no. The guys crawled along beside us until the traffic began to honk and they moved on.

Before we reached the restaurant, I saw a fabulous snowbank on the side of the sidewalk. I needed to try it out. I ran ahead of my mother and dived into it. She pleaded with me to get up. I refused. I lay there thinking about Eskimos and igloos and Santa Claus.

"Rikki Nelson," she said. "Don't you do that," she warned. "That's just how mountain climbers give up."

She'd won my interest. "What do you mean?" I asked.

"When they get lost," said my mother, "when the fat dogs with the kegs of whiskey can't find them, they lie down just like you are right now. It's a kind of rapture of the deep, sweetie. A love affair with ice. Now, that's just too weird. You get up."

I dozed while I walked and I had dreams about not getting out of things. For instance, swimming deep in an ocean—seeing the sunlight ripple on the surface—pulling my way toward what I knew would be clean air—but the climb was taller and steeper than I'd imagined—I became terrified there was really no surface.

My walk was like the dreams. Where did I think I was going? Who did I believe would rescue me? I clenched my fists and didn't let myself limp. Robin's oversized T-shirt was soaked with sweat and urine and spotted with blood. I tried not to look or smell. I used dreams to convince myself I was alive.

Another dream was about escaping from a hooded killer in a sewer, crawling through the tunnel in the darkness with the dreaded fear that the tube only joined others, interconnected like the organs of a monster. Perhaps I was walking in a circle, headed right back to where I started from, and I'd end up with the dying tribes in the ashes of the camp with no food or water, no family or language of my own. But I forced myself to see a circle of light. I fell down, slicing my left hand, and crawled in that tunnel, in the jungle toward the opening so far in the distance.

Sasha had warned us that the jungle was the greatest master illusionist. He said all you had to do was walk a hundred meters from the campsite and you'd lose all sense of "differentiation." Every direction would look the same. Once he made us go out there in separate groups to prove his point. Bruce ended up lost all night. When he returned, the circles under his eyes were black and he sat with his hands folded for a couple days just staring into space.

"I'm a Jewish boy who hated summer camp," he said, breathing hard. "What's wrong with loving Ovid? What's wrong with a love affair with grammar? Metaphor? History? Can't I be your scribe, Sasha? I'm too weak to live out the myths."

Sometimes at night Jonah would let me stand on his bare feet with my feet in socks and he'd lift me up and down and we'd step forward and back and sideways in lines and circles. He'd whisper in my ear the names of the landscapes . . . "Now we are on a road! Now a bridge! Now we're climbing a hill! A tree! We're rolling into a ditch! Jumping into a lake!" When we fell, we landed in the ocean and swam to a Hawaiian island where a fat man played a ukulele and sang.

When I squatted down to relieve myself, I cried from loneliness, but of course nobody heard me. When I saw blood spotting the leaves, I began to cry until I lost control. I held out my arms in the middle of the nameless cavern of trees, waiting to be picked up, to be walked, to be whispered to by Charles or my mother or even Sasha. It took a long time to come around again, to stand up and decide it was worth walking for another immeasurable distance.

I didn't try mathematics. Mathematics could only lead to insanity. I didn't know how to calculate how many stories filled up a quarter of a mile. Or how fast my brain invented images in ratio to seconds, minutes, hours. I was tempted to calculate how many people had died all over the world since I set out on this sticky hidden trail, but it would've been a lie. I didn't know any statistics. I couldn't let myself ask if Sasha or Charles had died. How long could a person go without water? I didn't want to estimate. Sasha loved to talk about a kind of claustrophobia people got in the jungle—a specific madness in which one hour becomes a year. I didn't want that to happen. I kept walking.

I tried not to remember walks with Charles. The specifics hurt too much. He walked with me every minute anyway. Where my feet stung, my face ached, or my cut hand dripped blood, he forced me to sing all the Cole Porter, Rogers and Hart, and Frank Loesser tunes he'd taught me. I also sang through *The Boy Friend.* I went through the operatic arias he'd taught me—*La Traviata, La Bohème*—in sobbing, phony Italian. I recited Sophie Tucker jokes, but I couldn't remember punch lines. "Da Da Da," I shouted in a nasal voice, "and *you* know da da da!" Charles and I listed all the Tarzan plots. Jane lost in the jungle, boy kidnapped by Arab traders, Cheetah stolen by heartless collectors from traveling zoos.

"Did you ever look at those films," Charles asked me, "and wonder who does Jane's nails? Where does she get her lipstick?" What if Charles was dead?

I remembered a walk with Sasha sometime in my first year. We were doing a teaching workshop at a college upstate somewhere right after I'd joined the group. We were doing an improvised show about Native American animal myths. Sasha wanted a child lifted into the beak of a huge eagle puppet and I was the chosen one. We rehearsed it with me hanging from the paper beak of one of Kosher's oversized puppets. I couldn't tell Sasha I was scared of the height. Every day they swung me a little higher. I trusted Kosher, but was still scared I'd fall onto the heads of the audience. And I was going to be naked—a "newborn" Sasha said. It was autumn, and the college crowd was gathered outside for the workshop. When the eagle soared through, their faces looked up. Seeing all those eyes, noses, and mouths intensified my terror. I lost control of my bladder, sending a spray of urine onto everyone. I was mortified. Charles, of course, found it hilarious. He called it "peepee warfare," but I was sure Sasha was going to send me back to Jonah or my mother.

After I'd washed myself and changed my clothes, he took me for a walk. The leaves were in their peak of change and I remembered feeling filthy in front of nature and Sasha's immaculate presence.

"You shouldn't be so ashamed about what comes out of you," he said, "or even when it comes. But you should think about why you lost control. You must have control. A great actor learns to control all the basic needs and desires. When you lose yourself in your work, your concentration controls your body. Your work is more important than your body."

I hung my head.

Sasha gave me a quick hug.

"The reason I tell you this," he said very quietly, "is because I had cancer when I was a child. I almost died, but because of my faith I had a recovery nothing short of miraculous. This is control. After the cancer I began to make theater pieces full of miracles and healing. I have terror and pain to thank for my greatest success."

I'd never heard about the cancer before. This had been Sasha's fifth version of his childhood, including one about a jealous cousin who bit him and drew blood when he made the honor roll at school.

"I will love you and protect you," Sasha said to me that day. "You have a safe home and family now. Your mistakes will not only be forgiven but transformed into miraculous strengths."

I thought about running back to him, but I remembered his eyes on the altar bed. I felt sick. I didn't even bother to squat. Something was wrong with my stomach. Defecating was so painful, I just let the sting go down my legs. Insects attached themselves to me. I got so tired, tiny rocks became hurdles to climb over. My lungs were raw and tight. I lost track of when I'd started. I began to say frightening things to myself. What's wrong with this place? It's not so bad. What's so scary about being alone? I'll learn to eat lizards and rubber leaves. I'll make outfits from snakeskin. Charles once told me desperate folks could adapt to anything in order to survive. He said, "If you have to live in one room your whole life with a ridiculously low ceiling, you just learn to walk bent in half." Then I calmed down. I accepted that I'd probably die. I wasn't as scared as I'd been before. I was curious about what I'd miss.

I wondered if I was too old to attend a ballet class or Junior High School Olympics. I thought about taking lessons and piloting a single-engine plane. I had no idea what my singing voice was like and I figured I was probably too shy to join a rock band. I imagined that I could have modeled Italian silks and long French capes with straight skirts—a slit to reveal my knees and thighs. Some photographer would tell me to cut my hair in a shag and buy false eyelashes, carry lipstick in my purse, and always have a pocket mirror handy. I wondered if I'd have made friends. Would I meet them for lunch in an open-air café where students played Bach on cello, violin, and flute? I wondered what a date would be like. Maybe we'd go to the movies and buy popcorn. My date would've put his arm around my shoulder and I'd push it off. It would've been an adventure to be a prissy girl. Death would steal nothing exotic or wild from me, only the small, normal moments I'd never known. A salad with iceberg lettuce and carrots. I tried to remember flowers. Irises, crocuses, lilies, azaleas, daffodils, tea roses, baby tears. I'd never had a telephone conversation with a girlfriend. I wanted to dial an area code, a number, and listen to the ring on the other end of the phone. It would be enjoyable to tell lies. I'd exaggerate my age, make up a new birthplace, re-create my family and my religion. I began counting all the missing days and months, all of them. I panicked. I wanted to live. I couldn't speak a foreign language or recite a poem; I didn't know how to iron blouses. I was counting all the declensions, conjugations, socks, nightgowns, comic pages, and barbecues. They were all missing. Like a body count in a war. All the nameless books and newscasts and television movies and ways to prepare chicken and styles of cookies and fast-food restaurants. All the constellations of stars and variations of architecture and ranges of mountains and historical episodes in chronological order. I didn't even know how to sustain my end of a simple two-way conversation. I wasn't even sure if I could lie down on a bed in a room and be alone without God hammering away at me, calling me into another dark and mysterious retreat. Charles told me lovers and prisoners repeat. He said it was why both lovers and prisoners end up back in jail. The cement walls were home. Darkness and silence were the order. Sasha's world was what I knew. Even without him the ruined dramatic jungle was his. Why was I running? If I made it out, would I die from freedom? Now that I was branded, how could I have any kind of chance in a cheerleading squad or bowling team? I wanted to try. I saw a flash of sunlight—the ceiling of the jungle breathed a little. In contrast, the earth became darker and more bare. I saw a flash of metal. The door of a jeep? The window of a car? Oh, God, that light scared me with its brightness. It was too harsh. Too active. What would happen to me? Once I sat on a white bed with a necklace of orchids around my neck. I imagined putting kerosene on myself and setting myself on fire like that college boy did in front of the United Nations. But I was playing. The flames were cool, like a waterfall. Sasha said whatever happened would always be best. My mother said nothing happens as it's advertised. I saw the tires of the jeeps. I was breathing hard. I was pouring sweat, emptying out. Dry as an old shell. I'd been too close to the sun too long. People were running toward me. Their outfits looked too clean. I think their hats matched their shorts. Their shoes had thick, ridged rubber soles. How Charles would laugh at those shoes. I took eight steps, I counted them exactly, and then I fell down. My vision went hazy. Voices, a chorus of hums. Someone turned me from my stomach to my back. I thought I saw curly blond hair. Then I realized it was the sun beating down on a silhouette. I heard several voices mumble in a language which either I couldn't understand or was too tired to recognize. The strong arms of a man curled under my back, and I let every muscle go limp and gave in to the rhythm of him carrying me. My only prayer was that he be a stranger, and that I hadn't walked such a long distance only to end up where I'd started.